AN *Elegant* SOLUTION

ANNE ATKINS

malcolm down
PUBLISHING

22 21 20 19 18   7 6 5 4 3 2 1

First published 2018 by Malcolm Down Publishing Ltd.
www.malcolmdown.co.uk

British Library Cataloguing in Publication Data
A catalogue record for this book is available from the British Library.

ISBN 978-1-910786-50-5
Paperback ISBN 978-1-912863-09-9

Cover design by Esther Kotecha

Art direction by Sarah Grace

Map of Cambridge by Katherine Baxter
www.katherinebaxter.com

Theo's College Illustration © Andrew Ingamells,
ink drawing & etching, 2006.

Printed in the UK by Bell & Bain Ltd, Glasgow

For my wonderful mother
MARY
best maths teacher ever
whose bedtime treat was puzzles and brainteasers

and my incomparable son
ALEXANDER
who is one

Acknowledgements

Over and above everyone else I must thank Alexander, without whom I couldn't even have imagined this story far less written it: for his tireless, careful – and often patiently repeated – tutorials in the workings of cryptocurrency; for his unflagging enthusiasm and support; for introducing me to experts who knew even more than he did; for investing my money in bitcoins when I'd never heard of them and filling the house with bitcoin miners which were so efficient at warming chicks, heating the loo and proving bread; for providing mathematical jokes; for his incisive literary criticism; for his unique relationship to time (or lack of it). Far more important than all this, for deciding to live when he was mercilessly bullied by grown-ups at the age of ten. Thank you, Alex.

Particular thanks also to Professor Nigel Smart of Bristol University, for explaining crypto-fraud and taking such an interest in solving plot connundra. To Professor Imre Leader of Trinity College Cambridge, for devising and monitoring Theo's research thesis and giving him such an exciting breakthrough. To Professor Jean Michel Massing, Fellow of King's College Cambridge, for telling me the Chapel's secret, showing me inside the roof and giving me lunch. To Sir Richard Dearlove, erstwhile Chief of MI6 and then Master of Pembroke College Cambridge, for generously giving up time to meet me. To Neil Seabridge, Head Porter of King's College Cambridge, for explaining college security and police work, and telling me about his silk top hat. To Julie and Michael Proctor, for so generously showing me round the King's Provost's Lodge. To Detective Constable Mark Bray, for giving up so much time on further explanations about police methodology and for his inventive ideas as to how to blow up a big building. To Dr Ed Anderson, for advising me on how Junior Research Fellows live and work. To the Trinity College May Ball Committee of 2013, for allowing me to wander around during the ball with my notebook.

Thanks, too, to our eldest daughter Serena, also a member of Trinity, for generously taking us to the same ball a few years earlier, for reading the book for consistencies with Cambridge in the twenty-first century and for such discerning editorial suggestions. To Nell Goddard for her recent experience as a young arts undergraduate at Durham, her helpful comments and so encouraging enthusiasm. To Dr Aurora Chen and the Bedford School Chinese Society, for so warmly giving of their time to make numerous helpful corrections and suggestions. To Haley Drolet, for kindly reading and commenting on the American dialogue. To my youngest daughter Rose, for supplying me with teenage jargon and advising on the corruptible morals of a modern young chorister. To Dr Peter Wilmshurst, Consultant Cardiologist at the Royal Stoke University Hospital, for his expertise on fraud in medical research. To my father David Briggs, for fulfilling my lifelong ambition and patiently teaching me Greek and Latin every evening, and for correcting the classical references. To Jack and Pina Templeton of the Templeton Foundation, for so hospitably showing me round Baltimore, particularly the site of the battle.

Heartfelt thanks to my cousin Fleur Lloyd, for caving in to many years of pleading and agreeing to be my writing mentor, and for being such an unfailingly supportive and selfless friend. And to hypnotherapist Tim Alberry for his patience in so gently encouraging me through many years of trauma-induced writer's block, and for being this book's first reader when it was in a very scrappy state.

Personal deep gratitude to Professor Simon Baron-Cohen, director of the University of Cambridge Autism Research Centre, for generously allowing me to name and quote him, and particularly for being so kind and sympathetic to an unknown desperate mother years ago, and almost the first person to show her son respect and understanding. And to Professor Ian Holyer of Bristol University, for his similar tolerance, academic admiration and understanding towards a student of a different way of being, who had already experienced far too much unkindness and idiocy.

Thanks to Katherine Baxter, for kind permission to use, and annotate, her beautiful map of Cambridge. To Sarah Grace for her attention to detail in the evocative jacket design; Chloë Evans for her intelligent and assiduous feedback; Rebecca Macdonald for her proof-reading; Rhoda Hardie for her tireless professionalism and zeal in promoting this book; and particularly to Malcolm Down for his enthusiasm in turning a book around in time for Christmas. The image on the spine of the Corpus Chronophage Clock by Dr John C Taylor OBE is courtesy of www.johnctaylor.com.

To Paul Walton, Thomas Foulger, Surj and Quentin Stott and Anthony Read for generously donating names to the story and money to good causes.

To my remarkable daughter Bink, whose supplementary jot-and-tittle proofreading, from hospital, shows the most meticulous mind I've ever come across.

Finally to my extraordinary late mother, for decades the best maths teacher in Cambridge and for ever the best mother in the world. For teaching me to love maths, love people, love life ... and be grateful for *everything*.

DISCLAIMER

There are a few characters in this story who are named and clearly recognisable (Simon Baron-Cohen, Bob Chilcott and the Duchess of Cambridge); and one who is referred to obliquely (in reference to his work regarding the discovery of public-key encryption). Our unlikely hero is closely, and shamelessly, modelled on someone I know well and love dearly. All the others – Master of College, Chaplain, Dean, Provost, Head Master, Fellows, choristers, undergraduates, porters, spouses and children – are entirely imaginary, and bear no deliberate resemblance to anyone, alive or dead.

THE AUTISM CENTRE OF EXCELLENCE

The Autism Centre of Excellence in Cambridge, an exciting new project under the auspices of the Autism Research Trust, is to be a unique collaboration – between autistic people and their families; world-class researchers; and clinical services – and the first centre of its kind for autism in the UK.

Currently autism research and clinical practice are not coordinated, so the benefits of research are slow to extend into clinical practice. There is also a shortage of funding for autism research and an acute lack of support services for autistic people and their families. ACE will integrate scientific innovation, for which the University of Cambridge is world-renowned, with wide-reaching lifelong support and intervention for autistic people, both within Cambridgeshire and via national referrals. This is an opportunity to transform the quality of life for autistic people and accelerate autism research in the UK.

A percentage of the proceeds of this book are being donated to the Autism Research Trust and its work towards this venture.

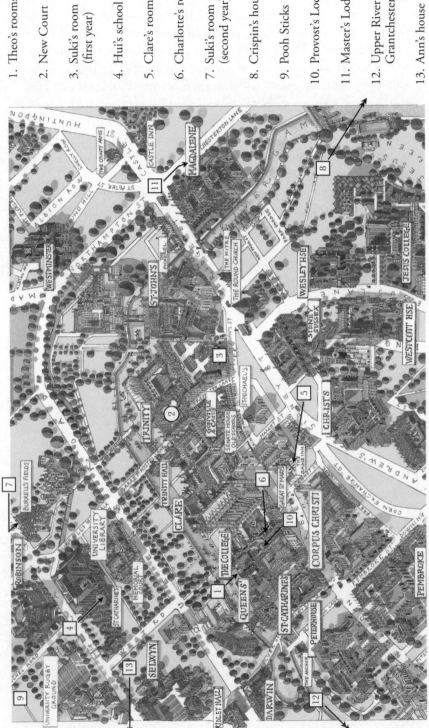

1. Theo's rooms
2. New Court
3. Suki's room (first year)
4. Hui's school
5. Clare's room
6. Charlotte's room
7. Suki's room (second year)
8. Crispin's house
9. Pooh Sticks
10. Provost's Lodge
11. Master's Lodge
12. Upper River and Grantchester
13. Ann's house

A colour version of this map will be found inside the dust jacket.

The Cam

East Window

South door

Founder & Fountain

Dining Hall

Tea Room & Bar

P'lodge

Cobbles

Theo's rooms

Charlotte's Room

Provost's Lodge

Chetwynd Court

PART I

Midsummer

Chapter One

The explosion came earlier than expected.

The two girls screamed.

"Hurry! Please, please hurry," they urged the young man. It's possible he smiled.

The sky burst into neon, yellow, purple. Sparks showered the darkness. The detonations were astonishing, shaking the night air.

The girls shivered, their faces illuminated. The younger one pulled her shawl around her and clasped her knees.

For a few moments neither said anything, transfixed by the heavens. They could hear distant squeals.

"Do hurry!" the more authoritative girl repeated.

Neither saw the figure on the bank of a murky tributary which was stealing off the river, his outline crisp against the stars, still as a leaf in the windless air and blacker than the night.

"Excuse me."

"Oh!" the younger one exclaimed. She peered into gloom. All she saw was a shadow blacking out the sky, waist deep in undergrowth. "It sounded like you asked for a lift."

"I did." His voice was gentle and low. "I've forgotten my key."

Everything was so strange, on her first night in this mystical city, that this seemed almost normal. "Can we pick him up?" she turned to the young man.

"I thought you were in a hurry."

"This is an emergency. Obviously."

Their pilot had to steer deftly into the tributary and find firm bank. He maneuvered efficiently.

The waiting shadow trod expertly into the middle of the centre of gravity. He was Stygian from head to toe, his face and hands blacked out. Only the whites of his eyes and his teeth reflected the stars and flashes.

"Do you often travel like this?" the younger asked.

The vessel pulled away. A thick chain hung looped over the water, impeding progress. The skipper attempted a seven point turn before giving up and reversing the way they had come.

"More often I bicycle. Or walk. But sometimes, yes, of course. I mislaid my bicycle in Grantchester a few weeks ago. Or rather my bicycle mislaid me. It was locked up outside the Green Man. I assumed it was in Cambridge. So I had to come home by river. And then, rather tediously, go back to collect it. How do you do."

"Dr Wedderburn," the older girl had been waiting to say. "Isn't it?"

He considered. The sky continued to explode behind him. The younger girl's face was like a child's at a birthday party.

"Not really," he said at last. "Who are you?"

"Suki Phillips. You supervised me last term."

"Ah. Hello. Have I supervised you too?" he asked the girl he was facing.

She laughed. "I'm Charlotte. I'm not here yet."

"Good. That it's yet. Or not yet. It's kind of you to give me a lift. We've passed my rooms now."

"Oh, we'll take you back," Charlotte said.

"Let's watch the display first!" Suki said. "We didn't mean to miss it. We weren't supposed to leave college."

"I promised the boatman fifteen minutes," their chauffeur objected. "The official river trips start after the fireworks."

"No one will be getting in punts during the fireworks," their passenger pointed out. "Not until the river is clear afterwards. Which will take at least ..."

"Fair enough," the steersman agreed.

"Thirty-six minutes. Approximately."

They passed under Clare Bridge, eerie and ethereal, swathed in green uplighting for its own May Ball, also tonight. The river was indeed crowded. Above and to their right the windows of Trinity

Hall were lit up, its high wall smothered in spectators, naked legs dangling over the water. On Garrett Hostel Bridge there was barely room to move. The dozens who had been waiting for some time, with hamburgers and cameras and one or two bicycles, were now closely packed, their backs to the travellers and their faces turned towards the sky.

The river in front was crammed: double-width punts twinkling with tea lights, tartan blankets over skimpy silken ball gowns, jackets in smart sable, bottles of Prosecco on punt floors between them; a traditional single punt with a middle-aged man holding it steady for his family, including a well-insulated granny; a couple of canoes, paddlers in track suits; a lone coracle with a father and young son.

"Can they all watch, for nothing?" Charlotte whispered. "I mean," she feared it a silly question, "aren't they within college premises, beyond that bridge?"

"The river is like the internet," their passenger said. "For the moment. Nobody charges us to watch the sky."

Only a family of geese continued upstream, one parent leading the way and the other bringing up the rear, their adolescent offspring drifting between them, ignoring the expensive display.

"Do you want me to press on?" the guide looked at Suki.

"Of course!"

"Please," Charlotte added. "As close as you can. This is Andrew," she explained to their passenger.

"Shh," said Suki. "Watch!"

Andrew nudged the punt forward, a narrow gap yielding as he eased between other boats. One or two passengers turned briefly to register the latecomers. Somehow he found space to turn the punt sideways so none of them needed to crane backwards, then jammed the pole hard into the soft river bed to stop it shifting.

The sharp smell of gunpowder overlaid with sausages reminded Charlotte of fireworks nights of her childhood. Smoke wafted over Trinity Bridge. Explosions peppered the darkness. Heart-shaped displays. Flares along the bank. Lasers skittering in the sky. The music switched and twisted from Mendelssohn to Ariana Grande, Bruno Mars to Albinoni, coordinating with the display. Inevitably the bangs, so loud now they sounded in their stomachs, lagged behind the flashes . . . exactly, Charlotte remembered, as the thwack arrived some time after the batsman whacked the ball at her brother's school cricket matches.

While the colours raced and burst overhead she stole a look at their passenger. Unlike others on river with their concerted gasps of wonder, he made no sound. He simply watched, expressionless. Neither aloof nor cynical: simply neutral. In the light from the banks and sky she could now see his clothes: a black towelling dressing gown over the satin stripe of his trousers. His shoes a slightly worn patent leather. Most curious was the blacked-out face. She would have liked to have studied him for longer, but feared he might turn and see.

The flares continued to criss-cross over the water. This is really happening, Charlotte thought. I belong here and I'm going to be here for three amazing years. It is as wonderful as everyone warned me it wouldn't be, and I am happier than I can ever remember being.

The firmament sparkled like an upturned goblet, the fireworks frothing it with champagne.

Earlier in the evening, as the two girls had walked up The Avenue of Trinity College on their way to the friend's rooms where they would change, the sun had slanted shadows of punt poles on the Cam, promising to give their lifetime's treat a bright and perfectly clear sky: the marquees swathed in flowers and drapes; the fairground rides being run for safety tests; loudspeakers booming sound checks.

The weather had been lovely all month. There had been no rain since the beginning of June, when enthusiastic waves had washed the buildings with extravagant abandon, soaking the river banks and sparkling the college gardens fresh with colour. Now there were tentative predictions that it might be the hottest since 1976.

The night would be perfect.

Many undergraduates, she knew, couldn't afford even one May Ball during their three Cambridge years. How fortunate she was to enjoy her first before she had even started . . .

As they had passed into New Court, Charlotte had looked up and spotted a swallows' nest under the archway, snuggled into the eaves and disguising itself among the neo-gothic gargoyles. A parent bird darted in.

"Isn't it amazing," she said. "It means nothing to them. All this money and security and preparations. They just fly in and out, regardless, as if in a parallel universe."

Suki's brow puckered. "They're birds," she said.

Now Charlotte remembered the swallows and wondered whether they minded all this noise and disturbance, after their bedtime.

A climax of rockets ripped the sky. "Must be the end," Suki pronounced confidently. Another volley thundered immediately, before sighing into the darkness. Charlotte sensed the collective suspiration of pleasure from the hundreds on the banks.

There was a hiatus, a few moments' breath merely, then the flotilla shifted. Far more boats than she had realised, thirty or forty, were now moving, mostly upstream towards Trinity Hall and Clare, some down in the direction of John's and Magdalene; back to other parties, other balls, or home to bed.

"Mate," Andrew said, "can I drop you off at Clare and you walk back?"

"I still don't have my key," the passenger pointed out, "to go through the front gate."

"Come aboard with us," Suki said. "You won't be checked from the river."

"Yes do!" Charlotte added. "Oh, but perhaps you need to get back," she added politely.

"I was working on something before I came out. I think it was: if p is prime and p squared plus two is prime, prove that p cubed plus two is prime." When he smiled, Charlotte realised he hadn't before.

There was silence.

"Because it's twenty-nine," he said. "My mother once told me if you have to explain a joke it's not quite so funny. Perhaps you have to be a number theorist. It would be amusing to join you," he agreed, "at the ball."

"Are you nuts?" Andrew said incredulously. "The committee employs an entire security firm, patrolling the river bank. Not counting the college porters. Even if you were dressed normally."

At this, the stranger took off his dressing gown, revealing a worn black jacket over a black T-shirt, leant over the side of the punt and put his entire head underwater. When he emerged, blowing water off his nose, he towelled his face vigorously with the dressing gown, rubbing the black makeup.

"I shouldn't collude in this" Andrew smiled despite himself.

"Thing is," their passenger objected, "gatecrashing is stealing."

Charlotte felt slightly shamed.

"But I needn't eat or drink, so I'd just be enjoying the air and the music."

"I wasn't thinking of the finer ethics," Andrew said.

"It's a bit like whether you think using someone else's wifi is wrong," the passenger continued. "Clearly, if the ball committee relied on honour, it would be unthinkable. But given that they have such tight security it is very tempting to accept the challenge. When I get caught," he reassured Andrew, "I could swim back."

"I'm on next year's committee," Andrew said. "It's already got me a pretty sweet internship this summer. And for God's sake get your face cleaner." They had drifted back under Garrett Hostel Bridge and were out of sight of the Trinity jetty.

"Your hands!" Charlotte pointed out.

"Well spotted." He dipped them in the river.

"Mind your jacket . . ."

He squeezed water out of his cuffs.

"Lucky you're dressed for a ball," Suki observed.

"These were my only black clothes. I had to buy the T-shirt and dressing gown. And black make up."

"Why?" Charlotte asked.

"I didn't have any."

"But why black?"

"And because I needed a tail."

"When I get to the Staithe," Andrew said, "you girls flash your wrist bands. This may not work."

"I'll leave the dressing gown in the punt, but I'd quite like it back. Can you leave it at the P'lodge for me?"

"You don't ask for much, do you?" Andrew grinned. "No promises. What name shall I leave it under?"

"Mine."

"Silly me," Andrew said. "Why didn't I think of that?"

"We don't know your name," Suki observed. "If you aren't Dr Wedderburn."

"Hello Jon," Andrew said casually to a distracted boatman with ponytail and leather jacket, supervising the rapidly growing queue. "Bringing back my early guests."

Jon barely glanced at them.

The two girls wobbled up the middle of the punt, exposing their wristbands. Their shadow followed.

All three had just reached the bank, when Charlotte turned. "Thank you!" She stepped back into the punt to give Andrew a kiss, but wasn't experienced enough to put her weight into the middle.

"Careful!" Andrew shouted.

Not-Doctor-Wedderburn, if such he wasn't, put one foot deftly into the punt – just off-centre, re-balancing it – lifted her up and placed her effortlessly on the bank, like a baby sister. He was stronger than he looked.

The boatman turned at the kerfuffle. Not-Doctor-Wedderburn steered the girls up the bank, towards the bridge into the crowds. They heard the boatman shouting, "Oi."

"You probably don't want to dip that frock thing," the Not-Doctor said, waving at Charlotte's swirling skirt as they crossed the Bridge. "The Cam's got lots of biology doing stuff in it."

"What were you thinking, Charlie?" Suki said.

"I wanted to thank Andrew. He'd been so kind. Anyway," she turned to their new friend. "You dunked your jacket in the Cam ..."

"My dinner jacket's been dipped in the Cam often before. Mostly by my great-grandfather. It's what dinner jackets are for. Rescuing girls and so on."

"Why the dressing gown?"

"I forgot."

"That you were wearing your dressing gown? Or that you had your jacket on under it?"

"No."

Charlotte was finding the conversation rather confusing. They stopped on Trinity Bridge to listen to a jazz quintet from the corner of Southfield.

"And if your name isn't Wedderburn, what is it?" Suki asked. "We called you Dr Wedderburn in supervisions."

"That proves nothing. You also wrote your implies sign backwards. Or was that Andy?"

"Adam," Suki corrected.

"You did what?" Charlotte asked.

"Which is about as illogical," he explained to Charlotte, "as putting your trousers on inside out."

"I really didn't," Suki protested.

"So instead of A implies B you had A implied by B. Not the same thing at all."

"It wasn't Adam either. There wasn't an Andy. Even though you kept calling him Andy. It was Tory, and she only did it once. Hello, Dave."

A tall redhead was bearing down on them. "There you are, Charlie!"

"On second thoughts it's more like putting them on back to front. Inside out would have the symbol going both ways: A and B are equivalent. Did you do that, too?"

"You said you'd be back for the fireworks," Dave grumbled.

"I'm sorry. We thought we would. David, this is Suki's maths supervisor. He either is or isn't Dr Wedderburn. He's gatecrashing," she explained in a whisper.

Not-Doctor-Wedderburn turned back to Charlotte. "What I forgot was that my dinner jacket didn't have a tail."

"I've got half an hour before the next set," Dave said.

"Not as in white tie and tails. I could have worn my father's tailcoat, if that's what I wanted. Tail as in jaguar. How do you do? That's why I had to buy the dressing gown."

"Charlie," Dave urged. "I haven't got long."

"Oysters!" Charlotte reminded them. "We all agreed oysters. The oyster tent's beyond the jazz."

"Except Doctor-Not-Wedderburn," Suki pointed out. "He can't have any. "

"Not-doctor would be more accurate than Doctor-not," he illuminated.

"Why does your father have a tailcoat?" Suki asked. "Is he a waiter?"

"He doesn't. Not any more."

"I wish you'd give me your attention, Charlie." Dave insisted. "I'll get in the queue." He didn't move. "Are you staying with Dr Wedderburn?"

"He's not Dr Wedderburn," Suki corrected.

"You said Dr Wedderburn can't eat oysters."

"No I didn't. I said Doctor-Not-Wedderburn. Until he told me he's really Not-Doctor rather than Doctor-Not."

"Like Eats Shoots Leaves," Charlotte said helpfully. "Except with hyphens."

"Don't you bloody start, Charlie. The place is pretentious enough without you joining in."

"And he can eat oysters. He just can't eat his own." Suki persisted.

"I think," the Not-Doctor said softly, "your friend would like to get in the queue. I'm very happy to queue for you, and we can bring you both oysters."

"And then you can have mine!" Suki said, delightedly.

"Bloody hell. You said he's allergic to oysters!"

"Dave, do stop shouting. Why don't you listen? He can eat other people's oysters. Just not his own. Because that would be stealing."

"Oh for fuck's sake." Dave abandoned them to elbow his way into the queue. The others followed.

"If your father doesn't have a tailcoat any more," Suki asked, "how could you have borrowed it?"

"It's not that my father no longer has a tailcoat. The tailcoat no longer has my father. Nor do I."

"I'm a bit cold," Suki said suddenly. "And I don't really like oysters anyway. I'm going back to the room to get my cardie. I could see you at the dodgems in half an hour? We've got the ceilidh dancing at two thirty. Apparently the Irish band is amazing."

Suki picked up her skirt a little clumsily and pushed her way onto the path towards the bridge and New Court. At the last minute she turned. "Eat mine for me!"

"Come on Not-Doctor," Charlotte said. "Let's get some not oysters. Or not queue for them. You're allowed to do that. Or not to. Or should that be to not? Do you mind split infinitives?"

"Not at all. I'm in favour of doing anything the French can't. But I'm not sure Sophie can gift me her oysters. Morally."

"Sophie?"

"Your friend."

"Your supervisee," she pointed out. "Suki."

"Especially if she hasn't even queued for them."

"That doesn't follow. You said you would queue on her behalf. And once you've given them to her," Charlotte continued, "she can bestow them on you."

"Charlie do stop blathering," Dave complained as they were pushed against each other in the oyster tent. Several people trod on Charlotte's skirt and another girl tripped and fell into her. "I've only got twenty minutes now."

"David's in a band," Charlotte explained. "He invited me instead of taking payment. So kind."

"Not really," Dave said dismissively. "There was an issue with the payment anyway. Though actually you can sell Trinity tickets for far more than they're worth."

"Well, it's kind anyway."

"You can't do that with a railcard," the Not-Doctor continued. "Just because something is legitimately yours doesn't necessarily mean you can give it to somebody else."

"Here you are, Charlie," Dave handed her the coveted treasure in its rough shell. "Well make your bloody mind up mate. D'you want this oyster, before you get chucked out?"

"Thank you," he accepted it graciously.

"Why would he get chucked out? He can pretend to be your techie."

"He doesn't look remotely like a techie. If he was my techie he'd be working. And he'd have a pass. He obviously doesn't belong. Tabasco?"

"That's ironic, David, considering he's part of the university and we're not."

"And I'm not sure you could sell a ticket for more than its worth. More than its face value, perhaps. I believe the general economic consensus is that something is worth what someone will pay for it."

Dave pushed forward to get more oysters, and finding Charlotte near said, "What kind of nut is he?"

"He hitched a lift on our punt."

"Figures."

By the time they emerged from the crush it was time for Dave's next set. "You coming, Charlie?"

"Maybe."

She gave him a little wave and stayed where she was. The two of them stood for a while on the bridge. Gorgeous dresses swept across the lawns: pastel raw silks, wide ball gowns, trailing little trains. So many girls looking so pretty. Men, a smattering in tailcoats and the rest in black tie, much more handsome than usual. They watched, resting in the still eye of the whirling revellers who were enjoying as many glasses of champagne, canapés, bands, jugglers, dances, entertainers, ices, as the few hours of the night could allow.

Then, by silent consent, they moved together into the archway leading to New Court. Charlotte paused to look at the swallows' nest again.

"Oh, they're still awake!"

"I like," he said, looking up, "that they care nothing for our concerns. Two ways to attend a ball. Work to get your place at Cambridge, swot for three years for Tripos, find a well-paid job in London to be able to buy a ticket, get lucky on the ballot. Or just fly home to bed."

"Or steal in on a punt?"

In Nevile's they found an unoccupied table and sat, within earshot of some students in conventional dinner jackets but with coloured bow-ties, singing close harmony under the Wren Library overlooking the sweep of the Backs towards the Cam and John's.

You may not be an angel, 'Cause angels are so few. But until the day that one comes along, I'll string along with you.

A few hours earlier she had barely dared to believe the dream. Now she sat in the core of contentment, with someone she didn't know and yet utterly at home. How had she landed in this strange, privileged world? Was she really soon to be part of it?

She shrugged off her pashmina.

"Why black? Were you going to a chess party?"

"Very good," he said. "An elegant solution."

"What fun!"

"If incorrect."

"So . . ." She waited. "Then what?"

"A jungle party." Obvious.

"Wait . . . You needed a tail. You were a negative comet spinning out of a black hole, which just happened to be flying overhead?"

"That's better than what I was."

"Actually, I know what you were because you told me."

He smiled.

"You blacked-up to go to a jungle party as a jaguar?" She laughed, incredulous. "Didn't anyone think it was a bit . . . politically incorrect?"

"I don't see what's politically incorrect about a black animal. If I'd been a Black and White Minstrel that might have been rude."

She shook her head and laughed some more. The singers had changed tune.

I dreamed last night I got on the boat to heaven.

"Political correctness doesn't have to be rational. People object to blacked-up Morris Dancers, which is nothing to do with race. I would expect someone to take offence."

"I can't worry about offending people. If I want to stay alive."

She considered this.

"What happened to your father?"

"He was murdered."

Sit down, you're rocking the boat. Be dm d d d dm.

"I'm sorry," she said quietly

"His college," he indicated the singers. "And mine now."

"What?"

"These choral scholars. That's where they're from. My father was the organist. Not recently."

"He had a tailcoat for conducting?"

"These are his organ shoes I'm wearing."

She felt, as she had never felt even with best friends or her mother, that she could say anything. Without really meaning to, she said, "You don't seem quite real. Or rather, more real than anyone. Just not ... ordinary. I feel like Alice, in another world. An equally valid one," she added.

For the next half minute he was quite still.

I would like to sit here for ever, Charlotte thought. Like this, doing nothing at all.

You've got to. Hide. Your. Love away ...

"When I was younger," he began, "about three I suppose, I was on the back of my mother's bicycle – sitting behind her, on the way to nursery school – and I realised there was no way of knowing she was real, or the sky was, or my teachers were, or any of it other than I myself."

"So did I!" Charlotte agreed, astonished. "Though I was five or six, I think."

"It could all be a figment of my imagination. The odd thing, of course, is that I couldn't know I was real either. But didn't doubt that, for some reason." He smiled again, his unusual smile. "It's the rest of the world I'm not sure about."

Goodnight, sweetheart. Well it's time to go. Ba da ba da boom.

The close harmony came to an end and the singers packed up.

"Sally said she'd meet you at the dodgems. Do you need to go?"

"I suppose so. Do you want to come? Or ... stay here?" she added, in case he didn't.

"I'll come. I can't have a ride, of course: that would be cheating."

They crossed back over the bridge, along The Avenue. Shadows were thrown against the trees: ghostly silhouettes, beyond the leaves, lurid green as if cast in a faerie spell from a Midsommer Nights Dreame. They passed marquees and bands, hamburger stalls and drinks portals and the Chill Out tent, arriving at the fairground rides near the back gate. They couldn't see Suki. The queue was short, and when the previous ride finished he handed her into a car.

"I'll watch you." He walked to the edge of the rink.

The other cars filled up. Nobody took the empty place next to hers. The toy vehicles jerked into life, and at that exact moment he leapt hazardously across the rink, darting like Mr Bean, dodging the traffic as it began to swerve.

"Oi," she heard for the second time that evening.

He jumped in beside her. "No point wasting a seat." They were rammed from his side. "Do you want me to drive?"

She was laughing too much to answer.

His steering was adept. Rather than aiming at other cars as everyone else did, he avoided them so adroitly that when the game ran out a few minutes later, they had hardly been touched. "Very satisfying," he said, and helped her out.

"I thought this place was supposed to be full of clever gits," an angry attendant complained. "Why d'you leave it till the last minute, you dick?"

"It would take rather long to explain," he said courteously. "I apologise for annoying you," he added, with genuine humility.

"Just worried you could have hurt yourself," the other conceded, confused.

They walked back up The Avenue.

"Anything else you want to see?"

"Everything," she waved her wristband at the security man on the bridge.

"Excuse me, sir. May I see your pass?"

"Ah. I think this is where I dive in the Cam."

"Mr Wedderburn?" A porter approached, intercepting the security guard. Mr Wedderburn – if such he was – smiled, delighted.

"Bernard!"

"Good of you to remember me, sir."

"Of course I remember you. You gave me some excellent tips on brewing ale."

The guard moved off to check on other guests, leaving the matter to the porter.

"Enjoy your evening, sir."

"That was clever," Charlotte said as Bernard moved on. "You've shown you can do it. You can stay all night, now."

"In which case," he said, "I really ought to leave."

"Should you?"

"I suspect Bernard knows, which puts him in a compromised position. I say, Bernard," he called to the porter.

"Are you lost, sir?"

"I hitched a lift from this lady and a friend of hers. Susie something. You'll know her: first year, mathematician, red. Curly. Pre-Raphaelite. I haven't got my college key-card, so I was on the river bank. Instead of taking me to my rooms they brought me here. I'm not exactly lost, but I didn't quite mean to be here."

"I suspected something of the sort. Would you like me to escort you out, sir?"

"I ought to go back the way I came. By river, really. I'm locked out."

"There'll be a very long queue for the punts. It's our ball tonight." Bernard indicated the hundreds passing before them.

"I thought it might be. If you have time . . ."

"Will you excuse us, Miss?"

"Of course."

"Er." He hesitated. "Goodnight." Charlotte thought he was about to shake her hand, but as she held hers out he put his in his pocket. "Mind you," he continued to Bernard as they walked away, "I could wait by the back gate until someone comes along." He turned again unexpectedly, and held her gaze as if slightly puzzled, before continuing, "Or I could go in by the front. The night porter should let me in . . ."

They were out of earshot.

Charlotte checked her telephone. On her wrist twinkled the white-gold cocktail watch her mother had lent her, inherited from a war-spinster great-aunt and studded with tiny diamonds. It never occurred to her to look at it. It was ten to one already. She shivered. Suddenly, the night seemed long. David's band was playing until one fifteen.

She sent Suki a text reminding her of the ceilidh, and went in the direction of the band tent.

Chapter Two

NIGHT

The ceilidh had been playing for half an hour and Suki still wasn't there. It was the act they had most wanted to hear. And dance to.

Suki's telephone went straight to her voicemail.

The music was Irish enough, but most of the dances were Scots and the caller at sea somewhere between the two. He managed to turn *The Dashing White Sergeant* into a complicated Rugby scrum before introducing something involving concentric circles, more like a cowboy barn dance than anything to the accompaniment of uilleann pipes and a bodhran.

Charlotte sat near the front: the harpist was too good to dance to.

After another ten minutes the band broke up. She took a last look around for her friend.

They had borrowed a third year medic's rooms in New Court so Charlotte sent a text saying she'd go there. She gathered up her long skirt and tripped up the stone stairs, worn in the middle with centuries of students running up and down and shouting to each other just as they were tonight.

Their makeup was strewn about in the sitting room, as they had left it in the light midsummer's evening. She envisaged the earlier gaudy queue below in New Court, the lavish costumes, the banter between friends as they waited merrily for the ball to start. The scene was now more bedraggled but no less celebratory. She left the window open and crossed the room to the bedroom to lie down for a few minutes.

She woke disoriented, her gown crushed. She rummaged in her clutch bag. Twenty past three. It was disappointing to have missed

28

any of the night, but perhaps worth it to feel so refreshed. She ran her fingers through her hair and scrunched it into place.

Suki must be enjoying herself. Charlotte straightened the bed and left it as she'd found it.

She didn't immediately notice anything in the sitting room: it was now in darkness. She switched on the light for her makeup. Suki sat on the window seat, hunched, her head on her knees, still.

"Hello!" Charlotte said brightly. "Were you having a great time? Suks?"

She knelt on the floor next to her. "Suki? You all right? Hey . . ."

Her friend barely moved. Charlotte realised she was crying. "What is it?" Suki rocked into her arms and sobbed. Charlotte wondered how long she should hold her, whether to get tissues, how to put the kettle on. It was a few minutes before she could let go.

"I'm making you some tea. Will you be all right?" Their roles reversed, despite Suki's whole Cambridge year ahead of her.

There were dirty mugs by the kettle, a box of teabags and a used spoon. Charlotte opened a cupboard but found only instant coffee.

"I'll be back in a moment. I'm going to find milk." She went into the corridor, opening doors. One led to the bedroom which must belong to the other occupant of the set. The bedclothes were in disarray and she saw Suki's pretty feather cardigan on the floor. She retrieved it. The next door was locked, but then she found a door saying 'Gyp Room'. It was a tiny kitchen. She took milk from the fridge, then returned for sugar.

"Here we are," she said, shutting the door carefully. She continued the chatter as she stirred tea bags and added sugar to one of them. Suki stared out of the window and went on crying.

"Come on, Suki. Take this. It's okay: I'm just moving your skirt out of the way. You don't want to wreck your dress, shaking your tea like that. I've put sugar in it."

"I don't take sugar."

"I know."

Suki winced at the heat. She gave the mug back. "Where were you?"

"I waited for you at the ceilidh. Like we said."

"The ceilidh," she said dully. "Have I missed it?" Tears ran down her cheeks again.

"The caller was rubbish: you didn't miss anything we can't do better another time. Have another sip." She waited. "Tell me what happened. If you want to. Do you want me to get anyone?"

"No! No, please."

"Okay, okay." Charlotte waited a moment. "Where did you go, after the punting?"

"I can't remember. We went to the photo booth. There was a long queue so we came back. Then . . . I don't know. I don't care. I met friends, and I was introduced to someone. A Fellow. He seemed really good fun." She started sobbing again and couldn't go on.

"Did you . . ." Charlotte thought of the feather cardigan. "Did you go into the room along the corridor?" Suki nodded. "Did he . . . ? What happened?"

Suki took a long, messy sniff, and wiped her nose on her wrist. "He . . . wouldn't stop. I couldn't make him stop."

A couple of years earlier there had been a series of crimes within a few miles of their Hertfordshire home. For those few months until the police caught the perpetrator, they were allowed dispensations. Girls who had taken the bus to school for years were driven by fathers. Boyfriends stayed over if parents were out. Charlotte took Folly with her everywhere, friendly tail wagging at the unexpected privilege: no shop protested. She had never felt such fear. At the time she thought she would rather be murdered.

Now she felt a burning, uncontainable rage. How dare anyone do this to her friend? He barely deserved to live.

"Tell me. If you can."

"Oh, Charlotte, it was horrible." The tears rolled. "I kept saying, Stop it, please stop. He just laughed. Eventually I screamed. Nobody heard me. It was really scary." She stared out of the window, and rocked on the seat. "Then he called me a frigid fucking cow. Like it was my fault."

There was a terrible silence. If he swore at her, perhaps he hadn't done worse?

"We report this," Charlotte said firmly. "Immediately."

"No!" Suki shrieked, keening afresh. "It was my fault. He's a Fellow."

Charlotte clenched her fists. She wanted to fling open the window, stop the ball, tell everyone to be outraged. And desperately, she wanted someone older to come and help.

Stay calm. Put Suki's feelings first. Look after her. And find out more. "Did he ... was it rape?"

"No!" Suki said, horrified. "Yes," more quietly. Then, "I don't know." She looked at Charlotte wildly. "I can't ...". This provoked a fresh eruption of weeping.

"Shhh." She wondered whether anyone would hear Suki's howls. And whether that would be a good thing. But there was far too much noise coming from the revelry below.

Suki's makeup-smudged eyes were like skull's sockets in the darkness. "He tore my dress."

Absurdly, this seemed the most pitiable thing. Torn silk doesn't knit itself together.

How could a Fellow do such an evil thing? He must be expelled from the university. Would he go to prison, even? Charlotte stroked Suki's beautiful skirt. "Your dress will mend." She knew how long it had taken to choose; that her parents couldn't afford it; her godmother had treated her. She had thought it would last for ever.

"Do you know who he is?"

"I know his college. Please, Charlie. Please don't tell anyone. *Please.*"

Charlotte had no idea what to do. Suki had always looked after her, in a gawky kind of way. She gazed at her mug of lukewarm tea, abandoned on the floor.

"I've decided." She said. "Finish your tea. We're going to find your friend."

"What friend?"

"Dr Wedderburn."

"What on earth for?"

"I don't know. I ... think he was kind." Suddenly, the plan seemed imperative.

"He was just my supervisor for a few weeks. And he's ... odd: everyone says so. Mathematicians are." She grimaced the ghost of a smile. "Cambridge ones."

"I don't know why. I trust him." She felt near to tears herself.

"Won't he be asleep?"

"I think when you're ... when you've ... It's allowed to wake him up." She was filled with a new certainty. "Come on. We can still be back long before the Survivors' Photo."

Suki stood. "Your first May Ball, Charlie. And Trinity. You may never go again. And what about Dave?"

"David's fine. His last set doesn't finish till a quarter to five. I'll text him. Wash your face in the bedroom. Your mascara's all over the place."

As the city clocks struck four, they stood outside the front gate of his college. It was only then Charlotte realised they had no way of getting in. Why had they come? There was a nurse on call at the ball.

As they dithered shivering on the Cobbles, the eye in the needle of the front gate opened from within. Charlotte dashed forward and held it while a student came out. Nobody looked out of the porter's lodge to challenge them. They walked around the Front Court, towards the river.

"Now," she said as they reached the great lawn. "Where are his rooms?"

Suki stared at her. "How would I know?"

"You went to his supervisions."

"They weren't here. He came to my college."

The two friends looked at each other and despite everything, began to giggle.

"I do love you, Charlie. You're nuts." As they hugged, Suki's sobs of laughter turned to tears again.

"We're going to find him. He said we'd passed his rooms, which suggests they might be along here." Charlotte led them into a courtyard, just before the bridge, with a gnarled old tree sagging benignly over the lawn. She gazed, trying not to feel despair, at the blind windows facing them. "We'll look for the name Wedderburn."

"I'm not sure he's even Wedderburn. Somebody called him Fitz. I only had two or three supervisions with him. And I don't know why we've come."

"I don't really, either. I'm sorry Suki. I'm a rubbish friend. I just ... look, there's somebody."

One light was on. The curtains were only partially closed. Charlotte ran over the grass to peer in. "It's him! He's up and awake." She started knocking on the window. "Mr Wedderburn!"

"What are you doing, Charlie!"

He opened the window. "Hello," he said. "Would you like some tea? I just heard the clock strike four and realised it was teatime."

"Yes, please!" Charlotte said.

"As you can see, I'm through the doorway, on your right."

The door under, "Mr T. A. F. Wedderburn," lettered in white, was open by the time they reached it. He ushered them in and looked from one to the other, then more carefully at Suki. "Would you like a hug?"

"No!" She said vehemently.

"Have this while you think about it." He dug in his pocket and handed her a clean handkerchief, with 'Monday' embroidered in mid blue. "Wait a minute. Is it tomorrow now?" He took it back, rummaged in a drawer and produced one in slightly different blue embroidery: 'Tuesday'.

The girls stared at him, then each other, then started laughing. Really this time. Like water tumbling over the rocks.

"Perhaps I would like a hug," Suki said. He put his arms around her. That was all. He didn't pat her. Or say, "There, there." Or rub her arms or stroke her hair. Just held her. Like a mountain, Charlotte thought. Like the Cam.

As if Suki were a child, or a frightened dog. Almost as if someone had taught him, Women need to be hugged, sometimes.

"I'll make the tea," Charlotte said. "I knew we were right to come."

Chapter Three

DAWN

It was after four when Mark came to bed. She heard drawers opening and shutting, the wardrobe door complaining, shoes hitting the floor. The springs moaned as he sank heavily in the bed without touching her. Within minutes she felt his low snoring growl.

The darkness was diluting into grey. A lone bird attempted something. Now she'd been woken, she wouldn't sleep again.

What had he been doing? Working? Emailing? He used the room he called his library. She preferred the comfort of reading in bed, though once Mark was there she had to turn the light off.

She was not entirely pleased with what she had worn last night. It was a calf-length dark red velvet dress, an unusual choice for midsummer, especially one as balmy as this, and one of their guests had commented on it.

The conversation had crossed back and forth about the table, as it should, until Shirley said, "You know all about this, don't you Liz? Aren't you on the Museum Committee?"

That was the moment at which Mark finished saying something to Tom's partner Rachel at the other end of the table, and addressed her. "Would you get the coffee now?"

"I'll get it in a minute. Yes," she turned back to Shirley. "It's a complex issue. He told us his terms upfront. He was very courteous, and quite happy to take his money elsewhere. His ideas are extremely well researched." She was about to explain his vision for the modern collection.

"It's been a minute," Mark said from the other end of the table. The conversation stalled and faces turned to him. His iPhone was in his left hand, timing her.

Silence. The room waited.

She pursed her lips into a smile and tilted her head attentively. She was surely used to it by now.

Everything Mark did made sense. He made the money so she did everything else. Brought up the children. Cleaned the house. Tidied the garden. Arranged the holidays. Produced the dinner parties. Down to every detail such as laying the table and filling the dishwasher. And, of course, getting the coffee. Even if she was in the middle of a question from Shirley, in the middle of a sentence.

Mark's contribution was to threaten the guests' glasses with wine.

If she had asked him to help with any of it, even carrying the bowl of olives because she hadn't had enough hands, he would have said, "Do I ask you to help me when I go to work?"

As she waited for the kettle to boil she took down from the window sill the tray of herbs she had planted and tended, and pulled at the little dead twigs on the sprigs of thyme and the brown parsley leaves. It was a job better suited to scissors than fingers, and after a few tugs she had dislodged the plants from their soil.

She carried the coffee into the sitting room, punched a few cushions and waited for Mark to bring the guests through. If he didn't she would call brightly that coffee was ready. If still no one moved she would presumably go into the dining room and ask if they would prefer it in there.

After the last of them had gone she stared into the empty summer grate. Mark sat opposite her swilling dregs of coffee.

"Shirley is a boring woman. I wonder why Brian stays with her." He drained his demitasse, glanced at the tray where some of the guests had put their cups to save Liz a few seconds of clearing up, placed his beside his chair and left the room.

She took a long breath . . . and remembered what the scent was. Lilies. That was why she stayed. Nothing to do with the home or social status or the fact that they could afford anything they needed, even if she didn't get to say what that was. But because every other Friday, mid-morning, the doorbell rang. She never went out on Friday mornings, now. The shop had come to know her. Fabulous Flowers. And it was indeed rather fabulous that every fortnight her sitting room was smothered with the scent, often before the previous bouquet had died.

At first she had assumed it was just one bunch, a birthday present. When another arrived two weeks later she thought it a mistake. At the third or fourth delivery she rang and told him they were still coming.

He laughed, and said he hoped so!

He was the reason she kept going. The reason she rose in the morning. They hadn't seen Selina for nearly eighteen months and had no idea where she was.

She never expected to be top of his list of priorities. Wouldn't want to be. She went over to the occasional table and took out the photograph she kept in its unobtrusive drawer. Nobody needed to say how handsome he was. It was so vibrant it hit you in the face.

Clever. Ambitious. Successful.

He wore the hood with the dull white fur which signified something, she couldn't remember what. Now he had a different hood. Not because he'd achieved anything, he said laughing. Just because he'd stayed out of prison and collected his MA. That was how Cambridge worked.

He would next be home late on Christmas Eve: he was far too busy to come sooner.

Occasionally, she imagined something awful happening to him, indulging in the searing pain of it so she could enjoy the sweet relief afterwards.

Suppose a lorry swerved when he was on his bicycle. It was ridiculous that he rode a bicycle when he could surely afford a car. But that's what they all seemed to do: a kind of inverted snobbery, perhaps. Suppose an ambulance, flashing, wailing, responding to a call from a passer-by, swerved to the curb and wheeled him into the back of the vehicle on a trolley. Elizabeth was not a woman of great imagination, and the picture stopped there.

If that happened, she would have nothing left. She would walk out, leave Mark for ever and never come back.

Mark had gone up to his study before midnight. He hadn't wanted to disturb her. And he'd had work to do. Keeping her in new outfits.

Now the night was starting to drain away. He poured himself a decent malt from the collection in his cabinet, and flicked through some crude porn on his laptop. He thought briefly of Rachel, and wondered what it would be like to have her a couple of times. If she used the number he'd slipped into her hand. He didn't expect her to.

In relationships as in business, Mark believed in a musket-shot approach.

He went upstairs at about four.

Lizzie had been asleep for hours. He got into bed without waking her.

A grubby dawn was leaking through the closed window when she felt the slight chill from the duvet being yanked over to his side.

The shadows shifted slightly in the room.

Chapter Four

DAYBREAK

"Theo," he said. "After Mozart," he added after quite a long pause.

The girls looked at each other.

"Theophilus?" he suggested.

Charlotte said, "Ah."

"Don't get it," Suki said.

"Amadeus," Charlotte added helpfully. Before she had a chance to explain further her mobile chirped. "Hello, David. Fine. Just went for a walk. Er . . . now? Okay. Bye."

"What time is it?" Suki asked.

Theo looked at his wrist.

"Whatever is that?" Charlotte stared at a gadget which surely belonged on a spaceship.

He unstrapped it, and handed it to Suki. She studied the rows of purple luminous dots. "Wow, that is so cool! Binary?" He nodded. "How?"

"Top: hours. Middle: minutes. Bottom: seconds. Least significant on the right. Obviously."

"Hang on . . . Off, on, off, on. Five o'clock?"

"Good."

"And, um, twenty-nine minutes."

He looked over her shoulder. "And thirty-three seconds, thirty-four, thirty-five. Et cetera."

To Charlotte it might as well have been a washing machine control board.

He showed her. "This light on the top row represents eight, then four, two, one. Eight isn't lit; four is; two isn't; one is. Four and one equals five. Easy." Suddenly, it was. "Next row represents: thirty-two, sixteen, eight, four, two, one."

"Third row . . . the same?" Charlotte hazarded. Some number of seconds as minutes.

"Well done. Read the minutes: middle line. The first light, thirty-two, is off. All the others are on. What does that add up to? Never mind: boring arithmetic. Thirty-one. It's an exciting moment because they're all about to change. What will thirty-two be?"

"First one on and all the others off?"

"Yes!" And all the little lights switched over.

He took a card from his desk and drew a line of four dots, six underneath, then another six, representing his watch face. "Look at it before you go to sleep. Then you'll remember next time. It's fun watching someone who's just looked over your shoulder hoping to read the time."

"It's gone half past five in the real world," Suki pointed out. "We were supposed to be back for the Survivors' Photo. Do we really want to?"

"Yes," Theo said.

"Why?"

"Because you are. I'll walk you to the porters' lodge. Where's my key-card?"

"You'd lost it," Charlotte said. "That's why you hitched a lift with us. Is this it?" She pointed to a blue university card under the watch he had just put down.

"Thank you."

As they were walking towards the porters' lodge, Suki said, "He mentioned you."

"Who, me?" Theo asked. "I mean, 'Who, who?'"

"The . . . person I was telling you about." She didn't want to say it. "Dr Thorpe."

"Ah." They walked on.

"He told me to call him Crispin," she added uncomfortably.

"Did he say anything interesting?" Theo asked. "People don't, usually."

"He . . . offered me stuff. I was a bit slow realising what he meant. He said I had you to thank."

"For supplying you with illegal substances?"

"Not quite, but yeah. Implied you were responsible."

"What did he say? Exactly." The sun was beginning to glance the tops of the trees in Scholars' Piece, the young light making everything fresh and clear in the vast courtyard, as if they were the only people in Cambridge. The golden hands of the clock above the porters' lodge showed a quarter to six.

The air smelt of midsummer, of the hedgerows of Charlotte's childhood, the sweet sharpness of dawn. The days would be halcyon as long as youth could last.

Suki's brow puckered. "I told him about you joining our punt. Because it was fun." She faltered. "I'm sorry. So much happened afterwards. He suggested you're a bit, um . . . naïve?"

"It would be more useful to know."

It came out in a rush. "He said you're a total dick. You sold him bitcoins, or something?"

"That's much more interesting."

"I don't think it meant anything." Suki was uncomfortable.

He started walking again. It was hard to tell whether he was preoccupied, or always like that.

"And," Suki was trying to lighten the atmosphere, "he said you always bloody call him Tristram."

"Seems a rather trivial objection. He surely knows whom I mean."

"Not like writing your implied sign back to front, you mean?" Charlotte smiled.

"Not like that at all."

Somewhat to their surprise his key-card worked in the porters' lodge gate. Just before Trinity Nevile's Gate he said abruptly, "Goodbye then." Before they had a chance to say anything he was walking away.

"I like your supervisor."

"I see what people mean though."

It was nearly six o'clock. There was no longer any check on people coming in and they joined the clusters gathering in Great Court. Charlotte saw Suki looking around nervously. They shivered, realised they were sore and tired and craned their necks up at the tower when they were told to say, Cheese.

Others chattered of punting to Grantchester for breakfast, or going to one another's rooms. Charlotte had intended to fill her morning with memories. But when Suki suggested going back to her room she agreed, thankfully.

"Up early," the porter observed as Theo let himself back in.

"It feels rather late but perhaps you're right." He checked his pigeon hole, picked up a couple of letters, decided they had been there some time and put them back.

The relatively new porter shook his head. He had been to the University of Hard Knocks. You wouldn't last five minutes if you couldn't tell which way up the day was, there. Cambridge is a funny old place. You can be daft as a brush and still get on. Some of them just mess about on computers. Must be useful to someone.

For his thesis, Theo's supervisor had suggested the snappy title: 'Transference Principles for Pseudorandom Sets in Additive Combinatorics.' He thanked him, agreed it was more or less accurate and some time later called it: 'From All Numbers to Prime Numbers.'

Which, as he said, was virtually the same.

Back at his desk he arranged in front of him the notes he had been making on Szemerédi's Theorem and the density of primes, and considered the sequence he was working on. Why was it pseudorandom? It seemed intuitively that it should look random . . . but this would need to be proved.

He stared at it, waiting for his brain to work. It wouldn't.

He gave up and wandered over to his piano. His mother Ann had bought it for him when he was an undergraduate and couldn't find time to visit the college practice rooms. He began on what he remembered of the first movement of the *Moonlight Sonata*. He had never before noticed the underlying eroticism inherent in the scrunching chords, the solid bass and skipping treble striving for harmony through dissonance. He played on, remembering the full moonlight softly stroking the college lawn, then suddenly couldn't remember any more. He searched in his piano stool, strewing his music about, then plunged into the fierce third movement. He was forced to give that up too after a few bars. As always, his competence frustrated by lack of time.

He poured himself a bowl of cereal and took off his shoes and socks. They had finished his milk in their many mugs of tea so he picked up a carton of orange juice, contemplated it, then poured it over the cereal. Looking around unsuccessfully for a spoon, he experimented with his key-card. It was a delicate operation: if he bent it too much it might crack; he also had to avoid his signature, written in old-fashioned ink.

After two mouthfuls – and the obvious conclusion that the more commonplace utensil was superior in design – he discovered that the feeling wasn't hunger. Which presumably meant he wanted a bath. Or bed. Or something else altogether.

He tossed a coin and ran a bath, set an alarm for ninety seconds so it wouldn't overflow into his neighbour's room along the staircase, returned to his room to take off his clothes, folded the outer garments carefully and put his underwear into his laundry bag. When the alarm went off he put on his dressing gown, took his pyjamas into the bathroom, got in the bath and fell asleep.

When he woke he was puzzled that he had his pyjamas with him when it was so obviously day, decided he had made a mistake and returned to his room to dress for college breakfast.

Unusually, Theo was ahead of the game. It was mid-afternoon before Charlotte and Suki woke for breakfast.

The weather, which had smiled so courteously for the photograph, the breakfast trips to Grantchester and the lovely trailing dresses walking back to various rooms, still beamed benignly on the buildings of Trinity Street. Perhaps it would continue to hold good all week?

"It's teatime again," Charlotte surveyed the flotsam of their discarded silk dresses washed up on the froth of Suki's books and papers.

Suki had done little to personalise her room. There were a few postcards blue-tacked half-heartedly to the mantelpiece; an old-fashioned metal tea-light holder with a beaded shade given by a family friend; a couple of paperback novels; a weekend bag shoved under the desk. No scatter cushions, posters or throws on the backs of chairs.

Her bedroom at home contained nothing but maths books. Charlotte sometimes wondered if her friend had had an artistic bypass.

"Seems only half a day since it was teatime last. Shall I buy something to eat?" She offered.

"Dunno. When are you going home?"

"Tomorrow, maybe? My lift went with David at the end of the ball. Um . . . Suki?" Charlotte didn't quite look at her friend.

"Yup."

"You must report it, you know."

"Report what?"

"It's assault."

Suki picked at the carpet, cross-legged on the floor. "It feels my fault."

"It isn't."

"I must have given the wrong signals."

"Bollocks."

"Really?"

"He's nearly twice your age."

"Shit, I suppose he is. But he's good looking, and successful, and everything. Honestly, Charlie, I felt ungrateful."

"You do know that's stupid, right? That's not your brain talking."

"It was Theo's reaction that made me realise."

"Yes."

"Everybody laughs at him. Theo, I mean."

"Everybody?"

"My supervision partners. What was it he said?"

"'It's always the fault of the bully. Always.'"

"He seemed really upset, didn't he? Why was he?"

"I think he's a nice person. I mean, truly." Charlotte had put on her sandals and was looking for her mobile. "That's settled then. We get something to eat, then ring the police. Or go to the station."

"What will happen?"

"You'll have to give evidence. And . . . I don't know."

Suki rubbed her face "I won't have to tell my parents, will I?"

"Why wouldn't you want to?"

"I still feel it's my fault. And it's horribly embarrassing. I wouldn't want to upset them."

Charlotte pulled her friend to her feet.

Half a courtyard from where Theo, feeling unaccountably sleepy, sat in front of pages of scribbles – capital sigmas, lower case English letters, equals signs and pluses . . . rather as if an educated spider had got very drunk and then set out to impress a lady spider with a sonnet – Dr Crispin Thorpe had also risen slightly later than usual. But not much. He had been to plenty of May Balls and expected to go to plenty more, and three am was way beyond the point at which he usually got bored.

He had lasted longer than usual.

Chapter Five

MORNING

Hui stared across the playing field. The lime trees shimmered in their pale green gowns. The English summer was much more soothing than summers back home. Even one like this, which they said was 'better' than usual. You could sit in the classroom with the windows open and no air conditioning. And at break time, burst out of the door with the other boys – like lemonade exploding through a constricting bottleneck – into the mild, fresh air which would nudge you gently as you ran into it, rather than smack you in the face like the punishing heat in Shanghai.

All the grown-ups were saying this summer could be the driest since . . . way back in history.

He closed his eyes and thought of his mother's soft voice and unique smell: freshly boiled rice and clean laundry. Fabric conditioner perhaps. With an occasional hint of lemon grass. There was no smell like it at school. When they had rice in the dining hall it was tasteless and dry, nothing like the delicately sweet-scented rice of home.

"Hui?" Mr Scarborough pronounced his name as almost three syllables, "Who-you-ee." No one in England said his name properly. Some of them said his surname as Zang. Only the elderly Irish English teacher, who read them Shakespeare and Keats like music, lilted it like the beginning of 'wheat' with her softly breathed 'h'. The boys called him Hoo-Wee, occasionally Hwee-wee or Who-We-Ooh-We-Are; but they didn't do it unkindly.

"How do you calculate that?"

"Pardon, sir?" His mother had told him that it wasn't English to say 'Pardon?'. English people say, 'Sorry?' or 'What?' and he usually remembered this.

"Your mind seems elsewhere."

"Sorry, sir."

He was in the top set, but nevertheless usually arrived at the answer first. Mr Scarborough had told his parents he could be quite a promising mathematician if he wished. Hui had noticed that English boys didn't always follow in their fathers' footsteps, and his mother had been a teacher of mathematics before she became his mother. His uncle owned a factory making computer parts in Zhejiang Province, so he was nearly a mathematician too, or at least a computer scientist.

He stared at the rows of numbers which swam in front of him. He should have told Mr Scarborough why he couldn't concentrate – it wasn't his fault – but the bell was ringing now for the end of class.

The boys shoved their books into satchels for a quick getaway while the girls patiently finished off whatever sums they were doing. Hui packed up and went outside.

"Hoots!" a voice called across the tarmac. Hui was popular.

"Hey, Marcus." They weren't allowed mobiles during the day but Marcus had a new game on his. They ran to the bench beyond the cricket pitch, hoping the gappy wouldn't follow and offer to kick a football. Teachers are more canny than gappies and notice more, but they usually supervise from near the school, hugging a mug of coffee.

"What's with you? You're normally the swot."

"Couldn't sleep, with all that thumping."

"What thumping?" Marcus was a chorister too, like Hui, so he boarded even though his family lived within walking distance. Hui's family was nearly six thousand miles away.

The others had all slept through it, so what was the point of explaining? The bangs and explosions had woken him up, but it was the throbbing beat which had kept him awake. Gedunk, dunk, dunk. Mindlessly pounding deep beneath him.

Hui didn't usually miss his mother. He loved being at the choir school. In half terms and exeats he went to his grandparents in Hampshire: his British grandfather and little Chinese grandmother, who had come to England when Grandpops retired from business in Hong Kong. They spoilt him there. Only occasionally did he think of his Chinese school, and the boys he had once played with. And his mother sitting on his bed with a glass of warm soya milk.

He had seen English parents, even sometimes fathers, hugging their sons, occasionally kissing them. His half-English mother would never indulge in such embarrassment. So he would have felt silly if any of his friends had known he had wished for her in the night.

A teacher was out on the tarmac ringing the bell for the next lesson. Hui wished he could go back to bed.

"Darling?" Peter called up the stairs of the Provost's lodge. He liked to snatch a coffee or lunch with Caroline between meetings, when he could.

He threw his briefcase under the hat stand and took the stairs two at a time. Though just over retirement age he carried himself like a man twenty years younger, and still had the lithe grace of the cricketer he had been at university.

Her study door was ajar. She sat at her desk overlooking the college lawn, her hair a mess as it was when work was going well. She held up her left hand to indicate she couldn't be interrupted. Against all domestic protocol Peter came up behind her, kissed her head and read her screen as she hated anyone doing.

"Mmmm!" she protested.

He wandered over to the window. "Do you remember our first year?" He asked, knowing she would never forget. "That summer was like this."

One of his Junior Research Fellows, Theo Wedderburn, was walking along the river with a teapot. He had known Theo as a young chorister when his father Alan was still alive, and was fond of him. Generally, it was those who didn't know Theo who found him annoying. There was no malice in the boy whatsoever. Almost as if he lacked the selfish gene – so that, Peter realised, he could be far too easily crushed by a world too busy to wait.

They had been friends with his mother Ann, in a less busy time. She had been a musician in her time, but seldom played now. He saw Theo stare over the river and pour himself a mug of tea. As far as Peter could tell it came out already mixed with milk.

"What I can't work out," Caroline said, still typing rapidly, "is whether he has been to bed. He's been up since before six o'clock."

"How do you know?"

"I saw him, from this window."

"What on earth were you doing at six?"

"You may not have noticed this, being at some boozy dinner last night and for most of the preceding week . . ."

"Development Committee. Extremely boring and very little booze. Or not until afterwards."

". . . but the day starts around four at this time of year and some of us have work to do."

"Going well? How is little Atticus?"

"It is, actually. Despite your getting his name wrong and your patronising lack of support, superb, thank you."

"How can a *lack* of support be patronising? And what was Theo doing at six o'clock?"

"Escorting two rather lovely young girls in gorgeous gowns. It was Trinity and Clare balls last night, wasn't it?"

"Inter alia. Those were the main ones. They could have been to a concert."

"And still up at half past five? Anyway, I doubt if he's had time to go to bed since. Seeing as it presumably takes him half a day to change into pyjamas. But if he's been up all night why is he still on his feet now?"

"Perhaps he got up early, like you?" he suggested.

"Theo?" she laughed. "And why were the girls in evening dress?"

"Maybe they'd just bumped into him," he said, losing interest. "Lunch."

"Since you've completely wrecked my concentration I might as well give up."

"Jolly good."

Down in the kitchen she took a bag of M&S Baby Leaf and Wild Rocket out of the fridge. "What do you want with this?"

"Not a lot. Another dinner tonight. Havoc for the waistline, this job."

"You don't have to eat all you're offered. The Queen copes with tiny helpings. It's a shame," she said, adding some cold ham, "that you were out last night. The fireworks were the best I've seen."

"There would be something wrong," he pointed out, "if fireworks weren't always the best you've seen them. If human endeavour can't progress in the making of entertainment out of gunpowder . . . Damn," he said, seeing a clock he'd never noticed before. "I've got Tom coming in five minutes."

"It's fast. Probably just over five minutes, this time of day. No, don't," she said, as he rose to adjust it. "I set it eight minutes ahead at breakfast and the day catches it up. I know exactly where I am with it."

He stared at her as if she were demented. "Why on earth don't you get it fixed? Or throw it away? That is going to drive me nuts."

"I haven't yet had time. And it was a wedding present."

"Good grief, where did you find it?"

"In a box left over from our last move, among about twenty boxes of books, all still unopened. Which we really should get rid of," she digressed, committing the ultimate blasphemy. "If it's important, it's online. Anyway," the argument was familiar, and pointless, "it was given us by some cousin or other who had just come back from chalet-girling in Switzerland. Presumably why she gave us a cuckoo clock."

"Saints preserve us. Why not move the pendulum up?"

"It's glued on."

"You can't remember her name but you keep her hideous clock, which is neither functional nor fetching. Thanks for lunch. I'll see Tom in the sitting room."

"Want me to bring you coffee? What's it about?"

"The 'Visit.' Which I haven't told you about. Lovely if you have time, thanks."

"The Christmas Eve one? I've got time. Hope I can remember where I was, you pest."

"Any news from the publisher?"

"They've definitely dropped me. I don't care," she said quickly. "It's my best yet."

"What a bugger. I'm sorry. I'm sure you'll prove them wrong." He kissed her and collected his briefcase. "This 'Visit' is such a waste of time," and he went into their vast oak-panelled drawing room which looked out towards the river.

"Caroline," the Head Porter greeted her at their kitchen door, wondering whether to give her an air kiss and deciding against.

"Tom. I was just making coffee. How's the June Event?"

"It would be fine if it wasn't being organised by undergraduates. None for me, thanks. Missis' orders."

"Pete's in the drawing room. Do you want what my children call decoffeenated? Peppermint? Lemon-and-ginger?"

"Sounds suitably disgusting. When is your daughter next on the box?'

"Tonight, as it happens. BBC two. Medieval charnel houses of Europe. We won't be at all offended if you don't watch."

Mr Thomas Foulger, Head Porter, accepted nettle-and-dandelion without enthusiasm and went through to discuss with the Provost the security for an afternoon six months hence.

The stranger sat outside Café Nero in King's Parade, diagonally opposite the porters' lodge. Or P'lodge, he'd noticed they call it now. Guarded by a member of staff on the Cobbles, wearing the college purple stole. Didn't have female porters back then. Boring job. Turning tourists away. He knew better: he would simply stroll in. If challenged, he could tell the truth. The secret of lying, he knew, is keep it to a minimum. He had nothing to hide.

Yet.

He took a last pull on his cigarette and stubbed it out. If he had stayed with singing, would he be smoking now?

He hadn't been back for a long time. He had been part of this, once. This privileged, sun-soaked, tourist-admired, grey-stone-and-pinnacle world.

At the next table, a couple of mid-West Americans consulted a guide book. "The cahlege was founded by Henry Six. It was George

One that was mad, right?"

"He was the one with the eight wives," her consort asserted, "and a beard. He locked them up in the attic and murdered them. And then founded the Protestant church."

"Oh my. So this is Protestant?" She waved her booklet at the Chapel. "It's quite fine."

He pursed a grim smile. There had been a time when he preferred to be in the Chapel than anywhere else in his young world.

He pinched his fag-end between thumb and forefinger, and when he looked up found his past staring at him. Theo fucking Wedderburn. Caught between panic and excitement he half rose from his chair.

Theo had been one of the decent ones. Perhaps the only one. In that split second there wasn't time to work out the implications, but he already knew that this could change everything.

He was about to say something when he realised Wedderburn wasn't going to acknowledge him. Instead he had stopped dead, in the middle of the street a few paces away, staring straight at him. Then he turned and went back towards his college.

Well fuck you then.

Hadn't they been friends? Shared a passion for music? Even more crucially, maths?

He rose. He would stroll into college and wander down to the river: it was the weather for it. The first visit of many. The porters couldn't possibly know the identity of every member. The more familiar his face became, the less likely he was to be challenged.

He was wearing faded pink shorts. He had always understood camouflage: students never mind standing out.

And afterwards? He wouldn't care. It would be a tide mark in history. Those two Americans would need a new guidebook.

If Wedderburn had greeted him, said hello, sat down for a coffee with him, it might have become impossible. Wouldn't that have shifted something, so that he would have taken a different route for the rest of his life?

He avoided asking himself whether Theo had really done this on purpose. Whether he hadn't always been a bit ... unintentional.

Tom left the Provost's Lodge just after 3 o'clock. He loosened his tie as he stepped into the beautiful afternoon. They would have to start sprinkling the college lawns, if this continued.

He was beginning to get over his astonishment at being given this job. He had enjoyed his time in Special Branch, but frankly he'd risen as high as he was ever going to. So when his thirteen-year-old, after being voted 'Man of the Match', had said, "Never mind, Dad. You never make it to my matches," he had handed in his notice. As Charys had said, he had his pension.

He didn't tell her he'd applied to be an employee of Cambridge University. He didn't bother to let her know he'd been called for interview, either. Especially when he discovered that several other applicants had been working for the university for years. Decades, one of them.

Charys wasn't as astonished as he was when he was offered it. She considered being a porter a bit of a come-down for a Chief Inspector. Tom knew better. These old institutions had ways of doing things . . .

Before he even took up the post, he was measured for a silk top hat, the most expensive item of clothing he had ever worn. He would have to lead the college processions twice a year: once for the degree ceremony at the Senate House, and the other for the Founder's Feast, whatever that was.

He would not, thank goodness, be on the telly at Christmas. Just as well, now they had this 'Visit' to contend with. He would have quite enough to do. And only about three dozen further security concerns, since his meeting with Peter this afternoon.

If they ran the police like that, organised crime would rule the country. All the most basic security measures were ruled out for one reason or another, most of which had been in place for centuries.

Take that chap who had just passed him, walking down towards the river. Tom's antennae were immediately alert. Dressed like a student, yes, in absurd ostentatious shorts. Behaving like a student, nonchalantly ignoring everything around him as if he did it every day.

So what was it? Copper's instinct. Some aura of adrenaline around him, as if he was keeping a tight lid on something.

Tom wouldn't do anything about it, of course. Unauthorised people came into the college every hour of the day. There was no proper system of checking ID, as there would be in any business or school or the BBC – even in the polytech Tom had been to, with nothing valuable in it whatsoever.

In his first week he had been told a story dating back decades. Two blokes had walked into college under everybody's noses, dressed in white coats and carrying a step ladder; marched into the dining hall; and removed two portraits from the oak-panelled walls. One of Henry VIII. Both priceless. And walked out again. Nicked to order presumably.

Never seen again.

After another week in the job, Tom realised they could still do it today.

So there was no point in challenging the intruder in the pink shorts. All he had to say was that he was visiting a friend, and reel off a name Tom hadn't heard of. Or that he lived nearby but had forgotten his ID, and then invent a Cambridge post code. Non-members could be there for any number of reasons. He was probably taking a short cut.

Tom let it go. As he now let things go dozens of times a week.

But at least now he understood why he had got the job. Security was one thing he did know about.

And come Christmas Eve, the College would need all the expertise he had.

Chapter Six

EVENING

A few years after Theo's father died, a consultant psychiatrist had telephoned his mother Ann, one rare afternoon when she was enjoying the one thing she loved almost as much as her son: her beautiful Greiner violin, which her parents had remortgaged their house for.

It had turned into a longer conversation than she had expected. Though 'conversation' is perhaps a misnomer.

"They don't marry, these people. Thank God!" the eminent man assured her. "You won't have looked to him for empathy when your husband passed away." But she was not to despair, he said. "They often find a niche, a landlady to look after them, some clerical job."

No empathy? Theo had been the only star in her desolate night after Alan was killed: had made her tea and poured her wine and buttered her toast, and hugged her whenever she needed it.

"You will make a wonderful husband," she told him. "You understand what so few men do: that women sometimes need to be held, nothing more."

"Sympathy perhaps," the psychiatrist had continued, "very occasionally. To a limited extent. Empathy, never." She felt almost embarrassed, that he made so much of the difference between two words which are surely virtually synonymous. To prove his thesis, he quoted some study involving Smarties and baskets and people who were not in the room. He never even used the words, 'Asperger's syndrome'. He didn't need to.

For the rest of that summer, Ann felt numb. It was a second bereavement. He had taken her brilliant, considerate, talented and golden son from her. And left her with a mutant, deformed as if he had been melted down and crudely re-made in plasticine.

In the light of his pronouncement Theo's reaction, over a decade and a half later, is noteworthy.

After his unsuccessful attempt at study, he fell asleep in the afternoon and rose in the night. He wasn't sure whether he should be eating breakfast or supper, so played safe and had both. Happily he had now found the spoon for his cereal, under his pillow, being used as a bookmark in something he had been reading when he last changed his sheets. Then he made his standard sandwich, of ingredients he kept in stock and always arranged in the same order: wholewheat bread; ready-made mayonnaise; as many leaves of lettuce as could be persuaded in; quorn, preferable to meat since it didn't grow as many whiskers when tucked into a bookshelf; cheese ready sliced; bottled pickle; no butter.

He made this into what you or I might call a perfect square. To Theo himself it was not at all square and certainly not perfect. He then cut it in half.

Before getting to grips with proving his sequence pseudorandom, he needed more intuition. At the moment he felt he was blindly hoping it was pseudorandom: rather like a weak student working for a supervision, who tries to prove something without first getting a feel for it. Doomed to failure.

He had forgotten to eat his sandwich. That could explain it.

As he took the wherewithal to fix this out to a bench near the river, he thought over the events of the previous night.

Theo had never been sexually assaulted. He had never felt vulnerable as he assumed all women do, at some level, in a way men can never fully appreciate. But he had been bullied. He had experienced cruelty from grown-ups far more powerful than he was. And he could transport his soul – whether with 'sympathy' or 'empathy' he neither considered nor cared – to a room overlooking Trinity New Court, into the mind of a nineteen-year-old who, though academically competent, was far too naïve and uncertain of herself to stand up to a senior member of the university. Who was trying to be respectful to her academic superior as well as enjoy herself at her first Cambridge May Ball, the ticket for which had cost her far, far more than it ought and required her to go half a term without proper food and rather longer lacking books she would have liked for her course. He considered too how her precious youth and enthusiasm had been so carelessly and callously ruined as surely as the beautiful frock of which she had been so inordinately proud.

When his imagination reached that point (with far more empathy, in truth, than the eminent psychiatrist had shown his mother long ago) he experienced his anger in the form of an intense and almost unbearable physical pain.

Another man, in the grip of such rage, might have hit something or (depending on his educational disadvantages) someone. Perhaps competed vigorously with a ball – or in earlier times a more brutal weapon – according to rules set down by other men. These outlets were not available to Theo: from an early age he had been excluded from all sports he enjoyed, by teachers who were far more competitive than their pupils and didn't see in Theo's enthusiasm anything that would advance the school's reputation or their own careers.

He considered it uncivilised – and more to the point, unconstructive – to go round to Crispin's rooms and punch him in the face.

So instead, Theo wept.

He wept for the trusting nature of a young woman he had only just met. He wept because from now on she would have to be a little harder and more cynical. He wept because the treasured memory of her first May Ball had been spoilt for ever. And because her friend, even younger than she was, had been made to grow up far too soon.

Without knowing it, perhaps he also cried for a little boy long ago. Tormented by teachers, hounded for attainments he couldn't reach, squeezed brutally towards a mould he couldn't fit, punished for failing at tasks God had never intended him to do.

To the neurotypical night porter who happened to be doing his rounds at the time, it was half past eleven. The midsummer Cam lapped, dark and pungent, a few feet from the bench the Junior Fellow sat on. The sounds along the water, random shouts and knocks from other colleges, were sharper in the near-darkness. He hesitated. The correct thing was to walk on by and say nothing. Grown men don't cry. Most of his colleagues – ex soldiers, or security guards –

would have done just that. But he had been, albeit briefly, a porter on a hospital ward. He had not lived in England two years yet, and still kept the emotional expectations of his home country.

"You all right, sir?"

Theo's crying continued, untidy and uncontrolled. But he took his handkerchief from his pocket and contained his face in it, slightly nodding.

After a moment the porter sat, leaving manly space between them, looking out towards the river.

"You want a cup of tea, sir? In the Lodge? I'm on my own."

Theo blew his nose. "Thank you. Carlos."

Fancy the gentleman knowing his name. The younger academic staff seldom asked and never remembered. "I've got to check the back gate, and finish my round. Take me about seven minutes, okay?"

It was not done in Theo's college to call the young gentlemen sir, as it is in a more traditional place like Peterhouse. Nor indeed to think of them as young gentlemen. Carlos didn't care. The young gentleman had taken the trouble to remember his name.

Fifteen minutes later Theo arrived in the porters' lodge with a jug of home-brew ginger beer and a pack of cards. Carlos was not supposed to drink on duty, but ginger beer didn't count. Even at 7.2% proof, which Theo had recorded, in his careful brewing notes, this current concoction to be.

And which probably helped them to overcome the deficiencies of a 49-card pack.

A couple of hours later Theo went back to his room, unsure whether it was time to start work or to go to bed. It was, however, not long till teatime. It never is.

When Carlos finished his stint – warmed in his belly from Theo's strange drink – and got home to his wife just getting up for her early cleaning shift, he told her it was a mystery why anyone scoffed at that particular young man. He was the one of the best there. Excepting of course the college clergy, who don't count; and the Provost, who was above other mortals.

Even including them, he continued as his wife shut the front door behind her to catch her bus and he took his coffee upstairs to bed, he was one of the nicest people in the place.

Though they were all nice, of course . . .

Chapter Seven

THURSDAY AFTERNOON

"Oh, look!" Charlotte said involuntarily.

"What?"

"Doesn't matter."

Suki followed her friend's glance. "Oh," she said, jumping up.

Charlotte stared into her teacup, determined not to catch his eye but unfortunately peeking through the window just as Suki, now outside and talking to him, was pointing to where they were sitting.

A few feet into the tea shop he tripped over a woman's handbag. He entangled himself in apology, arrived at their table, realised there were only two chairs and went off for another while Charlotte hissed, "What are you doing?"

"Inviting him to tea."

"He's a tutor!"

"Supervisor. You were the one who said we should have tea with him at four in the morning."

"Shh . . ."

"Here," he said triumphantly, bearing the chair aloft and only stepping on one other customer's toes. "Shall I buy us all some tea?"

"We have some already," Charlotte said as he sat down, comfortably. "Don't you want some?"

"I usually do. But I can make it in my room. Was I going there, or somewhere else?"

Suki looked blank.

"You were going in that direction." Charlotte pointed up towards Trumpington Street.

"Perhaps I was going to get a basket from Ben Haywood's. Have you seen the chronophage yet? On Corpus."

"The what?"

"Oh, come!" And he took Charlotte by the wrist, pulling her between all the chairs and tables and out into the street, where they broke into a run till they reached the corner of Bene't Street.

"There," he said. "Isn't she beautiful?"

Charlotte had seen the clock before. The vast grasshopper grabbed the cogs of time and pulled them, ticking towards itself, each second sweeping in an electric blue arc and expiring just beyond where it had started, to make way for the next. When the minute was up, another blue light swept around after it, and in turn expired a notch on from its starting point.

"Yes," Charlotte sighed.

"It has true mechanical action," he explained.

For a few minutes they stood, admiring the savagery of the beast, munching, devouring, relentless, the seconds interminably digested with nothing to show.

"What oft was thought, but something . . ." Theo said.

"Ne'er so well expressed," Charlotte supplied. "I think," she added apologetically.

"This was the nightmare of my childhood."

"Did it frighten you?"

"The beast did," Theo said. "Time itself. I thought I was the only person being chased. Everyone else seemed to get away. It wasn't until the clock appeared that I realised it's the same for everyone. Others are always much further out in front, so I didn't realise they were losing the same race."

"I'm surprised you would want to be like everyone else," Charlotte said as they turned back for the tea shop.

"I'm surprised you don't already have a bicycle basket." Suki had caught up with them, and indicated the shiny new bikes ranged smartly outside Ben Haywood's.

"Did you ever play Grandmother's Footsteps?" he continued. "I don't know why grown-ups devise such cruel games. There's that other one about being eaten by a wolf."

"Our dog loves Grandmother's Footsteps," Charlotte laughed.

"It was the only game I ever won," he admitted. "Like Æsop's tortoise. The other children were so much faster they were always moving when the grandmother looked. A bike basket?" He turned to Suki. "Of course I have. How else would I carry my teapot?"

They returned to the tea shop and sat down. There was a lull. Theo seemed content to say nothing. Suki looked awkward, but then she often did. Charlotte cast around for something to talk about. Are you going away for the summer? Too boring. Did you get to bed all right the other morning? Too intrusive. What's your favourite colour? She was just deciding this was probably the question he would answer most readily, when Suki jerked into conversation.

"It's Charlie's birthday."

"Oh, it doesn't..." Charlotte began.

"Sorry?" he said, returning – perhaps reluctantly – from wherever he had been. "Who's Charlie?"

"Charlotte," Suki started, as Charlotte explained, "Some people call me that."

"Ah," he said. "Hence the tea outing."

"I'm not really celebrating."

"I thought you might like us to sing Happy Birthday," Suki said.

"Certainly not!"

"Sorree. Dr Wedderburn? I mean, Theo," Suki changed the subject, "did you say, in one of our supervisions, that it's possible to trace where bitcoins come from?"

"Yes."

There was an expectant pause.

"So... where do they come from?"

"Where do what come from?"

"Bitcoins?"

"Unanimous agreement of their existence."

"I see," Suki said, baffled.

"From the definition of bitcoin."

"Suki, I didn't mean you to..." Charlotte interrupted.

"From consensus," he elucidated further.

"Right," Suki nodded.

Charlotte squirmed. This was worse than Suki's announcing her birthday.

"From the block in which they were mined, if you prefer."

"It's just that Charlie's father . . ."

"Suki, please! Drop it."

"From miners that mine them. I've got some in my bedroom, if you want to see. Useless now, and have been for a long time. For a while they broke even, heating my room. Although the college pays my electricity and I got the coins, so I tried to give college the proceeds, but it became extremely complicated . . ."

"I meant can you work out where someone has bought them from?" Suki explained. "Charlie wanted to know."

"I'm not sure she does," Theo observed. Charlotte shifted. Her private question, to Suki earlier, had not been a worthy one.

"You want to place an order?" A pretty waitress with a romantic French accent and matching moue hovered at their table.

"What you meant was, is it possible to work out their provenance? Of course." He stared at the waitress. "Most people say it's impossible. It isn't. It's just difficult."

"Excuse moi?"

"I don't think so." Charlotte said helpfully. The girl looked very young, even to her.

"You need to work out the algorithm," he explained to the waitress. "And when you've done that you can trace an account."

She pouted prettily and moved off.

"Which is not difficult at all, but – oh!" he called after her. "Do you need me to buy something, to sit on this chair? It's perfectly reasonable if so."

She shrugged.

"Charlie wondered about something her father is doing."

"I was just being stupid," Charlotte said. "And he's not my father."

"Stepfather," Suki corrected.

"Ah," Theo said. "I have one of those."

Charlotte felt suddenly transparent: as if all her workings were as visible as the chronophrage's. Far from disconcerting her, this felt almost reassuring.

"If you come back to my rooms, we could start. We won't get it solved in a day. However, it is a birthday. We must have a cake. Did you say you are one of my pupils?"

"I had a couple of supervisions with you last term," Suki conceded.

"Here's my card. My PIN this week is a Mersenne prime. Choose something at Fitzbillies. We'll give you ten minutes." And he looked at the purple dots on his binary watch.

"A Mersenne prime?" Suki echoed.

"Ah. I was forgetting you're not a CompSci. A prime of the form two to the n minus one. That should tell you enough."

Suki wandered off, staring at his card as if for the answer. She would have fallen over the same handbag had its owner not snatched it up.

Charlotte glanced at Theo's watch. She thought she could remember the method but it involved too much mental arithmetic. The college clock outside was behind her. The unmeasured minutes stretched before them in luxurious silence.

She couldn't remember who started the conversation, but Suki was back at their table just as she was saying, "So do I."

"So do you what?" Suki settled back in her chair, spilling her tea and putting a receipt, his card and change on the table.

"Success!" Theo noted the signature white cardboard box with purple ribbon.

"Have a difficult stepfather," Charlotte explained.

"I didn't say he was difficult," Theo objected. "I find him difficult. My mother is a sensible and intelligent woman. Why would she marry a difficult man? It's all right not to like him," he continued. "But it's better to be truthful about why."

"My father was the best man I ever knew," Charlotte said, her eyes threatening to betray her.

"Of course."

"I remember your dad," Suki chipped in.

Charlotte turned to her, face shining. "What do you remember?"

"Him telling us off when he was trying to watch the telly!" Suki laughed.

There was a moment's discomfort, before Charlotte let it go. "I still remember the day he left. It was the most beautifully sunny afternoon. We were having tea in the garden. I asked where he was, and my mother said, 'But he's never home at this time.' I just knew. I don't know how."

"I'm sorry," Theo said. "I didn't get to say goodbye either."

"My dog knew too. She came out and sat with us, miserable. My mother said he was the best father in the world and he would always love me."

"You know it's not your stepfather's fault," Theo said, "that your father was the best man you ever knew?"

"S'pose."

A different waitress passed their table. Theo handed her his card before the girls realised. By the time they had finished protesting, the conversation had slipped away.

"You got it without too much difficulty?" Theo asked Suki.

"Sorry?"

"My PIN."

"I didn't have the nerve to use it in the shop. If I got it wrong they might think I'd pinched it. I went to the cash point to give me three goes."

"And?"

"I got it at the second attempt."

"Good. Caught out by 2047?"

"Yes." She blushed. "4095 was easy, because it ends in 5. 1023 wasn't difficult either. When I got to seventeens into 2047 I took a guess. Which didn't work . . ."

"Because?"

"Of 23."

Charlotte turned to each in turn, like a spectator at Wimbledon.

"Good again."

"8191 was my next try."

"Very good."

"I wouldn't do very well if I was a criminal in a hurry."

"You aren't. Next term I'll choose something harder."

As he was putting his card away Charlotte asked, "Your father . . . You said the other night . . ." She hesitated. "How . . . who . . . ?" She couldn't quite say it.

"Who killed him?"

"Yes."

"His murderer," Theo elucidated. "Shall we go? We'll eat the cake over tea-and-bitcoin-provenance. Like so much else, it's easier to understand the principle than execute the practice."

"Like tightrope walking?" Suki suggested randomly.

"Playing the violin," Charlotte offered.

They stepped out into the sunshine.

"Understanding emotions," Theo concluded.

That evening, the night of her eighteenth birthday, Charlotte arrived at Stansted Mountfitchet railway station just before seven. She had told her mother when to expect her but it was her stepfather Guy who was there, waiting in his silver Alfa Romeo.

She hid her disappointment. "It was kind of you to come."

"Of course we would come. Good ball?"

"Fantastic!" she said, before remembering Suki and feeling guilty.

"Dave's band?"

"All right."

"Only all right? Poor bloke," Guy smiled as he drove.

The implication irritated her, unreasonably.

She looked out at the dirty white may in the hedgerows, and the glaring yellow rape ripening in the still dazzling sun. It seemed very different from Cambridge. She had always loved coming home, rushing up to her bedroom in their old farmhouse, overlooking the rolling countryside through its little dormer windows. She would greet Folly. Have a mug of tea with her mother. Michael would look up from his homework and grunt.

It hit her that it was her eighteenth. She had been so preoccupied with A levels, and then her birthday treat of the ball, that she hadn't stopped to think about the day itself. She felt another slight pang of disappointment, which she dismissed as ungracious: why should her mother do everything for everybody?

Besides, she hadn't made anything of it either. She'd only come home because Theo said she should, for her birthday. How odd, when he barely knew her.

"Your thoughts?" Guy said.

"What?"

"Did you meet some nice people? Revisit your college?"

"Oh, yes, thanks. Met a Fellow there."

"Fellow classicist?"

"Mathematician."

"Oh, I see. I thought they called them dons. Was she at the ball?"

"He," she said without meaning to. How could she explain? If she told Guy that Theo was hitching a lift, he would think David picked him up on the way to Cambridge, and then Theo would seem somehow dodgy. She didn't know why this mattered.

Guy wouldn't get Theo at all. "We had tea in his room. Suki and I," she added, so he wouldn't get the wrong idea.

"So you think you'll be happy there?"

How could she explain? She understood why Suki felt she had come home, in her first Michaelmas Term. Charlotte loved her home and her family. But Cambridge was . . . everything. All her dreams rolled into one. Where she belonged.

"Yes, thanks," she said flatly.

She left Guy to bring in her bag. "Folly!" The labrador-retriever waddled out, tail belying her indifferent gait, followed by her mother, wiping her hands from the kitchen.

"I've run you a bath."

No 'Happy Birthday.' Not even Michael pretending he wasn't pleased to see her.

Fine.

When she went up to the bathroom she found a flute of sparkling wine, breathing mist into the air, dewy from the chill. Perhaps her mother hadn't forgotten after all. It had that dry, biscuity flavour which Guy had tried to teach her only came with real champagne. How hopeless she was: she would never know the difference.

Half an hour later, barefoot, and still in her dressing gown, she followed voices through the drawing room to the French windows.

Their garden was full of people, in black tie. "Sorry," she said, starting to back inside.

They burst into Happy Birthday. Charlotte winced at the different keys vying for the first few notes. Helen, her best friend, gave her a hug. "You are such a muppet, Charlotte. How did you ever get into Cambridge?"

"You can stay in your dressing gown," her mother said. "Or go and put on your gown."

"How did you all know?"

"Duh," one of her friends said.

By popular demand, Charlotte went back upstairs to put on her ball dress.

When she took it out of her suitcase it no longer seemed like a faerie gown, as it had in Cambridge. Nor even like something from *Period Piece,* which she had read in eager anticipation, about Gwen Raverat's Edwardian Cambridge. Just a little squished, and very over the top.

But they all said she looked gorgeous, so she smiled graciously. And realised with a start that she wished she were back in Nevile's, listening to close harmony.

Her mother had braved Beef Wellington, Guy his signature tiramisu. Helen gave her a silver necklace. Someone else, a picture for her new room; a bottle of champagne; earrings; her college scarf. She didn't think she would ever wear it, but was touched by the effort.

Michael had painted a cat, in funky geometrical lines. She loved it, and said so.

Her mother had already given her the ball dress. Guy saved his present until last. As she opened the thin envelope a cheque fell out. She spread it open, and couldn't take it in. No one had given her such a generous present before: not even her dress, which had taken half a dozen fittings.

"Gosh. Thank you, Guy. That's . . . I mean. Wow."

He beamed.

"I don't know what to say."

"You don't need to say anything. Just buy something you really want."

"Oh, I will." Without thinking, she added, "I'll go to Washington, to see Daddy."

"Fab!" "Terrific." Her friends chipped in.

"Or rather . . ."

Guy looked at her mother, who looked away.

"That is, if I may?" She had wanted to go on that trip since she was six. But she didn't need to say so, and spoil the evening.

Guy said nothing for moment. Then, "Charlotte, sweetheart, I gave it to you. There are no strings." He was carefully not looking at her mother. "If that is what's important to you and will last you a long time, that's what you should have."

"Thank you, Guy. Flights to Washington are only a few hundred," she added quickly, knowing exactly how much. "I'll save the rest."

She paused, to give the promise weight. "For something very special. Something else very special. Perhaps you could advise me?"

She crossed the room to hug him.

Her friends cheered and clapped.

"Guy?" one of them said. "I think we should toast Charlie, and uni, and her birthday, and her trip. May we?"

"If that's a hint for some more bubbly," Guy said, "I think it's a damn good idea."

Shortly after midnight her mother and step-father, having loaded the dishwasher for the umpteenth time, left the young people and went upstairs. Sara had a quick shower before joining him in bed, where she lay staring at the ceiling.

"Sorry," she said eventually.

"Not your fault." Guy didn't look up from his book. "And you mind a lot more than I do."

"My fault for choosing badly first time around."

"But then we wouldn't have Charlotte or Michael. Must have been something decent about the bloke, to produce those two."

"He was clever," she conceded. "Intellectually. Not at anything else, unfortunately."

Guy continued to read.

"Anyway, I'm still sorry."

Guy finished the page, closed the book, took off his spectacles and looked at her.

"I'm not. At first I thought oh hell, her eighteenth birthday present, that I'd looked forward to giving her for months, wasted on that bastard. I had wondered about all the things she might get. Perhaps a decent violin. Even a little car. I never expected that. But I'm glad."

"Why?"

He sighed. "For twelve years she has resented me. Don't. I know it, she knows it. She has promised to save most of it, and being Charlotte, she will."

"True."

"Sadly, she will have a shitty time. Or maybe she won't."

"She will."

"You're not impartial."

"Thanks."

"However much I love you, Sara, you can't possibly be neutral on this one."

"Go on."

"Suppose she has a lovely trip, reconnects with her father . . . can only be a good thing. She'll resent me less."

"How do you work that out?"

"Happier is better, wherever it comes from."

"What if it comes from booze? Drugs, cheating?"

"That's not long term, wholesome happy. Being at one with your biological parent is."

"Moving on to what will really happen."

"What is likely, sadly, is that she will get a big let-down, and realise I'm not the home-wrecker she's always thought I was."

"What happens then to your theory that happy is always better?"

"With hindsight, I'm not sure your policy was right."

"Policy?"

"Of never saying a bad word against him. It wasn't truthful."

"It's not for me to demonise their father to my own children."

"The truth will set you free, I believe someone said."

"The truth sometimes makes people very unhappy. But yes, perhaps it sets them free."

They both lay for a while in silence.

"Anyway, do you?" she said.

"What?"

"Love me?"

He smiled. "That's for me to know and you to find out."

"How would you like to prove it?"

He turned off the light.

Downstairs, the conversation had moved on to Existentialism. As this was a topic none of them knew much about, it was generating more wild theory than accurate illumination.

The night was still warm, the young people dotting the lawn. Charlotte sat slightly back from the circle, on the wooden swing seat, her knees up and her arms around her shins. She listened to her friends arguing, content.

She thought of the journey she had wanted to make for so long.

Upstairs, almost as content, Sara murmured, "You'd think she would work it out. She's a bright girl. Why has she never wondered why he doesn't come and see her?"

There was no answer.

"Are you asleep?" There still being no answer, she joined him.

Chapter Eight

FRIDAY

As she had for several years, Liz woke thinking of Selina. At four, a quarter past five and six thirty, after which she drifted in and out of sleep until seven, when Mark turned on the television he kept in their bedroom.

It was an addiction. She rehearsed her speech over and over again. Begging her daughter to come home. Getting angry. Asking why. Then apologising. Giving vent to all the months of sorrow and anguish.

"What are you thinking?" Mark never spoke to her in the mornings. He was putting on a tie, looking at his reflection.

"I was thinking of something she said to me."

Liz had long stopped sharing her feelings but Mark knew she thought of their daughter every day, perhaps every hour. "When she was thirteen, she asked if I was sorry I'd had both of them, instead of just Crispin. I said, 'Of course not. No mother ever regrets her children.'"

Mark didn't answer.

"I do. Now."

She had the satisfaction of seeing his surprise.

"All that pain we wouldn't have."

Unusually, Mark was delaying leaving. He shrugged on his jacket. Liz hadn't made him breakfast for years. He sometimes grabbed a quick espresso, leaving her to clear up. More often, he just left.

"I had a friend at school . . ."

He wanted to go. Perhaps she wasn't talking to him at all. She was looking out of the window, addressing the trembling trees, their leaves beginning to thirst.

"Youngest of five. Killed on her bicycle aged eleven. I wondered whether it was worse, because there were so many in her family to be sad about her; or better, because they wouldn't miss her so much. Anyway it wouldn't have dragged on like this. Her family wouldn't be tormented, wondering where she was. And why."

She paused, and Mark took his chance. "I'll see you this evening." He briefly wondered what would happen if he were to kiss her goodbye.

She didn't even look at him.

"Suppose we just had Crispin," she continued after he'd gone. "Wouldn't we think we'd done well?"

And she crumpled and sobbed.

"Shit," the Head Master said, hanging up.

Then he panicked and checked that he really had ended the call. He didn't always hang up properly and frequently pocket-dialled. And he never used bad language in public. Only in front of his wife and very occasionally, his children.

It was all right. He had hung up.

Not only had the bishop, due to give away the prizes on the morrow, dropped out last night because her father had died ("And why does that mean she can't do it?" Martin asked Jane crossly when she gave him the message) but now his maths teacher had put his knee out playing Rugby and wouldn't be able to go to Shanghai.

It felt as if Hui's father had emailed Martin several times every day, all term. What had at first seemed an exciting opportunity had ended up costing hours of negotiation. And would now need more, the day before Speech Day.

"Have you remembered you're seeing John?" Jane said, putting her head round the door. "Gosh, you look cross."

"This bloody trip to China. It's an absolute headache. See what I did there." Martin cocked his head playfully. "Head. Ache . . . never mind."

Jane survived prep school life partly by ignoring its humour. "China?"

"You know. Hui's father. Invited Simon Scarborough. 'Kill two birds in the bush with one stone,' he said. Take Hui home, and visit the boy's old school to see how they teach maths."

71

"Generous."

"Thought I told you."

"Nope."

"And now Simon has gone and dislocated something. His flight's already paid for. What am I supposed to do now: go myself?"

"Why not? Asian pupils keep a lot of the private schools in the country solvent." she observed. "See it as jammy market research. And don't be late for John."

"How did you know I was seeing John?"

"It was fixed the other day, over dinner."

"You don't know why, do you?" he asked hopefully.

"You suggested popping in to talk about the choir trip to Copenhagen. Said you'd be in college anyway."

"I wonder what that means I've just missed."

It was a glorious midsummer afternoon – June already looked set to break all records since records began, as records do – and Martin enjoyed the smell of mown grass mingling with late blossom along West Road. Having been brought up in Central London and attended university in Durham he wasn't a fan of bicycles, and it didn't do to admit to liking driving in a city where using a car for less than three miles was considered immoral bordering on microwaving kittens or smoking.

Walking, however, he enjoyed.

Undergraduates overtook him, cycling three abreast, chattering merrily. A couple of young men in shorts and polo-shirts strolled the other way, real-tennis racquets slung over their shoulders, heading for the courts in Grange Road. The Mr Whippy van outside the back gate spewed forth a tinny rendition of Greensleeves, as if played by tone deaf toddlers on a set of bells given free in Christmas crackers.

"Afternoon," the purple-stoled custodian at the back gate nodded.

"Beautiful," Martin agreed.

The river seethed in the sunshine. Martin watched a hapless father ramming the bank while his wife paddled furiously in the wrong direction, shouting in a foreign tongue. Unbelievably, she was wearing a life-jacket. He would have liked to linger, amused, but was already late.

John only had instant coffee so Martin opted for tea. He liked John. He had only recently been promoted from Chaplain to Dean and Martin thought he might have been right to be reluctant. John was a pastor, not an administrator or public figure, and Martin wasn't sure that his new gravitas and the evidence of too many college dinners over his waistband entirely suited him.

"You don't know any mathematician who would like a free trip to China?" he said, after they had wrapped up the Danish tour.

"Odd request," John said. "Tell me more."

"Boy in the choir, Hui Zhang" (Martin pronounced this, 'We Chang') "has a Chinese father."

"You amaze me. He looks Aryan from head to toe."

Martin was stumped by this, but continued. "Hui's father has paid for his maths teacher to go out to Shanghai for a week. Says they get such fantastic results, they should share their success."

"Cambridge also has one or two decent mathematicians. Possibly not quite as many as China."

"More Nobel prize-winners in Trinity College . . ." Martin began.

". . . than in the whole of France, yes, yes," John completed the cliché for him, having lived in Cambridge too long for this to be interesting. "And more Cambridge undergraduates have travelled to India than to Girton, and so on."

"Really? That's quite funny. I'm not sure I've ever been to Girton College myself. Where was I? Oh yes. Hui has an uncle . . ."

"Don't tell me. Also Chinese?"

"Oh I see. Joke. Anyway, he has a factory that produces money, apparently. I got a bit confused, to be honest. So, Hui's always had someone accompany him before."

"And why isn't the maths teacher going?"

"Simon used to be a blue."

"Is a blue," John corrected. "Once a blue, always a blue. Like members of a college. Or the university."

"Whatever." Martin noticed with irritation his slide into teenage patois. "Stupid idiot still plays Rugby. In the summer! He's injured himself and I'm landed with a return flight to Shanghai and a father who was enough of a fusspot when everything was going well."

"Why don't you go yourself?" John asked. "Government directives keep telling us to fortify our links with China."

"Odd: that's what Jane said. Anyway, I'm looking for a vaguely personable chap, preferably with CRB clearance, who'd like a free trip to China and could show a modicum of interest in a class full of maths pupils."

"You mean DBS clearance. Any payment? And what's the uncle got to do with it?"

"I didn't understand a word of it. Has a factory. Makes machines to make money, or something. Perhaps that's where the Zhangs' comes from."

"Do you mean forgery?" It sometimes surprised John that Martin had made it to head teacher.

"Zhang insisted it was legit. Digital money? Digital-dodgy I'd say. Give it some thought, could you? Preferably by yesterday."

"Do you mean bitcoins?"

"That's it. Have you heard of them?"

"Martin, everyone's heard of them. In ten years' time you'll be buying groceries with them."

"I certainly won't. I still use cheques."

"So do I – as bookmarks. If there are bitcoins in it the answer's easy. You want Theo Wedderburn. He'd probably go half way round the world to learn about a bitcoin-business, unless he knows it all already. Oh for goodness' sake, Martin. Alan Wedderburn? Before your time, but even so. Organist before Amschel."

"Ah. As you say, before my time. Wasn't he, um . . . didn't he, er . . . ?"

"He was, yes. Murdered, is what you're trying to say. Theo was a chorister at the time. Now a Junior Maths Fellow. Happens to have a bunch of bitcoin miners in his bedroom, though I suspect he now uses them as coffee tables. He explained it to me once. No idea why he thought I could understand. His thesis is on transference, which as far as I'm concerned is what shrinks are into. Digital currency is like Structuralism. Or why instruments are transposed. You can understand it for about four minutes before you have to start again."

Martin, who had never tried grasping Structuralism but didn't have any difficulty transposing instruments – though he couldn't have begun to explain why, not being gifted in the classroom, which possibly answered John's question as to why he had become a head – was losing interest.

"This could make my life a lot easier. Will he be all right looking after a small boy on a twelve hour flight? I'm afraid no payment was mentioned and it could be awkward to ask, now."

"Don't worry. Theo will either be interested, or he won't. I'm not sure he's motivated by money. Though I believe he made quite a lot in bitcoins, in the early days."

"Good Lord. Is that legal?"

"As legal as the stock market. And possibly more ethical. More democratic, anyway."

"Don't suppose he has CRB?"

"DBS. Don't suppose so."

On that, however, they were wrong.

Five minutes later Theo, answering his telephone as he always did, was able to inform John that yes, he, Theophilus Ambrose Fitzwilliam Wedderburn did, as it happened, have Disclosure and Barring Service clearance. Until recently he had helped with teenagers' Christian summer camps. Till he became exasperated with cleaning the loos for the third year running. In truth he enjoyed cleaning the loos: a necessary and satisfying job. But he deduced – correctly, as it happens – that the reason he was still on toilet-cleaning-duty was because the organisers didn't understand him, didn't know what to do with him and didn't really want him looking after the children or giving talks. He decided to find some other way of expressing his faith.

Theo didn't like last-minute plans. His rule was not to do anything without a fortnight's notice, particularly if it involved meeting a girl. But when there was a sensible reason for it, that was completely different. And yes, he was available next week.

When he was told it might include a visit to a bitcoin-miner factory, he was so excited he said yes immediately, without considering the logistics.

Thus Martin was able to email Mr Zhang the next morning – before an obscure Member of Parliament, who had briefly attended the school as a child, arrived to bore four hundred children, eight hundred adults and a smattering of put-upon siblings with numerous clichés and not a single joke (though at least, for once, it didn't rain) – that, sadly, Mr Scarsborough had been rushed into hospital but they had found a replacement.

Theo would chaperone Hui to Shanghai, leaving in just over a week.

Chapter Nine

THE FOLLOWING WEEK

Theo's friends, of which he had a surprising number, knew that if he had said he would meet you in the pub one Sunday evening a month hence, he probably would. Changing plans, he explained, is like lying. The primary difficulty isn't morality, so much as confusion. Once you start, how do you know when to stop? Life would lose its fixed points.

He wouldn't say exactly *when* he would meet you in the pub. 'Evening' was about as specific as it got. (Or, 'breakfast,' since as long as it contained bacon, egg, tea and preferably hash browns – and was one of the first meals of the day – it still counted, even at 7 o'clock in the evening.) So it was a good idea to give him as much notice as possible, and welcome him warmly if he turned up on the correct date, in more or less the right half of the day. With trousers on. He liked to claim his unfamiliarity with time was derived from his Irish heritage . . . Which was curious, as his mother Ann adhered rigorously to the punctual habits she had learnt at music college.

He hadn't organised anything in so short a time since he left school and could choose for himself. He had a week before going to Shanghai. His tickets and itinerary were arranged for him. He had recently checked his passport for the conference in Baltimore he was attending in early August. He would need his laptop. And perhaps his Ancient Greek grammar, since (unlike the New Testament) that wasn't available online.

Anything else, he could buy at the airport.

He was vaguely uneasy that he might have missed something, but went over it several times and couldn't think of anything else.

He had discovered, to his considerable excitement, that Hui's uncle didn't own a bitcoin-miner factory at all but one that constructed miners for a currency called Marigold, which almost nobody had heard of. Theo *had* heard of it, just, and on Sunday afternoon – he kept Sundays sacrosanct for non-work-related activity – he read all that was available in the public domain on Marigolds . . . Which wasn't much.

He was intrigued.

Everyone knows bitcoins are environmentally unfriendly, eating unecological amounts of electricity. And unlike old-fashioned currencies subject to inflation, bitcoins tend to go up in value, encouraging hoarding rather than spending. Ideologically, Theo was on the side of demurrage: currencies designed to decrease, keeping money active and working. Bitcoins are interesting, but flawed.

By contrast Marigolds seemed to have some very pleasing characteristics.

Such as a facility for escrow, or a delayed payment via a third party. (Obviously, the third party is a block chain not a human being, but it amounts to the same thing.) Suppose Ann wanted twenty bags of compost delivered on Thursday morning, without the bother of staying in. She could make a one-way, non-refundable transfer of Marigolds, show the compost-seller the transaction, tootle off on her bicycle – to a rehearsal with her fiddle if she had any sense, or more likely a counselling session if she hadn't – come back that evening, count the bags, and then press Go for completion. Neither party could cheat on the other.

Neat.

More striking was the Marigold Foundation. When a bitcoin transaction is made, a small commission goes to the owners of all the bitcoin miners in the world. When a Marigold transaction goes through, instead of being raked off as profit, that same commission goes into the Marigold charitable foundation. All the Marigold owners in the world have a vote as to what the foundation will support that year. Democratic. Philanthropic. He liked it.

The world could become a better place . . .

In under an hour Theo had exhausted all the available information on Marigolds. So he opened his emails.

Theo didn't believe in reading emails often. He had seen too many colleagues lose hours every day which he couldn't spare. Once every couple of weeks or so he would skim-read them all as quickly as possible. First though he emailed someone he was looking forward to meeting.

To: americangeek13@hotmail.com
From: tafw@cam.ac.uk
On: 02 07 18 at 10.32.14
Subject: Provenance

Dear Evan

I've been asked about tracing bitcoin provenance.
I thought it would be fun to design a programme.

Do you have pubs?

Yours sincerely,
Theophilus Ambrose Fitzwilliam Wedderburn.

He then turned to his inbox. He had designed his own Spam filter, but no system can accurately interpret every kind of junk. He had eliminated several dozen or so when he came across one he hadn't expected.

To: tafw@cam.ac.uk
From: clsebastian@gmail.com
On: 02 07 18 at 10.57.27
Subject: Hello.

Hi Theo,

Thank you for telling me to go home for my
birthday. My mother had arranged an amazing
dinner party for me. It was brilliant!
    I think you said you might be going to Baltimore?
I was given some money for my birthday so I'm
going to Washington DC to see my father (I've
wanted to since I was six) and apparently it's quite

nearby. I can't remember when you might be there but if it's the first week in August it would be quite a coincidence!

    Do you want to let me know?

Charlotte.

Why did the words in front of him not quite fit the girl he had observed? As with any discrepancy, he needed to factor in the new specifics to improve the model. Eventually he put his finger on it: she had seemed rather shy. He might have expected her to mention going to America in conversation, but not to write to him 'specially.

He updated his mental database. Shy *most of the time.*

(He was not, of course, in possession of quite all the relevant intelligence. It could not have occurred to Theo that anyone could write an email several times, edit it, let it sit in her Drafts for several days, rewrite it, then press Send before she lost her bottle. Then wish she could rescind it, with immediate and agonised regret.)

He read the email again, and replied:

To: clsebastian@gmail.com
From: tafw@cam.ac.uk
On: 02 07 18 at 15.06.17
Subject: Clarification

Dear Charlotte

Know, what?

Yours sincerely,
Theophilus Ambrose Fitzwilliam Wedderburn.

It was touch and go, in the end.

He had arranged to pick Hui up by taxi on the last day of term, Saturday 7th July. Having done most of his packing the previous Monday he had forgotten about his trip for the rest of the week, until Saturday itself when his mind went blank.

Theo had no idea how to hurry. He couldn't see how. If it takes a tennis ball a certain amount of time to fall a certain distance to the ground, how can it ever be faster? (Unless an objective change has taken place, such as in the atmosphere.) If boiling an egg takes four and a half minutes and brewing tea three, how does it make a difference to be in a hurry?

Ann had observed him, trying to catch a train. His shoelace broke as he was getting ready. He put down his bag, went in search of the old wooden box in which she kept shoe polish and brushes, emptied the contents carefully (one by one not to make a mess) and eventually found a pair of shoelaces in a packet at the bottom. They were black. His shoes were brown. He looked again until he found two loose brown laces. He measured the lengths against each other and decided they would do. Then he put everything carefully back in the box, cleaned the table, removed his old shoelaces and replaced them with the new.

It was agonising. Ann didn't shout at him, tell him to stop being a bloody idiot, snatch the box from him or bundle him out of the house. Not because she didn't want to. But because she had learnt the hard way that this would confuse him and slow him down more.

Long after he had missed his train and been so late for his friends that they had gone into the cinema without him and he had missed all of the film (for which he had paid in full) apart from the last seven minutes, when she was debriefing him some days later, she explained. "When you're in a hurry, there are things you don't do. Perfectly reasonable things, which would be good to do if you had time. Such as fixing a broken shoelace."

"But how do you know," (he only needed each such lesson once, but he needed to understand it) "which things to skip because they don't matter, and which are essential regardless of how much hurry you are in?"

Ann sighed. "I don't know. How do neurotypical children know, before they can speak, what mood their mother is in? Okay. Let's devise a formula. If there's a fire, you don't wait for anything."

"Not even clothes?" he asked her. "Suppose you're a housemaster, and you're in bed with the matron, and the fire alarm goes off but you suspect the fire is quite a long way away in another building and could even be just a fire drill. Do you not put your dressing gown on before running outside, with the naked matron? In the middle of winter if it's pouring with rain?"

Ann burst out laughing. "Most people can work it out without thinking."

"But those people can do all sorts of things, without thinking."

"Yes, we can," she agreed.

So this was yet another simple life skill which Theo put years of his life into learning. Which steps you can cut without the consequences being worse than missing your train.

And that morning he didn't get the balance quite right. He knew it was important to get to Heathrow on time, with Hui, or the consequences would be troublesome, distressing and probably – though he didn't mind this nearly as much – expensive.

He also knew there was no point in turning up without his passport, and that his trip could be much less enjoyable if he forgot something like his laptop. Or, worse, left it on the train because he was panicking.

To gain fifteen minutes, he rang the school and asked if a member of staff could take Hui to the railway station to meet him there instead of his picking the boy up as previously arranged. This was agreed, whether reluctantly or not he neither knew nor could afford to care: working it out was one of those tasks he was in too much of a hurry to do. Nor did he now have time to walk, so he would lock his bicycle at the station.

He was half way down St Andrew's Street when he realised he had left his wallet behind. Credit cards, driving licence, railcard. Was this a step he could skip?

He decided it wasn't.

By the time he arrived at Cambridge Railway Station the teacher waiting with Hui was visibly annoyed.

"You've missed the train."

"It was delayed in Ely," Theo said. "It will arrive," he consulted his iPhone, "in seven and a half minutes. We'd be better with the train waiting on Platform One. You must be Hui. Have I pronounced that correctly?"

"Yes, you have."

"I'm Theo. Thank you," he turned to the disconcerted young teacher, "and sorry. Let's go."

The teacher followed, trying to steal back some credibility. "Excuse me," he said to a pear-shaped man in railway uniform with a name badge saying Faisal. "Will the train standing at Platform One reach London before the delayed fast train due in?"

"He won't know," Theo said cheerfully. "They won't even know behind the windows: their computers don't give them enough information. I could show you if you like," he offered his iPhone, "but then we might miss it. It's due to leave in thirty seconds."

"I should listen to him," Faisal said.

Theo showed the guard at the extra-wide barrier his iPhone screen with his e-ticket, confusing him so much he let them through; took Hui's enormous case; and they entered the train just as the doors beeped and started closing.

"Now," Theo said, working out how to subvert the window lock to get some fresh air and settling them both into seats reserved for someone else.

"I have cards," said Hui, producing a new pack and undoing the cellophane.

"How about Snap?"

It was fortunate they hadn't chosen the quiet carriage.

They touched down in Shanghai shortly after ten am. The heat greeted them like a wall. Theo looked carefully at the sea of Chinese faces, searching for characteristics he had painstakingly memorised, like a map. It was hardly necessary but he recognised Hui's father before the boy did, waving excitedly with his wife.

"So honoured to have you visit." Mr Zhang offered Theo the front seat next to the driver, then gave him a continuous commentary on Shanghai, its architecture, industry and people while Mrs Zhang chattered softly with Hui like the gossip of dawn birds.

Theo nodded politely, as Ann had taught him, to indicate he was listening. He wasn't, but this doesn't constitute a lie. Not even a white lie: simply a white impression. It is fine to smile when your girlfriend turns up in a hideous skirt, for instance. And while he faced the front he allowed his eyes to close. He didn't think the driver would mind. He had deduced that the driver must be the Zhangs' personal driver: in Theo's experience, taxi-drivers never stop talking, and this driver looked implacably ahead and never spoke a word.

The city of Shanghai seemed to be all noise and people and car horns. And bicycle bells. As if New York had bred with Cambridge.

"You don't have to tip him," Hui said, tumbling out of the car when it pulled into the curb and pre-empting an action which had not occurred to Theo.

"Welcome," Mrs Zhang said in impeccable English as they entered an expensive-looking block of flats. "Perhaps you would like to recover from your flight, Mr Wedderburn? I am Monica by the way."

Theo was shown into a huge bedroom with a stunning view of the city. Below him skyscrapers soared. Traffic swarmed, silent as ants. In the misty distance a yellow river twisted in the searing sun.

He took off his shoes, lay on the vast bed in the middle of the room and fell instantly asleep.

The change of light told him it must be evening. He found the en suite bathroom and plunged his head under water.

He opened the wardrobe thinking to tidy away his few items, and found clothes belonging to his host and hostess. Theo would have liked to have said he would prefer to sleep on the sofa rather than displace them, but this was a negotiation too hazardous to attempt without Ann.

In the hall Mrs Zhang appeared, looking as fresh and calm as before. "Tomorrow evening we would like to take you out and show you the city. But we thought tonight you might be tired."

She ushered him into an elegant dining room overlooking a different view of the evening city and furnished with opulent sparseness, while she called her husband and son. A woman he hadn't been introduced to brought in plates of steaming food.

A fork and spoon had been considerately placed by his plate. He took up the delicate porcelain chopsticks.

"In the morning," Monica said, "Hui will take you to see his old school. You can observe."

"I'm not a teacher," Theo explained. "Of children."

"You've been through the English educational system," she pointed out.

Theo wasn't sure how to explain. "I didn't . . ." He scissored his chopsticks together, and missed. "Learn much at school. Not maths."

Mr Zhang frowned. "Are you not a mathematician? The Head Master told us you doing doctorate in mathematics."

"Number Theory," Theo corrected. "That doesn't mean I learnt anything at school."

He pushed his chopsticks together again, and flicked rice over Hui's head.

"You've got it all wrong," Hui screeched delightedly. "Look."

Theo was spared any more explanations by his tutorial in eating three grains of rice at a time.

Long before he was conscious Hui was in his room, asking what he wanted for breakfast. The sun slipped through the paper-thin blind. Theo always wanted tea so that part was easy.

"My mum bought you some American orange juice. She'll make you congee when you're ready. Or would you prefer you tiao?"

Theo took a mental step back from this interrogation as from a complicated calculation. The initial thing, presumably, was to ascertain what type of question it was.

"That first one. Congee? Has your mother already got it ready?"

"Yup. Won't take her minutes."

"What about the you something? Has she prepared that too?"

"No, but we can easily go out and get some," Hui said cheerfully.

"In that case," he said, relieved, "I would much prefer congee."

"School starts just after eight. We've got ages."

Theo knew what 'ages' meant in other people's minds.

He found his short-sleeved cotton shirt and shorts, and a framed print of Cambridge which Ann had chosen, wrapped and added to his bag for his hosts. He never stopped being amazed at the things she did for him. The numerous tasks he performed for her – far more than his brother did – he never even noticed.

Monica was in the kitchen, smiling and ready, with the woman he had seen last night bustling about. Everything smelt of fresh popcorn.

"I hope you slept well."

Theo wasn't sure whether this was a question, so he said nothing.

"What would you like for breakfast? Fried egg?"

"You promised congee, Munaly!" Hui complained.

"I would like Theo to have what he would most enjoy."

"Do you . . . do you drink anything with it?" Theo asked slightly desperately.

"Warm water. But we can give you English tea and toast if you prefer. Or Chinese green tea. And a pancake or egg with it?"

"Yes please," Theo said. "All the above. Especially the English tea and Chinese tea and another mug of English tea. And no toast," he remembered in time.

Jian, as Theo had learnt Hui's father was called – not John as Anglicised for European friends – had arranged for Theo to visit Hui's school that morning. He offered a taxi.

"How would you normally go?" Theo asked.

"Bicycle, of course," Hui answered before his father had a chance.

"I'd prefer that then."

"Don't you know Daddy, everyone in Cambridge rides a bicycle. It's like home."

"It's not very like home," his mother pointed out. "We can provide a bicycle. Be careful, though. We have rather different road rules."

Chapter Ten

THE NEXT TWO DAYS

Theo wasn't sure why he was being shown around Hui's school. When he had mentioned his trip to another PhD mathmo in the college bar a few nights earlier, he had been told how fascinating it would be to see how the impressive Asian results were achieved. Theo suspected it was probably similar to the Suzuki method of learning the violin: the children were drilled so young that they learnt all the boring bits before they could protest.

When he was younger Ann had told him he must tell somebody when he was upset. He had registered the instruction obediently as he did everything. But it was only the beginning. His difficulty was that he didn't know when he was.

He didn't think to ask her. Like children the world over, he assumed his experience was no different from anyone else's. He had no reason to believe anyone knew the answer.

So he started to examine himself. After several years he noticed that when he was 'upset', for want of a more accurate term, he forgot things. What he had done that weekend, that day, that hour. How he left the choir. His entire senior schooling. Eventually he deduced that he must have been distressed. Forgetting was the sign. Once he had interpreted the data, his method was sound. If somewhat cumbersome.

Continuing from these deductions, given that he couldn't remember most of his own schooling, it was unlikely he would want to enter another school. He hoped he could survive the morning without undue distress.

Hui was very excited to show him his old classroom. Theo himself was struck by the contrast with the little he did remember. Here were thirty-five or more children, looking shockingly young, sitting in obedient rows, not saying anything. He looked politely at the maths they were learning and it seemed standard. Boring even, for bright children.

It wasn't this which troubled him: he too had experienced boring maths. Dismal, wasteful, enervating . . . but not unbearably painful.

What was a child supposed to do, though, who didn't know what was expected of him? Who knew all the answers and didn't know what to do next? Who could work it all out in his head but couldn't commit it to paper? He looked into the eyes of the children and couldn't tell whether they were alert or dead. It was hard enough to read faces in his own culture: that had taken half his life-time.

There was only one question he cared about. Are they happy?

"Oh yes, yes, yes," the teacher said, misunderstanding entirely. "Very, very happy. Love mathematics. Yes."

"Thank you," Theo said, and hoped.

Out in the playground, nestled in the busy city, several grass basketball courts were necklaced with a tarmac running track.

"Did you like it here?" he asked Hui.

"Yes. But I much prefer the choir school."

"Good," Theo said. "Liking school is good." He stared across the wide sky at the circling specs of birds high over the distant skyscrapers, dimly aware of the chirruping joy of released children. "I wish I had."

"Pardon?"

"Nothing."

When they arrived back at the flat Monica greeted them with the smell of freshly steaming fish. Theo couldn't remember whether or not he was hungry, but he was all right. He had been liberated from his tour of the gulag.

He hoped there would be plenty of vegetables.

The Zhangs' driver was waiting outside the apartment the next day to take them to Zhejiang. The car was comfortable, and efficiently air-conditioned. From time to time as they travelled his host pointed out waterfields, or red beans growing. Having been told by his wife and son of Theo's enthusiasm for tea, Jian showed him lush fields, striped like lurid green corduroy. The scenery seemed both strange and familiar: farmland, bereft of trees.

Thus they drove for half the day, till they came off the motorway, zigzagged for a while through hills and arrived at the main street of a small town. A mule, apparently without a driver, stood absentmindedly in the middle of the road, carrying what seemed a completely unreasonable amount of fencing. Mr Zhang's driver waited patiently, answering his employer's comments without turning. One or two cars hooted.

Eventually a precarious scooter arrived, the rider tying a rope to the animal's bridle before revving up. The mule stood stubborn, the outcome hanging in the balance. Then the animal seemed to shrug and followed, scuffing its hooves like a teenager.

Their car turned a corner and stopped outside a small new-build two-storey house. Children playing a game similar to hopscotch gazed at the car with large eyes.

"My brother's cottage," said Jian.

Theo could see from their faces that the brothers were delighted to see each other, but they didn't even shake hands.

"Hullo hullo how are you today very good thank you very nice." Jian's brother Li smiled and nodded. "My wife make green tea?"

"Queen tea?" Theo asked.

"Very good, Chinese tea, you like."

He was shown into a house no bigger than his two rooms in Cambridge. A woman was squatting on the floor, feeding a stove with batons of wood.

"Ah Lam," Li said, "my wife."

"Does Ah Lam mean wife?" Theo asked. "Or is that your wife's name?"

"Yes, Ah Lam, my wife."

Ah Lam rose and nodded, solemn and silent.

That evening the men sat up late, drinking tea and smoking. Theo, wise now to the etiquette, insisted on sleeping on the floor with the others so Ah Lam could have the bed.

The next morning the noise started with the sun. Jian showed him where the men's communal loos were, off the next courtyard, and gave him a towel, soap and coins for the shower.

Back at the house Ah Lam greeted him with another silent smile. The room was sweet with the tang he was becoming accustomed to, of delicious fried aromatic food. He noticed a new packet of sliced white bread and an unopened jar of jam, and realised with dismay that someone had gone to considerable trouble for him. Ah Lam handed him a plate with two slices and the jam. He wondered how to put the jam on the bread: if he gestured for chopsticks it could get complicated. He rolled the bread up to dip it into the jam jar: it was either that, or his debit card. When Ah Lam saw she clapped her hands, laughed, and found him an enormous chopping knife.

Theo was not a fussy eater but he needed to eat healthily: if he went for half a day without fresh vegetables he would lose concentration until he chewed on a cabbage leaf or found a raw carrot. Although he could happily exist for weeks on Huel powder, giving him all his nutrients in a grey and muddy glassful, he nevertheless enjoyed different culinary experiences: sheep's eyes, fermented camel milk, the brains or testicles of unspecified mammals inspired him with curiosity. He would have much preferred the local cuisine.

Li and Jian returned with another man. Theo was introduced, but the food had left him with an unpleasant coating of sugar on his teeth and insufficient nutrition and he failed to take the name in. Outside four bicycles stood untethered against the house.

The Marigold-miner factory was the other side of town. Bicycles surged, as in Cambridge during Full Term just before the hour and lecture change, but more chaotically. Wheels wobbling, bells shrilling, friends calling to each other. Jian pointed over the road and they converged towards a squat building, its metal door standing open to the rising heat.

Inside it was cool and Tardis-like: ordered aisles, metal shelves stretching in all directions, cardboard boxes, components ranged like soldiers, innards of computers. Theo could have been anywhere in the world. He was too captivated to attend to the criss-crossing twang of the men around him.

Instead, he saw parts. Chassis, small to large. Boards containing chips, ready to programme controllers. Displays on the outside of cases, arrayed in lights, connected to computers the size of wallets. Fans, cables, power supplies. Someone stepped forward to show him which bits went where, but Theo had already assembled a Marigold-miner in his head.

He wandered from shelf to shelf, noting with interest a Peltier heatsink. Back in Cambridge he would remember everything, and now understood the inside of his own bitcoin-miners. Like da Vinci witnessing a postmortem, he was seeing the detailed muscle and ligament structure invisible from the outside.

Theo had bought a few bitcoins as soon as he heard of them in 2011, and persuaded Ann to do the same. Brian had thought her most unwise but she had her own money from Alan, and trusted Theo's judgement. He told her not to give him any more than she was happy to lose, so she handed over a thousand pounds, now worth a hundred times more.

From the beginning he was interested, not primarily to make money, but for the sheer fun and academic appeal. In the autumn of 2012 he signed up for as many bitcoin miners as he could afford.

Some of his experiments were more successful than others. He paid for several machines from someone called Darren, who then (as far as Theo could make out) drank a whole bottle of bourbon, changed his mind and sent Theo's money back.

Another company offered to lease miners for a fee, but Theo heard of them too late and missed the waiting list.

Yet another, called Butterfly Labs, put out expensive advertising and caught everyone's attention, which meant all their clients were competing with each other. Theo paid for several machines, and waited and waited . . . By the time they were delivered, over a year late, they were worth far less than the bitcoins he had bought them with.

Early in 2013 he noticed a company called Avalon. Unlike Butterfly Labs they had delivered almost on the day they'd agreed. Immediately he put in an order for the next generation, promised in a few weeks. Of barely three hundred machines in the world, Theo soon had half a dozen: four and a half for himself, one for Ann and half for Charlie, who had thrown in the few hundred quid he had earned with his Saturday job.

From these Theo did well, earning himself the equivalent of about fifty thousand in sterling, selling a handful when bitcoins soared to eight hundred pounds, buying more when they dipped to a couple of hundred and everyone thought they were finished. By late 2017 he had enough to put down a deposit on a decent-sized house. In Cambridge.

He had learnt what he already knew: because there was no check on supplies of miners, it was impossible to make money reliably by buying machines six months in advance. An excessive supply, on pre-order, meant the market was flooded by the time the miners were delivered.

Li's factory operated a different system. Jian had already explained this to Theo, helped by Monica's translation. Li and his colleagues didn't take money for their machines in advance, but only when they were ready to ship. The company would make far less profit immediately, but would build up a reputation for honesty and a loyal customer base.

It pleased Theo greatly. The purpose of digital currency is to stand outside governments and corporations: everyone in the industry should be as ethical as the currency itself. Knowing the integrity of those involved – Li and his colleagues – Theo's interest was piqued.

Against all this, he weighed his dream.

He planned, with most of his bitcoins cashed and a modest mortgage on his meagre but stable Junior Fellow's salary, to buy a house in Grantchester Meadows, where he could work peacefully and live for ever. The Cam at the bottom of his garden winding slowly from Grantchester into the city, reassuring him there was no hurry. Ann a few minutes' walk away. Perhaps one day a wife, and children, and a mongrel who would jump in the river and swim in happy, barking circles – on summer dog-days the family would all jump in too – and he need never move for his whole life long. A punt kept upside-down at the bottom of the lawn.

There are only half a dozen such and none had yet come up for sale. In the meantime, his savings were in bitcoin. He couldn't cash all of them at once: such a sum would cause absurd money laundering charges and throw conventional banks into a lather.

Changing them to a different digital coin, however, would be easy.

Excited as he was about Marigolds, he must not lose his Grantchester Meadows house. Having money had liberated Theo from misery. He could eat in a pub rather than waste hours chopping, stirring, and burning his supper; buy another train ticket when he missed the train he was booked on; walk into a shop for a clean shirt when he had forgotten his laundry.

Digital currency had bought him freedom.

His instincts had proved reliable. He had taken enough risk to make money. Not so much that he lost it. He hadn't become a multi-millionaire: his success was built on common sense and a little skill. He wasn't clairvoyant. But he understood cryptocurrency, approximately what it was doing and why.

There was no reason for Marigolds to go wrong. Unless there was something significant he didn't know – which seemed unlikely – the currency was as safe as bitcoin. And more likely to increase because it was newer and underpriced. It should not fail.

When he got home, if his research bore out his initial impressions, he could transfer most of his bitcoins to Marigold.

"Drink?" Li interrupted his thoughts.

Theo followed him into an office, where Li gestured to a chair by a desk, "Please, sit. Very hot. Time for water." And he went out again.

The desk was awash with bills and invoices, incomprehensible scrawls in Chinese characters, Post-it notes crawling with unreadable strokes and pictographs. Theo wondered how long it would take to learn Mandarin, one of many things he had not been allowed to do at school.

One piece of paper alone was comprehensible to him. At the top was a transaction of money, in Marigolds, destined from one domain to another. It didn't matter that the explanatory notes above and beneath were in Chinese: he recognised the horizontal line, the shorter vertical lines branching off it, the numbers above and the way they were set out.

What caught his attention was the arrow pointing to the junk space within the transaction, with a series of equations as if they should be inserted there.

It was clever. In effect, it was a way of writing a message into the transaction. So that when the currency was transferred to the new owner, the receiving computer would be told to do something else at the same time.

When he was a boy and Ann was doing paperwork at her little desk in the dining room, she had written her name and address on the reverse side of a cheque.

"Why did you do that?"

"To save writing a letter," she smiled.

"Won't it invalidate it?" It was a word he had just learnt.

"No, it's fine." So you could write something on the back of a cheque without affecting the front. The agreement would still be honoured.

Nor would this invalidate the transaction of Marigolds. He wondered why it was there and what the message was.

Li came back with one of the other owners and a tray of water. "You interested what you see?" he asked Theo.

"Yes. It's good."

"Thank you. Most honoured. You have questions?"

"Yes, actually. This is cool," Theo picked the paper up. "What are you doing here?"

"Ah, 'scuse, 'scuse!" Li bustled rapidly over to the desk. "Come. I show you something." There seemed some urgency or excitement. He clearly wanted Theo to go back into the warehouse.

"Look," Li said, and took him to the far side. "We put pieces together here. I tell man to show you."

Li left him doing nothing for some minutes, watching the work. "I promise you drink," he said, returning. "I bad host. Perhaps prefer tea?"

"Thank you."

This time Li preceded Theo into the office. He spoke to his colleague in Chinese and received a reply. He clicked his tongue. "Sorry. Tea not ready. I thought he make while we gone."

Theo turned to the desk to ask about the message and what it was for.

The piece of paper was no longer there.

"I wanted to ask," he said to Li, "about a very interesting idea you had written here." He wasn't sure Li's English was good enough for the question, but he would surely know what he meant. "You put something into the blank space of the transaction. I wondered why."

"You take milk in English tea," Li said, with inscrutable Asian politeness. "Jian told me. You have wife?"

"No," Theo said. "I have no wife."

"Theo," he heard his mother saying, years ago. "She was trying to help you."

He had been telling Ann about a member of staff behind the ticket counter at the railway station who kept telling him he was fourteen. Every time she said it, kindly, he corrected her, politely. No: I am thirteen. After three unsuccessful attempts at correcting his age upwards she told him, sadly, that he couldn't travel on his own and go home for the weekend from his new school. He was too young.

It was all right in the end because a man behind him in the queue overheard it all and said Theo could travel with him. The lady behind the counter even lent Theo her telephone so he could ring Ann and get her permission. So when he got home, she asked him about it.

She laughed. "Sometimes people are telling you something, 'between the lines'. There's a message behind the words they're actually using."

"Why don't they say it normally?"

"Because they can't, perhaps? Presumably there is a rail-company rule about unaccompanied minors. She could see you were competent to travel and the rule shouldn't apply in your case. But she couldn't openly bend – sorry, break – the rule for you, because if she had done that knowingly, she might lose her job. If she didn't officially know you were only thirteen, it wouldn't be her fault."

"So she wanted me to lie?"

Ann weighed this up. "I don't think she'd have called it lying. Perhaps, 'Playing along.' After all, you could have just nodded. You could have fudged it too."

"Surely that amounts to the same thing?"

"Yes, it does really."

Li and his colleague were saying something between the lines. They wanted him to play along.

They wanted to 'fudge' as well. Or rather, lie.

And the lie they wanted him to tell was that he hadn't noticed anything.

Chapter Eleven

HIGH SUMMER

When Clare opened her eyes the sky was still muted, grey as a seagull's wing. She hugged the warm, comfortable arm which enveloped her. Then drifted back into sleep.

The next time she looked the light was golden, the sky fading into blue. She listened to the rhythmic suck and shush of the sea and lone squark of a gull, before kissing the sleeping shoulder and getting out of bed. She would take the dog down to the beach before getting breakfast, which they would eat in the back garden in the rising warmth overlooking the misty blues and pale yellows of the glorious view.

The summer was exceeding all records. Unbroken sunshine for nearly two months. Why go abroad when North Norfolk was more fabulous than Cyprus? Day after day, week after week, over thirty degrees. Every weekend, every bride in the country enjoying perfect wedding photographs, while her guests sweated gently or fanned themselves under trees and parasols. Clare had always loved the heat. Nothing could go wrong in conditions as idyllic as these.

The dog yapped on the descent. Looking after it was the (extremely modest) cost of borrowing the cottage. Clare scrambled down the cliff, poo bags in one pocket of her beach robe and mobile and hair band in the other.

The beach was deserted. She left her robe, towel and flip-flops on a large boulder while the little dog ran about. The water was milder, and clearer, than she ever remembered its being: not even the slightest gasp as she stepped into the North Sea. The early sun scattered diamonds in its path; curiously, Clare found the water warmer when she swam towards it than with the sunrise at her back.

The spaniel skittered, sniffing and exploring. Colours were washed pale in the morning air. A faded watercolour: primary colours of the beach huts diluted into pastels; horizon hardly even blue; barest sliver of diaphanous moon above, calling to the tide. The scant clouds had been splashed transparent onto the sky. In the heat of the day they would clump into storybook cotton wool, if they hadn't been burnt completely away.

The little translucent waves turning and falling on the sand loosened any knots of tension she might have imagined. Her life seemed so perfect she hardly knew what to long for any more.

She had won the doctorate, with distinction, she had dreamt of before she left school. She had one of the loveliest rooms in Cambridge, overlooking the Market Place and University Church. And she was – she admitted, with rare force and passion – in love. She hadn't been sure at first: hadn't wanted to share her life. She had weighed up their intellectual incompatibility, and the challenge of living with someone who earned money rather than broke new academic ground. And of course, the tedious concerns about their parents' friends, which had turned out to be groundless.

None of this mattered now. What they had was more important than everything. Even, if possible, the career she had worked so hard for. Her decision had been taken on another plane altogether, where differences had no place.

The little dog looked out to sea, wondering when Clare would return.

"Good girl." It was a girl, wasn't it? Everything was good on this gilded morning.

When her feet touched the soft sand again she stood, cupping her hands into the sea and splashing her face, throwing waves into the air and scattering shards of light. The dog barked.

She had formed her resolution the evening before. They had walked across green and white cliffs in the Mediterranean warmth, the sea swishing its skirts on the drying sand far below, whispering its secrets along the shore. Sand martins dipped and swerved, and a lark ran along the path before darting low above the rough grass, then rising in song that filled the sky like a resounding bell. The red-gold sun dipped into a Turner sea. They talked, as they always did, of everything. The Booker long-list. The underlying cause of Communism. Why grouse rise from the ground like bullets.

After pints and chunky soup in a homely pub they walked back in the dark, stumbling on differently worn paths, Clare holding out spread fingers so they could walk hand in hand and not fall. The dog ran to and fro about their feet.

As a child, Clare never wanted to marry. She told her parents she didn't need a man getting in her way. Stopping her from reaching the top, she meant. And now, only twenty-six, she wanted commitment and one person for life. Even children perhaps: why not?

Little girls are not taught how to propose. Wait until a leap year? She laughed. She would pick wildflowers for the scrubbed kitchen table. Make tea and take it up to their bedroom. Walk into town and buy a still-hot white bloomer, and bloaters from the one-man fishmonger. Champagne wouldn't be right for their rustic five-day cottage: that could wait for Cambridge or Clapham.

She would say, "Please will you marry me?" as lovers have said since the dawn of time.

Her life would be complete.

As she came up from the beach the wildflowers she had noticed earlier, dog roses and poppies, buttercups and one she thought was cow parsley, all seemed to have disappeared. She found a thistle which scratched her, and a couple of dandelions staining her fingers with milk. And the spaniel pulled and tussled on the lead, so that even these were broken by the time she neared the cottage. It didn't matter. You could engineer a perfect proposal and the Metro might still break down on the way to the Eiffel Tower.

In future years they would laugh over her squashed weeds in a jam jar.

Gulls squabbled overhead as she let the dog into the house. Upstairs, unusually, she found their bed tousled and empty. She went down into the sitting room and saw the screen busy already. Money doesn't sleep.

"I thought you'd still be in bed. I'll go and get breakfast." She had the self-control not to add any more. Clare prided herself on her will-power.

The clear hazel eyes dragged themselves from the screen. "What?"

Clare put her arms around her. "You're supposed to be on holiday. Though I have no objection to your earning money. Lots. For both of us," she joked. "I'm never likely to, am I?"

"Sorry," Kathryn said, pushing her laptop away. "Crisis in the office. Did you say breakfast?"

"Yes."

"Good. I've got something I want to talk to you about. Or perhaps, say."

Clare's heart skipped. Ever since she had known Kathryn they had thought, even moved, as one.

"I'm just going for fresh bread and bloaters."

"I'll finish before you're back." Kathryn was already on her laptop again. Clare wouldn't understand any of the figures in front of her, just as Kathryn wouldn't grasp Clare's A level syllabus, let alone her doctorate. There was time for all that. Two years together now . . . They didn't have an 'anniversary': it had all started so tentatively. She ran her fingers through Kathryn's soft, mousy hair, kissed the dimple on her cheek and left.

In the weeks afterwards she agonised over why Kathryn had let her go. Why didn't she say, forget the bloody bloaters! We don't need bread, for the love of fuck. Not for what we have to say.

Then she would pull herself back. It wouldn't have made any difference, would it?

She had walked into the little town, its twee red tiles smiling beneath a seaside-blue sky alongside the holiday bunting. She pushed through the beaded fly-door of the baker's, waiting behind other early-morning holiday-makers. It was already hot enough for the cool of the shop to be welcome. She chose two silly little green cakes shaped like smiling frogs, for their tea. The bread was warm and soft in its paper bag.

She crossed the road. Sorry, love: bloaters not in yet. Come back at lunchtime. In a moment of extravagance she bought a dressed local lobster. Perhaps champagne was called for after all.

She hesitated over brut Cava. Unlike Kathryn, Clare couldn't afford champagne. But you only propose once. She took her card from her shorts pocket.

On the way back to the cottage she wanted to embrace the vibrancy of sky and sea; to sing aloud; to thank the universe for her doctorate, her prospects, the unnatural sunshine . . . and most of all for Kathryn. She hadn't known it was possible to be so happy, all the ducks in a row at once.

This time Kathryn shut her laptop and rose immediately.

"I'm not really hungry," she admitted, seeing the spread. "But thank you. It's kind." Then added, with the characteristic calm Clare so admired, "There is never a good time to say this."

When Clare left the cottage, alone, the bottle of Moët was in her bag. The lobster wouldn't keep, and she couldn't see herself eating it any time soon.

There were no tears, no entreaties. She almost wished there could have been a row, some throwing of crockery and accusations. But she would not have been Kathryn if she had behaved like that and Clare would not have loved her.

There was nobody else, no. She wasn't bottling out and going straight: that would be totally unlike her too. It was Kathryn who was unequivocally gay; Clare simply loved her because she loved her. She just didn't want marriage enough to commit. And once you have decided that, it's the end, isn't it?

The view from the little two-carriage pay-train back to Norwich which they had so enjoyed together – cream-coloured Scout tents clustered in a field; purple loosestrife painting the verges – now seemed a savannah wasteland. Suburban gardens reduced to shrivelled patches. Chestnut leaves browning in the glare. The compartment baked. Hadn't there been thunderstorms and flash floods at the beginning of June, almost impossibly long ago?

Even as she thought this, the welkin turned as if on a sixpence. Rain started to whip the windows and streak the glass. Soon hailstones bounced in through the meagre top window. How was this possible from such heat? Visibility reduced almost to the edge of the tracks; the sky lowering behind the onslaught. And still the ground parched.

Clare arrived at her room in the early evening.

She didn't want to tell her parents. Perhaps not ever. Perhaps she would just leave them to work it out. It was no one else's business and not many friends had known about their relationship. Those who had, hadn't been particularly enthusiastic. They had turned out right, hadn't they?

She put the champagne at the back of her wardrobe, grabbed a friendly old jumper though the evening still sweltered, and went out onto the barely damp pavements, to eat alone.

She would get on with her life. Particularly, her work.

Chapter Twelve

EARLY AUGUST

Theo arrived at Heathrow in such good time that he nearly missed his flight.

It was due to leave at two. He was there just after eleven. He went straight to the British Airways counter to check in, after which he would go for a beer.

There he was asked for an Esther. When he said he didn't know what that was, he was told no one could embark in the US without and it would take seventy-two hours to apply.

It took a bit of unravelling to decipher this confident assertion. The two officials by now advising him didn't mean what they'd said. They meant seventy-two hours to arrive, *after* he had applied. The earliest he would be able to fly would be Friday.

He explained he was due to attend a conference starting in Baltimore that evening through which he had booked both flights and accommodation. Upon which he was told that the conference organisers themselves probably didn't realise he needed the Esther.

"It's like a visa," one of them explained. "Electronic System for Travel Authorization," as if this made more sense. "You can't fly to the US without an ESTA," she repeated for the nth time.

Theo could be surprisingly tenacious. Just as a deaf person can tolerate noise which would be agony to the rest of us, so Theo could wait for the seas to run dry and the rocks melt with the sun, without boredom. It was nothing to him if he spent three days at the check-in counter: he wasn't going anywhere else. Nor was anyone, while he was holding up business.

After he had been at the desk, quietly insistent, for so long that the staff had been obliged to call up reinforcements, it became less troublesome to resolve Theo's problem than ignore it. Somebody rang someone and faxed something to somebody, the requisite form was filled in and signed and approved. Not seventy-two hours at all, then. As usual, this didn't constitute a lie.

He now had his ESTA. He could go for his beer.

He had always factored in the beer. Fifteen minutes for a check-in which should take five. A comfortable hour before going to the gate. There was no obvious catch. Unfortunately, when an unexpected or (particularly) stressful event happened, Theo sometimes forgot a vital step. Such as recalibrating his brain.

He found a bar, bought a pint of Abbot, took it to the window and sat down to enjoy his anticipation of the conference. The grass outside looked like sand. A waiter came to wipe the table.

"Thank you," Theo said.

The waiter, who looked about fifteen, beamed. "It's my first day."

"It will be my first time in America," Theo reciprocated.

"Cool," the waiter replied politely. "When's your flight?"

Theo looked around for the information board, having momentarily forgotten he was taking a flight. He scanned down for Washington and deduced there was some mistake. It was flashing a closing gate.

"What's the time?" he asked the waiter.

"Just gone twenty to two."

Theo jumped to his feet, grabbed his laptop and nearly knocked over the beer. "Goodbye. I mean, thank you."

"Hey! Your wallet!"

He turned, looked longingly at the beer and realised this was just one of those things – like new shoelaces – and ran, dodging, searching frantically for the gate.

It seemed about half a mile to his required destination. He tore down escalators, past shops, along corridors. Not until he found himself, sweating uncomfortably, in a lift with several Americans laughing at their delayed connection did he believe he might arrive at his conference after all.

He collapsed into his numbered seat, leant back, shut his eyes and felt sick. He had left his room just after eight o'clock that morning. He had no idea what he should have done differently, to have avoided such an unpleasant few minutes.

"Are you all right sir?"

"Yes, thank you," he told the stewardess. "Do you have any whiskey? Or tea?"

"Not until we've taken off, sir. I'll bring you both as soon as I can."

Charlotte knew his face off by heart. This man was heavier, shorter, his features stubbier than she had long ago memorised.

And he looked straight past her, eyeing those disembarking. She had imagined for so long calling "Daddy!", waving like someone in a film. Her voice faltered. Still he ignored her.

She approached, touched his arm and said, "Daddy?" again.

"Oh my Gahd!" He appraised her briefly. "Makes me sound ancient. Not bad." He kissed her lips, turned and started walking towards the exit. "Journey all right." It didn't sound like a question.

She wiped her mouth briefly and quickened her step. There was no reason he should take her suitcase. This was America. And the twenty-first century. She was quite strong enough herself. "What do you want me to call you?" she said, a little out of breath.

"Selwyn. What the hell else?"

She hadn't expected the American accent. Stupid.

"Waddya want me to call you?"

"Charlotte is fine." Hadn't he had lots of pet names for her? She suddenly couldn't remember any.

"Haven't changed your name to Princess Trixabelle then?"

It wasn't until they reached a car, he flicked it unlocked and opened the boot for her that he looked at her again.

"Hmm," he said, approvingly. This time she moved her face and the kiss landed on her cheek.

In the passenger seat she crossed her legs tightly and pulled her skirt towards her knees.

"Where ya staying?"

"Oh, I . . ." She was stumped. "I thought I could stay with you?"

"I wish. We'll find you someplace. You gonna see the sights?"

"Yes, please." The shock was so sudden she struggled not to cry. Hadn't she written, with such excitement, that she was coming to stay?

"What you wanna see?"

She managed to stop herself from saying, Whatever he wanted. "What do you recommend?" Perhaps she had said she was coming to 'see' him? Nobody's fault. Except hers, for being muddled.

"You haven't planned your sightseeing? That's so English," he laughed shortly. "Well, I can advise."

She stared ahead of her, seeing nothing. How could there be no room even on his living room floor? "Um," she started, before clearing her throat and forcing her register down. "I haven't got much money." She had to say it. And then quickly added, "Are there youth hostels? I don't mind where."

There was a long silence while he negotiated traffic. His car seemed swish, the seats beige leather.

"Just like ya mother, aren't you?" He looked sideways at her with a thin, crooked smile. "We'll find somethin'. There's nothin' cheap in town."

She blinked, the lights dazzling into a blur. Then turned her head away to look through her window while she wiped her cheeks.

Almost as if he might have wished it otherwise, he said, "Don't blame me. Barbara can't cope with visitors."

The streets sped past the window.

It was exactly a week until her flight back home.

As soon as he arrived in the hotel, Theo triggered off the following text exchange:

"Hotel bar?"

"K. When?"

"Yes."

"??"

"'Do you want your tea now, or when it's ready?'"

"Pardon?"

"Hibernian phrase. It means you choose."

"You brits make me die."

"Didn't you chaps have a War of Independence too? I'm Irish."

While he was waiting, Theo asked what the local brew was. The courteous barman showed him an array of bottled beers, meeting with Theo's ill-disguised disgust. "What do you drink yourself?"

"Pardon me?" The barman asked, astonished. "What do I drink?"

"Yup."

"Why d'you wanna know that?"

"If I want to ride the best horse in the stable, I ask the groom for his. You work here. What do you drink?"

"Cranberry juice."

"What on earth for?"

"Sir, I'm a Seventh Day Adventist."

"Blimey. Hard luck."

"Okay, I get it," a voice said behind him. "You're Theo."

Theo turned. "That doesn't mean I'm going to drink cranberry juice."

"I'm Evan."

"What do the natives drink? Obviously not tea or beer. Is it cocktails?"

"We don't drink like you guys do. We tried to prohibit it. I'll take care of this. You find a table."

Theo settled near a window overlooking an open square, watching the people rather as David Attenborough might observe penguins. About sixty percent of those sitting down were crowded into approximately twelve percent of the space. They didn't seem to notice they were blocking a path. It would be far more efficient if some of them were moved: that family of five should swap with these two old ladies; the gentleman taking up a four-seater table should move to a two-seater; those lovers would be more comfortable in a corner. But of course, that would be difficult because they're people. The path, however, was definitely in the wrong place and that would be much easier to move.

Evan arrived with a large tulip glass of red wine and a fizzy drink of a frighteningly lurid colour. "Welcome to the Land of the Free."

"How did you get on?"

"Excuse me?"

"With the provenance programme?"

"Oh, pretty good. Coupla little glitches. You might be able to fix. Good trip?"

There was an apparently meaningless pause. "Oh, I see." There was another. "Well, I got here. Which was the important thing."

"Not enjoyable?"

"The tea was pretty awful. The stewardess was interesting. Has a widowed mother in Virginia Water, and her fiancé was killed in Helmand."

"Oh my! I'm sorry. Who's this again?"

"The stewardess. You were asking about my flight."

"You crack me up."

"I like this. I didn't know whether Americans drink wine."

"When we want wine, we do. Not when we want tea."

"When you want tea, you drink something completely disgusting and virtually pointless. Everyone does, apart from the English. And Irish. And Chinese. And possibly the Scotch and Welsh though I wouldn't trust them entirely."

"We have decent coffee. I've tried the coffee you guys drink, when I was in Ahxford, and it's very bad. Now, which seminars tomorrow?"

Evan swung onto his lap an expensive tooled leather briefcase, clicked it open and produced a brochure thick enough to stop a door.

"I dunno why they waste paper on this stuff."

Theo consulted his telephone. "The sell-by date seminar."

"Sell-by Date Seminar?"

"Village in Italy," Theo explained, searching. "Middle Ages. Economic crisis, so the mayor introduced a law diminishing the currency. Negative interest, technically called demurrage. The longer you keep money in your pocket the less it's worth. Rescued the community from destitution. Here we are. 'The Wörgl Experiment.'"

Evan skim-read. "Austrian town in the Tyrol in 1932. Are you usually this particular over detail?"

"I'm a bit the same with names, Ann says."

Evan wondered if Ann was his partner.

Theo read on. "The results were so miraculous and so many other towns wanted to follow suit that the government banned the practice. Here's the medieval connection. Bracteates: coins which diminished in value."

"Interesting."

"It's what we should be doing. With digital currency. And there's credit card fraud in the afternoon. Shall we get a bottle of this stuff and take it up to your room?"

Evan took a moment to assess this. He was not at all sure he had read Theo's sexuality correctly – nor Theo, his – but decided it was a cultural difference merely. "Sure," he said. "But bear in mind I'm only a yank: I can't keep up with your British drinking. And I think ya'll be shocked at the price . . ."

But Theo was already at the bar. "A bottle of anything you recommend, please. Except cranberry juice."

Charlotte had never known such misery. Not even when she was six, when her father had walked out. At least then she hadn't fully understood the nature of the rejection. And she hadn't had other worries to contend with. Five minutes earlier her father had put her in a taxi and given the driver the address of some hostel he had just Googled. That was all.

She thought of tapping on the window and asking the driver to put her out. She couldn't summon up the courage. And what would she do then, anyway?

She had brought ninety-three dollars and sixty-three cents – the remainder of the five hundred pounds she had allocated for the trip – as spending money: for presents, postcards and a thank you present for her father. The cab clock already showed nine dollars fifty.

Even if she hadn't given Guy an undertaking, there was no more birthday money left. The day after booking her flight, she had gone with her mother to try a violin, fallen in love with it and paid slightly more than was left. Careful though she was, she was near her overdraft limit. And Suki had told her how important it was to have enough money at Cambridge. "It sounds awful, but if you don't, you can't make friends. People meet up in bars and clubs and things."

How heartbreaking if, as a result of Guy's kind present, her first term was blighted by anxiety . . . How much better if she had used it to have a bit extra in her first year.

And yet she was only mistily aware of all this, so sick with worry was she over the cab fare. How would she eat? How pay for tomorrow night?

"This is it," the driver said.

She fumbled in her bag. "How much do I owe you?"

"Y'okay?"

She looked at the brash, confident neon of the night buildings. "Yes. Thank you."

"That your pa, back there?"

She nodded.

"When you last see him?"

"When I was six."

"My da walked out before I was born."

She looked away again to hide her face. "How much?"

"Nothin'."

She stared, stupid, not knowing how to thank him. "Are you . . . sure?"

"Only hope you get on okay."

"Oh, thank you, thank you! You've no idea . . ."

"Yeah I have. You okay now?"

"Yes. Thank you."

He waved through his open window. "Good night, ma'am."

From: clsebastian@gmail.com
To: tafw@cam.ac.uk
Subject: Sightseeing?
Time and date: 07 08 18 at 21.53.07

Hi Theo,

I'm in Washington! I realise you're probably busy at your conference, but it turns out my dad is quite occupied this week so I've got time to see the sights. If you have a free afternoon would you like to come over? Apparently there's a train.

Charlotte.

PS You can bring your friend.
PPS I'm not sure if my phone takes calls abroad, but there's wifi in my hostel.

Theo laughed out loud. His mother wouldn't know either.

From: tafw@cam.ac.uk
To: clsebastian@gmail.com
Subject: Sightseeing?
On: 07 08 18 at 23.29.13

Which friend?

Theophilus Ambrose Fitzwilliam Wedderburn.

From: clsebastian@gmail.com
To: tafw@cam.ac.uk
Subject: Sightseeing?
On: 07 08 18 at 23.37.48

Hi Theo

Sorry: I thought you knew someone at the
conference. You mentioned it when we were
talking about the provenance thing.

Charlotte

Theo often analysed his behaviour, thoughts and feelings. As with
most things – mathematical equations or computer programming
or musical performance – he did this far more accurately than
'normal' people. But it took him longer.

So it might have taken months, even had it occurred to him, to
work out why, when there was no down-time in the conference he
had been looking forward to since the Lent Term, he replied:

From: tafw@cam.ac.uk
To: clsebastian@gmail.com
Subject: Sightseeing?
On: 08 08 18 at 00.16.37

Tomorrow?

Theophilus Ambrose Fitzwilliam Wedderburn.

"You're nuts," Evan said. "You've been planning this trip for eight months. Why doesn't she come here?"

"Maybe she didn't like to invite herself? Perhaps she couldn't afford the train fare."

"It would be kinda cool to meet a real Cambridge stoodent. Classics, you said. That's like Latin and Greek and stuff?"

"I'm a real Cambridge student," Theo pointed out. "And Charlotte isn't, yet."

From: tafw@cam.ac.uk
To: clsebastian@gmail.com
Subject: Sightseeing?
On: 08 08 18 at 01.02.19

Change of plan. (Do you mind changing plans? I do, but I seem to be in the minority.) You come here. Evan and I will split your train fare, which will still be cheaper for us.

Evan says Washington DC takes a week whereas you can 'do' Baltimore in an afternoon.

Theophilus Ambrose Fitzwilliam Wedderburn.

Evan had not, in fact, offered to share the cost of Charlotte's train fare but he was very happy with this latest arrangement. He was in the tentative early stages of a new relationship back home, and liked to know which side Theo played for.

First thing the next morning, Charlotte received a text from her father. He told her he was extremely busy but could see her for twenty minutes at a coffee shop the other side of town. She asked the hostel proprietor for a map.

He said it would be crazy to walk – it was several miles, goddamn – but seeing how determined she was, remembered a few errands in that part of town. She almost cried with gratitude, and ran upstairs for her backpack and a book.

She waited for her lift for the best part of an hour, and was still early for her father. Normally when Charlotte had her nose in a book, hours passed as minutes. After reading the same paragraph half a dozen times she gave up, and watched the street. To her surprise not many people seemed overweight, or stunningly beautiful, or any different from a crowd in England.

She didn't notice him approach. "You wanna sit here, out on the sidewalk?" He sat down heavily, the table between them suddenly fragile. She hadn't taken in how very American he had become.

"I didn't want to miss you." She jumped up, apologetic. "We can go inside."

"Ah siddown."

After a minute she got up again. "What would you like to drink?" She didn't know what to call him.

"Skinny latte. With hazelnut corn syrup and cream topping."

She returned, with water for herself, and they sat for a few moments saying nothing. On the opposite side of the street, a stall was hung with woolly hats. They looked like braces of dead birds, the bobbles hanging like heads, thigh-shaped earflaps and ties like dead feet tossed in the breeze. A tormented plastic bag was kicked across the road by the wind. The passers-by didn't seem so familiar any more.

"It's no good blaming me, ya know."

"I'm sorry?"

"Ya don't fool me. She's bin pissed with me since the day I left. Always dissin' me."

"No ... you don't ..."

"Come ahhn. A man can't stay with a woman who can't love him. Things happen. Jenny loved me."

"Jenny?"

"Janey. Don't try an' catch me out."

Charlotte tasted the name on her tongue. "Is she ..." Partner? Girlfriend? If she didn't ask now, she would always wish she had. "Is she your wife?"

"Ha. I'd had 'nough of that." His accent seemed to be slipping. "And it was a long time ago. Jus' like your mother, ain't ya. I was not to blame for the breakup of that marriage. You hear me?"

Charlotte glanced around to see who else had heard him. Nobody blamed him here, for sure.

She heard a light toot on a car horn, and saw the proprietor of the hostel waiting, engine running.

"I've got to go. I'm really sorry." She stood up. "I have a lift."

Instead of relief, her father looked as if she'd thrown water over him.

"Sorry. Um. Bye. Dad." She hesitated for a moment. "Thanks for the . . ." She looked at her untouched glass of water.

Charlotte had watched the DVD of *Cabaret* at a friend's house when they were fifteen. She had always wanted to emulate Liza Minelli's wave with the back of her hand, without looking back. She did so now, as she went towards the car, before feeling the pretentiousness of the gesture and putting her hand in her pocket.

"Good meeting?"

She shrugged and maintained her smile. "Thanks for the lift." Their table was receding into the row of shops. Her father was staring after her.

I will not cry. I will not I will not I will not.

Then realised she didn't want to.

Chapter Thirteen

THURSDAY

"Okay, I don' really know Baltimore at all."

Theo was paying for lunch – seafood, Evan had insisted: Baltimore was famous for its crabs – and Evan was responsible for the rest of the afternoon.

"I dunno if you guys will be offended: the Battle of Baltimore is where we beat the Brits."

Charlotte and Theo both laughed. "I'm not sure you've understood the English," Theo said. "We don't really do success."

Charlotte, obeying instructions, had ordered a prawn cocktail, Theo a chowder. The piled-up plates were placed before them. And these were just starters.

"You came over to see ya pa?" Evan asked conversationally. Charlotte nodded. "Ya see him often?" She shook her head. "What does he work in?" She shrugged. "My parents are quite boring: still together an' all." Charlotte raised her eyebrows.

"I dunno how you Brits put it away," he said admiringly when the waiter cleared their plates. "I'm sorry bud, I'm done. And you're so tiny," he said to Charlotte. "What are you, size nothin'?"

Charlotte blushed. Americans were straightforward: everyone said so. "Um. Do you think the waiter would put yours in a doggy bag?"

"Buddy, put this in a container for the lady. You kind of hungry?"

To her horror, a tear rolled down her face. "I'm so sorry," she mumbled. "I haven't . . . eaten since Monday night. Well, the flight on Tuesday."

"Say wat?"

"Oh, you could have shared my fish soup thingy."

"We've got more coming," Evan said. "Didn't work out with your pa?"

In England, making a scene in a restaurant would have been awful. Somehow, it didn't seem to matter here.

"Stupid of me. I'd idolised him."

"Easy to do."

Theo nodded. "My father showed us all his faults when he was still with us. And I loved him anyway."

"This will do you the second half of the week." A vast oval of salad and cheese-heaped crabshell was put in front of her. "That why you turned up with your luggage?"

"That was a mistake."

She hadn't meant to tell them: she wasn't going to spoil the afternoon. But Charlotte, as her mother had observed, was as transparent as a blue sky on a summer's morning.

After her meeting with her father, she had asked the hostel proprietor how to reach the National Arboretum. It wasn't most visitors' choice, but he dropped her off and told her how to get a bus back.

She had climbed the green slopes of that peaceful world and allowed her sadness to fall from her. She lingered over the Bonsai, marvelling at the tiny White Pine which had been in training thousands of miles away when Charles I was on the throne. She sat by the water in the slanting sun under the Georgian columns, and decided to be glad.

Which made it all the harder when she arrived back and the proprietor's wife explained that they had tried every which way they could, but they had taken a group of students from Australia a long time before and there was nothing they could do. She gave her a list of recommendations.

She packed her suitcase, abandoned her plan of seeing the *Gutenberg Bible* in the Library of Congress with her heavy case in tow, and told herself everything would feel easier once she had seen someone English. She had nowhere to store her case so she brought it with her.

By the end of lunch Theo was seeing if he could bring forward her flight and they had agreed that, after learning about the utter humiliation of the English in 1812, they would all go back to the conference centre.

"I'll sleep in Evan's room tonight so you can have mine."

"Will you hell. I bet you snore, you British bastard."

"Irish."

"So you said."

"If I go home early," Charlotte protested, "my mother and Guy – my stepfather – will know. You know, that my dad didn't . . ." She petered out.

"You think your mother doesn't know?" Theo said gently.

"It was Guy's eighteenth birthday present to me. And I wasted it."

"You realise how stupid that comment is?"

"Do I?"

"You've learnt something critically important, which will inform the rest of your life. How can that possibly be a waste?"

They spent the afternoon on the Baltimore peninsular. Charlotte was in a thin summer dress, unprepared for the wind despite the temperature inland. As a huge star-spangled banner was spread out on the ground, their guide asked if anyone could guess which American writer might have been named after Frances Scott.

"Fitzgerald?" Charlotte suggested.

The guide stared. "Well there you go," he said, affronted. "Brit, are you?"

She slid behind Evan, embarrassed. They went inside and heard a lecture on the defeat of the British. Theo teased Evan for American chauvinism. "This Battle seems to have been a bit of a draw."

"I'm going to buy Charlotte a memento in the gift shop," Evan retorted.

As they looked at prints of warships at sea, sails unfurled and straining, he and Charlotte were rudely blasted by an ear-piercing blare behind them: a bass note, then a fifth up, then a desperate octave. Theo stood, bugle in hand.

"Bud, I'll buy it," Evan begged him, "if you shut up."

"That's what I'd like," Charlotte said, "for my present."

In the cab back to the conference Evan tried. "I can't get a squeak out of it," he complained.

"Do you mind?" Charlotte leant forward and asked the driver.

"Go ahead, lady."

She wiped the mouthpiece, pursed her lips and played the first few notes of the Reveille.

"Holy shit," Evan said. "That's knocked you into a cocked hat, bud."

"My baby brother plays the trumpet," Charlotte admitted. "I shouldn't have told you that."

They hadn't made any arrangement to meet at breakfast. As Charlotte sat waiting for the waiter she heard a familiar voice from behind the pillar.

"Is Pedro here, please?"

"Pedro, sir?"

"The waiter on duty yesterday."

Her first impulse was to join them, but she didn't want to impose.

"Any of us will serve you to the best of our ability, sir."

"I'm sure. It's just that I'm English . . ."

"That's okay sir. We have a full English option. French fries, white and black pudding, two eggs, beans on toast."

"We're a bit particular about our tea."

"Sir, we have a selection of fifty-two teas. I'll go get them right away."

Gathering up her book, Charlotte went round the pillar and waved.

"Charlotte, siddown. You're just in time for the Vaudeville. The Irish rebel has become an English imperialist."

The waiter was back, sporting a smart wooden tray as if selling ices in a cinema, arrayed with teabags dressed in every colour of sachet imaginable. "Sir, we have English Breakfast, Lady Grey, Afternoon Blend, Rosehip and Ginger, Lemongrass and Seaweed . . ."

"It's not quite what I meant." Theo sighed. "The secret of tea is boiling water. Now, here we have an ominous thermos flask of warmish water . . ."

"Sir, our water is completely safe. It was all boiled first thing this morning."

"It's not that," Charlotte joined in. "You have to pour the water, just before it boils, into the pot. Which has previously been warmed."

"Thank you," Theo said emphatically.

"Ma'am?"

"And it should be the first time it boils, really," she warmed to her theme. "Otherwise there isn't enough oxygen to bring out the flavour."

"Pedro couldn't get it either," Theo turned to her. "We were getting somewhere yesterday. Part two of the supervision should have been today."

"Could I," Charlotte suggested tentatively, "perhaps come into the kitchen and show you?"

"You guys make me die," Evan laughed. "Does it matter? It's tea for Chrissakes."

"Does Democracy matter?" Theo said. "Does the First Amendment matter, whatever that is?"

"Ma'am, if you want to visit our kitchen, you're most welcome."

"Now you see, in England that would never be allowed," she beamed, giving credit where it was due. "Elf and Safety. How sensible America is."

Five minutes later she returned triumphant.

"There was an American in my First Year," Theo said, "called Gabriel. Or possibly Daniel. Decent mathematician. Kept tea bags in his room for English friends. He offered me tea, then put a mug of cold water in his microwave."

"Oh dear," Charlotte said.

"When I asked, 'What are you doing?' he said, 'Sorry, we were having such an interesting conversation' – we were arguing about the rules of the Assassins' Guild: obviously you can't use a weapon labelled 'Oil Tanker' in the university Chemistry Lab; it's clearly spelt out in Clause Seventy-Six that you can't use water weapons in the Computer Lab – 'that I forgot to put the tea bag in.' This is Gabriel speaking again. And then . . ." He paused for dramatic effect. "He put the tea bag *into* the mug of cold water. And turned his microwave on."

He waited for the shocked silence.

"And?" Evan said.

Theo and Charlotte looked at each other. America fell away. The age difference between them fell away. She thought of a summer garden, back home, blackbird darting across the lawn and her mother arriving with a tray of fresh tea.

The waiter was at their table, bearing a teapot.

"I even found a pot!" she said proudly. "They were so kind. They thanked me. For explaining how it's done. The point of the story, Evan, is that you don't make tea with cold water. Though," she glanced at Theo apologetically, "I'm not sure I agree with you about the temperature. Ninety-five degrees is supposed to be optimal."

"Theophilus, marry this woman! Let's try this tea."

Charlotte fumbled with her napkin.

"See if I can tell the difference. Buddy, you look like you've just worked out how to solve an NP-hard problem in polynomial time."

"With black tea, anyway," Charlotte backtracked. "Green is supposed to be eighty-five. And loose leaf. I expect boiling's best for teabags."

"Or Archimedes' Paradox maybe. Tastes okay I guess. Not quite sure what the fuss is about."

"What did you just say?" Theo asked him.

"So what did you do about the tea bag and the mug?" Charlotte asked brightly.

"What?"

"Gabriel."

"Who?"

"And the microwave. Or possibly Daniel?"

"Oh!" Theo said, enlightened. "You mean Raphael. Drank coffee."

Charlotte spent a glorious day alone in Theo's room, reading the second of her three books. She had decided to be kind to herself: the trip was her treat from Guy, and she was spending it doing what she preferred to anything else in the world.

The men had said the plenary session ended at half past three and they could meet up after that. It wasn't until nearly five that she realised they hadn't arranged where.

They weren't in the dining room. Finding them proved harder than expected. Eventually, Reception suggested E McDonald, University of MIT, staying in room 603.

She knocked gently on the door. She was just about to give up when Evan opened it.

"Come in Charlotte. No tea, I'm afraid."

Theo was at a desk, two laptops open in front of him, a bottle of wine on the floor and a glass at his elbow. Charlotte settled herself on the bed with her book while Evan produced a toothmug and poured her some.

It was gone half past seven when Theo said, "That's good now. All we've got to do is run it."

"What is it?" Charlotte said.

"You remember that question whatshername asked? About bitcoin provenance?"

"Before you do all that," Evan said, "shall I ring down to Reception for something? Sushi? Pizza?"

"Evan designed a programme," Theo continued. "We've been ironing out the glitches."

"With a bit of help from Dorit Ron and Adi Shamir."

"Who?" Charlotte asked.

"Couple a quality geeks," Evan explained. "Wrote an academic paper about the bitcoin graph."

"This, you see, will do all the calculations we couldn't do by hand." And Theo launched into an explanation which she couldn't follow at all. Evan tried to stop him a few times, but it was quicker just to let him run to the end like a wound up toy. After ten minutes Charlotte stood up, Evan gave her a $50 note and half an hour later she returned with several boxes of Mexican takeaway and another book.

As she and Evan ate, there were long easy silences, broken only by Theo tapping his keyboard interspersed with Evan occasionally asking her about her family or what she was doing for the rest of the summer. Theo topped up his glass.

"I've put in someone I've been trading with, as some of the transactions are known to me. Ooh, food!"

He helped himself, went back to his laptop, stared at it for a moment – taco halfway to his mouth – then lowered himself into his chair and started tapping again.

"What is it?" Evan asked. There was no answer.

Evan offered Charlotte more food and was just spooning sour cream over it when Theo said, "Have I read this right? See this company here?"

Evan got up and read. They were so absorbed that Charlotte rose and looked over their shoulders.

"I think you have," Evan said, moving over to the other laptop and putting in a search. After a few minutes he said, "Not very nice."

"It's a lot more than that," Theo said. "Crispin is a psychologist."

"So I guess he'd be interested in this kind of thing."

"That's not the point," Theo replied. "I sat next to him on High Table a few months ago and he was telling the woman opposite about his thesis. The effect on children of seeing pornographic images."

There was a long silence. "Holy shit," Evan said eventually. "Though it may not be what it appears. They're probably over eighteen. I bet they've covered themselves. Legally. They obviously haven't covered the kids."

"That is totally not the point," Theo repeated. "It is *a* point. But not the point I'm interested in."

Charlotte was looking at Theo's laptop, but there was nothing intelligible: just numbers and figures. Then she saw Evan's and gasped.

"This friend of Theo's, here . . ." Evan started.

"Not exactly a friend."

"Co-worker. Appears to be receiving large amounts of money . . ."

"Very large. And carefully hidden."

". . . from this company here, Kute Kittens. Which seems to make underage porn movies."

"What do you mean, seems?" Charlotte no longer wanted to look.

"They use stars who look about eleven," Evan continued. "Or less. They may not be, but that's what they look like."

"Surely illegal?" Charlotte hoped.

"Doesn't ultimately matter," Theo explained, "regarding Crispin's interest. As Evan says, the actors or whatever you call them may be twenty-five. They look like children. And the company's market undoubtedly is. Look at the adverts."

Down the right-hand side were computer games; pop-up toasties; acne concealer.

Theo stood and went to the window, looking out on the pinpricks of night-life far below struggling not to be extinguished by the night. Neither Evan nor Charlotte said anything.

"In other words," Theo turned back, his face very still, "Crispin is engaged in supposedly independent research. Whilst going to a lot of trouble to hide large payments from an interest which would very much prefer his findings not to be independent at all."

"Hey, man," Evan said soothingly. "It's not that bad. So, his research is compromised."

"Not that bad?" Theo demanded, moving his spectacles very slightly on his nose. "Not that bad? His integrity is compromised. The college is compromised. The entire University of Cambridge is compromised."

"Surely not," Charlotte said. "One bad apple . . ."

"The foundation on which we all conduct research is compromised." He looked away, collecting his thoughts. Letting the colour in his face subside. "Kute Kittens," he resumed after a long, slow breath, "is campaigning for freer access to porn. Wanting the internet, all websites, to be uncensored. No frontiers. Crispin is researching how porn affects young viewers. Whether erotic images have a permanent effect on children's neural pathways. Whether this later affects their relationships, influences how they view the opposite sex, creates an acceptance of violence. His findings will be published in peer-reviewed papers. Reviewed by other psychologists who will assume his research was kosher. What he 'discovers'," he paused, "will enter the field of expertise, become part of the body of accepted fact. Some journalist on the Daily Mail – or perhaps, in this case, the Guardian – will skim-read it in five minutes and summarise it in an argument for free access to porn. At some stage the House of Commons will decide to vote on some related piece of legislation. Busy MPs will ask their unpaid interns just out of journalism college who have never been introduced to the concept of independent thought let alone proper research, to investigate the issues. These dippy, not very clever stooges will find the Guardian article. It wouldn't occur to them to consider first sources. Even if they did, all they would find would be the lies Crispin has been paid to produce. Overworked politicians will vote on the basis of those lies. Do you not see?" He took off his spectacles and wiped his face. "Somewhere down the line, Crispin's bribed and far from independent or indeed academic research will abuse the minds of children, who might then go on to abuse others. Maybe they will grow up and hit people, or abuse other people's children, or their own. Or even just get divorced and wreck more childhoods. I don't know, because I haven't done an independent study. Neither has he. Or they will hurt girls who can't fight back because they've seen this stuff too," he said, turning and sweeping their meal off the coffee table in a gesture as unexpected as his mood.

"Don't you see why academic research matters? How can you be so stupid, both of you!"

There was a long silence before he added, "As it happens, I believe access to the internet should be free and unfettered. That's the point of it. But it's not the point of his research. And I've been facilitating the fraud."

Charlotte salvaged what was left of the supper, and put some in front of Theo. She scrubbed with a paper napkin at some meat sauce which had spilt on the carpet.

"I have no idea whether children can be influenced by porn," he went on, "or in what way. That's why we have academic research. And why it must be independent. They're *children*."

Evan poured the remains of the wine out for the three of them. "I guess you're right," he said quietly.

"Of course I'm right."

"So," Charlotte said, "what are you going to do?"

"Was I rude to you two, earlier? Sorry. I sometimes am. I don't usually mean to be."

"It's okay," Charlotte said softly. Evan nodded agreement.

A calm stillness settled between them.

"Stop him, I suppose," Theo said eventually.

PART II

Michaelmas

Chapter Fourteen

NOUGHTH WEEK

When someone mentions the City of Cambridge you probably think of an iconic building, its four corners stretching out of the once medieval mud through the imagination of Henry VI and his architect Reginald Ely and into the arms of everlasting heaven, its white limestone yearning into eternity, its graceful face overlooking the sighing river, smiling enigmatically on the loves and ambitions, the hopes and dreams, the volumes of slim poetry and glancing kisses of those who have ever travelled the lazy Cam in midsummer ... and without knowing exactly what ephemeral joys or permanent wonders the vision brings to mind, it's a safe bet that the one thought which doesn't occur to you is that the Chapel might not be there by Christmas.

Charlotte went up on the last day of September. They agreed to set off in the late morning after she got back from church; and that Guy would buy lunch. Charlotte sat in the back, cradling her new violin, made by John Baptise Vuillaume in Paris in the mid-nineteenth century. It had needed work done to it and she had only picked it up the day before. She wanted the first time she played it to be a special occasion. Her old one was in the boot, to shove in her bicycle basket for orchestra rehearsals.

She gazed out of the window. The leaves were just beginning to turn: when she had stayed in college for her interview the previous year they had been blackened and cold. Without consciously intending this, she had chosen a jumper which was the russet of the autumn trees, her trousers dull green, her scarf golden yellow.

They went straight to college and Guy asked the porters if they could park on the Cobbles. They could have ten minutes, no more: half the students were moving in that day.

Parents were carrying boxes from cars to rooms: balding fathers, well-dressed mothers, seeping pride.

They went past the dining hall where she had eaten at interview, upstairs and into an ugly labyrinth that was not as she had imagined Cambridge at all. Her room was poky, overlooking a courtyard where surely no sun could shine. She rested her elbows on the sill, thinking of the next three years. She had dreamt of having a room near the river. Like Theo's.

"Where do you want these?"

"Oh, thank you. On the coffee table. I'll go down for my Vuillaume."

"Guy's bringing it."

Charlotte didn't like the idea of anyone else carrying her new violin. Irrationally, she felt as if Guy were establishing that the gift was his. She ran downstairs and found him leaving the car, violin in hand.

"Our ten minutes is up," he said. "There's a restaurant I'd like to try in Grantchester. I've been told I can leave this in the porters' lodge."

"I'll take it upstairs."

"Like I said, our time's up," Guy was carefully not sounding tetchy. "Leave it with the porters like a good girl. That's what they're for," he said, knowing nothing about Cambridge.

It was the same old battle, played out with new weapons. She knew she shouldn't take issue.

"It will be fine, darling," Sara said, oil on water.

Charlotte hated her own stubbornness. "I'd rather take it with me."

Guy looked away across the lawn, toward the eternal fountain springing around the Founder's statue. It wasn't about the violin. It never had been. She saw the nerve of tension pulse in his cheek.

Pacifying, Sara said, "That would be all right. To bring it with her. Wouldn't it, Guy?"

"Hello!"

Charlotte smiled even before she turned. "Hello, Theo."

"I know you."

"Mummy, this is Theo. Wedderburn. Not doctor, yet, though."

"These your people? Hello, people."

Guy approached to shake his hand, charming again. "Theo!"

"So am I. I expect you're hiding a violin in that machine gun case."

"We were just leaving it in the porters' lodge," Guy said. "Charlotte was worried it might not be safe. I was telling her it will be safer there than anywhere. Won't it, Theo?" Men together: silly women.

Theo looked at Charlotte, then back at Guy. "Oh, no. Tone deaf they are, to a man. They'll probably use it to hold up a bank. I'll put it in my room if you like. It'll be safe with my laptop."

Charlotte handed it to him. "Thank you."

She didn't need to see the look Guy gave her mother.

Much as she wanted to, she didn't collect her Vuillaume straight away. She must get her room straight first. Mugs and teapot on a shelf under the coffee table. Candles along the mantelpiece, at least until someone told her she wasn't allowed them. Books on the only bookshelf, in chronological order: Homer first.

Finally a photograph of the four of them, taken shortly before Selwyn left, when she was five and Michael two: a picnic, all smiling happily into the sun.

By six thirty she had done enough for the day. Before she could go for her violin her mobile squawked.

"You up?" It was Suki.

"Of course. When did you get here?"

"Where's your room? I'm outside. Downstairs. I'll come up."

For some reason, she wasn't ready for Suki yet: she wanted her room to herself a little longer. A couple of minutes later there was a thump on the door and her friend fell into her room. "Oh," she said. "It's not that bad."

Charlotte sat on her own floor, hearing how everything was going to be all right. There was no issue: it was not a problem. Suki didn't care. She was completely over the incident. She had moved on.

Charlotte was pleased to hear her say so. Her carefree, funny, idiosyncratic friend had changed so much since midsummer. They used to laugh so much, at the daftest of things.

Suki didn't leave until gone eleven o'clock.

Charlotte wandered down to River Court, wondering whether Theo was still up. A light shone from his rooms but the curtains were drawn.

She decided it was too late.

The Freshers' Fair was overwhelming. Noise, dynamism, hard sell.

"What *is* the Monday Club?" she asked several young men who looked dressed as their fathers should be.

"We're the Monday Club of the university."

"But why do you meet on Mondays?" They looked puzzled and didn't answer.

"Could I learn to fly? For free?" she enquired at the RAF stall. Half way through the enthusiastic explanation, she decided she couldn't be bothered.

"Oh, I'd love to play polo!"

"Have you done it before?"

"No, but I ride." The girl in the light blue university Polo Club shirt could hardly contain her excitement. When she told Charlotte she spent every afternoon, after finishing in the lab, biking three miles along the Barton Road to look after her own polo pony which she'd brought from Shropshire, Charlotte felt obliged to tell her that she couldn't spare more than an afternoon a week and didn't have her own pony.

"Some in the team can't commit every day. You can be a Reserve."

She took away a brochure.

She hesitated at the Christian Union stall – girls with neat clothes and pretty hairstyles and modest makeup; lantern-jawed young men in chinos and clean sweaters – and decided to give it a miss for now. She would try the tea party she'd been invited to in the Chaplain's rooms.

And there was Suki. "You aren't a fresher!"

"Good spot. I'm supposed to be helping man the Maths Soc stall. Can't be arsed. Let's go for coffee."

As they headed for the door they passed an unprepossessing counter, the women badly-dressed, the men worse-shaved, drinking out of plastic cups, with nothing on display except a few old, battered books.

"What are you?" Charlotte said.

"Pooh Soc," one of them replied without looking at her.

"What's that?"

"Pembroke College Pooh Soc. Open to anyone. The Queen has been invited to join."

"And has she?" Charlotte asked the earnest large girl in plaits who didn't seem to have a sense of humour. Or bra.

"Not as yet," replied one of the men.

"What do you do?"

"Have meetings. Take minutes. Drink tea and eat cake. Read."

"AA Milne?"

"Take minutes, mostly. Who else? Sorry, whom."

"Come on!" urged Suki.

"Sounds hilarious," Charlotte said as she was dragged away.

"Look at them," Suki whispered when they seemed out of earshot. "Complete geeks. Why would you join that?"

"To meet the Queen?"

Illogically, Charlotte had expected Suki to be in the same room as last year. Instead, they walked fifteen minutes over Queens' Road, along Burrell's Walk and behind the University Library to Grange Road, before Suki proudly showed her into a glorious large room with a bay window overlooking a beautiful garden, somehow rambling and well-kempt at the same time.

"Suki, this is stunning!"

"Yeah. Bit of a bummer it's such a long way from everything."

"Do you like the others in the corridor?"

"Don't know any of them yet. No mathmos."

On Suki's bed was her beautiful signature coat: calf-length, full-skirted and made entirely of tapestry. She had bought it in an Oxfam shop in Camden Town on a visit to a cousin. With her flaming hair, she could be recognised from the other side of Trinity Great Court.

"I love this." Charlotte stroked it admiringly.

It proved a mystery why Suki had invited her for coffee, when she hadn't unpacked any of her mugs and hadn't a clue where to find coffee. "I know it's in here somewhere," she said, pulling out another pair of high-heeled shoes Charlotte couldn't imagine her wearing, and drowning in a sea of bubblewrap, books and clothes.

"I'll go and forage." Charlotte wandered along the corridor. "Sorry," she said, opening a room containing a young man in boxers looking out of the window. At that moment a girl came up the stairs in an anorak and bike helmet, carrying a rucksack. "Can you tell me where the kitchen is?"

"Just here."

"You don't know where any coffee and milk is, do you, please? My friend's just moved in."

"Have mine. The name's Petra and I've labelled everything. I'm sure you can borrow anyone's mugs, as long as you put them back."

"Thanks."

It transpired that Petra had a cafetière, ground coffee and fresh milk, so Charlotte gratefully poured out a couple of mugs and replaced the washed-out cafetière, before making her way carefully back to Suki's room.

"Oh, goodness, sorry." A policewoman in hi-viz flack jacket, walkie-talkie beeping at her shoulder, filled the space.

"PC Willet," she flashed her ID. "Ms Phillips may want this to be private. I should emphasise that she's not in trouble."

"Well, of course not." Charlotte said sensibly. "Would you like a coffee?"

PC Willet turned to Suki. "Would you like your friend present?"

Suki looked blank with misery. "I don't know."

"I'll make myself some more," Charlotte said. "You have mine."

"That would be best," PC Willet replied.

When Charlotte returned with a third mug of coffee the atmosphere seemed to have shifted. "Ms Phillips says you are appraised of the situation."

"Oh. Okay."

"I'm here to ask if she wishes to press charges."

"Um . . . Is it allowed to ask why you didn't ask her three months ago?"

"We didn't have her address. We were told she had left Cambridge for several months."

Well, yes. It was the summer vac. "Couldn't you have asked her college for her address?"

"We didn't have that information."

What information? Charlotte sat on the window seat, at a loss.

"Now . . . would you like me to call you Susan?"

"I don't care."

"I've given you a lot to think about. You can talk it over with your friend, though we strongly advise you to come to your own decision. Survivors do report finding it helpful to bring someone to justice. And we have a strong case."

"How many?" Charlotte asked.

"Pardon me? How many what?" PC Willet had positioned herself so that she had to turn uncomfortably to look at Charlotte. She compromised by talking over her shoulder.

"How many victims find it helpful to appear in court? Rather than finding it traumatic and wishing they hadn't?"

"We prefer to refer to survivors. 'Victims' suggests something has been done to you which you can't control."

"It has," Charlotte said very quietly.

"I'll let you think it over. Nice to meet you. Thanks for the coffee."

Her mug was still full, on the floor.

Chapter Fifteen

FIRST WEEK OF TERM

Clare was annoyed.

First she had indulged herself: expensive haircut, handmade chocolates, designer clothes. Items she couldn't afford. Be kind to yourself.

Then she lectured. Pull yourself together. No man would behave like this.

She'd had the entire summer to get over it, but felt in more turmoil than when it happened.

She threw her biro down on her desk. What did she care about Aliénor d'Aquitaine and the power of women in the late Middle Ages?

Right now, very little.

She did, however, care about the position of women in the twenty-first century. Clare had seen older women, supremely gifted, still disadvantaged. How many were Masters of Colleges in the university? Off-hand, she could only think of one or two . . . despite more women entering as undergraduates. She had always vowed not to be one of those girls who come top at school, then disappear in their thirties.

It had just gone nine o'clock. She would finish the chapter, write up her notes and then have a nightcap. Perhaps to a pub for a glass of cheap plonk. On second thoughts, something decent. Treat yourself better than you've been treated.

An hour later she had done more work than she had set herself.

She might as well see if there was any post for her in the P'lodge. From there, the college bar was closer – and cheaper – than any pub.

She bought a gin and tonic and took a table near the French windows opening onto Chetwynd Court. For a few minutes she looked out at the dark space, smaller and more welcoming by night.

Ever since she was fourteen, this was what Clare had wanted.

Being at a girls' school, neither she nor any of her friends had yet invited boys to their parties. Tammy's was the first. She was the most sophisticated girl in their circle: women's boobs since the age of ten, subtle makeup and honey-blond highlights. Her parents had enough money not to flaunt it. Tammy's fourteenth birthday party was dinner in a restaurant. Clare's parents, who seldom took her out even to a pizza parlour, said a meal there, for twenty teenagers, might set Tammy's parents back nearly four figures.

The girls were wildly excited. Their mothers worried what they could do for their own daughters' birthdays in return.

Clare was to be picked up, with others, in a pink stretch limo just before seven. At half past six her mother came in to see if she needed anything. She was still in her school uniform, her face shining in the light from her lamp, her head in a book.

"Aren't you going to change?"

Clare looked up. "S'pose so. Wish I didn't have to go."

"Why?" her mother asked carefully, expecting some agonised tale of the wrong boy or no suitable clothes.

"Oh, it'll be all right," Clare kicked off her school shoes and looked half-heartedly into her wardrobe. "Such a waste of time. I'm so nearly at the end of my book."

After she left, in acceptable jeans and a pretty jumper but with no more effort than a brief shower, her mother looked at what she was reading. Not what she had expected, a gripping historical novel: Clare had recently read every Philippa Gregory and just discovered Elizabeth Chadwick. Instead, *Elizabeth Woodville, a life*; according to its jacket the most authoritative text book on the Winter Queen since 1938.

Clare was delivered home safely before midnight. By the time her father went in to wish her goodnight she was already in bed and had just started a new book.

"Good party?"

"Mmm."

"What does that mean?"

"They're all a bit silly."

Her father sat on her bed watching her. "What do you want to do when you leave school?"

"History."

"I meant after that."

"After history?" Clare seemed · disappointed. "Do I have to decide now?"

"Not at all. I just wondered if you'd ever thought of being an academic."

"Why?"

"A girl your age who'd rather be with books than friends . . . And of course," he bent down and kissed her forehead, "you're very clever. Good night, love."

From then on, she had no other serious purpose. She went out with boys, had friends, tried sex when the others did. But nothing fired her up as the kings and queens, the ordinary people and politicians of the past did.

Her history teacher told her she hadn't a hope. "The most brilliant girl I ever taught wanted to be an academic. She went to Oxford, got a First, stayed on for her Masters and then her DPhil. Every essay she ever wrote for me was of prize-winning quality," she looked pointedly over her spectacles. "She's now in her thirties and tutoring spotty kids who can't pass their GCSEs."

Clare fumed. Her parents had always encouraged her. The put-down didn't diminish her self-esteem but it did make her angry. When the teacher added that after Clare had taken time out for a family she'd never catch up with the men, she determined to ignore all further advice: she didn't apply to the college in Oxford where her head teacher vaguely knew someone; nor agree to Murray Edwards as a less competitive Cambridge college; nor even accept the opportunity from a kind classroom assistant to teach in an American school for her Gap Year.

She went up to Cambridge before her eighteenth birthday and missed a First at the end of the year by a whisker. She was furious with herself, made up for it in Finals and won funding for her PhD. Her parents said they would have supported her anyway, but she couldn't have accepted: they would have re-mortgaged their house.

She wanted to make them proud. Prouder even than at her graduation. She would not be distracted by romance until she was at least thirty and successful.

She was invited to the career event hosted by Morgan, Grenfell & Co a year into her PhD. She didn't have any intention of working for them, but since her teacher had humiliated her she had secretly considered a safety-net option: it would be no disgrace to leave Academia for a six-figure salary in London. She wouldn't stay long, could grab a sandwich instead of college dinner and be back at her desk inside an hour.

She and Kathryn struck up an instant friendship, exchanged contact details, arranged to meet. When they did, Kathryn naturally treated her to the meal and theatre ticket because she was paid a lot more. Neither of them was awkward with this. When on their third or fourth evening together Kathryn asked her courteously, putting no pressure on her, if Clare would like to consider a relationship as lovers, she realised that no man had ever had the consideration to ask her permission before fumbling at her. Nor had anyone else won her affection and respect as quickly. She would far rather be in Kathryn's company than anyone else's. Why not? Somewhat to her surprise, when their friendship blossomed into love she found her passions awakened as they had never been by the clumsy attempts of friends' brothers or boyfriend-castoffs.

It wasn't until that seaside summer that she acknowledged she had met the person she wanted to spend her life with, the person she loved more than her parents, the one at whose feet she wanted to lay her glittering doctorate. Had she decided? Or simply recognised the inevitable ...

She imagined taking her home, her mother's friendliness, her father's careful acceptance. She didn't want a conversation about sexuality. She didn't identify herself as gay, or indeed not-gay: the word almost made her flinch. She was just in love.

Added to her deep, fulfilled joy in Kathryn's company and the tight fist of longing that ached beneath her ribs when Kathryn looked a certain way, Clare had to admit there was a comfortable satisfaction that she would never have to teach spotty-faced kids who couldn't pass their GCSEs. Already they shared everything, acknowledging that each brought something different to the relationship and there was equality in asymmetry. Both living on Kathryn's generous income: both enjoying Clare's intellectual status.

And now dumped, like a schoolgirl with a crush on a teacher.

She knew with utter certainty that Kathryn would not change her mind. With scrupulous discipline she had got rid of everything which reminded her of their happiness together. Even the beautiful oil painting of the willows at Grantchester which Kathryn had given her for her birthday, which she had spotted in an art gallery in King's Parade and which had cost a fortune. As she did so she knew she would regret it: it was a superb and valuable picture and she would always love Cambridge. But she had to move on.

She finished her gin and tonic and decided on another. She wasn't planning any more work tonight.

At a table outside in the darkness of Chetwynd Court, Theo Wedderburn sat smoking an incongruous cheroot. Three girls who looked like freshers were with him. Clare had a sense they had followed him out there.

She had made Theo's acquaintance during their first year of research. They'd had rooms along the same corridor and had met by the washing machines. She had no particular objection to him, though she found him annoyingly nerdy and harboured a sharp suspicion that he did much of it on purpose. Though in truth, she retracted the thought with the meticulous honesty of the academic, she had no evidence to that effect.

She was surprised to see him as a magnet for pretty girls. Good-looking, yes. Almost absurdly so, given his gawkiness. He also had the slightly winsome, endearing air of a man completely unaware of the attraction he held; rather as if it were a mistake, which presumably it was.

The girls giggled. They seemed very young.

Was there anything else she could have done? No: Kathryn was decisive in everything she did. She had simply concluded they were not permanently compatible. Why hadn't she given any warning?

Because there hadn't been any. There was nothing spiteful or unkind about Kathryn. Indeed, not much unnecessary about her at all. As soon as she knew, she said so. She must have decided when Clare was down on the beach with the bloody dog, picking flowers for her.

She was absolutely not going to get sentimental in the college bar. It was a waste of energy and time. With a burst of resolve she jumped up to leave.

"What the hell!" she cried at the explosion of red wine. "What the fuck d'you think you're doing?"

Theo Wedderburn stood, glasses half empty in each hand and most of the drink spilt down him. She had stood up and turned in one movement. He had simply been walking past. She waited for him to be annoyed.

He was quite calm. "You all right?"

"You're in my way." She looked away. When she turned back to say, "Excuse me," so that she could pass, Theo was already at the bar asking for a cloth. "Here," he said, and dabbed at the few splashes on her jeans.

"You'd better clean yourself," she said grudgingly. Then surprised herself: "Why aren't you cross? That was entirely my fault."

He thought for several seconds. "How would that help?"

"People don't get cross in order to help."

"No," he said, wringing wine out of his jumper. "Have you changed rooms?"

"No."

"You've stopped eating college breakfast." Half way to the bar, he came back. "Who are you again?"

"Clare," she said, without meaning to.

"That's right," he said, as if remembering her own name was an achievement. He returned to the bar. She thought about offering to pay for a fresh round and knew she wasn't going to. She had no idea why she was so angry.

As she watched, she realised the barman had given Theo another round without charging him, and wondered how he had achieved that.

The next night Clare found herself in the same place at around the same time. Her previous evening's work had been successful so she tried the same formula again. Which made more visits to the college bar in a week than all the previous year.

She arrived just as Theo was giving the bartender licence to invent any cocktail he liked and he, Theo, would drink it, and the delighted staff was tipping Campari into a pint of Adnam's.

To her astonishment, she laughed. Then realised it was the first time since that dreadful and beautiful summer's morning in Norfolk. Her soul felt as if it might one day almost be glad again.

"You're really going to drink that?"

"Hello."

"Sorry," she indicated the wine stain on his jumper.

"My mother gave it to me. I'm not sure how to clean it."

Something unaccustomed stirred in Clare.

She surprised herself again. "What can I buy you? To take the taste away."

She wasn't sure how they got talking. Once or twice she simply switched off and let her mind go back to her work. They got on to a second drink, and a third though it hadn't been in her plan to stay up late or have more than a couple of units. On the other hand it could be an evening well spent, if it made her feel better about herself.

"Are you going to the Middle Common Room dinner on Friday week?"

"What?"

"In Hall. Courses, wine, good food. Neither am I," he added.

Theo had never been 'dumped,' having never enjoyed the kind of relationship from which he could be. Indeed he had not yet noticed that the effect he now had on women had changed since his adolescent misery. But he had experienced plenty of rejection, at school and afterwards, and had spent so long studying his own emotions that he was now quite adept at reading others'.

"You know people sometimes do exactly the opposite of what they need?" he went on. "If you're drowning, for instance, you thrash about and swallow water, instead of putting your head back and letting your body float calmly so that someone can rescue you."

"What the hell are you talking about?"

"Counsellors call it Fight or Flight. But then, counsellors spout a lot of tosh. It's supposed to be the adrenaline rush you get, for instance, when a tiger is chasing you. Instead of making you better equipped to get away it can petrify you so you cower in a corner. There is presumably some evolutionary point to it. If you're a rabbit."

Clare opened her mouth.

"Sometimes, when people are miserable," he continued, "instead of spending time with friends who cheer them up and going for walks with dogs, they shut themselves away and feed the miserableness."

"I'm really not into college dinners."

"You might remember it afterwards as something that was fun. You dress in a pretty . . . thing . . . which makes girls feel better. Apparently."

"Doing a productive evening's work makes me feel better."

"Good."

Suddenly, spontaneously, she said, "I'll go if you will."

He thought for a moment. "All right."

"Come and pick me up," she added almost coquettishly.

"You've got a room in Market Hostel, haven't you?"

Clare was impressed. The evening before, he hadn't known her name. She didn't realise that Theo knew all sorts of things: how to read bar codes; where the college hoovers were kept; every beer served at the Red Lion in Grantchester. That it didn't necessarily signify. And that he still didn't know her name.

He programmed the appointment into his iPhone. "Bye then."

Theo did not arrange appointments for specific times, as a rule. He had learnt that it could lead to great stress and disappointment. Which made him unhappy, and he didn't like unhappiness. By the same token, he didn't like unhappiness in others, either.

Even in someone he had no connection with at all, he hated unhappiness even more than time-keeping.

Chapter Sixteen

SECOND WEEK

It was nearly the end of her second week before Charlotte saw Theo to collect her violin.

On Monday, by the time she got back from Suki's she only had a few minutes before college dinner. On Tuesday, her hair was grubby. On Wednesday she called at his rooms just after four. The door was ajar. She pushed it open, and found his room extremely tidy in the main but with small explosions of clothes and papers in corners. She couldn't see her Vuillaume. There was tea paraphernalia out, rather as if he expected visitors to help themselves.

She took a piece of paper from an in-tray labelled 'Rough Paper', wrote, "Came for my violin. Will call again. C." and left it in the middle of the desk. She omitted her usual 'x'. She wondered whether she should sign it, "Charlotte". But then she thought he might not know who Charlotte was and that would be worse.

She left without helping herself to tea.

On Friday of Second Week, after a Christian Union mug of tea that was not quite warm enough and a welcome a tad too warm, she tried again and was successful.

"Oh," he said as he opened the door. He was wearing a pristine dress shirt, bright blue boxers with teddy bears romping over them, black ankle socks and tatty brown suede shoes. "Would you like a cup of tea?" He stood back to welcome her in.

"You look busy."

"I was just thinking about the Provost."

"The Provost?"

"Do you know where I keep my cufflinks?"

"Drawer?" she suggested.

"Tried them all."

"Desk?"

"That too."

"In one of those mugs? Or that little inlaid wooden box?" He examined each in turn. "My step-father keeps his on a shelf at the top of his wardrobe."

"Tried that." Nevertheless, he went into his bedroom and opened the wardrobe. "Ah. Here's my tie." He took out a rather dog-eared, long black silk bow tie and slung it round his neck.

"Theo?"

"Yup."

"How are you going to get your trousers on if you've already done up your shoes?"

Theo looked down at his feet, and ran his hands rather wildly through his hair. "I don't see the topological difficulty: it still has two holes." He picked up his black evening trousers and wandered back into his sitting room. "They seem to be the wrong shoes."

He took off his brown shoes, went back into the bedroom and returned with his patent leather black pair, putting the left one on and tying the shoelaces.

"You're still putting your shoes on without your trousers."

"I mean three, of course. Otherwise there would be nowhere for the waist."

"I'm not sure it's a topological challenge," she hazarded, wondering how well she understood the parameters, "so much as whether your trouser legs are wide enough to accommodate the heels."

"Ow," he said, trying the other shoe. "Ah. Yes. This was so I couldn't forget where they were." He extracted his cufflinks from his right shoe, put it on and laced it up. "He should be there," he explained.

"Who?"

"The Provost."

"That's nice."

"No. He's an old family friend."

"Oh?"

"When I was at school, there was a thing about not snitching. I didn't know, and Ann had told me if I was ever bullied I should go to a teacher. When I was a 'new bug', the other boys all hid my satchel."

She assumed she wasn't supposed to interrupt the long pause.

"I was always there at a different time from all the others as it was. If it hadn't been for Alan, I would have been in trouble all the time. I found it very upsetting to be late. So losing my satchel was even more upsetting. Than it would have been for most children. Because it would make me even later. Presumably the other boys realised that."

"Why are children so cruel?"

"They aren't, particularly. Adults just hide it better. So I headed for the staff room. All the other boys jogged alongside me asking me what I was doing, so I said, 'I'm going to tell the teachers. That you've hidden my satchel.' They begged me. 'Please don't. They'll kill us.' And took my satchel out of the cupboard."

"What a sensible mother you have."

Charlotte wondered whether to tell him he still hadn't got his trousers on, but judged the risk of his going out without them to be small. He would feel the cold on his knees.

"Why am I telling you all this?"

She hoped the shrug she gave him was encouraging.

"Snitching," he continued. "I didn't know until years afterwards that it's not allowed. Breaks some code. Schoolboy thing. Like the Mafia."

"Sounds as if it was good you broke it."

"Unless that's why the teachers bullied me. There's nothing you can do about that."

Charlotte wondered how to frame her question. "So . . . why *are* you telling me this?"

"Crispin. Snitching. Necessity of. More fashionable now. With paedophiles and so on."

They both said nothing for a while. Eventually, Charlotte asked, "Do you want help with those?"

"What?"

"Cufflinks. I never know how men do them one-handed. Looks as if you don't either."

"His career will be over I suppose. And it will be very unpleasant for Pete."

"Pete?"

"The Provost."

Charlotte had seen the name Professor PJ Langdon Murray FRS on College literature. She hadn't thought of him as Pete. "I think Crispin's career might be over anyway. You remember Suki?"

A shrill ringing like an old-fashioned alarm rent the air. "Pick up Clare! Pick up Clare!" It sounded like Stephen Hawking on speed. Theo shook his wrist till a band appeared with a miniature screen. He turned it off.

"What happened to your binary watch?"

"It needs a new strap. It usually does."

"You'd better go and pick up Clare."

"Yes." He sighed.

"And put your trousers on."

"Oh, that."

"And, Theo?"

"Yup."

"My mother would say, if you know you're doing the right thing, don't agonise."

"Thank you." He smiled, and everything was all right. "Do you think that's how soldiers feel before they shoot people?"

"I should think they feel awful. But I expect the successful ones learn to put it out of their minds."

The alarm went off again. 'Pick up Clare!'

"I'll leave you to get ready," she said. "Don't forget your trousers."

She was halfway to her room before she realised she hadn't collected her violin.

Theo reached Market Hostel just after a quarter to seven.

Clare didn't seem quite ready, so presumably he wasn't late. "Red or blue?" she said, opening her wardrobe door.

"Blue please," he said.

"I thought the red suited me better."

"Oh I see. I thought you were offering me a drink. Blue sounded interesting. One of those would be fine. And the answer's no."

"Not the red dress?"

"The answer to the trick question."

"What trick question?"

"'Does my bum look big in this?' A girl I fancied asked me that. Ann told me the right answer. Afterwards."

"What answer had you given?"

"After she had laughed a lot."

"What is the right answer?"

"Ann's my mother. I had said, 'No more than usual.'"

"You told a girl you fancied that her bum looked no bigger than usual?"

"It didn't."

"I wouldn't have dreamt of asking you if my bum looked big in anything, but now I will know not to."

"On the contrary, you can now. Same answer fits every situation, girl or frock. 'How do you do?' Answer, 'How do you do.' 'How are you?' Careful: slightly different. 'Fine.' 'Would you be good at this job?' 'Yes.'"

"Can you help me get it on? The zip's a bugger." Clare stepped into a pillar-box red shimmery sheath and turned her back to him.

"Though I refuse to say yes to the last one if it's not true. That could be miserable."

Clare waited.

"Am I supposed to do something to this?"

"Could you zip it up for me? It gets stuck."

"I don't see how," Theo said, zipping it up with ease. "There's nothing for it to catch on." He unzipped it again. "That's clever, the way it's sunken in like that." He zipped it up and down again several times. "Men's zips don't do that. I can't see how you could get that stuck."

"Perhaps it's harder when it's on you." She stepped into a pair of matching shoes.

"That's clever too."

"What?"

"Your shoes match. And your bra and things. Though there seems less point to that because no one will know."

"You know."

"I meant someone who matters."

She smiled in a way Theo wasn't familiar with.

144

"That's seven o'clock," he said, as the Great St Mary's clock began to strike. "There's sherry from seven, and we go into Hall at seven thirty so we mustn't be late for that. Do you have to do your hair and face and things?"

"I've done my hair and face and things." Clare waited momentarily for the compliment, knowing how she looked. "Would you like a drink?"

"Yes." He opened the door.

"I meant, here."

"It's free in College."

Clare decided to leave her Moët in the communal fridge and hope it would be safe.

They arrived in the Senior Combination Room before ten past seven.

"Bloody hell, Theo," a colleague looked at his watch. "Clare's obviously a good influence."

"Who?" Theo asked, pouring her a sherry. "Oh I see." He started pouring for everyone else. "I don't think it's that, no. I didn't know how much time it would take to collect her so I had to allow a lot. Excuse me." He broke away, empty-handed, and approached an elegant woman in late middle age, with a blonde bob and a striking, calf-length black dress. "You're Lady Morgan-Langton aren't you?"

"Caroline is fine, Theo," Caroline Langdon Murray (Mrs) smiled encouragingly.

"Oh, good. Nice, um, frock thing."

"Thank you," she smiled again.

"Who's Caroline?"

As she wondered how to respond to this, he said, "Oh, there's Pete. I have to talk to him. It's a bit, er. Maybe I should fix an appointment."

They looked across the room to where the Provost was engaged in conversation.

"If it's something you don't want to discuss over dinner," she suggested, "you could ask his secretary for a time. How is your mother? And how lovely to see you with your beautiful companion. Is it Clare?"

"Ann," Theo corrected.

"I thought her name was Clare."

"My mother has always been Ann."

Competent though she considered herself in most social situations, Caroline was beginning to feel a little dizzy. "I know your mother well, Theo. I meant your lovely girlfriend."

"My girlfriend?"

"Dr Savage, isn't it?"

"I don't know. That would be quite useful. I mean, if you have a girlfriend, to know her name."

"Didn't you come in with Dr Savage?"

"No. Someone called Clare. She's over there." At that moment the Provost broke away. "Excuse me, Lady … um … thing. Do you need any more sherry or anything?"

As Theo walked away, Caroline Langdon Murray felt as if she had attempted a slightly too complicated Sudoku. She engaged a fresh smile and looked around the room. "Sergio!" she spotted a painfully shy Research Fellow. "It is Sergio, isn't it?"

On the other side of the room Theo hovered near the Provost. "Did you want to talk to me, Theo?" he broke off after a minute or two.

"Yes, please." In the pause that ensued, someone else butted in.

"Tell you what," the Provost said. "Let's find a moment over dessert. There's no seating plan after dinner so grab a place near me."

They were called to go into Hall. The Provost turned to the visiting professor in the Philosophy of Physics. Theo nipped back to the sherry table and finished off several abandoned half-full glasses.

Clare seemed to be waiting for something. They filed into Hall, and Theo noticed their name places next to each other on High Table. He wondered what topic of conversation he hadn't exhausted with her.

After dinner they moved back into the Senior Combination Room room for dessert wines, cheeses and fruit. The Provost had kept a space next to himself. Theo asked carefully about his summer holidays and what book he was working on.

After a few minutes during which Theo wasn't listening to any of the answers, the Provost poured him a glass of Marsala and asked him what he wanted to talk about.

"Dodgy funding."

"Sorry?"

"Dodgy research funding."

Peter smiled. "Can't you fiddle with your virtual coinage?"

"That's what somebody's been doing."

"You're serious aren't you?"

"Somebody in college."

"Let's talk about it in my study." Peter glanced about him.

"I discovered it at a conference in Baltimore in August."

"Can you pop into my secretary's office first thing on Monday, and book the earliest appointment she has?"

"We were designing a programme to trace the provenance of bitcoins . . ."

"Theo," Peter's voice was quiet but clear.

". . . and Evan had done some work on it before I got there. I thought it would take several months, but he'd largely designed it in just a couple of weeks, only it had a few things which needed fixing . . ."

"Theo, stop."

"So we worked on it together, and it was quite simple. What was wrong with it turned out to be . . . Sorry, what?"

"I don't think this is the right place to discuss it." Peter looked across at the visiting professor, fortunately engaged with the Vice Provost. "I'll ask Sarah to email you an appointment. In the meantime, I shouldn't mention it to anyone."

"Of course," Theo said. "I haven't. Except Evan. He's the person I was working on the programme with. And someone who was in the room at the time."

"Who was the someone?"

"She's a member of college."

"I'd be grateful if you could ask her to be discreet." The Provost looked at Clare.

"Okay," Theo said. "What do you think about introducing red deer to the college?"

The Provost inclined his head. "Red deer?"

"I thought I might start a campaign for a college deerpark. Peterhouse has one. Sadly denuded of deer. It might be classier to have a deer and no deerpark, than a deerpark with no deer."

"The Fellows would have to vote it in. Best get it proposed when they're all on holiday. The catering manager would no doubt welcome the venison. Scholars' Piece, presumably?"

"I was thinking of the lawn just outside my room. I don't know much about deer. Would it run away?"

"They're herd animals. One on its own would be very lonely. Unless it had been domesticated when very young, and learnt to treat the college as its family."

"I hadn't thought of that."

Theo assumed, having got Clare there, he had done his job, but she came and told him she'd like to leave.

"Do you want me to walk you back?" he said, hoping she wouldn't. He hadn't yet enjoyed the evening, having looked after Clare during dinner and then broached the difficult subject with Peter.

"Yes, please."

He collected their coats.

"Goodnight sir. Goodnight miss," Carlos said at the porters' lodge.

"Why does he call you sir?" Clare asked.

"Because he's Portuguese, I think."

"Presumably I could ask him to call me doctor."

Theo could think of nothing in response to this.

"Come in for a drink," she said at the door to Market Hostel. Theo started to accompany her in, until she smiled winsomely and said, "If you like."

That he might not like was a liberating thought. "Oh. No, thank you." He left her, wondering quite what she'd misjudged.

A bicycle on King's Parade barely missed him, its bell ringing furiously.

"Sorry."

"Tosser," the cyclist offered.

Crossing the Cobbles back into college, he collided with someone standing facing the P'lodge in the dark.

"Sorry," he said again.

He continued for a couple of steps. Then stopped, turned, and came back to look at the person he'd bumped into. Generally, this strategy worked. Theo failed to recognise so many people that when he actually noticed a face, it invariably belonged to someone he knew. Approached by his questioning expression the face would say, "Hello, Theo," and remind him to whom it belonged, with its name-tag and so on.

On this occasion the face just stared back at him, and turned away.

"Fair enough," Theo said, and walked into college.

Chapter Seventeen

NIGHT

The stranger – if he really was – didn't go far.

After a moment he went back towards the porters' lodge and stepped through. That's all you had to do: look as if you owned the place.

"'Scusi? Can I see your pass?"

"I'm just going to see my friend, Theo Wedderburn. I missed him by minutes so I'm hoping he's just in front of me."

"He just come in. But the gate ees abou' to be locked. Mr Wedderburn 'e will have to let you out."

"No worries. I'll catch up with him another day."

"I tell 'im you call. You name?"

"Naa. I'll ring him."

He turned, and didn't stop until he was in the Market Square. Easy as that.

He stuck a cigarette in his mouth. Wedderburn was a fucking jammy bastard. Always late, always behind, always in a dream. He would arrive at the changing room with the other boys. Couldn't fail to: they all walked in a group together. Everyone else would be changed and out on the pitch. Halfway through the game Wedderburn would wander out . . . and then the teacher would notice he had yellow socks on instead of purple. You'd think he must do it on purpose.

Must've done, since he was never late for a service. Never came into Evensong five minutes after it started. Didn't stroll down the aisle in the wrong cassock, after the Dean and Fellows, and take his place half way through the Introit, as he did for everything else.

So it was a choice, right? If he could be on time for Chapel he could have been on time for everything.

And Wedderburn was never even bloody punished. Whereas he himself was slung out for one misdemeanor.

He stamped his cigarette out on the pavement.

He had just over two months. Until that moment, until he bumped into Wedderburn for a second time, he hadn't been absolutely sure. Despite all the preparation, years of it, there had always been the tiniest niggle at the back of his mind. Not any more.

Wedderburn had lit the touch paper.

Crispin had been at the same dinner.

He owned a terraced house off the Chesterton Road. It looked small from the front and had a minuscule and grubby garden, but it had three bedrooms and he had taken on two lodgers straight away. These days he didn't need them to meet the mortgage payments, but he kept one anyway: no point arousing suspicion.

His bike was parked at the front of the college and it was a crisp autumn evening. As he stepped out of the bar he saw Theo walking towards the river. Crispin stepped back into the shadows. He didn't quite know why.

His mobile rang just as he was unlocking his bicycle.

"Selina, hi."

"Returning yours."

"Just going home. Can I ring you in five?"

"Sure."

"Make that ten."

It was more like half an hour. He greeted the lodger, poured a large Scotch, had a quick shower and returned her call while reclining on his bed.

"How are you, Sel?"

"Is that what you rang for?"

"Mum's going schitz."

"Soz."

"You're upsetting her a lot."

"Yeah. Well."

"You all right?"

"Never mind. You said you're in shit."

Crispin took a pull at his whisky. "Maybe I exaggerated."

"My arse."

"Tell me something. If you were at a do, dolled up to here, acting all flirty, and went voluntarily alone into a bedroom with a bloke . . ."

"Fuck me."

"No thanks."

"What happened?"

He took a deep breath. "I honestly don't know. We were getting on fine. She suddenly went Arctic on me and started screaming. Scared the shit out of me."

"And?"

"What do you mean?"

"What did you do?"

"Stopped of course. What do you take me for?"

"So what's the problem?"

"I've been called to appear in court. Sexual assault."

He could visualise her face in the silence. Eventually she whistled. "Must be a bugger."

"You could say that."

"Will you get off?"

"How the hell do I know? They must think they have a chance. The consequences are too awful to contemplate. End of everything."

"Come on," she said, not unsympathetically. "You'd get a good job in business."

"You haven't got a clue, have you?" He needed the outburst: he was dangerously near tears. "Selina, this is my life. The people, values. Everything."

"Should be more careful where you shove your prick then."

He was wondering why he had told her.

"Look, I'm sorry. Truly. But it must have been a near thing or you wouldn't be in this mess." This was too close to contest. "What do you want from me?"

"Thought you might advise."

"Last time I looked, I didn't have any legal qualifications. I'm happy to understudy as your defending barrister but even I have to admit you might do better."

"Should I tell the old man?"

"If you're limbering up to becoming a suicide bomber, could be good training."

"Seriously."

"What the fuck would you tell him for?"

"For all his faults, he's good at getting out of scrapes."

"Yeah, well he's been doing it all his life. Know what? He'll probably rise to it. He won't tell Mum, so you needn't fall off your pedestal. Until you have to explain why you're in the clink instead of . . . whatever's the poshest bit of your campus."

"Cambridge doesn't have a campus."

"It wouldn't."

There was a companionable silence.

"Yeah, tell him. Not now: they go to bed after the Archers. I'll come and see you. Tomorrow?"

"Sorry: can't. Sunday?"

"What makes you think I'm free on Sunday?"

"From your life of doing sweet FA?"

"He'll probably be chuffed to find you're a chip off the old."

"I'll take you into college dinner."

"I'll think about it. Bye. Thanks for telling me."

Crispin put his mobile on his bedside table and finished his whisky. He'd had a lot to drink in College, but he needed another.

His limbs ached all over as if he hadn't slept for days.

He would ring the old man. But not tonight.

153

Chapter Eighteen

THIRD WEEK

Charlotte was battling in the rain along Sidney Street when a woman staring at a map stepped in front of her bike, causing her to brake and topple into a puddle.

Two of her books fell out of her basket. As she bent to retrieve them, a taxi drove by and sprayed her.

"Bother!" She muttered under her breath, as a passer-by stopped to hold her bicycle. "Thank you," she said. "Oh, hello."

"Hello."

Why now, she thought? With my hair a mess and I haven't even got any mascara on.

"You look wet," he said.

"Is that a compliment?"

"Which direction was I going in?"

"I didn't see."

The rain dripped off his hair and onto his nose. "I'd had lunch, I think."

"I was going towards Magdalene, if that helps."

"That's it." He started to push her bicycle. "Are you coming to Hugh's recital?"

"Hugh?"

"Yes, I am."

Charlotte was stumped. "Whose recital, did you say?"

"Yes."

Not for the first time, Charlotte had the sensation of having swum slightly out of her depth.

"When I was a little boy," he swerved her bike to avoid pedestrians and nearly knocked a cyclist over, "I went to the baptism of a boy called Hugh. Why, I asked my mother, is that baby called me? Curious name."

They walked along in silence. Eventually she ventured, "Recital of what?"

"Double violin."

"Double violin?"

"Do you not like it?"

"Not like it!"

"I'm beginning to feel narcissistic. I should be nodding into this handy big puddle. Echo was in love with Narcissus, though."

"It's my favourite piece," she said quickly. "How could anyone not like it?"

"Well," he circumnavigated an overflowing gutter, "ignoring the obvious," nearly colliding with an elderly Fellow, "such as being tone deaf or only ever having listened to punk," and disregarding a hooting taxi, "suppose you'd only ever heard pentatonic music, say? Or you're an early medieval monk whose experience is limited to plainsong. Though I suppose you wouldn't have to be a monk . . ."

"You could still enjoy Bach." She had recovered herself. "If you've only seen El Greco and someone introduces you to Rembrandt, you'll still recognise a work of genius."

"Sorry: too clever. Too much of my education spent on maths."

"It wasn't a good example." Charlotte felt pompous. "I don't know enough about art to think of a better contrast."

"Anyway, that's because a painting by Rembrandt," he said unfairly, locking her bicycle against the wall of Magdalene College, "looks like something. You don't need cultural conditioning to recognise a likeness. Have you got a ticket?"

"What for?"

"The recital."

"I didn't even know there was a recital."

"Lucky I bumped into you, then. I was at school with Hugh," he explained.

"Really? I never noticed you there."

"Very good," he smiled.

"I don't know him," she continued. "Does that matter?"

"All the better." They entered the porters' lodge. "The more people you don't know, the more friends you can make. Like the Numbers Game: the more often you get turned down the nearer you are to the next job. Or the Irish statistician's argument that it's safer to get on a plane which has a bomb on it already. Can you direct us to the Bach Double Violin Concerto, please?"

"Chapel," one of the porters said, barely looking up from a pile of post.

"Though . . . Thank you . . . it's not a good idea for proposals. You're supposed to persevere with the one rather attempt as many as possible. I suppose that's less relevant to you, being a girl and so on."

"Explain the Irish aeroplane and the bomb thing?"

"You could use the Fiancé Game: you reject the first n applicants, then accept the next one who is better than the best one you've turned down. Gives you a thirty-seven and a half per cent chance of getting the best available husband. Quite good odds."

"You're assuming . . ."

"The aeroplane doesn't have to be Irish. Suppose the chance of there being one bomb on an aeroplane is one in three hundred and fifty six thousand. If you get on a plane which has a bomb on it already, the chance of there being another is one in three hundred and fifty six thousand, squared. Safer, obviously." He stood back to let her in, their voices dropping as they entered the dimness of the Chapel. "Hang on," he said. "I've done that wrong, haven't I?"

"It does seem counter-intuitive."

"It has to be your own bomb. Always pack a bomb. Reduces the odds. Could be quite dangerous, getting that wrong. Mathematicians really shouldn't attempt statistics."

The Chapel was already well populated, but in true Anglican style the front row was still empty, so they sat down a few feet from the podium.

The scritching cacophony of tuning had just begun.

"Perhaps Hugh will be this side," Theo whispered hopefully.

"I'm this side already," she whispered back.

The conductor entered.

As the applause was dying down, Theo turned to her. "'Let others have the harmony if we can have the counterpoint.'"

"What?"

"Dorothy Sayers. *Gaudy Night*. Women's lib, or something. Ann told me. She's a violinist."

"Shhhh," came from behind. With a few little coughs and rustles.

And then they plunged in.

Charlotte held herself still, not wanting the tiniest moment to slip away. The violins chased each other, arguing, following, one and then the other. One offered an idea; the other threw back a different suggestion. They danced, they played, they whispered to each other, then jumped over one another for sheer joy. Like friends, with much in common but not committed to one another yet . . . And then suddenly somebody slipped.

She opened her eyes.

Something had become derailed. It was all disjointed, like a sense of déjà vu. As if an event had happened and then happened again, a beat too late. All looked as it should, conductor continuing, soloists skipping together.

She glanced at Theo and he glanced back, a slight smile of amusement.

Before she knew quite what had happened they were back on track, confidently drawing together for the end of the first movement.

The audience sighed contentedly, and shifted a little.

"Close," Theo whispered.

"I wasn't sure it was happening."

"Oh, it was."

The players took a breath to swim again into the second movement, and without meaning to Charlotte did too.

Now they were lovers. Charlotte longed for the music to be suspended like an insect in amber: for the afternoon to hang for ever. Down, the first one plunged. The second swooped after it, from higher. On an ardent tryst, calling to each other. Again they plummeted and copied. Each time she heard the four careful notes stepping down, she knew they would soar again. And yet each time she feared it couldn't happen. Gentle discord, sweet reconciliation, a wildly exquisite slow crescendo till she thought nothing could grow more lovely . . . and finally they agreed, far too soon.

A few strings tuned up again.

Then the mad, frantic, insanely quicksilver third movement. Fighting, disagreeing, teasing. Was that how the story must end? From careful friendship to deep passion to the tussling for independence of middle age? They skipped and crossed and overtook each other in an endlessly stimulating partnership. Loving, asserting, entwined: impossible to tell which was in the ascendency, who led and who followed.

Finally the crunching embrace, as they died in each other's arms.

The audience cheered and a few stood. Theo applauded slowly. Charlotte sat still, stunned.

The conductor stepped forward as the applause died down. "It's not often," he said, "that one finds oneself in charge of a runaway train. What can I say? The least we can do is play the first movement again."

There was a momentary tuning up, and Charlotte heard someone behind say, "Did something go wrong?"

"Sounded fine to me."

Back they went, to the beginning, all the more delicious for being a repeat. Applause again, bows again, filing out.

Tea reception.

As they all moved, Theo stopped to help a lone elderly woman no one else seemed to have noticed, asking if she'd enjoyed the performance. "We seem to be going in here," he said, turning into a lecture room where sandwiches were laid out. "What can I get you?"

"Theo, you goofy! I can't believe you made it. Right day, time and place and everything!"

"Hello Hugh. This is . . ."

"Charlotte," she said before Theo could forget who she was.

"She has a fiddle but doesn't play it," Theo explained. "I'll get tea."

"Why not?" Hugh asked her.

"It's not quite true," Charlotte smiled. "My best violin is stuck in Theo's room."

"There was a mouse, once, stuck in his bedside cabinet when we were at school."

"It's not his fault, actually."

"First time, then."

"Was the mouse alive?"

"Oh yes. He fed it toast from the dining hall. It's all the school toast was fit for. We need some rather better violinists in CUMS, the university music soc. Will you join?"

"I might be worse than the ones you have." Charlotte had thought of auditioning for CUMS, and knew the standard was formidable.

"Couldn't be. Well done, Theo."

It seemed impossible that anyone could balance as many tea cups, saucers and plates of sandwiches in the pyramid Theo had achieved. His attempt to offload was thwarted by Hugh's hand being shaken.

"Hugh, that was a triumph. I hope your parents are here?"

"Thank you, sir. They'd love to meet you." Hugh looked around the room.

Theo was concentrating hard on not dropping his large collection of college china.

"Would your friend like a cup of tea?" Theo asked. "I'm rather hoping somebody will."

"This is the Master," Hugh said. "Doctor Chanticleer. Sorry, I should say Sir Christopher."

"Chris, please." The Master said. "And you are?" he divested Theo of a couple of cups.

"Theophilus Ambrose Fitzwilliam Wedderburn. Thank you. Can I ask a couple of personal questions?"

"Theo . . ." Hugh warned nervously.

"Of course," the Master inclined his head.

"First, what is your favourite sandwich? There is egg and cress, ham and mustard, and cucumber. If you don't mind either way my favourite is egg and cress."

"Cucumber. But I'm out for dinner so I won't, thank you."

"Can you use 'either' when it's of three?"

"Yes. Was that your second question?"

"No." By now Theo had shed all but two wine glasses and a cup of tea, all tucked into his left hand. He extended his right. "How do you do." He tilted the tea to his mouth, pouring the contents of the wine glasses onto the carpet.

"And I'm assuming that isn't either."

"Are you the Chanticleer of asymmetric key encipherment?"

"Yes."

"Oh." Theo sighed deeply. "That is the most exciting thing that has happened to me since . . . the Bach we've just heard. Or being born. Or something. Do you mind if I . . . um . . . sit down or say oh again or something?"

"Theo, what are you wittering about?" Hugh asked.

"Public key encryption," he explained. "Christopher Chanticleer." He waved his free hand. "Solved it overnight at GCHQ. Only, obviously they couldn't tell anyone. Took a team of Americans about two decades to do what three people in Cheltenham had done in an evening."

"Not quite," the Master corrected. "Only five or six years."

"'You made rather better use of it than we did,'" Theo quoted.

"That was Jim, not me. On the way to the pub. A rare moment of indiscretion."

"Feels like meeting God," Theo sighed again. "Or an intelligent version of James Bond."

"I'm mostly known for my work at MI5," the Master said. "Though of course that's secret too."

"Of course," Theo smiled with satisfaction.

"Theo, you remember my parents?" Hugh had procured a couple in their mid-fifties. "Mum, this is Sir Christopher Chanticleer."

"How lovely to see you, Theo," Hugh's mother said. "And you're here at Cambridge? I'm so glad everything turned out for you."

Theo's watch suddenly crowed with the rudeness of dawn. "Supervision alert! Supervision alert! Supervision . . ."

"Excuse me," Theo said. "I have a supervision to supervise. I'm very happy to have met you," he turned back to the Master, and for a moment it looked dangerously as if he could talk for another half hour.

He was already at the door when Charlotte remembered her bicycle key. She was just wondering whether she would make him late if she ran after him, when a dapper, slimly built young man introduced himself. "Piers Braithwaite. I'm just dashing off, but I wanted to say . . ." and with breathtaking efficiency he gave her his contact details and invited her to a black-tie dinner and debate at the Union the following week, where he was on the committee.

The party was dispersing. Charlotte looked around the nearly empty room. She still had Theo's egg sandwiches on the plate he'd handed her. He'd said they were his favourite. He had managed to gulp two lukewarm cups of tea and half a glass of wine on his way out, but hadn't eaten anything. She wrapped them in a paper napkin: she could give them to him when she collected her bicycle key.

When she got outside Magdalene porters' lodge she found her bicycle was gone. She was intensely annoyed with herself: she knew she should have got a better lock.

Just as she was going through her own porters' lodge she spotted it, behind the octagonal pillar-box. He must have unlocked it, biked it home and carefully locked it up again.

She smiled, and went up to her room.

Charlotte had never got used to locking her door. She lived in a house where the front door was kept on the latch. Neighbours would let themselves in and call from the hall. When Folly was younger she had barked to let them know, in place of a doorbell.

It would be different when she had her expensive violin in her room: perhaps that's partly why she wasn't in a hurry to recover it. In the meantime, she locked her iPad in a drawer and expected friends to let themselves in.

They didn't. Everything else in Cambridge was locked assiduously.

Which meant that on this particular afternoon, when she came in and dumped her bag on her bed and wondered whether to attempt half an hour's work before dinner, she was a bit unnerved to hear the loo in her room flushing. She would have preferred an older and more beautiful room over one with an en suite, but she hadn't been given the choice.

She stood stock still. The memory of Suki's being assaulted at the ball flashed into her mind.

Then she heard her toothmug clattering and smashing. "Oh!" came a familiar voice through the wall.

No work before dinner then.

"Hello," she said when Suki emerged, hair twirling more frantically than usual.

"I broke a mug."

"I guessed."

"It was already chipped." She held the shards, Mrs Tiggywinkle's head on one piece and her prickly body in its dumpy frock on another. It was the last thing Charlotte's father had given her.

She just stopped Suki throwing it in the bin, took the pieces and placed them carefully on her desk. "Have you cut yourself?"

"Doesn't matter." She sucked the palm of her hand. "Charlie, the police want to press charges."

"Sit down," Charlotte said. "I'll make tea."

Suki hovered. "I don't know what to *do*," she wailed.

"Do what you want." Charlotte swirled warm water around her pot – a matching Peter Rabbit one, the only teapot she had – and went to tip it away. She saw tiny chips in the basin.

"Here." She gave Suki a fresh mug of tea. "Now, what do you want?"

"I don't want the hassle."

"Then don't."

"Trauma. I mean trauma, don't I? But then I'll go through life feeling he's got the better of me."

Charlotte couldn't think of anything helpful to say. Eventually, she said, "No one else matters. You don't owe anything to other, future women. You don't owe anything to him. You certainly don't owe anything to the police."

"No," Suki said dully. "Obviously."

"You owe yourself a degree. Concentrate on that."

"Okay, then." Suki stood up, leaving her untouched mug on the coffee table. "I'll press charges."

"You don't have to."

"Bye, then," Suki said. "Oh, sorry, my tea," and she reached for it and knocked it over.

After she'd gone Charlotte surveyed the little chips in the basin. She picked them up with one finger and placed them in the palm of her hand. Back in her room she put them with the other pieces of her mug.

Her mother kept used string and brown paper and household items going back generations. Everything salvaged, broken items glued. But even Charlotte could see that piecing her long-loved mug back together was virtually impossible.

She knew exactly what her mother would do: put a search on eBay, and long before Christmas replace it with an exact replica, probably for under a tenner.

But it wouldn't be missing the little chip, lost when she dropped it the day Selwyn left. The day her mother had let her leave her satchel at the foot of the stairs instead of taking it to her bedroom, and made a tray of tea for them both, with homemade cake, and served it on the lawn. And Folly had come and flopped between them, looking more desolate than Charlotte could ever remember her: not even thumping her tail.

Much later, after her brother had been brought home from a party by someone else's parents and they had both gone to bed, Charlotte got out of bed and went downstairs. There she found her mother sobbing crazily in the kitchen.

She put her little arms around her, climbed on her lap and said, "Mummy, what's wrong?"

"Your daddy is the best daddy in the world, Lottie. He's given me the best daughter, so he must be."

"When is he coming home?" Charlotte asked.

Her mother blew her nose, and seemed to decide not to cry. "I don't know darling." She looked out of the window at the still golden evening. "I think probably never again. I'm sorry." She turned and smiled bravely at her daughter.

Charlotte swept the pieces of mug into her hands, being careful not to cut herself. She thought back to the man who had greeted her in Washington.

She tipped the pieces into her wastepaper bin. One of them broke further.

Chapter Nineteen

Fourth Week

Charlotte might be able to survive several weeks without her Vuillaume violin. She couldn't go a day without her bicycle.

The next morning she was late for a lecture.

It proved to be an extremely boring fifty-seven minutes on 'The Advantages and Disadvantages to the Ancient Historian of Inscriptions versus Literary Texts.' Long before the hour was up Charlotte concluded that the main advantage of writing on stone is that you can't write as much. Particularly if you're a very ancient historian. She would not attend the rest of the series.

But that wasn't the point. It is bad manners to arrive after the speaker, even though half a dozen others slipped in later than she did.

The walk back from the faculty, along West Road and through the back gate, meant passing Theo's rooms. She would call for her bicycle key. And not invite herself in. As before, the door was not locked. She saw her bike key straight away, on his coffee table. Underneath it was an omnibus *Winnie-the-Pooh*; beneath that, a much-used *Study Bible*, annotated; *Feynmans Lectures on Computation*; and one or two maths books.

She glanced around again for her violin, hoping not to see it open to view.

That afternoon she attended a seminar in Sidney Sussex. As she unlocked her bike from behind the pillar-box on the Cobbles she noticed a discarded envelope in the basket. It is a truism that an empty bicycle basket abhors a vacuum, and any passer-by feels obliged to toss his used cigarette packet or water bottle into it. Charlotte stuffed it in her bag to throw away later.

The seminar was being given by someone she had looked up to at school. It seemed unreal that Katy Osmond from the Upper Sixth should have a doctorate at Cambridge. As they sat in a circle discussing 'Gods taking the form of humans in the *Iliad*,' Charlotte felt yet again that she'd rather be here than anywhere in the world. Homer, wine, song and war. Three glorious years . . .

The young Fellow had another meeting to go to, but invited Charlotte to call on her any time. Still smiling with happiness, she biked back to college to finish her essay.

At first she didn't recognise the unopened envelope in her bag. She tossed it in the wastepaper basket, then reconsidered and picked it out again. It didn't look like ordinary rubbish. It wasn't crumpled, except by her. The envelope was sealed. She might as well open it: it might have a return address.

It didn't, as it happened. It didn't have anything, except a single paragraph of text.

'Late again. If you hadn't been late all those years ago, you'd still have your father with you. I hope you remember that . . . And that you don't deserve Cambridge. Private schooling. All those privileges. You don't even bother to notice me. But I see you. All the time.'

At first, Charlotte's reaction was detached puzzlement. Why would anyone write such a vile note? And then why throw it away? It obviously hadn't been opened.

Then she read it again . . . and again. She began to feel a nauseous churning. She never usually found it difficult to be on time. It mystified her that others did. But that morning, anyone in the lecture hall could have seen her coming in late.

This was not random rubbish. Her bicycle had been tucked out of the way, behind dozens of others. This had been written by someone who knew she'd been late and had then sought out her bicycle.

As it had so often, her mind went back to that sunny tea with her mother in the garden. When she still had another couple of hours of her childhood left. Except that it was already too late. Her father had left even though she didn't know it. The beginning of years of tearful agonising. Why? What should she, Charlotte, have done to prevent it? Had he gone to another family, where the children were nicer?

The thought tormented her young soul. Her mother, hearing nothing of this from Charlotte, would hug her after her prayers, and reassure. "You do know, darling, that when parents split up, it is always the fault of the grown-ups." She knows, Charlotte thought miserably. My mother is only saying that because she is so kind. "We failed to do what we'd set out to."

If it wasn't Daddy's fault – and it certainly wasn't Mummy's – then it must be Charlotte's. Charlotte's and Michael's, perhaps. But Michael was only three.

As she grew older, so her guilt became more sophisticated. By senior school she knew, of course, that she couldn't possibly be held responsible. She had too many friends it had happened to. But that didn't stop the bilious feeling in the pit of her stomach which felt so much like guilt, sickening her every time she thought about her father and often when she didn't.

When her mother remarried, she knew she had to dismiss thoughts of her father's coming home again. But even that she struggled with. Somewhere, in part of her heart she hadn't examined yet, she knew she only gave up hope in Washington DC that summer. Instead of relief, she felt a dull disillusionment.

And now that lurching, qualmish, guilt-larded fantasy was back. If only she had been there. Where? Should she not have gone to school on the day he left?

It was ridiculous. Perhaps it was a joke. Something to do with the Assassins' Guild: students who stalked each other with lengths of spaghetti labelled, 'semi-automatic shot-gun.' Was it part of that game?

She knew it wasn't. She had an idea that harassment could be reported. She could at least take it to the college authorities: the Chaplain perhaps. She had met her at the Christian Union tea party and she struck Charlotte as approachable.

But she had work to do. She opened her notepad. "Do a Prac Crit of Book XXIV, lines 718 to 776 of the *Iliad*."

For the next fifty minutes Charlotte immersed herself in Homer. She loved this tight-textured work: analysing every word; building up the effect; noting alliteration, imagery, scansion. It was straightforward, and didn't need much structure or planning.

She revelled in the repetition: the 'στονόεσαν ... στενάχοντο,' lamentation from line to line. The onomatopoeia of the wailing γόοιο. The image of white-armed Andromache embracing Hector's severed head: it wasn't until she pictured the stark white and vivid red that she understood the horror.

The closer she read, the more pitiable she found Andromache's sorrow. *The Trojan Women* had moved her deeply at school; she remembered the helpless Astyanax, a little boy in a cruel world after his father's violent murder. ἡ γαρ ὄλωλας ἐπίσκοπος. ('For you the defender died ...' Surely 'trusted one' was more accurate?) In her searing bereavement, Andromache found consolation with Hector's mother. Both loved him: mother and lover.

She looked up. To her surprise it was dark outside. She had barely noticed the summer's passing. Soon the clocks would go back and it would be night by teatime. She thought of her mother's kitchen, Folly lying in front of the Aga, a steaming casserole and bottle of red wine open on the table, and quite unexpectedly she burst into tears.

She was astonished. Here, where she loved it so much.

She had missed college dinner. She went into her little bathroom and splashed her face. She would perhaps go down to the bar and get half a pint of cider, and bring it back into her room. She was a couple of days ahead with her work so there was no hurry.

How silly she was being. That stupid, vicious piece of paper ...

The bar was so full and so noisy she recoiled. She stepped outside, into a bunch of other First Years, new-minted friends.

"Charlie, howya." "Come to a club."

"I'm in the middle of an essay."

"Do it later!" "You must have till tomorrow." "You look like you need to party!"

"Do I?" But they had moved on.

Tattered clouds raced across a steady moon smiling down on the Chapel, the autumn sky chasing itself for excitement.

The Trailer of Life van had kebabs. She went through the well-lit P'lodge and out onto the Cobbles.

"Hello."

She was surprised that he had noticed her first. It cheered her in some indefinable way.

"How are you, Theo?"

"I assume that's rhetorical. What's the matter? That was not."

"What do you mean? Or rather," she corrected herself, more truthfully, "how do you know?"

He considered. "You didn't look straight at me, as you usually do. Your face is . . . a bit grey maybe? That could be the street lighting. Your eyes look worn. Perhaps you're not good at putting your contact lenses in."

She smiled, rather feebly. "I don't wear contact lenses."

"In which case you've probably been crying. Do you drink beer?"

"Um . . . I could try. I like cider, 'specially if it's interesting," she offered hopefully.

"Good. Eager or Ankle?"

"Sorry?"

"Which pub?"

"Oh, I see. Eagle," she said by mistake, wondering whether the spoonerism was genuine.

They barely spoke again until he had a pint of ale and she a half of dry cider, and they were looking onto the Elizabethan yard, too cold to sit out, where troupes of actors allegedly performed four hundred years ago.

She considered whether she was supposed to speak first and eventually decided she was. "I found something unpleasant in my bicycle basket. It upset me. Probably silly."

He took a swig. "Probably. Pigeon? Seagull, perhaps. They come inland in the winter. Or is it summer?"

"Not a seagull. A letter."

"That does seem more likely."

"What?"

"That a pigeon would drop a letter. Seagulls have webbed feet I suspect. Certainly more likely to drop it than write it."

"Theo . . . um."

"You need me to be serious. I'm sorry. I learnt to laugh at school. Eventually. After Ann told me I couldn't kill myself. I hadn't realised how much Alan had protected me."

"Did you want to?"

"Of course not. The instinct for life is very strong. I just couldn't see what else to do. Tell me about the letter."

"Someone has been watching me. Who knows about my childhood."

He listened, not making any more flippant comments. After he'd drained his pint he said, "I expect you have tea in your room: you strike me as civilised. Let's see it."

Her room was dingy, small and modern. But she didn't have to worry that she'd left dirty underwear on the floor (or worse) or a mug of mouldy coffee on her desk. It was always scrupulously tidy.

She put the kettle on and closed the curtains against the unfriendly night. They drank their tea, companionably.

"You'd be better with an Apple," he said, without looking round.

"Oh?"

"Do you want to show me the letter?"

She realised she didn't. Drinking tea with him in her room, she didn't want to spoil anything. She reached for her desk and passed it over.

For a good five minutes he did nothing except look at it. Then he said, "When did this appear in your basket?"

"This afternoon."

"When were you late for your lecture?"

"This morning."

There was such a long silence following this that Charlotte wondered whether to offer more tea, or ask a question, or make some movement. She did none of these. Mostly, she wanted nothing to change.

"My father died when I was ten." He held the letter between them. "If my mother had walked into a room a few minutes earlier than she did, he would still be alive."

For the first time since Baltimore, Charlotte thought she could detect emotion working Theo's face.

"You may have noticed, I . . ." He stopped. "I don't know how to explain. SBC understands."

"SBC?"

"Professor Simon Baron-Cohen. Most intelligent man I've ever met. Director of the Autism Research Centre in the Trumpington Road. Don't. Do time."

"I'd sort of noticed."

"It's a dimension I don't have."

"That's all right."

"Thank you. In an absolute sense it should be. It's not like being unkind, or stupid, or something that matters. Whole cultures don't do time. My mother Ann is Irish. I sometimes think I'll go and live there, though she says it wouldn't make any difference. I can catch trains and things, though it takes me about twenty-four hours and a lot of effort. So I can't do it very often. Because when I do, I can't do anything else."

Charlotte wondered how to help. "Is your mother the same?"

"So it means I'm sometimes late for things. It's not late really, because I get there when I can and I don't fix times for appointments. But when I was younger . . . when I was at school . . ."

"You got into trouble?"

"What did you say? My mother? Who, Ann? Oh, no, no, no. Not at all. She's abnormally normal. Not normal in a bad way. She's very . . . neurotypical. She was a musician. She probably finds it harder to be late than I do to be on time. She wasn't late going into the room. She was just late in terms of my father not being murdered." There was another long pause. "That's why."

She said very softly, "What is why?"

"Ann told me it would be wrong to kill myself."

"Theo, do you know who wrote this?"

He stood up. "Do you mind if I leave now?" Before she could say anything he was at the door. She thought he was going to turn back and say goodbye, or thank you for the tea, or something. He didn't. He just went.

Some time later Theo returned to his rooms. He had got systematically and steadily drunk. Hour after hour, alone in a nasty pub he had never visited before nor ever wanted to again. By midnight he was feeling awful.

He went to his bathroom, cleaned his teeth and submerged his face in water. He stumbled into his sitting room and kicked off all his clothes straight onto the floor. He was just about to fall into his bed when he noticed someone on it.

"Hello," he said without enthusiasm.

"Hello," Clare said. "You were so long, I had to open the champagne. It's a very good one. It won't keep, so we have to drink it now."

"Oh," he said dully. "Why?"

"Why?"

"I mean, thanks," he corrected, confused.

"Don't you like champagne?"

"Doesn't everyone?"

He longed for his bed, alone. He sat down on it, and sunk his head between his knees.

She had brought flutes with her. She poured him one.

Perhaps this would dull the pain, or help him forget, or make it more bearable.

It tasted of nothing.

Chapter Twenty

Next Morning

Theo woke late. He was alone. And relieved.

He wondered if he had dreamt. He hoped he had.

His retro mid-1970s Teasmade – which he'd bought on eBay and which reminded Ann of her student days – had nearly-cold tea in it. He had never overslept his Teasmade before. That could mean he had overslept other things. He reached for his iPhone.

Supervision, Thursday, 10 am, 'Analysis'. The time was now 10.12.43 seconds, 44, 45, ... He slammed his iPhone down and sat up, then lay down again and picked it up more gently to check he hadn't hurt it.

His iPhone was all right. Nothing was cracked.

The supervision. Damn. He sat up more slowly. He couldn't take a supervision. If he left immediately he would arrive half way through: his students would have left. Well, they might not have done, if they knew him, but he hated letting them down. Really. Hated it.

They weren't even particularly good. They flipped between convergence and absolute convergence without being aware, apparently, that they were different things. Last week he had given them some examples, and they simply stared blankly back at him. Eventually he had pressed them as to what a particular question was asking – always a good fallback – and the most talkative one had admitted, 'I'm not really sure . . .' and then dropped her notes.

The last thing they needed was a missed supervision.

He pushed himself out of bed and looked for his trousers. He had a confusion, a muddle at the centre of his soul that he didn't want to examine. If his trousers were in his bedroom everything was all right.

They were in his sitting room.

He picked them up.

Charlotte's bicycle basket. He held on to that thought as a friendly one. He had sat with the pretty, uncomplicated girl in the Eagle pub and tried to help her. So far things were fine.

Shirt. Also on the floor in his sitting room.

Oh for goodness' sake, he thought angrily. Face up to what you've done! He used some rather crude Anglo Saxon to himself, which made it worse.

He stared out of his sitting room window onto the gloomiest he could ever remember the Cam looking. Most unusually, as he was gazing hard into the corners of his mind to avoid the elephant in the middle of it, something clicked and he realised it wasn't yet Thursday. He couldn't remember ever having had more time than he expected. Perhaps he was six days behind rather than one ahead, but that didn't matter as long as he hadn't just let down a couple of struggling undergraduates.

In his first Michaelmas at Cambridge he had signed up for a rowing eight because he had heard his mother say, years before, that people should enjoy all university had to offer. One cold, wet November afternoon he arrived at the river bank and was a little surprised to find no one else there. He waited for some time before getting back on his bike. He discovered in the college bar that evening that seven rowers, a cox and a coach had stood shivering in a soaking drizzle for nearly two hours waiting for him, only giving up minutes before he arrived. After that, the Chaplain had kindly suggested he might want to contribute to the College Music Soc instead.

The thought of students waiting for him was far worse. He checked his iPhone. It was Wednesday. The supervision was tomorrow. Or last week.

Thank God.

He leant forward until his head was on his knees. The letter. He had received a very unpleasant letter, or the girl had. He wasn't ready for this thought yet so he scrolled on to a different part of the evening and a different woman. He found he wasn't ready for that either and it was far more painful in a much less obvious way.

Then to his huge relief he realised he hadn't had any tea and perhaps that's why everything was so terrible.

Ten minutes later, with a mug in his hand and some tea in his system, he looked out of his window again. The world looked exactly the same. For the first time ever, Theo wondered if he didn't feel quite as at home in Cambridge as he'd always thought. Perhaps people here were normal too, and he was still a stranger.

That girl. The other one. The one he had taken to that dinner, to cheer her up. Was this what it was then, to have a girlfriend? Right. That was what he'd always wanted.

All through his years at school, even his undergraduate years, he had longed for this. He would then be like all the other boys and he wouldn't be lonely and he wouldn't be different. Even when he grew into being proud of his difference and had a proper diagnosis from SBC, he had always assumed that girlfriend = happiness as simply as $e^{i\pi} = -1$.

He hadn't expected it to happen quite this way. And he no longer felt the crushing need to be like everyone else, anyway.

Theo had never quite got it right with girls. When he invited them to the cinema or out for a cup of tea, they always found something else to do. In his first Lent Term, during Rag Week, he had put in a bid to take a pretty girl out for a date. The higher you bid, the higher-ranked partner you got. All the money went to charity so Theo put in the highest bid allowed. His friends had ranked him as one of the least attractive men to date, so she had hardly had to pay anything.

Her name was Gloria, she was at Trinity Hall and he had to take her out within a week. He sent her an email, arranged a place to meet and suggested a film. Ann had taught him that he should always call for a girl to pick her up, but the rules of this game didn't allow it. So he had suggested the ADC Cinema because he had always wanted to see the film *Fatal Attraction* and it was Classic Film Night. Afterwards he was going to take her for a Chinese meal. He was much more careful of that expense because it wouldn't go to charity. Never before had he spent so much on an evening.

He bought the tickets in advance and rang the Chinese restaurant to book a table but they said it wasn't necessary.

The weekend after the date, Theo remembered.

He sent her another email apologising and offering her a different date, but she never replied. He supposed that was what you did when you were a high-ranking girl.

It was a year before he discovered that the film he'd thought was *Fatal Attraction* was in fact *Brief Encounter* and that he hadn't wanted to see *Fatal Attraction* at all, far less take an expensive girl to it.

Now he appeared to have succeeded at the girlfriend thing. Without trying. Clare. He must be careful not to call her Kate or Cathy or even Jane. Jane would be a perfectly reasonable substitute – also one syllable; and two letters the same – but girlfriends mind that sort of thing.

He realised he didn't want to think about it any more and his telephone was ringing.

"Yes?"

It was DC Andy. "Sorry I couldn't respond to your text last night. I'm free now, and nearby. Shall I come and have a look at this poison pen?"

"It isn't, after all," Theo said.

"Prank from a friend, eh?"

"No." He was about to say it wasn't directed at the person who owned the bicycle, when he realised how much he would like to see his friend and told him to pop in anyway.

Andy was one of those people who preferred coffee to tea, and instant to ground, and Theo found he was out of both so he went upstairs with an empty mug and knocked on half a dozen doors until he found a girl he barely knew, who gave him a teaspoonful of Nescafé.

Andy had said he was twenty minutes away. He managed to turn up long before Theo noticed he wasn't dressed yet.

Clare was not the type to sing to herself. She was almost completely unmusical. Despite the drear morning, however, her mood sang.

Her very limited experience of minor hardship combined with her rapid and successful career trajectory had not yet taught her the joys of being magnanimous. And yet she was appreciating having done a kind deed. She was honest enough to admit she found Theo Wedderburn desirable, in a somewhat urgent way which was probably more to do with her immediate circumstances than anything more lasting. But that she had done him – as well as, yes, herself – a favour she was in absolutely no doubt.

She looked out over the Market Square from her double-aspect corner room which she had jostled so successfully on the ballot list to win. She had left Theo's rooms early, not because she had any appointments but more because she considered it tacky – rather 'undergraduate' – to be found in someone else's room. She had been mildly amazed that he continued to sleep, but relieved.

Since then she had got several hours' work done and now wanted breakfast. She contemplated buying a fresh croissant from the bread stall below and putting it in the communal microwave.

Something in that thought triggered a memory of Kathryn, and Clare felt an unexpected and most unwelcome pang. She replaced the sharp longing with annoyance. Theirs had been the perfect relationship: enough in common and enough contrast. Stimulating, exciting, stable enough to last for life. Not for the first time Clare wondered what had gone wrong. What she not metrosexual enough? Not gay enough, perhaps?

It was like picking at a scab. She felt as the jilted always do, that she was of less worth as a result. She knew this was absurd – plenty of people are incompatible – but the feeling lingered. Whenever she had dumped boyfriends she had felt superior. Now was pay-back.

She had heard nothing since, except an infuriatingly considerate notification of an exhibition in London which Kathryn thought Clare might be interested in. She knew, with the brutal integrity on which she prided her academic work, that there was no hope whatsoever.

Her mind went back to Theo. He was, by all accounts, a competent academic. And it was . . . the first word which came to her was 'necessary', which she dismissed as heartless. Therapeutic? Expedient. They would have fun. She could understand the appeal, to some women, of his rather endearing inexperience.

She would forgo the croissant and have a quick slice of wholewheat toast. And return to the scorned fury of Aliénor d'Aquitaine and how she used her anger to great political effect.

Barely a stone's throw away, just inside the window of the Copper Kettle, the stranger sat, irritated with himself. He had turned thirty the day before, but hadn't marked the day. He was not on any social media any more and no one, not even his mother, knew his postal address. He wasn't entirely sure he knew it himself.

He had acted spontaneously, and that is how mistakes creep in. When he saw Wedderburn floundering up to the college – late as always, ridiculous on a bicycle far too small for him – he boiled over. Just like when they were boys.

Early that morning he had lingered outside Wedderburn's room and seen a woman come out. Looker, if you like that crisp, intimidating style. Which, as it happens, he had, in the days when he was interested. Fuck me. Totty sneaking out of his room before breakfast. How was that supposed to sit with his butter-wouldn't-melt Christian façade?

Presumably God indulged him just as teachers had.

It didn't matter. What mattered was that his rage had got the better of him and he had posted into that cycle basket. He'd have to follow it up, or it wouldn't be 'excellent.' Or whatever the fuck it was that obsessive teacher had taught them maths answers had to be. He must be more careful. He, who was so strict on security he only saved anything onto memory sticks: never his laptop. His next step had better be bloody good.

It would be. He might not have a college degree. But he had all the money he wanted, now. Thanks to his own brilliance.

He could barely remember the git in the pub who had mentioned it. Late 2009 or early 2010. No one had heard of them. He understood the concept immediately. And he'd recently learnt how to syphon money from a bank account and had stashed away several thousand. It wasn't his so he didn't care one way or the other. He blew it all. On bitcoins. At less than a dollar each. Then forgot about it.

His big project might take most of his crypto-millions. But after that he could find himself somewhere where he couldn't spend them easily anyway.

In the meantime, why not have some fun? Make Wedderburn look the prat he was?

Anything could set Liz off. A story on the radio; a picture of them as a family; a leaf revolving in the sun; any could incapacitate her for hours.

'You must eat,' her NHS counsellor had told her. The sessions never did her any good. But they were free. And she could talk about Selina for fifty minutes to someone who was paid to listen.

She put a slice of bread in the toaster. She stared out of the window, seeing nothing. The toast was ready before she expected it to be, before she had made her coffee, so she opened the kitchen door and threw it to the birds. She deserved her toast hot-buttered.

'Happiness is a choice,' her counsellor said. Perhaps she preferred to cry and cry, rather than forget her own child. But then she would come across someone with depression, such as Mark's secretary Rosa who was so miserable to be around that Liz wanted to throw her into a cold bath, and she didn't want to be like that at all.

Mark had been saying for a year and a half, "Forget about it. You have a brilliant son. That's more than most people."

She was just about to treat herself to a walk in the low autumn sunshine when a flier came through the door. Instead of being the usual glossy 10%-off voucher for a pizza, it was decorated with pictures drawn by children, announcing the Christmas Fayre for the local Church of England primary school: homemade cakes, toys for children, socks for granddads, 'hook the duck' challenge and pin the nose on Rudolf.

She flopped onto the hall stairs. Without warning the tears came, uncontrollable, overwhelming. She remembered Selina the cheeky little imp, clever as Puck, much faster than the older and steadier Crispin. Able to do anything: ballet, art, music. First in cross-country and captain of games.

She sobbed now, as in the after-shock of bereavement when the far worse depth of pain has set in. Loudly enough to bring someone to comfort her from the next street, almost. But there was no one. Mark would have told her – if their relationship had still been intimate enough for such advice – that she should move on.

They had a son to be proud of.

Chapter Twenty-One

FIFTH WEEK

"Hello." Theo opened his door wearing pyjama bottoms, shirt, silk cravat and tweed jacket; and holding a screwdriver.

"Had you remembered I was coming to tea?" Ann proffered a white cardboard box with a purple ribbon.

"Nearly."

She removed a pile of clothes from the most comfortable-looking chair.

"I would go out and buy you something to eat," he said, "but fortunately someone's just given me this cake," and he undid the ribbon on the Fitzbillies box.

"Do you have tea, milk, and things to drink out of?"

"I always have tea, milk and things to drink them out of."

"That's fine then."

"Would you like a hug?"

She stood up again. "Yes please."

That done, he took the kettle to fill it upstairs. "Why am I carrying a screwdriver?"

Ann shrugged.

Left alone, she sank happily back in the chair. She found her son the easiest person in the world to be with, more even than her husband. Either of them. On his coffee table were some maths books; *When We Were Very Young*; and an *Interlinear Greek-English New Testament*, Ed. Nestle and Marshall. She turned idly to 1 Corinthians 13.

"I didn't realise your Greek was good enough for this," she said as the door opened.

"It's not." Ann turned to see an expensive dark haircut, a red cashmere jumper and heels under tight jeans.

"How d'you do. I'm Ann."

"Hi." The dark haircut went into the bedroom. "Where's Theo?"

"Filling his kettle. I don't know why he doesn't do it in his bedroom," she added, to be friendly.

"Basin's too small."

Ann was wondering what to say next when Theo came in.

"Ah," he said. "Tea. I mean, introductions. Ann, this is Clare. Clare, my mother."

"I came to remind you of dinner. Don't be late, will you?" She kissed him on the lips. She didn't look at either of them on her way out.

Silence.

He laid a plate on the coffee table and lifted the cake onto it.

"I see," Ann smiled.

"Yup," Theo agreed. "I'll get the milk. Where's my screwdriver?"

"You took it with you."

"You didn't like her, did you?" he said, as he returned with the screwdriver but without the milk.

"Didn't I?"

"Surely you realise that?"

"I was going to give her a bit more of a chance."

"Why not?"

"Surely *you* realise that?"

"I wouldn't ask if I did. I think I wanted the milk, didn't I?"

"You did."

He went out again with the screwdriver and came back with the milk.

"And?"

"Because I was being rather old-fashioned and predictable. Some very nice people have been brought up without any manners. Or rather, some good people."

"Why isn't the kettle boiling? Ah yes: it needs propping up."

"Perhaps that's what your screwdriver was for?"

"Good point." He left the room again with the milk and came back with the screwdriver. Ann called after him, too late.

"I suppose she was. Earl Grey, Lapsang, Assam or girlie tea?"

"Was what? You have Lapsang?"

"Of course not. But I know you hate it so it was safe to offer."

"Ditto the girlie tea?"

"Actually I do have girlie tea. A bit rude."

"I didn't quite say that. Why girlie tea?"

"Clare."

"Uh-huh," Ann said slowly. "Is her toothbrush in your bathroom as well?"

"Sort of."

"I'm not always right, you know."

"Let's hope. Where on earth is the milk?"

The next hour and a quarter passed without incident. Ann loved talking to Theo and listening to him even more, and this afternoon was no exception.

Even when she couldn't follow a word, his company was soothing. "I am trying to get to grips with some Fourier estimates. The convolutions suggest that Fourier is the way to go, but Parseval seems to give me the wrong answer. I must be getting something wrong." Ann smiled encouragingly. He didn't need her to understand. Not his maths, anyway.

Clare was not mentioned again. She didn't bother to remind him not to be late. One woman nagging him was probably enough.

As she got up to go, she saw the letter on his desk.

She took in the paragraph in a flash. Late again. If it hadn't been for that your father would still be with you. Always, late, all your life.

She stood still. The words blurred. She became aware of feeling hot, and being careful about her breathing.

All through his adolescence: demands, punishment, belittlement. Why can't you be on time? Where have you been? What do you mean by it? Four pages of A4 on my desk by tomorrow morning: 'Why it is Necessary for Children to be Punctual?' Until the boy tried to take matters into his own hands, and nearly didn't come back.

Why is it necessary for adults to be kind? There was no point in railing. The teacher taught PE: no one had explained to him, he wasn't particularly bright and it wasn't his fault. It was confusing enough even for Ann – even for Theo – that he could be able to programme computers at the age of seven without ever having been taught. But couldn't, simply could not, be on time for breakfast.

She had thought he was happy: not subject to cruel and unimaginative teachers any more.

And now this.

"Where did this come from?" she asked when she could control her voice.

"It was left in the basket of a bike I borrowed."

"Know who wrote it?"

"No."

"Why have you kept it?"

"In case the police want it, I suppose."

She turned and he gave her another hug, different this time. Not a routine-welcome-hug, but a hug to put the strength back in her and tell her it would be all right.

He released her and she looked round for her bag. She put her handkerchief to her nose for a moment.

"What did you do?"

"Got very drunk."

"Did that help?"

"It. Changed things."

"Thanks for the tea," she said, wondering what and how.

"Pleasure."

As Ann crossed back over the river she stopped, and gazed towards the Mathematical Bridge of Queens'. So many absurd myths. That Newton built it, though he died two decades earlier. That it was made without nuts and bolts and held together by tension. That when the college took it to pieces, years later, they couldn't put it back together again, hence the black studded ironwork which now decorates it.

"All rubbish," Alan had pronounced cheerfully when he first showed it to her. "Like so much of Cambridge. Like the nonsense abounding about the missing segment of one of the stone balls on Clare Bridge," he said, punting her beneath it. "The number of people I've heard claim their great-grandfather removed it for a drunken bet could populate a very boring dinner party."

Now she crossed over and looked North, towards that same bridge, spanning from Clare College's courtyards to her lawns and gardens, the graceful arch stretching back to the fourteenth century, back sagging like a tired old horse. She had heard all the stories, now: that the builder had been underpaid, and removed it out of revenge; that a Fellow had a bet on the number of balls, and when he found there were fourteen not twelve he cut off a segment one night, so as not to lose. The most likely explanation was the dullest: that a mend in the ball had been cemented in and fallen off.

She wondered if it had hurt anybody when it fell.

A lone punter was passing underneath it towards her, a couple of tourists taking photographs. They must be cold.

Alan. Theo's father. Did she still miss him? Of course. You get used to it but never over it. She loved Brian, and his familiarity: life with him was calm and uneventful. But yes, she missed Alan, probably every day. With an acuteness out of step with the rest of her life. There was no comparison between her two husbands, at all.

As she left the Cam and walked home, she wiped the rogue tear from her face. Perhaps it was the wind, whipping the coming winter up off the Fens. So much bullying Theo had put up with. So many unkindnesses and punishments and cruelties.

He once told her he found losing Alan easier to bear than all that came after it. She was astonished: surely death is the Last Enemy? He was about fifteen. "Alan's death was given to us by God. It wasn't designed to be unkind. Whereas people, teachers who do it on purpose . . ."

Her heart felt worrisome. He would be thirty soon. Surely he could look after himself?

He'd have to. He would not be looked after by the expensive dark haircut.

To the stranger himself, those few Cambridge years of his childhood seemed so magical it was almost incredible he had really been there. Everything had happened so unexpectedly.

His uncle Bob had seen something on the telly about Salisbury Choir School, found there were two similar schools in Cambridge, and told his mum Sally – Bob's sister – to take her boy along.

"You're always saying he's musical, Sal. Wishing you had a piano. I'll give you the money to get there."

He just turned up, sang, and was told he would be moving school the following term.

He had no idea how much of a fluke it was.

On the day of his Voice Trial, three places were filled by unanimous agreement. For the fourth, the panel was split. There were two boys, equally good. The others – the Head Master, college organ scholar and the school head of music – favoured the no-risk candidate. The boy's father was a local doctor and his mother a piano-teacher; he was likely to come to the school anyway; he would fit in, win a scholarship to his next school and do well. And probably become a doctor or musician himself. Mr Wedderburn overruled them. Give the boy a chance. Single mum, never a music lesson in his life (other than one singing lesson his uncle had treated him to) and he would never get such an opportunity again.

So at the age of eight, his uniform paid for and fees waived, he found himself among children who didn't know what council housing was let alone what it meant to wait for a Giro before you could eat. One girl said to him, "I'm from a single-parent household too, you know." Sure. With a cleaner and an au pair, and a father who picked her up in his Merc every other Saturday, and took her on holiday to Italy.

Oddly enough, he was happy. He loved the stimulation: the music, the maths, the challenges. What he didn't like was being an outsider, knowing he could never afford what the others took for granted. He didn't notice the two clergy sons in the choir, who wore pass-me-downs at weekends and were also on bursaries. Nor that plenty of others had parents who were teachers or academics who had never bought a new car, who clothed themselves from charity shops and scrimped to get their children the best education they could. These children never complained for lack of pocket money: their houses were full of books and musical instruments and interesting conversation.

One day he went up to the dormitory and found himself alone. They were supposed to hand pocket money to the housemother and not keep valuables up there, but he knew some ignored this.

He opened the locker of a boy who was notoriously careless and saw a five pound note just sitting there, on a book. Before he had time to ask himself what he was doing he pocketed it and left, heart thumping. For the next day or two he wondered when it would be missed, and burned every time a teacher spoke to him.

As far as he knew to this day, it never was. Perhaps the boy never even noticed, or simply asked his parents for more.

It was two years before anything untoward happened. The Head Master called him into his study. It was then that he learnt about the Voice Trial and the other boy. He had a duty to repay their trust. He resented that conversation still. What was he supposed to do? He had pipped another candidate to the post, not because he was better but because they pitied him.

They couldn't be a hundred per cent sure, but everything pointed to him. Numerous little losses and petty thefts, going on for months. He raged. He felt as if they had set him a deliberate trap. How dare they accuse him before they were sure? Because he wasn't one of them, they had decided he was guilty without any evidence. In his moral indignation, he ignored that he had done all they accused him of and more.

He was being given one more chance . . .

It was this that made him commit his last, unforgivable crime. Certainly not because he wanted to be expelled. But because he didn't belong. He wanted to more than anything. To be one of those who knew instinctively how to behave because they drank it in with their mother's milk. Because they had been fed mother's milk, for fuck's sake, not formula from a bottle. Because they had lawns and teapots and tables to eat at instead of laps to balance chips on in front of the telly. One or two of the kids had parents who were Nobel fucking prizewinners.

He would never have a right to any of it. Take Wedderburn. When he looked him up he found he hadn't even passed all his A levels. Got a D in Physics or something. And the university claimed to be fair, into open access and only interested in academic potential!

So that was why he had nicked the most valuable item. It was insane.

A NeXT computer was on loan to the school science lab, from the university Computer Science Department in the New

Museums site. It was the size of a frigging picnic box – exactly a foot cubed – and there was absolutely nowhere he could hide it. Did he even want it? In an ultimate sense, of course: it was worth several thousand pounds. But it also wasn't worth anything, since it could never be sold. He wondered if he had been inspired by a story they'd been told by the Dean at a Christmas party, of thieves walking in to the college and taking priceless works of art which could never be passed on.

He hid it, absurdly, under his bed in the dormitory.

Stupid though his teachers were, they could surely tell such a pointless theft wasn't for the thing itself. That he wanted the Head Master to invite him back into his study, and say he understood. That his behaviour wasn't acceptable but because he was one of them, they would make it work for him. He longed for what Wedderburn had: to be so much part of the family that he would never be thrown out. Because he belonged.

The shock was so great that he didn't believe it until he had left the choir school for good.

His next few years were not comfortable. Bullied ruthlessly for having been at a posh private school, his mug on the telly at Christmas looking angelic. The teachers worst of all.

The sole solace left him was his appetite for maths, whetted at the choir school by the best teacher they had. He spent all his free time on a second-hand computer his uncle had procured from an office upgrade.

He never sang again.

When he was fifteen, his life changed. Chrissie arrived from Canada. She had skin like cream, a few beauty spots setting it off, and unfashionably wavy, glossy chestnut hair.

Being Canadian she had no understanding of class hatred. Being pretty, she had no fear of bullies. She sided with him.

His mother was so pleased he had a girlfriend, it was embarrassing. He would leave the two of them to it, in his mother's poky kitchen too small for anything more ambitious than pot noodles or microwave meals, mugs of instant coffee in their hands, putting the world to rights. He would go back upstairs, then, to his lone cyber world at which he was becoming more and more proficient.

Chrissie had one love in her life, apart from her family – and now, him. They had left their husky back in Toronto and she missed him acutely. She had an uncanny ability to acquire anything with four legs or two wings. A hamster. A budgerigar (he had thought budgies went out with maiden aunts and antimacassars). Even a garter snake which he had to handle enthusiastically every time he called, and which came to a sticky end when the rescue cat bit its head off.

Her passion for the animals she knew was nothing to her passion for animals generally. Battery chickens; veal calves; frogs heaped in live twitching piles after their legs had been cut off to satisfy the gourmet market . . .

To his shame he had known none of it. He swallowed her propaganda whole. When he heard of the suffering geese endured to produce fois gras, he was more disgusted than she was.

Chrissie was the gentlest person he had ever met. He had got over her long ago, but he still recognised her radiant goodness. She never hurt anyone. Except him, of course.

What distressed her most was laboratory experimentation, perpetrated by educated people. He played Devil's advocate and argued that the animals' suffering might be justifiable, to find a cure for cancer or other serious illnesses.

At this she cited beagles forced to smoke fifty a day though everyone knows smoking kills; rats blinded with totally unnecessary women's cosmetics; the damage done by Thalidamide despite extensive testing on rabbits, mice, even primates; finally the Nazis' experimentation on humans, which could have pushed back the boundaries of science but that didn't make it justifiable.

The day they went on their first protest remained one of the happiest of his life. He was spotty, unprepossessing and sported the world's worst haircut. And he was with the most beautiful girl in town. Neither of them quite sixteen.

They spent the day in drizzling rain under cheap anoraks. Their placard, made so painstakingly the evening before, fell apart in a soggy mess before they arrived. At the end of the day they went back to her parents' house soaked to the skin, made themselves cocoa and stripped down to their underwear.

When they realised Chrissie's parents were out she raided their drinks cupboard and poured them both a large brandy. It did what the adverts said: burned into parts of his body he hadn't known he had.

Half his lifetime ago. He put her name into Facebook a couple of years back, then realised he didn't want to know.

Increasingly, they had spent weekends demonstrating and campaigning, intoxicated by success. A research company was wiped off the New York Stock Exchange, its share price reduced by a thousand per cent.

He started thinking about university. He had a sympathetic maths teacher at last, who said he was capable of the best: Leeds or Warwick. Perhaps London. When he mentioned Cambridge, the teacher went quiet. The last time a pupil had gone to Cambridge was so long ago none of the teachers remembered him, and it wasn't for maths.

With an obvious effort at politeness his teacher told him he could include that among his choices. It was always a good idea to put a spread. You never know.

He decided to apply nowhere else.

His interview did not go well. Before he was five minutes in, he was out of his depth. He was only ahead at school because the others were so stupid. He'd had no idea the standard was so far above what he was used to.

If he had stayed on at the choir school . . . He told himself that if he had stayed at the choir school, he wouldn't have met Chrissie.

He never spent another minute on maths after that, barely scraping his A levels.

They joined DEN! (Drop Experimentation Now!) – supposedly non-violent but not averse to arson, blackmail or worse. An academic on the advisory board of a research company was beaten up and left unconscious in front of his small children. This was against the group's stated principles, but animals suffer far greater atrocities.

The day he realised he had become more dedicated than Chrissie was a revelation. He recalled a conversation lasting long into the night, when she said it was supposed to be about the animals, not politics or proving a point. She seemed more interested in her own happiness, her dog and the people she loved . . . and having a family of her own.

After Chrissie it was perhaps inevitable that he would return to Cambridge, to settle old scores.

The success of the group became legendary. He made sure he was never senior enough in the ranks to be held responsible, which proved very useful. He also learnt what made influential people take decisions. The rest was history. The university research continued to limp on and the Government claimed success over terrorism. The group had made their mark, the ringleaders received recognition on Wikipedia. And prison. He didn't regret the dissolution of the group in 2014. Cracks were beginning to appear.

By then he could afford to go solo.

The new Provost of the college was appointed the following year. Animal behaviouralist. Very interesting. Wedderburn's college. His own college, by rights, if he had stayed at the choir school.

From then he knew, with a burning passion he had never experienced before, what his life's work was destined to be.

Chapter Twenty-Two

SIXTH WEEK

At Cambridge Charlotte no longer stood out as she had at school, but unlike many freshers she felt more comfortable with this comparative anonymity. Nevertheless within a few weeks she could barely walk from her room to the porters' lodge without being stopped half a dozen times to be asked whether she was coming to this gathering or that dinner.

Hopeful male undergraduates, mostly in their first year, issued her with various invitations she happily accepted without reading anything particular into them, any more than if they had been from young women. She took little interest in the torpid sexual undercurrents raging around her, and was happily oblivious to the predatory games played by some of the Second Years, competing over how many freshettes they could shark in the first week.

She would not have a use for the little packet in her Freshers' Pack of freebies supplied by a bank hopeful of clients destined to be much richer one day. She hadn't been brought up to throw things away, but these went in the bin.

She would have been amused to know the use to which Theo had put the same item some decade earlier. He too didn't like to waste something fit for purpose, so put his away in a drawer along with receipts for biros and used train tickets. Towards the end of his first term, his neighbour in the next room hammered on his door after 11 pm, said it was an emergency and asked if he still had his free packet. Theo was only too glad to give them a home. What he wasn't so enthusiastic about was the detail his supplicant then gave him about his girlfriend's menstrual cycle.

"Work. Party. Sleep. Pick two," is the Cambridge advice so oft-quoted no one quite remembers whose Supervisor or Director of Studies it originated with. Under the intense pressure of an eight-week term relationships that might take years to form in an office can resemble settled domesticity in weeks.

Thus Charlotte found herself, without quite intending this, in the company of one more than others. Piers was personable, charming and urbane. He was reading Law at Magdalene. His family lived in Esher. Charlotte hadn't quite ascertained why.

After that first evening at the Union he had continued taking the initiative, inviting her to plays and concerts, giving her dinner. He didn't put unwelcome pressure on her. After a few weeks he invited her to visit his parents' place after Christmas.

By rights she should have been happy. As she biked through the slanting sunlight from lecture hall to college, or dashed through gusting leaves after a rehearsal or before a party, or searched for an academic paper in the University Library to skim-read in the few hours allocated for reading twenty such, she knew she was where she had always wanted to be.

So why the longing? As if she were trying to snatch an exquisite piece of music played almost out of earshot, or had smelt a hint of heady blossom on the breeze but couldn't quite find the tree that was frothing with flowers. She yearned for something.

But she had everything.

A propos of nothing, she remembered the end of *A Passage to India*, Aziz and Fielding riding hand in hand at a canter, the earth rising up between them. She thought of Piers walking her home from the theatre, his arm around her waist, after an indifferent student production of *Look Back in Anger*. Then she thought of Theo and flinched. It was quite irrational. Theo even had a girlfriend.

Nevertheless she didn't want him to see her hip to hip with Piers. Nor did she fool herself that Piers could be content with such courteous restraint for long. She found a polite excuse to decline his invitation.

By the following week Piers was in another girl's bed.

Crispin had invited his parents to Cambridge before. His graduation, of course, with lunch in the Provost's garden. A concert in Chapel, with internationally renowned alumni and a conductor his father had never heard of.

His parents' reward for all they had done for him: his mother's for living with his father. She relished such events almost too gushingly. Crispin believed the way to enjoy Cambridge was to take it for granted. Buildings are born hundreds of years old. The banks of the Cam are destined to be carpeted with flowers. There will always be numerous gardeners to tend the effortless elegance. Those who make much of it are newcomers, tourists, or moneymakers who have spilled North from London. Real Cambridge people assume as of right the breathless beauty of the Backs, and enjoy it as they take pleasure in their own children.

Now, however, he needed to treat his father to the sort of evening Mark could easily afford for himself: a smart restaurant, not a medieval dining hall. One of his father's traits which Crispin admired (and suspected his mother despised) was his directness. He scanned the menu, chose the second most expensive item (only because he didn't like lobster), handed it to the waitress with a gratuitous eyeing up of her bottom and asked Crispin what all this was about.

He had been dreading the moment. To his surprise, as he began to talk he found it a relief. Yes, he'd had a bit to drink. Yes, she was far younger than he was. But an adult. Perhaps for the first time he felt an affinity with his father. Mark had always been the shit of the family. Crispin began to wonder if perhaps all men are, together. Why can't women accept us as we are? His father's rôle was to provide money: the boorish lout who shagged anything that moved. His mother took the credit for everything. She was content to live in a large suburban home and have smart clothes and plenty to eat. For all her Guardian reading. That's what women do: put themselves in the right.

Mark twirled his wine (one of the most expensive on the list) by its stem, contemplating its tears. He was always stingy with it at home. Presumably because he really preferred spirits and beer. Crispin realised his father was enjoying himself. Half way through his fillet steak (well-done), he was already talking to a lawyer.

"She'll ring back shortly," he said, hanging up. "Where's the ketchup in this place?"

"Dad! Please . . ."

"I think you're becoming a bit of a snob. Too good for your roots, my parents used to call it."

Crispin took a sip of his crisp white (his father had insisted on a different wine for each of them) and played with his Dover sole. Mark was right. Crispin thought him coarse. And Liz a bit pathetic. It was low of him.

"Can we see the sweet trolley?" He'd be asking for melon balls next. Crispin suspected he was doing it on purpose. He had never before noticed his father's prodigious appetite. He ordered apple pie with clotted cream. "I got in a similar scrape myself once." Crispin did his best to look surprised. "Not that it mattered so much then. Could have done, though."

Crispin put his head politely on one side.

"I was seventeen. My first time, if you can believe that. Went out for the afternoon, to a farm. Years afterwards, she cried rape. Said she'd been traumatised ever since. Okay, I didn't ask her to sign on the dotted line, and we'd both had a load of cider."

"How old was she?"

"Twenty-two. Teacher."

"Yours?"

"French. Taught me something a hell of a lot more useful than French."

"What happened?"

"What do you mean? Nothing happened. It was, like, years later. Her first time too, apparently. Had the nerve to claim her only time. Said she just wanted an apology. Her therapist had told her it would help her 'move on'," he gouged speech marks in the air. "What do you suppose her lawyer would have done with that?"

"What happened to her? Did you keep in touch?"

"Topped herself," he said. "Nah, we didn't keep in touch."

The waiter shimmied over to their table with large flat white plates decorated with delicate desserts.

"Nearly missed," Mark said.

There should have been a deafening silence. Crispin didn't know whether to be more appalled at a teacher taking advantage of a pupil, or his father's blithe indifference.

"Did you feel guilty?"

Mark had just taken a rather large mouthful. "Pardon?"

"That she killed herself?"

"Bloody hell I don't know what happened to her. She was a nut. Normal people don't go screaming rape because the earth doesn't move first time."

Crispin folded his napkin into smaller and smaller squares.

The lawyer rang back. His father fixed a meeting; ordered cheese; demanded a brandy; and at last, when Crispin was nauseous with fatigue, ordered a taxi.

"That was all right," he said.

"Pleasure," Crispin hoped it sounded more sincere than it was.

"Your place now? Or on somewhere?"

"Mine, I thought." He had made a bed for his father in the little room at the front of the house, too small for the lodger.

"Garçon! Can I have the bill, please?"

"Dad, I'm doing this."

"Don't be bloody ridiculous. On your salary?"

"That's very kind."

Crispin wondered whether he had time to change his sheets so his father could have his room.

It was not quite the first time the stranger had made contact with Wedderburn. Some fourteen years earlier a young man his own age, in the US, had also dropped out – of university. To become a billionaire. He and Wedderburn both happened upon the American's website when hardly anyone else had heard of it. He was so surprised to see someone he knew that he sent Wedderburn a message. Gave him some news; talked of his involvement in the animal rights movement.

Everyone does it now. Contacts old schoolfriends they can't be bothered to see, and sends them news they don't want to read.

They both dissociated from Facebook as soon as everyone else started using it. He didn't suppose Wedderburn had read his message . . . nor would he have known who he was if he had.

Soon he would. Everyone in the civilised world would know his name. By Boxing Day, if not before. His pulse raced at the proximity of it. Within months – weeks – he would be a name in history. On Wikipedia, as the others were, though they had to trade it for a prison sentence.

They would get out of prison, of course. He never would. Not if it went according to plan.

He had plan and counter-plan and fall-back plan. If his main plan failed – it wouldn't – he had several more. And it was almost a one-man job. That was the beauty of it: there was so little to go wrong. There was even that wild, heady possibility that, unlike others, he might get away with it. He wasn't relying on it. Nor ruling it out either. In which case he would switch career and never be associated with animal rights again. His life was divided into the Before and the After. As indeed would Cambridge be.

He was not averse to having some personal revenge first, though. It would be a pleasure to fleece Wedderburn.

Somewhere deep in the dark rock of his soul he knew it wasn't really another child's fault. But that wasn't the point. Wedderburn enjoyed everything that had been denied to him: charmed childhood, golden adolescence, academic career. His schoolmate had stolen his life.

If the father were still alive he needn't have targeted the son . . .

Wedderburn's interest in cryptocurrency was on his University webpage. He dismissed the idea of fobbing off fraudulent bitcoins onto him. It could be months before Wedderburn needed to make any transactions. And he only had till Christmas.

He would devise a meeting.

It took him several attempts to hack into Wedderburn's computer. Mostly because Wedderburn was such an effing freak. Obviously, it was no good sending him an email from a colleague: most of his colleagues would be computer-literate. And Wedderburn might actually read it. Far better, from the Domestic Bursar. When Wedderburn clicked on some notification about breakfast and it didn't open properly, he'd just assume the college office was staffed by idiots.

There was no response to the first attachment, purporting to be the term's menus. Nor did Wedderburn open the next about a non-existent college dinner. The third attempt was an urgent notice about college linen, labelled 'top priority'. Wedderburn clicked. And presumably didn't react when it wouldn't open, because it was about bedsheets.

He was in.

Inside Wedderburn's computer, he ran the software. Within twenty-four hours it had extracted a security token giving access to his university Google Calendar account. It wasn't his 'Raven' university login password, which he doubted would have been possible given that Cambridge University's Computer Labs aren't run by complete jerks. Besides, it would be such a serious breach of security Wedderburn would go apeshit if he realised. Which could risk everything.

As he sat, in his dingy room rented from someone whose name he couldn't even remember, gazing at Wedderburn's life opening up in front of him, he had a sense of empowerment such as he hadn't felt since the early days with Chrissie. He had proved what he had always known: he had far more brains than Wedderburn.

He had entered his life. Like a parasite in the gut of a dog living in a stately home, he was now inside the club which had put up so many barriers to keep him out.

Ann poured herself a glass of Pinot Grigio. She was drinking more these days. Who wasn't? She and Alan had almost never bought wine. They drank at other people's houses and at college events, which he attended more than she did. And if they entertained. Now she and Brian almost never spent an evening without alcohol.

He was out at a rare work evening so she had decided on an early night and an indulgent read of her new book, *The Rosie Effect*. It was fashionable now: Asperger's syndrome. Presumably that would make life better, for younger versions of Theo. She had a feeling he had told her Asperger's had been abolished and it was all autism these days. How little she still understood her son. And yet she understood him better than anyone else.

"You worry too much," Brian said. Well he would, wouldn't he? In some ways she believed she didn't worry nearly enough.

No mother thinks another woman good enough for her son. Ann knew this not to be true. Plenty of women might not relish the rôle of absent-minded-professor's-wife, once so familiar in Cambridge: the sensible, down-to-earth woman reminding her brilliant but dippy husband of the names of his children and which train he should be on.

The woman who did, though – if such a species still existed, in Cambridge or anywhere – would get a fair bargain in Theo. Not the old-fashioned trade-off of income and status in exchange for raising the children and running his diary. Theo might not earn a living at all: young academics face futures as uncertain as actors' or musicians' now. But his wife would live with the kindest man imaginable. Who would never raise his voice, or off-load his bad moods, or even argue with her. Who would put her first in everything, quite simply because he put everyone before himself.

Or rather, he would put her on a par with himself. And with everyone else in the world, known or unknown. Ann had known Theo tell an interview panel that one of the other candidates would do the job better than he would.

This was how he related to everyone. To the tiny iotas of nameless statistics, the thousands and hundreds of thousands and millions of victims of tsunamis or earthquakes or terrorist attacks, in the same way that he related to someone he had known all his life. Every single one, every last tiny star of humanity, was as big to Theo as he was himself. Each pinprick in the sky, a sun.

No wonder it hurt so much that life was sometimes too much to bear.

Professor Baron-Cohen had once commented on the irony of the nomenclature 'autistic'. People who are autistic, he explained, often have no sense of self at all. Which is why they can make good scientists – presumably good academics of any kind – since objective truth can be so much more important to them than individual comfort.

She remembered Charlie's attempt to make Theo backtrack, after he had asserted that of course he would forgo medical treatment if giving his own life would save several unknown lives elsewhere.

"I don't believe you."

"Any rational person would."

Exasperated, Charlie had said, "Okay, suppose you could save your life, or just one other person's? Someone you'll never know?"

"In that case I'd save my own."

"Ahah!" he cried triumphantly. He didn't often better his older brother. "So you are irrational?"

"No: my life is probably more use than the average person's."

"Oh, you're so annoying. I still don't believe you, anyway."

"Nothing else makes sense," Theo concluded.

If everyone were like Theo, yes, it would make sense. If everyone lived rationally, Theo wouldn't be at a constant disadvantage.

Take Clare, for instance.

Ann knew, as surely as she knew her own name, that Clare would not live according to Theo's altruistic logic. Why should she? She will meet her own needs because that's what her genes, her upbringing, her career, all tell her to do. And then she'll dump him. Or worse, marry him if that suits her better.

Theo would do what was best for the world. His girlfriend – must Ann really call her that? – would do what was best for herself.

That was what made him so vulnerable.

At the beginning of each academic year, Theo transferred his university commitments, laboriously by pen, from the university Google Calendar into his desk diary. It took him an afternoon, but ensured that everything made sense. He sometimes lost the diary soon afterwards (this year, by chance, he hadn't) but that didn't matter. And because he also put commitments onto his iPhone, he didn't use his university Calendar much after that.

The next day, however, he was taking the penultimate supervision of a series. He wanted to be sure he had covered the syllabus. So he opened it to remind himself of the course he was teaching. It was the third-year Number Theory course. He wondered about continued fractions: he knew they mentioned them, but did they actually prove anything of interest? They characterise quadratic irrationals. He'd better be ready to explain this if needed.

Hmm. That was interesting . . .

One reason it was impossible for Theo to turn up for dinner on time or risk inviting a girl out or even catch a train without yanking his entire nature out of joint, was this. As a child will see every dew drop on each blade of grass, every individual feather on the blackbird which is pulling the worm out of the ground – sometimes each ring on the skin of the worm and the nostril on the bird's beak – and not come when its mother calls it for tea because it is simply too busy, so too Theo's mind was young always in the details he noticed, which no sane person had time for. Figures and numbers and small print in the margin of the screen, invisible to those of us who can catch trains. He had been known, when buying a packet of butter, to read the bar code to check it was correct.

Thus he noticed the discrepancy, in tiny digits in the bottom right hand corner, 'Last account activity 23 hours ago.'

He hadn't noticed being unhappy recently. Not unhappy enough to have forgotten – which was how he knew when he was unhappy – the last twenty-three hours. He clicked on 'Details', underneath the digits, to see if he was.

As he thought. The IP address which had logged in was not his. Indeed, it was not a Cambridge University one: they all had the same first few numbers, like an area code for a telephone number.

Theo's first question was not *why* anyone would hack into his calendar, but how. The details would probably be rather boring. But the method of access interested him. There was a niggle at the back of his mind: something he had noticed earlier in the term. Hadn't there been a communication concerning some issue of college admin, some topic even sillier than usual for which the attachment hadn't opened? Carpet mites or toothpaste or something equally pointless.

That must have been when it was done. He nodded, satisfied. Not a bad way.

Only then did he consider the far less interesting question of who and why.

Did Crispin know that he, Theo, had reported his compromised research? Was he spying on him? He must have disguised his own IP address if so, as his would be a university one. That was possible: whoever had done this was moderately competent.

But no, of course not. If the Provost had challenged him directly rather than instigating a discreet enquiry, he was far too sensible to let Crispin know his source.

It was intriguing. He would look again in a few days' time, to see whether it had been repeated.

What particularly amused him was that if someone had wanted to know his timetable – without using the most straightforward method, which was to ask him – he could have walked into his room and opened his desk diary. Without leaving a footprint.

As his adored maths teacher Miss Lormer, at the choir school, had taught him, taught all of them: the good mathematicians are the lazy ones.

The elegant solutions are the best.

Charlotte realised she didn't want Theo to know there was another note in her bicycle basket.

She could just leave it. The autumn winds might eventually blow it away. Sooner or later someone would throw an empty beer can into her basket, then a crisp packet or KFC box, and when she next took her bike for a service, if she didn't deal with it, all the detritus would still be in there. It was even possible, perhaps, that this time the envelope contained nothing?

But she hated litter. She picked it up quickly and shoved it in her bag. Then went to the college coffee bar, ordered tea and an Eccles cake and sat overlooking the courtyard.

In Charlotte's world, men protected women. Even Michael, nearly four years her junior, was already taller and stronger. When she took him to friends' parties or for his first visit to a pub, she looked after him socially: introducing him to friends and ensuring he enjoyed himself. But he walked her home.

Now she wanted to protect a man. Someone a generation older: a real grown-up. How dare she presume Theo was vulnerable? And yet she instinctively felt so: as if he had no shell.

She had a rehearsal at five and wanted to read a couple of papers first. She opened her bag, tore the envelope open and read.

"Baron of Beef, Friday night, 20.00 hours. *I'll* be on time."

She would not leave it in his pigeon hole. She would hand it over personally, or not at all.

Chapter Twenty-Three

SEVENTH WEEK

Suki asked her to be there.

Charlotte knew memories of that early morning back in June had infected everything for her friend. Every night Suki remembered the susurration of her skirt, or the slick of his tongue, or scrape of his cheek on hers. And worse. Then she would be filled with a wild, uncontrollable screaming. Charlotte was far from convinced she should go through with the court appearance. Nobody had witnessed anything: how could he possibly be convicted beyond reasonable doubt?

The barrister, who was called Jayne, had arranged to visit Suki in her room. Jayne didn't look like Charlotte's idea of a barrister. She had a soft round face, pretty blonde curly hair and blue eyes. Charlotte was reminded of Harriet Smith in *Emma*.

She rummaged through Suki's file. Charlotte offered to make drinks but Jayne refused and Suki seemed too nervous to make any decisions.

After several minutes she looked up. "Hmm," she said. "The defendant has Samantha McKenna."

As this meant nothing to either of the girls they didn't respond.

"Has he got a lot of money, I wonder?" She looked from one to the other. Suki looked to Charlotte for help.

"We don't know," Charlotte said. "Is it significant?"

"Not at all." Jayne said quickly. "Just wondered."

She read on.

"Now," she looked up eventually. "You'd better tell me everything. In case you're not familiar with the procedure, I mustn't have any nasty surprises in the court room. I don't want to pry, but I need to know about all your previous sexual adventures." And she smiled as if complimenting candidates in a local contest for Victoria Sponge.

"I thought," Charlotte said tentatively, "it was supposed to be illegal to comment on the witness's private life?"

"Supposed to be."

Suki piped up. "My father's a bishop."

The look Jayne turned on her took Charlotte right back to junior school, when her friend had stepped on the wrong flower bed.

"That is, he's only a suffragan . . ."

"It's my duty to warn you, Susan. Not judge you. Anything which comes out in court, unexpectedly, is going to damage your credibility."

"Suki is not on trial," Charlotte ventured. "She's a witness."

"Exactly."

The conversation went steadily downhill after that. At last Jayne shuffled her papers again, stood up and extended her hand.

"She was nice," Suki said shutting the door.

"Good," Charlotte took a deep breath. "So, what have you learnt?"

"Oh. I didn't know I had to learn anything."

She changed tack. "Okay, what has your barrister learnt?" Charlotte didn't credit her stepfather with much, but he had taught her to assess the value of any meeting.

"I'm not very good at this, am I?" Suki said dubiously.

"That's her job, not yours." Charlotte sighed. Perhaps she hadn't done her own job well either. "Let's go out for tea."

"I've got work."

"So have I. But we'll concentrate better. I know: there's a lovely walk near here, over a little brook, through fields with horses. We'll be back in our rooms in half an hour. And more productive for the fresh air." For some reason, she didn't add that her mother had told her that her father used to walk there every evening during Finals, instead of swotting.

The layout of the land must have changed since then: they followed a few dead ends. Nevertheless it was no more than fifteen minutes before they found the little stream.

"Pooh Sticks!" Charlotte decreed, and they leant over the darkly dashing, disturbed water, hurling sticks as far as they could to cheat the current. Charlotte won easily, until Suki darted ahead and claimed the winner.

"That's mine!" Charlotte protested.

"No, it isn't!"

"They do look very similar," she conceded.

She had passed the second note on to Theo. She had no need to be so apologetic, he assured her: she hadn't written it.

Maybe, she said; but Greek and Latin can't be the only languages to have the same word for 'messenger' and 'message'.

From this it was a small step to whether the music in Chapel wasn't proper worship because half the choir had no faith in the message: how could they be messengers of God if they didn't believe it?

"The official stance of the Christian Union," Theo said. "College Chapel is the last place you would ever find Christ, because not all members of the choir are Christians."

"I've heard Suki's father suggest as much. He's a clergyman," she explained. "I wonder whether members of the CU insist on bibles being printed by firms which only employ Christians?"

"That's interesting: you think like me. Well, obviously you don't think like me at all. But you think the same thoughts." She wasn't sure how to respond to this and was relieved when he continued, "Is he? Yes, that works. I suppose that's why she's not as reserved as she might be."

And thus the poisonous note was put aside on his desk, with the last few days' receipts from a couple of pubs and a stationer's.

Where it remained studiously disregarded for a while.

Many times in his life Theo had been required to tell himself that others didn't always behave rationally – by which he usually meant kindly – and he had to ignore them. This was easier in adulthood. Mainly because he was no longer at the mercy of adults being illogically cruel to him. But he had also become more practised.

So it was by chance that he happened to see the note again while looking for something else, and then notice it was twenty to eight on the night in question and the writer had suggested meeting at eight, with the strong implication that Theo would not be on time.

Thus he wasn't sure whether he was successfully goaded into going; or whether he had merely finished one task, not yet worked out the next, wanted a drink and felt curious. Or indeed whether there was a difference. When a hypnotist orders you to blow your nose, are you acting out his will or your own? Or does his skill lie in aligning the two? Thus he arrived seven and a half minutes early for an appointment he had never agreed to.

In truth, he was a hundred and sixty-seven hours, fifty-two minutes and thirty seconds late, not having realised that the invitation had originally been for the Friday before.

The evening didn't get off to a good start. Theo tended to choose brews with names like Feathered Pheasant, Hairy Hedgehog or Slimy Slug. The nearest he could find was an unpromising "Red Ale, 536". He bought a pint and sat by the window, looking out over the Cam where the punts would bob in summer.

Just after his third Michaelmas Term, a girl he knew slightly had disappeared from Magdalene late one night, as her friends waited in the street for her to go back for her keys. Her body emerged miles downriver shortly before the New Year. Theo thought of her family's Christmas, not just that year but every year afterwards, and lifted his glass sadly. It was empty already. He glanced at his watch: "twenty-nine minutes past eight" was spelt out in Helvetica. He would have preferred Book Antiqua but he didn't have a say over the font.

He got up wondering why he had come, then sat down again. There was a couple having a drink about four feet away from him. They had been together approximately five years: not animated in each other's company but still not entirely familiar. Beyond them, a group of rugger buggers, so obviously behaving as if from public school that they presumably weren't.

And someone alone, reading *Feynman Lectures on Computation*.

Theo went towards the bar.

"Have you spotted the mistakes?" he asked as he passed.

"Mistakes?"

"I haven't read it for about fifteen years so if it's a later edition they might have been corrected. Can I buy you a pint?"

"I'll have what you're having."

"I couldn't recommend it," Theo warned. "But there's nothing else."

When he returned to the stranger's table he launched into a conversation about the book, which he had discovered when he was at his most unhappy stage of life. He couldn't remember much before that. The therapist, the mad woman who asked what kind of a bedroom he had ("But is it a happy room?" she demanded, when he said it was painted yellow and had a window, a door and a bed in it), had told him you can't remember back beyond trauma. That traumas stack up and create barriers, and what lies beyond is mist and darkness.

He didn't know then that Ann had approched school after school, and all of them had turned him down. That in despair she asked her physicist cousin to give him some lessons. The cousin suggested Feynman, 'written for PhD students', which the twelve-year-old Theo read hungrily and spotted its mistakes.

From here it was easy for the stranger to introduce cryptocurrency. There were at least three pubs in Cambridge, Theo volunteered, where you could buy your pint in bitcoins. "More accurately, two. The Haymakers has stopped: the technology was too cumbersome. Worth going to the Devonshire Arms and the Queen Edith, just to do it."

And from there, it almost felt as if Theo himself had introduced the name Turing.

"I have some lecture notes of his," the stranger said. Theo took a pull on his third pint. "From when he was up at your college." There was barely a beat before he said, "Your university. You are at the university, obviously."

Theo said nothing for a while.

Even before Alan died Theo had experienced difficulties. At nursery school, he drove some of the staff half-demented. He was always inadvertently infringing some code. Since he tried to please harder than any other child, this caused him far more distress than it did his teachers.

In those days Ann hadn't yet taught him how to respond. Which was quite a disadvantage, because tellings-off happened so frequently. And unpredictably. As soon as she realised, she explained. "Consider two dogs. When they meet the more dominant one will put the hairs up along his back to look even bigger and more dominant. The weaker dog crouches to look smaller than he is, wagging his tail to look friendly. This concedes victory to the bigger dog, and stops him attacking the smaller one."

"If it's so obvious," Theo objected, "it seems unnecessary."

"Be that as it may, this behaviour protects the smaller dog. He acknowledges the other's superiority, so the bigger one doesn't have to prove his strength, and hurt him."

"Did you know animals of the same species rarely fight to the death?" Theo observed randomly.

"Which proves the behaviour works. Given that your teachers are, for the moment, a lot more powerful than you are, when they tell you off you've got to imitate that little dog."

"I can't."

"You can learn."

"I haven't got a tail."

Theo's first diagnosis, when he was seven or eight, was, 'Semantic Pragmatic Disorder.' The therapist explained, "If you ask someone with this disorder if he knows the time, he's likely to say, 'Yes, thank you', and walk on."

"That's not a disorder," Alan objected. "That's using language properly."

Theo always used language properly. Although he couldn't write essays, he often did well in English because he understood grammar so precisely.

"You don't have to wag a tail, Theo. Just look at the floor, instead of into the teacher's eyes."

"You taught me to look you straight in the eye."

"This is a further refinement."

"Like when you have to unlearn all the maths you learnt last year, because it wasn't accurate?"

"Sort of. Oh . . . Just look *sorry,* Theo, could you? Somehow?"

She could understand their frustration. Several times a day his teachers attempted to rebuke him. And when they did he looked straight at them, displaying no emotion . . . and went on being late. It was natural to conclude that the child was almost psychopathically naughty.

What they didn't know, he didn't know, even she didn't know until she spent years observing and watching and learning how to read him – until, indeed, it was nearly too late – was that Theo was *feeling* far more than the other children. He was trying far harder. And he was certainly hurting far more. It just didn't show on his face.

So Ann taught him to write suitable emotions on his face. As with so much, Theo had to become bilingual in order to survive. But that didn't mean he had to abandon his earlier mode. He was now adept at expressing the emotion appropriate to the situation.

It was not a skill he was obliged to use.

It would appear that they had done a deal. As an undergraduate, Alan Turing attended lectures by Wittgenstein on the nature of mathematics. Transcripts survived, complete with Turing's interjections. Theo was being offered Turing's notes. He had no objection to owning them, and could probably sell them on if he could be bothered.

The price was just under a bitcoin.

"There's a better currency," Theo said.

He explained how Marigolds included a facility for making a delayed payment, using the block chain as the intermediary.

"You've bought this currency yourself?"

Theo could tell he was excited. He sensed a shared enthusiasm. They could almost have been friends. He saw no reason not to be open. "I've converted most of my savings into them."

"So you want to pay me in Marigolds?"

"It's safer than bitcoins," Theo observed. "I transfer the money to the block chain; you give me the Turing; the block chain transfers the money to you."

They agreed to meet the following evening in a pub with proper beer.

"Evening, sir," Carlos said as Theo went through the P'lodge ten minutes later. To his momentary disappointment, Theo didn't seem to see him. He was even more focused than usual.

Charlotte came for Suki in good time the next morning, the first day of the trial.

"Have you had breakfast?"

Suki looked confused. "I think we've missed college breakfast."

"I'll treat you," Charlotte said, carefully cheerful. "As soon as you're dressed we'll go for a croissant."

"I am dressed."

Charlotte had seen Suki's jogging trousers and oversized green sweatshirt before, in the middle of whatever mathmos have instead of an essay crisis. They were just about okay for nipping to the college bar for a sandwich.

"Do you want to brush your hair, before we go?" Suki's hair was the best thing about her: fiery wild corkscrews, blazing above her bold and incongruous choices of colours. Now it looked as if it hadn't been washed for a week. Suki grabbed an elastic band and pulled it behind her, as if for school hockey or a chemistry lesson.

"Suki, I wonder . . . You usually look so pretty. Do you want any makeup?"

"Whatever for?"

"Just an instinct . . ."

"I'm not on trial."

"No. It's just . . . I suspect juries, like anyone else, decide in the first few seconds."

"This was not my idea," Suki said sullenly.

"It's your choice. You'll need something warmer though."

Charlotte held out her beautiful tapestry coat.

"Don't want it."

"I know it looks sunny," Charlotte argued, "but it's really nippy out."

For some reason, this prompted Suki to pull her hair out of the elastic band, savagely, so Charlotte could hear the ends of her hair tearing. Then she shrugged on her coat.

Charlotte followed her out with a heavy heart. She would have to miss a couple of lectures – one of which she had very much wanted to hear – and had been excused her afternoon's supervision.

She wasn't looking forward to any of it.

Chapter Twenty-Four

NEXT DAY

Charlotte thought those two days the worst of her life: worse even than when her father left and a fissure of pain scarred through her childhood and adolescence. If she felt so shamed and humiliated just hearing the evidence, how much worse must it be for Suki?

It was on the second day that she saw the placard. They walked past it so quickly that she didn't immediately register.

She had promised Suki lunch somewhere near the courthouse. Her mother had mentioned a restaurant which had now closed, but another had opened in its place. When they looked at the menu Charlotte was so preoccupied by what she'd just seen that she didn't take in the figures.

"Gosh this is generous," Suki said.

An intimidating waitress looked them up and down and showed them to stools by the bar. "Best we can do, without booking. As it's a weekday lunchtime we'll squeeze you in."

Suki indicated a framed award. "It's really posh. Thank you."

Charlotte looked at the prices, felt sick, and prayed that Suki wouldn't choose a main course.

"What are you having, Charlie?"

"Oh, um, soup I think. It looks really nice," she added.

"It just says, 'Soup of the day' in mine." Suki leaned over Charlotte's menu to see if it was different.

"It's probably homemade or something."

Charlotte waited anxiously while Suki dithered. "One soup of the day, please. Do you want more time, Suki?"

"I don't know. Maybe . . . Shall I have the same?"

"Two please," Charlotte decided. "You can have something afterwards if you're still hungry. I'm just going to the loo." She slipped outside when Suki wasn't looking and walked back to the newspaper stand.

CAMBRIDGE 'SEX' CLAIM: TUTOR NIGHTMARE.

Not just the Cambridge News, but the Daily Mail.

Suki filled the front page. Her hair flared out from her pixelated face above her distinctive tapestry coat, walking away from the courtroom.

She was appalled. Could that be legal?

"Sixty-five pee," the news vendor said.

"No thanks."

"The fact that this is genuine," DC Andy said, "doesn't mean the next one Mike offers you will be."

"Of course," Theo agreed.

"Haven't you seen *Hustle*? It's called the 'convincer'."

"I don't need to see a movie," Theo said. "And his name's not Mike."

"I thought you said it was."

"So these are from 1939?" Theo fingered the pages of numbers in faded ink. "When Turing was an undergraduate, in Cambridge?"

"They were quite easy to verify."

"That's so good." Theo spread the notes out on his knee so as not to risk beer from the pub table. The debate between the two mathematical giants was legendary.

They were in the Fort St George, overlooking a torpid river. They had been friends since an undergraduate had appealed to Theo for help, convinced her debit card was being used fraudulently but her high street bank wouldn't believe her. The bank claimed fraud was impossible with Chip and PIN.

Theo was so outraged by this absurd assertion that he had forged a chip himself to prove how easy it was. It wasn't a good forgery: he didn't have enough time, and his contact in the relevant university department hadn't been free to help. But he was able to demonstrate the principle, that a wafer-thin film placed between card and machine can dupe the machine.

He and Andy met at an acrimonious meeting with a young bank manager who was completely out of his depth, and kept reiterating that his IT department said it couldn't be done. Eventually Theo's student got most of her money back . . . though Theo wondered afterwards whether perhaps she was so absent-minded, she had spent the money and forgotten.

The friendship with Andy had been the lasting result.

"What I said was," Theo clarified, "'He said his name is Mike',"

"It's not?"

"No."

"How do you know?"

Theo thought back to their evening together. "He said, 'Mike', then immediately, 'Michael', as if it needed explanation. So when I went for another round I asked the barman to call 'Michael' to someone in the kitchen, so I could see his response."

"Would there necessarily be one?"

"If somebody called Theophilus in the Market Place I would look round even if I didn't recognise the voice."

"That's not quite the same."

"Next time we're having a drink I'll ask someone to say, 'Andrew.' You will react. Even if you're determined not to because of this conversation, your eyes will."

"Why didn't you call the name yourself?"

"He might have responded to my voice, rather than his name. And I wanted to watch his face."

"Ever thought of being a copper?"

"No."

"How much are you prepared to pay for the next one?"

"A few grand?"

Andy whistled. "It's going to be a forgery, Theo."

"I want to work out what he's doing."

"Expensive."

"Interesting."

"You have a pic?"

Theo handed Andy his telephone. A man was sitting at a table, reading a book. Andy enlarged it to read, *Feynman Lectures on Computation*.

"This is before he approached you?"

"He didn't approach me. He wanted me to approach him. Hence the book."

"Send these over," Andy said. "I'll see if we've got anything." He drained his pint. "You coming?"

Theo continued looking at the photograph.

"I've got to go," Andy slipped on his coat.

Theo didn't stir. Andy gave up and moved some chairs out of his way. Like a cat threatened with a closing door, Theo was suddenly there before him.

"Still think you'd make an interesting detective," Andy said as the November night air slapped their faces.

"There are lots of things I'd like to do," Theo said. "If I had world enough and time. Look," he gazed upwards. The sky bled dirty yellow with the light pollution but it was still possible to see a startlingly large silver star. "Venus. Very close to the earth tonight." He sighed with pleasure.

"Pretty," Andy agreed.

"Particularly time."

Charlotte's efforts to protect her friend proved as vain as a paper bag in the rain. The first person to say, "Have you seen the papers?" in Trinity P'lodge wasn't even someone Suki recognised.

There was a copy in the Junior Common Room. The porters all seemed to have seen it too. Even some of the Fellows.

According to editorial opinion, Suki was a malicious and mendacious mischief-maker who, out of sheer spite, had set out to ruin a brilliant, distinguished young academic who was selflessly dedicated to protecting children from the effects of pornography.

"Why?" Charlotte asked her mother that night, through hot tears of anger. "I just don't get it. Why invent such a horrible interpretation, out of nowhere? And isn't it illegal, before the verdict?"

"I would have thought so." Her mother was also at a loss. "I suppose if they've pixelated her face . . ."

"But her clothes! Her hair! Everyone knows who it is."

"Only people who know her already, sweetheart. It can't come up in a few years' time, when she's looking for a job. Whereas he is named."

"Mummy, he's guilty of a criminal offence!"

"Not yet, strictly speaking."

"He jolly well is, whether or not he's found guilty." Her tears had dried, leaving frustrated fury. "I found her, afterwards. She was . . ."

"I know, darling. I'm sorry. I agree they have made her recognisable. And that is wrong. It's possible she could sue."

"Anyway, I'm not saying he should be named either," Charlotte added inconsequentially. "The whole thing's vile." She started to cry again.

"Can I make a really old-fashioned suggestion?"

"Go to bed, I suppose?"

"That too. Have you got a good book? I don't mean work, for your course. Just a detective novel or something."

"Don't think so."

"Can you borrow one? Anything well-written, and preferably not too demanding. PG Wodehouse. *Wind in the Willows*."

Suddenly Charlotte remembered *Winnie-the-Pooh*.

"AA Milne?"

"Perfect. Have you got any?"

"I'd have to borrow from someone."

"Do that," her mother urged. "Have a mug of cocoa, and early-ish night, and *Winnie-the-Pooh*." It was on the tip of her tongue to ask whether it was from that nice chap who looked after her Vuillaume violin, but some instinct stopped her. "And don't read tabloids."

"They're hard to avoid." But she sounded mollified. "Goodnight Mum. Thanks."

"You'll be home soon," her mother reminded her.

"Oh, I was going to ask if you mind if I don't come home till Christmas. I've volunteered for the service of Nine Lessons. I'm carrying the cross."

Her mother hid her disappointment flawlessly. "Lovely! We'll watch you on the telly."

"I mean for the live service. On the radio. The telly's just a pre-recorded thing."

"Oh yes, I knew that really. We'll listen to you then."

"I hope not. You'll only hear me if I fall over."

"Joke. Now, go and get that book."

"K. Love you."

"Love you too."

Charlotte was aware that her mother's insistence that she borrow a book from Theo didn't necessarily make it a good idea. But at least it wasn't hers.

It had just gone ten. She would go immediately before she changed her mind.

His curtains were closed and his light on. She could hear a woman's voice. She had only come to borrow a book so she knocked before she had time to think about it.

"Yup."

"What would be the point?" the other voice was saying as she opened the door. "Of course I appreciate beauty but I can enjoy the architecture any time, it's not my kind of music and you know what I think of patriarchal superstitions."

"Sorry," Charlotte mumbled.

"Give it to someone who would appreciate it." She turned and stared at Charlotte.

"Hello," Theo smiled. "For what?"

"Sorry?" Charlotte asked.

"Exactly," he said.

"Oh I see," Charlotte said. "For, um. Interrupting."

"Would you like to go to the Advent Carol service?" he asked. "I have two tickets. Clare," his tone was not at all sarcastic, "believes the arrival of the Son of God will be wasted on her."

"Oh, I'd love to," Charlotte gushed. "It's my favourite service. Well, and Easter."

"I'm glad you've found someone," Clare said crisply. "And there's no need to mock someone else's ideology. Christianity has been responsible for some pretty shocking abuse, particularly of women and the oppressed. Most people consider atheism a perfectly acceptable and rational position."

"Why are you upset?" he asked, curious.

"I didn't mean to interrupt," Charlotte tried again. "I only came ..."

"I can't stand intellectual laziness. And offering the invitation to another woman before I've even turned it down is plain bad manners."

"I don't like it either," he said carefully. "I didn't describe your ideology, disparagingly or otherwise. You called mine patriarchal superstition. Christianity's track record is surely irrelevant to its objective veracity. And popularity is a poor basis for any intellectual commitment. More important than any of this: I apologise. I didn't realise you might want to come. You must have my ticket, as I've now given the other one away."

"Oh no, but ..." Charlotte started.

"I would be very interested to know why this conversation is distressing you, but I don't think it's the right time to find out so I suggest we change the subject. Will you be going home for Christmas?" It wasn't clear which of them he was addressing.

Clare swept up her bag and left the room.

Charlotte opened her mouth, then thought better of it. She breathed in the very different silence. There was a plash from the river, through the open window. A swan joining its mate, perhaps: it was too late in the year and the day for human river traffic. The night sighed.

She managed to stop herself saying, "Sorry" again. She had come to borrow a book, but it came out as, "Advent's far lovelier than Christmas. Though I love Christmas Eve too."

After a while Theo said, "It's certainly more important."

She wondered whether she should offer to make tea. Would he consider this presumptuous? Or even notice? She hadn't fathomed the difference between the imperceptibly tiny fern seeds he examined in close detail, and the massive great elephants stomping across his path which he didn't see at all.

"Yes, please," he said.

She crossed the room and switched the kettle on.

Her mother had advised an early night, a good book and an innocuous drink. When she reached her room it was the wrong side of midnight, she'd forgotten the book and had drunk a third of a bottle of homemade strawberry wine. By the way she was viciously attacked by her bedroom door she deduced it was stronger than it had tasted. Her mind was whirling with rags of conversation she longed to process.

She washed her face, threatened her mouth with a toothbrush and was under her duvet in minutes, looking forward to savouring her memory of the last two hours. The next thing she heard was Theo's voice telling her it was breakfast time.

She sat up, astonished, until she remembered he had put an alarm on her iPhone. She laughed.

Charlotte wouldn't have thought it possible to make a trial for sexual assault so interminably dreary. It was not so much what was said, as the underlying insinuation and antagonism.

Suki had ranted the previous evening about the stupidity of Crispin's barrister. She kept going over details which were completely irrelevant: Suki's home background, the kind of friends she had and how she had spent her first year. As well as Crispin's research into children and his involvement in college life. Nothing to do with the facts.

Charlotte had a dull and weary suspicion that, on the contrary, Samantha McKenna was very expensive indeed and knew exactly what she was doing.

She gazed around the courtroom. A few looked like reporters, scribbling on pads. Which one had savaged her friend? And why? How could anyone be so cruel?

Behind Crispin she saw a man who, she realised after she had been staring at him for a while, resembled him, though older. He caught her eye, set his mouth in a grim smile and then winked horribly. Charlotte turned away. He looked like a man intending to win.

She had a supervision later that day and had been unable to do any work for it. She had told her kind, elderly supervisor that she would be supporting a friend in a court case. By now he would have seen the glaring headlines.

She felt sickened.

It wasn't that Professor Postle never talked about sex. The previous week he had gone into graphic detail about the *suppostaque furta* of Pasiphaë's under-coupling with the bull at Minos resulting in the grotesque Minotaur, and of the hollow cow made for the girl to climb into to satisfy her bestial desires. So why should Charlotte squirm at the thought of his knowing the far less prurient details of a bishop's daughter and the flirtations she had had in her first year which even Charlotte had known nothing of? When Suki was persuaded to take her top off after a party before deciding she didn't want to go any further; or the President of the JCR who had thought she had invited him into her bed? Both of which were now in the public domain along with Suki's barely pixillated features.

The very clergy in Suki's father's diocese would be able to recognise her coat and hair. Those who had castigated the bishop for his gentle sympathy years earlier over remarrying divorcées – or was it same-sex partnerships? – would be rubbing their hands in unChristian glee.

She glanced at Suki beside her. She was white and trembling.

Theo was impressed that an even worse pub could exist. This time, the man calling himself 'Mike' suggested one of a chain. The website showed dark lacquered wood, steel tubular chairs and a promotional photograph of the new urinals.

Theo drew the line, not at folk dancing and incest, but at Applied Mathematics. Otherwise he liked to embrace every experience. So he asked for the most unpleasant-looking drink he could see and set himself the challenge of enjoying it.

The other man didn't seem to be there. Theo wondered whether he was late on purpose. He saw a sign saying 'Blokes' and made for it out of curiosity for the cynosure.

"What the hell?" the other man, his trousers open, almost shouted at him.

"Take your time," Theo said cheerfully. "They're supposed to be one of the attractions of the place." By the time 'Mike' emerged, slightly more composed, Theo was toying with something cloudy enough to be camel pee. "Reaper's Revenge," he explained. "I'm not sure whether it's cider or a Terry Pratchett novel."

'Mike' sat on the edge of a stool. "What did you think of the Turing notes?" The hands smoothing his hair seemed unsteady.

"Notes. Turing's. No more interesting than my own lecture notes. A bit like Picasso's shopping list."

"You're disappointed?"

"Not at all."

The pub droned around them: an irritating fruit machine; the murmuring of the other drinkers.

"I have access to others."

"You said."

"Wiles. His proof of Fermat. Maths's biggest prize of the last century, and Cambridge's."

"My teacher taught him. I met him at her sixtieth birthday party. The trouble is," he said, taking another swig, "that you can't really taste the apples. That's the test. The hops, the fruit, the malt."

The other drank his Foster's. "Or Gauss." He looked at Theo carefully. "Carl Gauss, you know."

"His shopping list?"

"*Disquisitiones Arithmeticae*. Maybe."

"You have Gauss's *Disquisitiones Arithmeticae*? The original? Or a copy?" A friend of Ann's, a theatre director, was fond of saying Theo should have been an actor. He was quick of study, and took direction faithfully. His eyebrows were raised. "First draft?"

"I've got photographs. If you'd be more interested in that than the Wiles."

Theo finished his drink. It was quite an achievement. "That would be exciting."

The other waited. He didn't want to move too soon. "Here." Out of the pocket of his donkey jacket he produced a memory stick. "Have a look."

Theo reached down for the laptop case which he carried almost everywhere except in a punt. He plugged the stick into his MacBook. One document showed in the contents.

It had taken him many years and far more punishments to learn that what passed as a moment to him could be a very long time to someone else. His companion fidgeted. "Want another?" he said, standing up.

"Thank you," Theo said. "Tell the barman to surprise me."

'Mike' went to the bar.

Control-shift; command; copy. Instinctive. His laptop would download the contents. Officially there was nothing else on the stick. But there would be shadows, memories of old transactions no longer visible to the naked eye. No memory is ever irretrievably lost. All Theo's life his curiosity had led him into trouble.

"It's called 'Harvester's Hangover'," he was told as another muddy pint was put before him.

"Very exciting, this," Theo said frankly, logging the memory stick out and handing it back. "How much would you want for it?"

"Forty-two point seven eight two."

"Marigolds?"

"This week. If it was more than a week I'd have to re-calculate."

"The currency will have changed by tomorrow."

"I'll take that risk. They're going down at the moment so it's more my risk than yours."

"This drink," Theo said, "is considerably more unpleasant than the last one."

"I asked for exactly what you said."

"I didn't think surprise was still possible." He took another pull on it. It was worse the second time. "I'll take it." The other man looked as if he didn't quite understand. "Do you want the money transferred tonight?"

The other drank, carefully. "It might take me a day or two to get hold of it. Tomorrow night?"

"Out of interest, how do you know it's genuine?" Theo asked.

"Didn't you get the Turing tested?" he said, too quickly.

"I assumed you had."

"I meant. I assumed . . ."

"You want to bring it to my rooms?"

"There are porters guarding the gate."

Theo laughed. "Tell them you're my guest. And those are custodians, not porters."

"I'd prefer a pub. Hat and Feathers, Barton Road, eight o'clock."

"I don't do eight o'clock, really. I just do evening."

"Oh for fuck's . . ." he stopped. Twice in one evening: not good. Finished his drink. Calmed down. "I'll see you then."

Theo watched him thread his way out of the pub. He tried the drink a third time, then pushed it aside. He opened his laptop and looked at it for a while.

He was thinking about something else. Some invisible memory. Somewhere, in the computer of his brain, an imprint had been made and then erased again.

It always remains somewhere, if you know where to look for it.

Chapter Twenty-Five

EIGHTH WEEK

"You were done," DC Andy said bluntly, throwing the manuscript onto Theo's desk and disturbing the ergodic theory he had been working on. "The Turing was genuine. The Gauss is fake. Rather a good one: he knows what he's doing, or has friends who do. I'll come on to that."

"Thanks," Theo said, adjusting the screwdriver under the kettle. "Oh, you drink coffee, don't you?"

"Please."

"I don't have any."

"I don't then, do I?"

"I can usually borrow some."

"Isn't it quicker to buy your own?"

Theo considered. "It depends how you measure it. If you're just looking at the time it takes to go upstairs and knock on half a dozen doors, say thank you, buy flowers in return and so on; as against taking coffee off the shelf when I'm in Sainsbury's anyway buying tea, then of course, yes. But if you factor in changing my mindset to imagine what it's like to want coffee instead of tea, re-programming the software to remember this next time I'm out, all the things it might then not do which it was programmed to do before such as remembering that I prefer full cream milk in my tea to semi-skimmed . . ."

"It doesn't matter," Andy said. "I just wondered."

"I'll work it out sometime."

"Please don't." He realised Theo's precision was important in the programming process. It seemed less useful for making beverages. "Just give me tea. Strong with sugar."

"I don't usually have sugar."

"Bugger me."

"I'm tempted to say something in response to that. Probably because I've been spending time with my younger brother and his humour is a little infectious."

"How much did you spend on this forgery?"

"Cryptocurrency or sterling?"

"Couldn't be worse, could it!" Andy shook his head. "Presumably the currency isn't traceable?"

"It's a lot more traceable than a picture of the Queen with 'I promise to pay the bearer' on it. Though that's not necessarily an advantage."

"Whose side are you on?"

"I mean generally, not in this instance. We need a wider choice of anonymous transactions. Including digital cash. The ideal would be a version of David Chaum's e-cash, sanctioned by the Bank of England."

"You realise I'm not following you at all?"

"In the meantime, cryptocurrency is the next best thing. About a third of us now have a telephone but no bank account. How can we make transactions, using the old money?"

"The kind of people who don't have bank accounts aren't the sort who want their money traceable. Believe me, I get to know some of them quite well. After arresting them."

"You're being very parochial," Theo said. "I mean people who live in villages several days' journey from the nearest town, who wouldn't know what a flushing lavatory was let alone a bank. They all have telephones. Cryptocurrency is the next thing they need after a clean well. And a mosquito net."

"So when you and your friend Mike here have finished doing time together . . ."

"That assumption makes me so cross. There's nothing dodgy about cryptocurrency. The fact that criminals prefer to operate at night doesn't make night-time intrinsically more evil. Silk Road was busted years ago."

"Might make it more dangerous."

"You have to be careful using any money. Ten grand."

"What?"

"Sterling."

"Wow."

"Gauss's *Disquisitiones Arithmeticae* would have been fun. I mean, a lot. Of."

"You prat," Andy said affectionately.

Theo pulled a chair up to his wardrobe, stood on it and started pulling boxes down. Eventually he found one labelled, 'Winnie-the-Pooh Soc' in felt pen. He emptied out plastic cups and spoons, a log-book and various files of paperwork before producing a battered and nearly empty bag of lumpy sugar.

"Here you are. I'll reimburse the Pooh Soc."

"I'm not going to nick you for taking a spoonful of sugar from a university society."

"It's Pembroke College, not the university. And the sugar doesn't belong to Pembroke, but to the members. As I'm one and I don't take sugar, you could probably legitimately have my share."

"Didn't you realise," Andy said, "that he was a con? Thought you had a nose for that kind of thing."

"Not a nose, no. That's exactly what I don't have. Which is why I compute all the details consciously. Takes me longer. But I get much more accurate results."

"So what went wrong?"

"And yes I did," Theo chewed his lip. "But I got over-excited. The Gauss would have been . . . well." He smiled. "Have you ever been in a situation," he thought for the right analogy, "when you know you ought to go to work, say. Or home to Wendy. But you meet a naked woman in the street inviting you to fuck her and you get distracted. I'm not sure I quite got that image right, did I?"

Andy was laughing so much he had to put his tea down so as not to spill it. "I've never heard you use that word before," he said, wiping his eyes. "But I get the idea."

Theo drank his tea thoughtfully. "It's sad that it's not. The naked woman. Wanting to make love to me for the rest of my life."

"They don't," Andy said. "Those kind of women."

Charlotte was trying to get her essay done. She felt doubly guilty: for excusing herself from Suki's afternoon court session; and for being late with Professor Postle's assignment.

'To what extent does Sophocles' use of dramatic irony win sympathy for the protagonist in *Oedipus Tyrannus*?'

She found the play challenging, but intensely enjoyable. She loved the poetic repetition: the way a speech would contain the same word in different forms, sometimes the negative immediately following the positive; reinforcing the sound while contradicting the meaning.

She read again Oepidus's eloquent commitment to hunt out the murderer and bring healing to his people.

She chewed her pen, wondering what it reminded her of. Outside, waves of late autumn leaves swam giddily past in a continuous relay. A heavy cobweb had formed beyond the glass, presumably overnight, presided over by a fat, silent spider with the sun glinting on its dull yellow cross-gartering.

Titania, that was it. Wrong play: right author. She had played the Faerie Queene in an edited version of the *Dreame* at school and was astonished, as she finished her angry speech to Oberon about their domestic squabble affecting the whole of creation, when an audience of other people's parents met her exit with a round of applause.

Thebes in the fifth century BC, like Athens at a distance of two thousand miles and years, was groaning under the discord of those in high places. Perhaps that was where Shakespeare got it from.

Irony.

Sophocles' audience would all have known, as the king did not, that he must eventually face his guilt. In a thoroughly anachronistic (and rather childish) way, she felt irritated with Oedipus for the brutal punishment he meted out on himself. At the moment she didn't feel any sympathy for him at all.

She resumed writing.

'Ignorance. Guilt. Punishment (self-inflicted). Exile. Blindness.' It didn't amount to much, but it shifted her thoughts. 'Intro' she wrote underneath.

There was a knock on the door.

She knew it was Suki even before she entered, hair distressed, face drawn down like a tragic mask.

"He's acquitted, Charlie. They found him innocent."

Charlotte's mind was still in a distant stone amphitheatre, dusty with the glorious Greek summer of some two and a half thousand years ago, an urgent Chorus intoning disaster in the undulating splashes and swirls of the woeful metre which punctuated the characters' plangent hexameter. It took her a moment to work out what Suki was talking about. How could they have the verdict the same day?

"What do you mean, innocent? You mean, not guilty?"

"I'm the one that's guilty. Apparently."

"Suki, stop." Charlotte was so confused she didn't know where to start. "You aren't a suspect. You're a witness, looking for justice. You can't be accused."

"You think?" Suki said. She had grown up, since the morning. As if she understood things she'd never known before. "If only I'd listened to you. I should have left things alone."

"You can't be thought guilty of anything."

"In whose eyes?" Charlotte was silenced. After the first twenty or thirty tweets, she had stopped reading. Suki was a liar; a slut; a vicious conniving bitch. The calls for her anonymity to be waived were clamorous. Charlotte wished she hadn't seen any of it. "The worst," Suki said, "was a text from someone in New Zealand."

"New Zealand? A *text*? How?"

"Saying I'd let down all Christians everywhere and should be thrown out of the church."

"Suki, I'm so sorry. I wish I'd been there for you."

Suki shook her head angrily, her few disregarded tears smearing her cheeks. "Wouldn't have made any difference. I thought . . ." She glanced round Charlotte's little room, as if seeing it for the first time, "having him all over me was the worst thing. It was so disgusting. Tongue. Fingers. Worse." Her face was ugly with distress. "What I didn't realise is that the press can violate you far more horribly." She kneaded her eyes with the heels of her hands, as if trying to rub it all away. "Shit. I'm not supposed to do that. I've lost a contact lens."

The next few minutes were spent trying to find it. Suki could feel it, stuck in her lid. Eventually Charlotte retrieved it, but it couldn't be put back in without saline solution. "Can't see a thing now."

"I suppose," Charlotte thought back, "that woman in the dowdy suit was his mother? They seemed very close."

"Who cares?" Suki said.

"I don't know why the press couldn't tell the truth. It's always more interesting."

"I've never felt like this before," Suki said so quietly Charlotte had to strain to hear.

"Like what?"

"That I want to die."

Charlotte sat next to her on her bed. "It will go. Trust me. That feeling."

"I suppose I'll be better away from Cambridge. Don't want to go home though."

"Next term ..."

"There won't be a next term."

"You don't mean that. Suki, you love it here."

"I did. Once. I can't stay."

Charlotte was at a loss. Where to start? "You worked so hard to get here. Don't you remember? When you were seventeen and I was still in the Upper Fifth, and you said this was the one thing you wanted. I'm only here because of you."

"Really?"

"Truly."

"Perhaps it's because it was what my parents wanted. My father was at KCL."

Charlotte wondered what it would be like to study in a bustling metropolis. Where would the autumn leaves be, drifting into the river? How would you go to the theatre at five minutes' notice?

"I'm a liar, Charlie. A privileged, stuck up, lying bitch."

"You are absolutely not. Though they did call us privileged ..."

"Over and over again."

"Well, we are. It's only in the Daily Mail that it's an insult. Look, I realise what I'm about to say is politically incorrect." Was it even wise? She didn't know. She simply knew she had to believe it. "What the jury decided ..." She wondered how to make it less callous. "For one thing, he was *not* found innocent. Not-guilty is not innocent."

"Amounts to the same thing."

"It really doesn't. It means there wasn't enough evidence. You know differently. That's what matters."

"He nearly raped me. He might with the next person."

"Yes, but he *didn't*," she pointed out. "He won't, after this. You have protected the next person. By going through all this. And there's a reason victims are called survivors. What matters is . . . I realise this sounds trivial . . . that you get your degree. Obviously I don't mean that, exactly. The piece of paper doesn't matter."

"It does," Suki said sadly.

"All right, it does. The point is, that you get on with your life. Otherwise, he's won. I don't mean Crispin has won, because I don't suppose he set out to wreck your life. What I mean is . . ." she couldn't think of a better way to say it, "evil has won."

"Do you believe in evil?" Suki asked, as suddenly as if they'd been talking about matters of academic interest. "My dad says some of his clergy do. They believe in a Devil. Literally. I'd always thought that was bonkers."

Charlotte wasn't sure how to handle the quicksilver change.

"Don't see why not, intellectually. If God exists, it's just as rational. But the Devil doesn't seem so credible emotionally, somehow."

"You'd better do your essay," Suki reminded her, standing up and shaking out her clothes. It was cold out, but she hadn't worn her beautiful coat.

"My supervision's in an hour."

"It doesn't matter anyway."

"What doesn't?"

"Whether I degrade or not. Everybody does."

Charlotte stood too, and took Suki's hands. "Suki, it really does. And no they don't. And a lot who do, don't come back."

"No, well. Write your essay. So you don't have to as well." She hugged Charlotte rather suddenly, and left.

It was barely four o'clock but almost black outside. Charlotte switched on the light.

Guilt. Sympathy. Punishment.

'Argent.' The word for silver and money is the same in ninety-two languages. For a long time we used commodity-money. Salt. Gold.

Silver. In the seventeenth and eighteenth centuries, we moved from commodity to representative money. Our banks still had gold behind them, which the 'money' represented. Until in 1914 the Bank of England, worried about a gold rush, took its paper notes off the Gold Standard.

If we hadn't done this – and Germany too – the Great War would indeed have been over by Christmas. We wouldn't have been able to afford the troops and armaments and other hardware of war. Perhaps the young blood poured out in Ypres could be laid at the door, not of politicians and generals and warmongers, so much as of economists.

By the nineteen seventies every country other than Switzerland had dissociated its money from the Gold Standard. By the eighties, electronic banking had become the norm.

Today, 97% of the world's money is not really money at all.

States and banks have acquired unimaginable power over a century. And half the adults in the world have no access to financial services. Three and a half billion people have a telephone but no bank account.

In a world which has developed a taste for democracy, this control by the few of the most important asset of the many had become unsustainable.

On 18th August 2008 a domain name was registered: bitcoin.org. Coincidentally there was also a global financial crisis such as had not been experienced since the Great Depression. On 3rd January 2009, the Chancellor of the Exchequer, Alistair Darling, announced his second bail-out of the British banks. And the first fifty bitcoins were 'mined'.

A currency had been launched which could change the world.

Theo had paid for his two items – the dull but indubitably genuine Turing notes, and the exciting but fake Gauss *Mathematica* &c., – with Marigolds. By transferring the record of cryptocurrency from his account to someone else's. Which is, of course, as secure as any other payment. Like a conventional bank transfer.

Long ago, when Ann told Theo he must talk about his feelings, his first task was to recognise what they were. Even Ann hadn't given him a map. 'Anger feels like this; happiness, fear, love . . . like that,' and so on. Eventually he realised that others, neurotypicals as he learnt they were called, knew all this already. It would be interesting to know how.

Unhappiness was the first he identified. When he was a child, if his pencil broke or he picked a stinging nettle, that was, presumably, 'unhappiness'. If a grown up gave him an ice cream that was a kind of 'happiness'. These feelings were manageable. So when Alan was alive he could assume he was mostly happy. At that age he'd had a good memory. If you'd asked him, aged seven, what he'd done on such and such a day when he was three, he could have told you. If he could have identified the day correctly.

By the time he was twelve or thirteen, he couldn't remember the previous lesson.

"Did you have a nice weekend?" some well-meaning adult would say, throwing him into a misery of doubt. What weekend? And what had he done in it? Let alone such a complicated question as whether it was 'nice'. He often had no idea whether he'd had lunch . . . until he looked at the school clock, saw it was two o'clock and didn't remember anyone shouting at him for missing it.

He looked for a pattern, and a pattern emerged. In the holidays, he could remember his cousin coming for the afternoon, Ann buying a new dress, everything. He operated more or less according to the instruction manual: played the piano; read books on computing; ate meals with Ann when she reminded him.

At school he couldn't remember anything. He must have got through lessons somehow or he would have been shouted at even more. But he didn't manage homework or exams or any of the other tasks.

So by the age of fourteen or so, he came to define the forgetting mode as 'unhappiness' and the remembering mode as, if not quite 'happiness', at least a reduction in his unhappiness. It wasn't very accurate as a coding system, but it was a start.

'Love' was what he felt for Ann, of course; Alan when he was alive; presumably his brother Charlie. 'Falling in love' was far more complicated. Obviously, he must be in love with Clare . . . He wondered what it would be like to live in a culture where Ann could choose a wife for him and they could just get on with it.

Anger was harder because he had less material. This emotion which was currently preventing him from working must be, if not quite anger, extreme irritation. Not with 'Mike', who had acted according to character so that wasn't annoying. On the rare occasions when Theo had been allowed to take part in competitive games – when he hadn't been excluded as a punishment for being late – he much preferred the best team to win, whether or not it was the team he was on. It was uncomfortable to be on the winning side if it wasn't the best.

So he must be annoyed with himself. He had known it was fake but had gone ahead anyway. He had done that about something else, earlier in the term . . . He remembered getting very drunk, sandwiched between two experiences he wanted to forget.

So far, 'Mike' had played better. The solution was for him, Theo, to improve his game. This shouldn't be difficult, now there wasn't any Gauss so he was thinking rationally again.

If you give somebody a gold bar, it is his. Until he gives it back to you. Or until you find out where he has hidden it in his bedroom and go and remove it. Which you might if he has sold you a fake, and you have read enough PG Wodehouse. You could even return the fake at the same time as removing the gold bar from the top of his wardrobe.

In the same way, if someone persuaded you to transfer money under false pretences, and you worked in the bank (say) and could transfer it back again . . . well, why wouldn't you? If you could do so with impunity.

All Theo had to do, to put the record straight, was put his Marigolds back in his own wallet. It might take him a little longer to work out the morality of the operation: ethics were outside his area of expertise.

But transferring Marigolds back into his account ought to be within his competence.

Chapter Twenty-Six

END OF TERM

To achieve this, Theo liked the idea of a side channel attack – a physical, rather than mathematical approach – for the same sort of reason that wartime codebreaking appeals to a schoolboy.

In the early days of computing in Cambridge in the 1960s, it was possible to crack passwords by listening. The machines were so unwieldy you could hear the data going through – like cracking an old-fashioned safe – for instance by attaching an oscilloscope to a power line next door. Sooner or later the password was bound to be typed in. Decades on, the method was more sophisticated but still basically the same.

Unfortunately, Theo didn't know where his adversary lived. Stalking him would be time-consuming . . . and cold at this time of year.

Being a member of the Assassins' Guild in his first term had arguably helped Theo's studies. The only places you can't be killed are in a lecture or a supervision. By Third Week he was getting up in the middle of the night, and arriving at lecture halls before anyone else could possibly be up stalking the streets in a high collar or low hat, sporting a calculator labelled 'pistol at dawn'.

Theo's weapon was a large polystyrene box on which he had written, 'grand piano'. After dashing into a friend's second floor room having spotted someone he'd been following for weeks, he miscalculated the physics and over-compensated for wind-resistance, and instead of braining the second year Engineer at Caius his lethal weapon fell on the delicate hat of the wife of a member of the House of Lords who was visiting the college for the purpose of being relieved of much of his disposable cash. The wife suffered a sense of humour failure over her beloved plumage, which she had designed (along with her milliner and quite a lot more of said disposable cash) originally for the occasion of her husband's ennoblement, and which had been pointing perkily upwards before it met a grand piano on its way down. Albeit a polystyrene one. Not being a university type and having only her looks to fall back on, she felt the humiliation keenly.

Theo was forced to make a run for it and abandon his grand piano.

The Caius Engineer survived far longer than Theo – who was killed by an eighteenth century musket disguised as a party popper (approved by the Committee only by a whisker, on account of potential danger to the eyes). He knew half a dozen Assassins had conspired against him, and took it as a compliment.

Thus he knew how long it could take to track someone whose college and subject you know in advance. Even with DC Andy's help (and he suspected there could be a legal issue here) a side channel attack was out of the question.

With a twinge of regret, he considered the memory stick instead.

When he had copied it – in the pub with the well-publicised urinals which seemed to feed the beer taps – it was not because he had any sinister intention. After all, the stick was wiped clean.

But everything leaves a footprint. It was no more clean than Theo's memories of his childhood. When he cast his mind back to before his multiple unhappinesses, his database presented a baffling blank. But his recollections must still be there. Someone with sufficient skill could find them.

Similarly, unless the stick had been brand new before the Gauss was imprinted, there would be treasure, or more probably dross, there. And then Theo might find the gleaming thread in the Labyrinth, leading into the moonlight.

Thus he dabbled in the digital backwater, looking at the grey shadows lurking in the Underworld of the downloaded. He found a lot of deleted rubbish: files with no names; unwanted contact details; dreary photographs; skeletons of system files. The usual detritus kicking around Gehenna along with other virtual refuse.

And a couple of password-protected files that looked interesting.

He looked out of his window towards the river. It was barely teatime but the panes were dark, the trees waving their black fingers against the night. Theo loved all seasons, the changing and turning of the English climate. And the season he loved best was always the one he was in. Now he revelled in the cosy afternoons, the night-time which started almost before he was dressed, the long productive evenings when he could study hour after hour without interruption – especially out of term, when he didn't even stop for dinner. He kept the same food, always, in the communal kitchen so he didn't spend time thinking about what to eat: a ready combination of carbohydrate, protein, vitamins.

By the sky he estimated it was between four fifteen and four thirty. He had that uncomfortable feeling in his stomach which sometimes denoted hunger (and sometimes something completely different), so he went to make his sandwich. By the time he returned it was nearly five by the sky.

He Googled for a password cracker and downloaded fcrackzip. It was crude, designed to break a password by brute force. He set it to work. Shortly afterwards it advised Theo that it should be able to find the password he wanted in 28,682,713.5 years, approximately. Call it thirty million.

Even for Theo this seemed a long time.

More searching produced John the Ripper, a word list and set of variations. It should guess any reasonable password invented by a human. It was Open Source, so there were as many different versions as there were interested developers. It took several failed attempts (the usual steps – 'configure'; 'make'; 'make install' – had never worked in Theo's experience) before he realised it couldn't operate on ZIP files. He found another version which didn't require compiling from source code. This, too, was free. Another search for a free word list, and everything was ready.

It was an odd experience. Cracking a password must be a common requirement. And yet no one had made it easy. It was like reading a paper on a difficult topic written by the only person who understands it, who hasn't bothered to make his work comprehensible to anyone else. Einstein's *Beiblätter zu den Annalen der Physik* (1905) came to mind.

He set it to run. By this time it was still an hour or two earlier (or perhaps twenty-three or -two hours later) than his usual bedtime . . . but as there seemed no more point in a programmer watching his computer work than in a householder staying up to ensure his dog barked at intruders, he went to bed anyway.

As soon as he was awake and without even waiting for his Teasmade, Theo leapt out of bed and checked for results. To his frustration his computer had gone fuzzy and was difficult to read. Perhaps it would calm down in the communal fridge. He went to get his kettle to fill at the same time, picked up his spectacles from his bedside cabinet and found they fixed the problem more simply.

The program had finished without a result. If he allowed it to try all variants it could take a month. Which was all very well, but he might want to turn his computer off occasionally.

He found a more efficient word list for $30. He had no idea whether the exercise was worth $30, but he had begun on a problem and this was the next step.

By lunchtime – for the rest of England: Theo was yet to remember breakfast – his computer handed him the password.

Henry1441.

No wonder it could be cracked by readily-available software in less than a day. Theo was seriously annoyed. How can crime be overcome if people who understand computing – as 'Mike' obviously did – are so slapdash? A password with sufficient entropy to be dependable should take billions of years to guess. Presumably his excuse was that he had deleted the files.

Still, it was more secure than the date of his mother's first marriage. And no worse than the passwords of most of his friends – other than mathematicians and computer scientists, who randomise theirs properly and then remember them with acronyms.

He opened one of the password-protected files. By fluke, it was 'Mike's' Marigold wallet. Now it should be straightforward to pay himself back.

Should he transfer the amount he had paid? Or adjust for fluctuations in Marigolds since? On balance, probably the latter. The downside was that 'Mike' wouldn't then recognise the sum and understand what had happened. Too bad. The currency had increased, so Theo would be short-changing himself.

Was it a criminal act? Certainly not legally, because British law still doesn't recognise cryptocurrency. Why, is as incomprehensible as it was that for years banks would take days to make transfers which took seconds in real time.

In 2013 Theo had tried to get himself regulated by the Financial Conduct Authority. He rang for advice and was told to read the website. Which, obviously, he had already done. 'What,' he asked, 'is a payment instrument?' The baffled advisor suggested consulting a lawyer. So he travelled to London and paid a solicitor to tell him that bitcoins don't constitute currency. There was nothing to regulate. And yet the Inland Revenue was willing to accept the tax he insisted he owed for the profits of his non-existent trading.

So removing Marigolds from 'Mike's' wallet could not be a crime in any sense that DC Andy would recognise. But was it morally a crime? Instead of acting unilaterally, should he go to the police, report the fraud, describe the perpetrator, admit he knew neither his address nor his name and wait several months for PC Plod to report back that he couldn't trace his defrauder, didn't understand the currency, hadn't grasped what had happened and was overwhelmed with paperwork anyway?

A bit like reporting bullying to teachers in the Staff Room who had just sat down for coffee.

Suki's tutor had done her sympathetic best, advising that she might feel differently after Christmas with her parents. The suggestion filled Suki with fresh horror. She imagined the party they hosted annually for her father's clergy, any of whom could read of the 'Cambridge student, daughter of a senior member of the Church of England', a description more recognisable than strictly accurate. Suki had already found a forum dedicated to finishing off what Crispin had begun. She had been named more times that she could count and had received several death threats. As well as exaggerated, fanciful and extremely uncomplimentary descriptions of intimate parts of her anatomy.

Dr Henley, the gentle Archeologist in charge of her pastoral welfare, wished Suki would tell her parents. She had met the bishop's wife and found her vaguely comforting in a sort of bustling way.

Suki's Director of Studies, by contrast, had seen very little work from her all term and had already accepted her resignation with arguably indecent alacrity.

When Charlotte called to say goodbye she found her friend surrounded by boxes, waiting forlornly for her mother.

"Woo-woo," the call came up the stairs, like a duck summoning its ducklings. The same for the waifs and strays she found under her husband's clerical wing.

"Hello Ruth." Charlotte went into the corridor to show her which was her daughter's room.

"Hello, Charlotte darling. Do you know what this ridiculous business is about?"

"She's in here." Charlotte indicated where Suki had heard their exchange.

Twice Charlotte let Suki go ahead of her as they carried her belongings to the car, in the hope of speaking to her mother. Eventually, Suki went to the loo.

"I think it would be good if she could talk to you about it."

"Couldn't you tell me, Charlotte, dear? A journalist rang my husband for a comment, and we didn't know what on earth it was about. Apparently Suki's all over Twitter."

"She's been very badly hurt. You mustn't tell her I've said even this much."

"It makes it very difficult. I hate any kind of deceit. We'll be having our usual Christmas party. You'll be home?"

"Not until Christmas Eve. I'm helping with the Nine Lessons and Carols."

"Lovely! I'll listen out for you. If I'm not too busy on the day, which I always am."

Charlotte went back upstairs. The abandoned room looked sadly onto the autumn-tousled garden. On the floor was a button from Suki's tapestry coat. Charlotte put it in her pocket, realising suddenly that she might never wear it again.

Just as she might never come back to finish her degree.

Theo's head was full of bees.

Having had fun cracking passwords, he had turned his mind back to work.

An idea was shimmering just out of his line of vision. Every time he turned, it shifted. If only he could get enough silence.

If his transference principles could be applied to a multiplicative structure – or a translate of a multiplicative structure – as well as an additive one, perhaps he could start to see interesting behaviour in the primes.

The implications were ... was 'momentous' the word he wanted?

He put the problem aside to think about itself, only to find his conscious mind making idiotic mistakes. He bought his advance train ticket for a conference in February, and booked the right weekday of the wrong week. The ticket couldn't be changed so he had to buy another, spending almost as much as if he'd bought at the time of travel. He then nearly got the time wrong, and finally forgot to book the quiet carriage. This could possibly be rectified, but in the meantime he went up to the kitchen to fill his kettle and broke someone else's plate.

Fortunately it was a college one. He decided to content himself with damage limitation.

He contemplated going to the Eagle for a lunchtime pint, but he wouldn't be able to think there ... or indeed afterwards. So he put on the woollen overcoat which had been his grandfather's, a knitted scarf Ann had given him against the knives of Fenland wind, his leather-and-tweed gloves bought in a moment of extravagance in Bridge Street, and finally a flat cloth cap which he found at the bottom of his wardrobe, the origin of which was a mystery.

He went out through the back gate and kept going West, soon finding himself on a path which began to suggest countryside. He reached a small bridge. Breaking a couple of twigs from a branch, he dropped them in the stream. There had been research results published a year or two previously as to the best weight and shape of stick for a competitive edge in the game of Pooh Sticks: short and stubby, rather than long and bent. Theo had little objection to the Research of the Blindingly Obvious – chocolate makes girls happy; being fat slows you down – but he drew the line at physics which an intelligent four-year-old could work out. Curiously, when the Pembroke Pooh Soc collected its own data, the only conclusive result was that a stuffed toy donkey would sink before it reached the other side.

Theo's short stubby stick came in a nose after the long bent one.

He returned to his rooms. The buzzing had softened to a low murmuring. It was over his second glass of decentish Irish whiskey some time after midnight that the distracting annoyance cleared as a mist dispersing, and he could see what he had been looking for.

"Yes," he said softly, pushing his glass aside to be found sometime after Christmas. "Yes, yes, yes."

He had the first, crucial step. After which it is mostly persistence.

He had, perhaps, solved the oldest problem in Number Theory. The problem considered by Euclid. Just as Andrew Wiles had proved Fermat's Theorem.

He had changed the world.

What he had done was so significant that for a while, he didn't do anything. Not throw his arms in the air. Nor swing on his chair. Nor whoop or dance round the room. He didn't fling open his window into the silky darkness and halloo anyone's name to the reverberate hills.

He did nothing. Except thank God.

The God who had made him to think a certain way. Which, yes, made him slower at some tasks: Christmas shopping or choosing his socks; working out whether he was happy or hungry; knowing how to catch a train or find his bicycle. But if he didn't think differently, he wouldn't be who he was.

And he wouldn't have done this.

He sighed happily. He wondered what was the time. For a while he couldn't remember where to find this information, so tried his pocket. 'Saturday,' his crumpled handkerchief told him. He had an idea that life might have moved on without him, so he looked in a drawer where he found a clean handkerchief with lighter embroidery than all the rest. A soft, Cambridge blue. "Sunday," it informed him kindly.

Day of rest.

He had done enough for today. He would write it up in the morning.

Morning being a loose term, meaning any time before dark. Or afterwards, if he hadn't had breakfast yet.

PART III

Advent

Chapter Twenty-Seven

FIRST SUNDAY IN ADVENT

"It's Theophilus Ambrose Fitzwilliam Wedderburn here."

"Hello Theo."

"I've been a bit delayed. My bicycle wasn't where I'd left it."

"Will you not be able to come?"

"That is, it may be. My bicycle's memory is probably more reliable than mine. But as I'm not quite sure where there is – or rather, where where is . . . What? No. I mean yes. I just wondered if you could queue."

Charlotte smiled again, in relief this time.

"You know where my rooms are? River Court, Staircase U. Right-hand side. The first one is my sitting room. Beyond that, my bedroom. Which you don't need. Choose a couple of clean pieces of paper from my wastepaper basket. Use these to replace the tickets which are acting as bookmarks . . ."

Luckily she had plenty of time: the service wasn't until six; they had to be in their places by half past five.

". . . then turn off my lights, in both rooms, and shut the door. Sorry, I never told you to turn them on, did I? The inner door and then the oak. Then get in the queue for the South door . . . I'll text further instructions."

She wondered if it wouldn't be quicker for him to skip the texts and just get there, but the suggestion could become complicated.

The messages continued. ". . . through the Antechapel, through the Choir as far as you can go without jumping over the table. Ignore everyone else wanting to sit near the choir stalls . . . as far East as possible . . . Put your bottom in one of the seats and save the other with your hat or gloves or similar accessory. Theophilus A. Fitzwilliam Wedderburn."

"And leave my ticket at the South door. Theophilus A. Fitzwilliam Wedderburn."

"Of the Chapel, not the college. Theophilus A. Fitzwilliam Wedderburn."

The moment the doors were opened she walked briskly the entire length of the Chapel. She was just in time to get the last two front seats by the altar.

It was soon surprisingly noisy. Coughs, rustles, the occasional chair scraping. Long after the Chapel seemed full the congregation continued to stream in. Pale, soft light smoothed the walls, emphasising in shadowy relief the Tudor roses and crowns. The fan vaulting stretched its chiselled cobwebs far above, stone fingers spreading their tendrils across the sky. She gazed up at the painted glass, blind and meaningless in the darkness, wondering why Theo had suggested they sit so far out of the way.

She read through the lessons in the service booklet, anticipating the music with pleasure. Half past five came and went. All the seats were full except the one next to hers. Several people had asked if it was taken.

The calm which now seeped in was filled with soft organ playing. Suddenly and with sadness she accepted that he wasn't coming, and in an unwelcome flash of understanding realised why people found him infuriating.

At that moment, flapping through the organ screen behind a couple of ushers, she saw an explosion of hair and, as he got nearer, quite a lot of mud on his trousers.

"Had to get my gown," he explained. She looked round: no one else was wearing one.

He sank to the ground and knelt directly on the stone floor, head bowed. In all the soaring building no one else was visibly praying. She shut her eyes. When she opened them he was in his chair. Not for the first time, she found herself confused by his contradictions. In some ways, he seemed easier to understand than anyone, saying things exactly as they were without a tangle of emotions.

"When they removed the Victorian wooden panelling to restore the stonework," he said, "they found medieval graffiti. See the red scribbles?"

"What does it say?"

"Oh, Fred wold Jenet konning or something equally rude."

A moment later, "When I was a chorister, we went through a hypnotism craze. There was a boy called Pottersworth. Anything swinging set him off: chains, conkers, string. The boy next to him turned the page of *I Was Glad* and he fainted in the choir stall."

"He wasn't really called Pottersworth?"

"I expect not."

After a while, "Ann taught me to make small talk, to make people comfortable. I get the impression you're comfortable already?"

"I'm really comfortable, Theo. You don't need to make small talk."

"I'm not sure it counts in church anyway."

And then, "You will know what Ergodic Theory means."

"Um. I know what the words mean. 'Work way'?"

"Dynamical systems that run for a very long time. Like, say, the motion of the planets about the sun. I did something very exciting this morning. Or was it last night?"

At that moment, inexplicably, everyone suddenly stopped talking. The organ was playing some Bach which Charlotte couldn't place. The lighting bled away. Only tiny bursts of candlelight, like yellow stars, shimmered along the choir stalls beneath the black oak of the Fellows' stalls. The fan vaulting receded. They couldn't see to read, and Charlotte realised it must always have been this tenebrous of a winter's Evensong.

"This is the best moment of the year," he whispered finally. "Except for all the others."

I look from afar.

The lone tenor sounded from the other side of the organ loft. Charlotte, used to the far more daunting distance of a cathedral, was surprised at its clarity.

And lo, I see the power of God coming, and a cloud covering the whole earth.

The ringing familiarity of Isaiah. The choir progressing into the stalls. The congregation heaving to its feet, flashes of mobiles lighting programmes.

Of the Father's heart begotten.

She hoped she could remember the words.

Theo's deep baritone underpinned the tentative fumbling voices around her. It was like listening to dark chocolate. As she joined her voice to his – finding the lyrics more familiar with him beside her – his voice seemed to vibrate deep inside her.

Anthems followed. Readings. The choir split into side chapels, the antiphonal singing eerie.

Hymns; shielded telephones; shuffling.

The choir processed to the East and suddenly she and Theo were bathed in candlelight. Barely a couple of paces from them the singing enveloped her in Heaven. Trebles threaded impossible heights, basses solid ground beneath their feet, the sound weaving gold, under and above and around them. She closed her eyes and sank into it.

No wonder they were sitting in the East End. What matter the rest of the service, when it ended in such glory? The boys – one a Christmas card blonde; another Chinese; several impossibly young – showing a seriousness of purpose as only small children can. Prayers, blessings, committals, then to their feet for the final hymn. A dear favourite of hers:

Lo! He comes with clouds descending...

Wesley's swelling words, the proximity of the choir, the understated magnificence of the medieval architecture made her relieved Theo couldn't see her face. The building rang like a chalice with its famous seven second echo. Without looking, Theo handed her a handkerchief with "Sunday" in pale blue embroidery in one corner.

The voluntary ebbed away, the crowds had been shuffling out for twenty minutes, before they spoke again.

"Drat!"

"What?"

"I've lost an earring. It caught my scarf." They were nearly at the West door. She dropped to the stone floor, feeling with her palms, trying not to get her fingers trodden on by the throng. Theo flashed his iPhone.

"Oh, you have a light after all!"

"Of course. But that would have been cheating. If they wanted us to see, they have plenty of electricity."

They found the earring quickly, embedded in a crack.

"I wonder what this is," she commented curiously.

"What?"

"This metal ring in the floor. I've never noticed it."

In all the milling and shoving of the crowds, there was suddenly a dreadful stillness. Had she said something wrong? He stood up slowly, not really there any more.

"Theo? Is everything all right?" The pushing and elbowing continued.

"Mulled wine," he said eventually, with effort. "In Hall. Usually."

"Don't we need to be invited?"

"Let's go."

They came out into the cold night, and set off across the sacred lawn. "I've never done this before," she said. "Walked on the grass."

"Worth being a senior member for. You know the Trinity story?" She shook her head. "Two undergraduates. Dress up as tourist and porter. Wait till genuine Americans or Japanese are walking round, admiring the ruins. Fake student 'tourist' steps on grass. Fake 'porter' shouts for him to get off. 'Tourist' ignores him. 'Porter' calls again. Et cetera. 'Porter' pulls out toy gun and shoots. 'Tourist' explodes with blood capsules. Real tourists gape in horror. Real porters emerge into the mayhem."

Her laughter frosted the air.

"They were sent down."

"No!"

"I struggle to believe it too, but that's how the story goes. Shall we do it?"

"Let's!"

"Need to wait for summer."

They had arrived at the Founder's fountain in the middle of the lawn. "The Head Master of the choir school," Theo said, "used to skate on this water."

"When you were a boy?"

"Nineteen twenties. He suspended all lessons when the Cam froze over, so the boys could skate too."

"The river froze over?"

"The summers were long, the winters cold and a boy could buy happiness for sixpence."

"Theo?"

"Mmm?"

"Back there. Something upset you?"

He said nothing for a while. "Did it?"

"It looked like it."

"I have shut down," he said. "Some memories." The lawn stretched around them in the darkness. "Presumably because I needed to."

"Then don't let's open them again."

They looked at the Chapel, already diminished to a model, the windows lit up like tissue paper.

"The most beautiful place in the world," she said.

"Yes."

"Imagine if anything were to happen to it."

"I can't. It would make me too unhappy."

The silence was mutual.

"Think of all the people whose lives it represents," she continued eventually. "Stone-masons, glaziers, carpenters. Little boys singing; townspeople worshipping; Fellows and Provosts and Deans."

"During the war, they removed every pane of glass. An old professor told me that in the gales of 1987 he climbed onto the roof, alone, with no safety equipment, to save the windows. There was scaffolding up to clean the stonework, and he feared a pole might come loose."

"Like Bathsheba and Gabriel. Sorry," she remembered he was a mathmo. "Just a novel."

"He wasn't a night climber or anything. Luckily he found workmen up there, and left it to them."

"It's stood for, what, nearly six hundred years?"

They sighed in contentment.

"Do you suppose," he said, "there are rules against senior members *running* on the lawn?"

"No one here to ask."

"You'll have to keep up. If you're on the grass without a senior member they'll shoot you."

She didn't.

They arrived, flushed and out of breath, into the warmth of the dining hall.

"I've read it, I think."

"What?"

"*Far from the Madding Crowd.* That was sad too."

And he gave her a glass of mulled wine.

He wondered if he had drunk too much of the sickly wine. Then he rather wished he had drunk more. Then he wondered if this was what it felt like to be neurotypical. This . . . noise; tumult; confusion. Raucous jangle of yammering.

The night itself was as quiet as velvet.

After the service, its being still Sunday, he had not returned to his breakthrough. Instead, for relaxation, he had looked at the second of the files he had copied in the Puddle and Roadkill, or Blackhead and Pimple, or whatever that ghastly mass-produced place with the undrinkable carbonated additives had called itself.

And it was in the virtual twilight of that second deleted file, looking for he knew not what but certainly not what he found, that he stumbled across it, as suddenly as an explosives expert might stub his toe on an undetonated bomb from the Second World War . . . possibly admiring what he'd fallen over before he even thought how nearly he might lose his own limbs or eyesight or even life. Thus Theo found himself looking at a plan whose thoroughness took his breath away. Everything was organised in meticulous detail. It must have taken years.

Admiration was not the only appropriate response: he knew that. But there could be a lag before the other reaction caught up. As if, in the moment of splitting the atom, Rutherford had also had to face all the implications not just for atomic energy, but for Hiroshima and Nagasaki and what that meant for each and every last child and dog and bird caught up in those devastating mushrooms. Perhaps this mismatch was something he had experienced all his life. It could take him months to work out that because a girl was pretty, he presumably fancied her.

He pictured the smallest boy singing in the front row, barely a few steps away from them in the service now so distant he saw it as if through the tunnel of history. He looked impossibly young. Hair so fair it caught the candlelight like a halo.

That boy's parents would be at the service on Christmas Eve. Perhaps he had a younger sister who looked up to him, singing on the telly. Or an older, resolutely not jealous of her younger brother's opportunity. Grandparents, listening proudly on the radio. Uncles and aunts, remembering to tune in at the last minute as they wrapped presents or stuffed turkeys.

This child should have many years ahead of him. A career in music or law, academia or finance; perhaps humanitarian aid. A wife to marry, children to have.

If this plan went ahead his grandparents would never laugh at Christmas again, nor hear carols without weeping. They would curse everything they had blessed: the day he arrived in Cambridge for his voice trial, nervous and trembling, to be offered a coveted place in the most famous choir in the world. They would wish he had never hummed a note. For the rest of their lives that little boy's face would look up from his photograph on their piano, frozen in childhood, and twist the loss in their stomachs like a knife.

The pain Theo himself had gone through – which had shaped his life so bitterly – would be nothing to what that little girl would endure, defined by trauma, losing both parents and brother in one tragic incident.

One boy in the choir. There were sixteen of them.

The one whose parents Theo visited in Shanghai, whose name was like wind whipping through a hedgerow. Whose grandparents had no one else to leave their futures to. Whose uncle had the Marigold-miner factory and no children of his own.

The tenors and basses and counter tenors in the back row, reading for their degrees. Whose parents would wish their son had gone to any other university: why had they celebrated his success?

The organist, successor-but-one to Alan, murdered as Alan had been. Theo had seen a small girl in Chapel with her mother, too young to be at school perhaps, with Burne-Jones auburn ringlets and an old-fashioned face. She would wait eagerly on Christmas

Eve for a father who would never come home, who would never again play ball in the garden with her or explain figured bass or the feudal system. Even in adulthood she would never escape the pity of it, affecting everything she did: the career she chose, the first boy she couldn't bring home to meet a father she didn't have.

The Provost and his wife. The Fellows. BBC camera men and sound girls. Members of the public who had queued all night. How fortunate, those feckless few who arrived too late and merely heard the explosion on the radio.

Millions listening in as the Chapel shattered into the air and crumbled onto every last man and woman and chorister, and perhaps a few in the streets outside, caught by plummeting masonry.

The night bled slowly in through his opened curtains. The college didn't sleep – there was always somebody studying or prowling the grounds – but it did sigh into a state of rest.

Ann had given her two tickets to him, for the Christmas Eve service. In the face of such devastation his own death hardly seemed to matter. Except to Ann herself, losing him twenty years after his father: everything of Alan lost to her.

The morning seeped sadly across the room, sluggish in the dreary cold. Was it Monday still?

And then he remembered. Charlotte. She had told him, eyes bright, that she had volunteered to carry the cross.

Slowly, very slowly, he picked up his favourite mug, saying, 'My Best Son', which Alan had given him twenty years earlier, and looked at the dull glass throwing so little light into his drab room. He threw it at one of the panes, propelling it so hard that instead of hitting the frame and clattering clumsily to the floor (such gestures so seldom come off) it went through the window and into the garden. The sound of splintering was horribly satisfying.

Much later, he went out with his wastepaper basket to gather up the shards. They had scattered widely. He didn't want gardeners cutting themselves.

And there, lying untouched on the earth, was his childhood mug. He held it up and examined it. Not a chip missing.

Chapter Twenty-Eight

MONDAY, MORNING AND NIGHT

Theo had no idea how long the numbed and listless Cam had flowed past his window.

He was approximately aware, as he assumed most vaguely informed people are, that the contemporary British police have extremely sophisticated anti-terrorism resources. But he also knew, from the Chip and PIN fraud which had introduced him to DC Andy, that even police officers specialising in computer crime don't know nearly as much as a moderately competent academic. More gravely, he suspected they didn't know how little they knew. So the average randomly-picked sergeant at Reception would be unlikely to take him seriously. It was too big for him to believe.

Even DC Andy wouldn't, really. He would pass it on . . . and there was no guarantee the person he passed it to would understand either.

The Provost might. But like Theo himself, he had too much emotionally invested in the college. The Head Porter would be better.

He cast his mind back to the Advent Service, and how long the Chapel had taken to empty. Half an hour? But of course there must be no congregation to empty. No broadcast service, for the first time since 1930: a terrorist publicity coup he didn't have the energy to care about.

Theo had been told, mostly by exasperated English teachers, that he had no imagination. Obviously it is absurd to accuse a mathematician of being unimaginative. Though they were right in that he found the truth so endlessly fascinating he struggled to invent such pointless lies as, 'The Loud Bang in the Middle of the Night', or, 'A story beginning: "I hid it at the bottom of the garden . . .'".

Nevertheless he possessed, in vivid detail, an imagination his teachers could barely dream of. The day he nearly killed himself, his imagination had been so stark it might have shocked even his English master. As he stood on the school roof, the wind blowing him like a whistle, he pictured it precisely: what it would be to fall and fail; to break his back and not his neck; to spend some months in hospital, with physical pain now as well as emotional; to be given quarter for a year at most; for the bullying to resume, only worse; to be constrained for the rest of life by quadriplegia, dependent on others for ever.

He imagined his body breaking. But not breaking enough.

Now he pictured a stump where the Chapel had been. That iconic image, on every photographic calendar of Cambridge, a marvel of the past. Please God, no one would attempt to rebuild it: like making a taxidermist's model of a woman you have loved, and taking it to bed with you.

Just as Theo could envisage a billion stars, each larger than our sun, in a million possible universes; and numbers in their trillions, all friendly and accessible: so he could see an almost infinite ripple of tears puckering out into blighted lives; all the six degrees of connection to those who had been there; the sum of suffering of all who would always have a shadow where Christmas 2018 had been.

The Christians would continue, praying and reading the scriptures – perhaps better than before, unimpeded by such a costly heritage. But he, Theo . . . he would be spiritually lost. There would be no still small voice of silence in the centre of his storms. The Chapel had been his spiritual home since he was so small that when Ann first took him up the black wooden steps, into a vast, dark-oak-clad Fellow's stall with its commanding view, he couldn't see over the luxurious maroon velvet cushion and huge, leather-bound book full of the golden language of Cranmer.

Here his father had created the music of heaven which Theo hugged to his soul with a joy too deep for happiness, the more precious for having been snatched away from him, along with his father, just as he was entering into the beauty of it. A place where he could step aside from the triviality and banality and ephemeral cruelty of this world for an hour at a time, and swim into the deep slow current where God assured him all would be well and all manner of things would be well, if he could only keep faith with himself.

All this, someone wanted to destroy for some political cause which would barely last half a lifetime.

And this was where both imagination and empathy did fail him. Theo's basic difficulty was that he didn't believe in evil. It wasn't that he rejected, intellectually, this dogma of the Christian faith. If good could exist, so could bad. But just as some struggle to trust in God while rationally conceding the possibility of a divine Being, so Theo could not really fathom the existence of genuine wickedness for its own sake. There must be some explanation. A cause so utterly compelling that the nobility of its aim outweighed the collateral sorrow. He would have preferred to understand what, and why.

The significance of the password hit him like an electric shock. The founder's name: the year of foundation. The person who had done this knew the college. And perhaps loved it too. As if the mind which had dreamt it up was itself prompting him to prevent it, he now knew what to do . . .

Where the hell is Magdalene Master's Lodge? How could he have lived in Cambridge for most of his life and not know? He Googled and found a map which didn't tell him. He looked at his watch: three oh seven and forty-two seconds. Then through the window: antemeridian.

The Magdalene porters wouldn't tell him at three am. He hadn't time to persuade them. That could take longer than persuading the police. It was well hidden, this bloody information. He would have to ask his own porters.

He grabbed the memory stick. A moment later he returned for his coat and the tweed gloves he had bought himself in that impulse of self-indulgence. Finally, he returned for his bicycle key.

And then he ran.

Carlos was alone, nodding over a magazine.

"Magdalene Master's Lodge. Where is it?"

"Ah, Mister Theo sir, I not know. I only work here. Can you not find on internets? You find everything. Is your job."

"It's not in the public domain. And rather urgent."

"Yah I see that sir. I not seen you hurry before. I not help you. Able."

"Blast and double damn."

"Ah, but wait," Carlos remembered. "Mattie. He was Magdalene porter before here. But maybe that was Magdalen Oxford."

"Not quite the same. Can you radio and ask him?"

"He home in bed. I ring him in the morning."

"Carlos, would you mind . . ."

"Or maybe he worked Fitzwilliam, and Jamie work Magdalene. Yeah, it Jamie. I don't have his number."

"Magdalen, Oxford. Good idea. They must continually be confused." He looked it up and dialled. "I'm sorry to bother you at this time of night," he said to someone whose job it was to stay awake all night. Some deep memory stirred him. "I have a bet with an old friend. Please could you tell me the location of the Master's Lodge of Magdalene, Cambridge? No, no, of course I wouldn't." He listened, and visualised. "That's really kind, thank you."

He hung up, and let out his breath. "Thank goodness porters are only loyal to their own. Thank you, Carlos. You are brilliant."

"You go to bed now, sir: you won your bet?"

"I'm afraid I'm only just beginning. This is no ordinary bet."

Carlos shook his head dramatically and decided to make a coffee.

As Theo left college he glanced briefly up at the Chapel. Some time soon he would take time to enjoy it, in case it wasn't there in a month.

He bicycled the wrong way up a deserted Trinity Street. If he saw a bored policeman he would turn the wrong way up Green Street and pedal faster.

He dismounted at Magdalene. There was a drive just beyond the P'lodge, to his right. By day it stood open, but now its high black ironwork barred his way. For a moment he considered the combination lock on the wall. It was simpler to scale the gates.

The gravel which now grumbled, dark, beneath his feet had appeared on Google Street View as a sandy beach on a summer's day.

To his right, a comfortable old building which ought to house the Master seemed to be student accommodation. The Master's Lodge was further along the drive: boring; square; the yellow brickwork grey with night. Somewhere far inside there was a light. The heavy brass knocker resounded so loudly on the dark oak that he wondered whether it could be heard by the porters, and one of them would emerge demanding to know what he was doing.

He heard a car moan on Chesterton Lane.

Fortunately for Theo – fortunately, perhaps, for the rest of Cambridge – Sir Christopher slept lightly. He was just getting out of bed (he had been at a college dinner, and several glasses of wine no longer agreed with him as they had) when he heard the thumping.

He was not often disturbed in the small hours any more. The last time had been when an undergraduate was found hanging in his room, two days before Finals. The Chaplain had said to Christopher's wife, answering the telephone on her side of the bed, "Can I speak to Chris? It is important." She had very much wanted to say, "I didn't think you were ringing to ask the time."

The boy had survived, after a fashion. His brain had been without oxygen for a while. It had certainly got him out of Finals.

The knocker banged again. Sir Christopher grabbed his dressing gown and went down to open it.

"We met," the figure said. "At the Double Violin Concerto."

Sir Christopher couldn't see him well, and met new people every night of the week. He waited.

"You worked for GCHQ. And MI5?"

"Come in. Remind me of your name?"

"Theophilus Ambrose Fitzwilliam Wedderburn."

"Mathematician." He was fully awake now. "I remember."

They sat opposite each other at the kitchen table. Christopher's wife was an accomplished cook, and had made her Christmas pudding on Stir Up Sunday to her own signature recipe. Tonight she had been making mince pies with the rest of the fruit: rich with chopped dates and finely grated carrot, and her secret ingredient of thick cut marmalade. When Chris was out, which he often was, she embarked on activities which didn't take much concentration: soon it would be wrapping presents. She had abandoned her cooking when he came in, intending to clear up before work in the morning.

"What can I do for you, Theophilus?"

"Could I use your computer? Please."

Christopher fetched his laptop. The young man would be able to read all sorts of stuff on there. He inserted the memory stick and turned the screen around for Christopher to read it.

"People call me Theo."

The fridge hummed. An owl hooted far off. The tick of the hallway long case clock soothed the passing minutes.

"You believe this. Otherwise you wouldn't have brought it to me."

Silence stretched.

"Do you know him?" The reaction this caused was the first genuine surprise of the night. Christopher rose, came behind Theo and put kind hands on his shoulders.

Theo had long learnt to exhibit emotions suitable for the occasion. To show anger long before he felt it, for instance, in order to pre-empt problems. Now, however, having once given himself permission, he had no idea how to stop. It swept over him in a deluge, full of past pain and confusion. Christopher tore some sheets off a kitchen roll which he was surprised to find in the correct dispenser, before he spotted the bottle of cooking brandy his wife had been putting in the mincemeat, still swathed in floury fingerprints. Sainsbury's Basics: a bit of a come-down from the cognac he had eschewed after dinner. He poured a finger into two tumblers.

"Here. How long have you had this information?"

"Ten days. I think."

Sir Christopher's eyebrows rose.

Theo looked at his telephone. "I'm not quite sure what today is but it was the twenty-first of November, just after seven minutes past nine in the evening. Oh," he realised. "You don't mean that. You mean how long I've known I had it. A day. Or a night, perhaps. It took me a while to remember who you are."

"Shown anyone else?"

"I could work it out if it's important. My computer will know. What? No."

Again, silence.

"Have mine." The older man pushed his glass across the table.

Theo blew his nose again, and wiped his eyes with the exhausted tissue.

"You did the right thing."

"Sorry about the time. Do you believe it?" Theo examined his face for clues. He was very good.

"It doesn't matter. I will treat it as if I do. You can forget about it now."

For the first time Theo smiled, through his tear-tired face. "Thank you. Those look good."

"Have one."

"Won't your wife mind? Or husband or whatever? I expect they're for Christmas."

"I will explain," and he smiled too.

"Can I put it in the oven? My mother doesn't like us wasting mince pies by eating them cold. And," he added, seeing the Master's intention, "she says the microwave spoils them. But it doesn't matter. Just, not for long."

The machine pinged, and the hot mince pie was in front of him. Christopher found a spoon, and a large lidded pot full of dark golden rum butter, dusted with cinnamon and clearly not to be started yet either.

"Thank you: tell her it's really good. Presumably you have to stay up now, and do things. You needn't tell me what." Theo stood. "This is going to sound very greedy, but please can I have a little more of that? I think might to struggle to sleep. And I'm very tired."

The Master handed him the bottle. "Thank you for coming to tell me."

In the hall, whipped by the sudden frisson from the opened front door, Christopher pulled his dressing gown tighter around him. "I'm still not clear," he said, "whether you know him."

The only light was from a distant lamppost in Chesterton Lane. He couldn't see Theo's face.

"Neither am I."

Chapter Twenty-Nine

TUESDAY

The gates opened before Theo reached them. He noticed at some exhausted level of his mind that there was a bicycle leaning against the wall outside which looked a ghost of his own. Cambridge is full of old-fashioned, sit-up-and-beg Pashley bicycles with big wicker baskets.

On Magdalene Bridge he gazed out over the black swishing Cam with its sleeping punts bobbing like ducks in the dark. He realised with a sudden self-awareness rare to him that he loved Cambridge. An academic career is precarious and he wasn't sure he was good enough, but there are plenty of jobs for the numerate.

It would be good to have a proper winter, to give Nature a rest. He felt tired as well as shivery. He wondered why he was on foot.

Hadn't he looked up at the Chapel, wondering whether it would still be there? Hadn't he been holding his bicycle?

Why could he not remember? That signifies something, doesn't it?

He longed for his bed with a tiredness that hurt. But he couldn't abandon his bike if it was out, not knowing where he was, tethered to a lamppost outside a college or pub somewhere.

He turned back. If the bike he'd seen leaning against the wall hadn't been the wrong colour he would almost think it could be his.

And there, just beyond Magdalene P'lodge, he met his dear, familiar bicycle, waiting patiently like a dog just where he had left it. A trick of the diverted lamplight had washed it into a shadowy blue-gray spectre of its daytime racing green self.

The iron gates were locked again, but there were more lights on in the lodge now. In the distance he could just make out Sir Christopher, sitting at his desk, on the telephone.

Theo pedalled slowly back to college and slept in his clothes for fourteen hours.

Christopher did not.

An hour earlier, he had thought he was tired. Sick of meetings, college politics and carol services; of pointless dinners and over-inflated egos; of colleagues who thought their latest paper or book or bid for a TV series was going to change the world. Now, his brain was neon clear.

Robin was his first protégé, a whippersnapper straight from a PhD in Engineering at Bristol, arguably the first rising star not to come out of Oxbridge. One of the finest minds Christopher had come across. Yes, including those he brushed shoulders with on a daily basis now. After more than two decades together, Robin had stepped into his shoes and Christopher's greatest hope and greatest fear was that his successor would outshine him.

Robin answered half way through the second ring, so quickly that his partner, a senior neurosurgeon at St George's, didn't stir. Christopher could picture him, on his feet within seconds, shrugging on a cardigan and walking into his study, throwing a fresh pad of paper onto the desk and grabbing a biro in whichever hand was not holding his 'phone.

They didn't ask how the children were or what the other was doing for Christmas. Far less did Robin express any surprise. Just an exchange of facts, as economical as possible.

Christopher would courier over the memory stick Theo had left him, to reach South London long before breakfast. Robin would get the IT boys onto it straight away: they should have something back before mid-morning.

"Will you contact Cambridge Special Branch or shall I?"

"I've got time," Christopher said. His first meeting wasn't until nine fifteen. He should be able to get hold of the person he wanted after eight.

If it didn't evaporate in the first puff of investigation, it would have to go through the Security Service. The Home Secretary would need to be informed. And of course, with the Duchess coming . . . But they were a long way off that yet. Much would depend on what he received back at lunchtime.

His wife came in, still in her dressing gown, bearing tea. She looked younger than her fifty-nine years, and he wondered why women wear make-up. Then immediately answered himself, knowing which were the women listened to in departmental meetings – in London, if not in Cambridge. What a lot of time it must waste, having to do that every morning.

"What was all that about?" She settled comfortably on the edge of his desk.

"We woke you? Sorry."

"Not really. Looked out of the window when I realised you weren't in bed, and saw an undergraduate walking away."

"Research Fellow. He thought it was urgent." She had long learnt not to be too curious of Chris's work. He got up from his desk. "He's right that we ought to rule it out straight away. I'll tell you about it when we have. Shall I have breakfast without you?"

"No, I'll get dressed afterwards." They went into the kitchen together. "Where's the brandy?"

"Mea culpa. One of your mince pies, too." He held his hands up in a gesture of peace. "He needed one."

"Ego te absolvo. Who?"

"The young Research Fellow. I've just worked out who he is. Do you remember Alan Wedderburn?"

When he had been at the choir school, outsider that he was, someone had paid for him to have piano lessons. He resented it still. All the others in the choir were learning two instruments. The head tried to put a positive spin on it, telling him he could progress twice as fast with only one instrument to practice. Thank you, sir.

He felt the seething hurt, the longing for a trumpet and a place in the orchestra, the determination not to like the tiny woman with grey hair.

"I play much better when you're not there," he told her angrily.

"Of course you do," she agreed. "So, what is the solution?"

"Only play to myself?"

"Then you would never improve. Let's say you play this well alone," she held her hands apart, "and only half as well with me," she brought them closer. "Suppose you learn to play three times as well to yourself," she stretched her hands as far apart as they would go, "you will still be able perform twice as well to someone else, which is much better than it was before, even if it's not quite as good as it is at home. Now, let's look at the bars that are giving you trouble, over the page turn."

He deplored her arithmetic almost as much as her assumption that he had access to a piano at home, but he remembered the lesson and implemented it when he worked for DEN! If a plan was several times better than it had to be, then when somebody was five minutes late or the police rumbled some detail, it was still a damned good operation.

Which was where his fall-back plan came in.

What he needed was somebody who cared about money more than anything else. Everyone likes money. But most don't like it enough. Do you want ten million quid? Yeah, of course. Okay, cut off your sister's arm. Well I don't want it *that* much . . .

It had proved surprisingly difficult. Someone needing medical fees in the States? A kidney for himself? A child for adoption? Even someone with an ideological objection to the West. He knew such people must exist: weren't they always destroying priceless artefacts in Iraq and places?

He had drawn a blank. Without the resources of the Intelligence Services, he had no leads.

As so often, it was serendipity which had eventually delivered.

Students were streaming into the Corn Exchange. Something about their self-entitlement had irked him.

He followed the flow, mostly to see if the security was as lax as he suspected. It was far worse. A false name, a spluttered indignation that they hadn't received his details, a hastily hand-written badge and he was in. He found himself in a limp-canapé recruitment-drive, and wondered why he had bothered.

Not for long.

He had spotted Yuri within minutes; chatted to him over the acidic white wine and curling sandwiches; explained that he was launching an exciting (and completely confidential) start-up; promised contact . . . and implied a lot more.

For the next two months he had cultivated him assiduously. Yuri was the greediest person he had ever met. He had no idea of his limitations and thought the world owed him far more than it was ever going to give him.

Yuri came from a grindingly dreary background in the Urals or Belarus or somewhere. He never quite worked out how Yuri arrived in Cambridge: he claimed it was something to do with the university. Far more interesting was Yuri's business ambition. He had a scheme that was going to make him a billionaire. Then he would go home, hire fast cars for a week or two and rescue his sisters to marry rich men in the West.

His plan was obviously doomed to failure because he was far more interested in the money than the method. He didn't care what he did: he simply had a wild and ravenous lust.

He explained carefully: it would barely take Yuri an afternoon. Then he could wipe his fingerprints off the control and throw it in the Cam. If by some bizarre freak of policing it was ever found – and what reason would they have to dredge the river for something the size of a handbag? – it could never be traced back to Yuri.

And perhaps Yuri, too, had a resentment against this university and city. He might not mind the job in hand.

Provided the money was forthcoming, Yuri would be. And the money certainly would be.

It was dark outside. Theo was remembering where he had got to. It seemed a long time ago.

Perhaps he had dreamt his breakthrough. Otherwise why wouldn't he have written it up straight away? Something was bugging him like a stone in his shoe. He wasn't wearing shoes, of course. Because he was on his bed.

He was wearing socks. And trousers. But no tie.

He abandoned the question of why he was dressed in bed (without a tie) as not very interesting and let his mind go back to where it wanted to be. His Teasmade didn't make particularly good tea but it did make him feel obliged to drink it after the trouble it had taken, and that helped him get up and make a decent brew.

He pulled onto his lap the pad of paper he kept by his bed. With considerable excitement he realised it was real. The idea had not slipped away like a guilty shadow in the night.

If the transference principles he had been working on could be applied to translates of multiplicative structures as well as additive ones . . . then he might be able to control some interesting expressions concerning primes. Perhaps relating to the sizes of factors of products of primes. Possibly relating to a sum of factors. Even, the sum of all factors of a product. It would be almost incredible. If he could force the sum of the factors to be the number itself, then he would have a perfect number. And if he avoided the prime number two – which his ideas should allow effortlessly if the transference indeed worked – he would have . . . was it possible? . . . an *odd perfect number*.

An existence whose likelihood was deemed by James Joseph Sylvester in 1888 to be 'little short of a miracle'. Whose probability of existence, according to some heuristics, might be one in several trillion. The number itself would have to be larger than ten to the power of three hundred, perhaps consisting of a thousand digits, or a million.

He started scribbling.

"Come in," he said.

"I can't. It's locked."

He was not in the habit of locking his door, and didn't know where he might have put the key. After looking in various obvious places he opened the window.

"You can climb in here," he called.

"Great." Clare came round to the window in a shortish skirt and rather impractical high heels. He could imagine they might not be very comfortable clothes for climbing through a window. "Well?" She didn't seem very happy.

"I'll come out and lift you in." He started to remove his socks so they wouldn't get wet on the ground.

"Theo for fuck's sake."

"You don't like that idea?"

"I like the idea of you being ready for once."

"Ready. For what?"

"The film starts at half past. We agreed we'd eat beforehand. Mainly so that we wouldn't miss the film if you were an hour and a half late. I'm not particularly old-fashioned but I do get pissed off always being the one to come and pick you up. And remind you. And choose what we're doing. And I don't like having an argument through a public window."

"But that's not true, is it?" Theo said reasonably, as if taking a supervision. "I came to pick you up for that dinner. Thing. Which kicked off in the Provost's Lodge. You remember." She seemed to be waiting. "What film would that be?"

"Forget it. I'll go with someone else."

"Okay." That certainly seemed easier. He wouldn't have to climb out of the window. "Before you go."

She turned back. "Yes?"

"Would you like to get married?" She stared at him. "Sorry, I didn't phrase that quite correctly. I think what I meant was, Would you like to marry me?"

"Theo." When Clare let her breath out again he could see it, silver in the darkness. "Have you been drinking?"

"No, actually. I think I've been sleeping, mostly. Does it make a difference?"

"You've never even told me you love me."

"Oh. I see. Would that help?"

"No."

Somebody walked through the courtyard. Clare turned briefly to see who it was. "I'm going to the film, Theo. I've been looking forward to it for some time. It was hard to get tickets. I'll see you another time."

"Good idea. Have a lovely time." As she began to walk off he called. "Half past what? I mean, Shall I take that as a no? Just so I know?"

She muttered, "Never mind," just loud enough for him to hear.

Theo shut the window.

He went over to his desk and opened his Bible. He read the first couple of chapters, and then shut it again slowly. He took a clean handkerchief from his drawer and saw that it might be Tuesday. He wiped his face. Then picked up *The House at Pooh Corner* and read the end, when Christopher Robin says goodbye because he is growing up.

Eventually he remembered what he had been doing, realised he needed the loo first, put on his shoes to climb out of the window and found his door key in the toe of the right foot.

Clare had told Theo about the film weeks earlier, they had talked about it several times and it was to be their last evening together before Christmas. Even for Theo the last ten minutes or so had been pretty spectacular. She was annoyed with herself for putting up with it and furious with him for dishing it out.

He even managed to turn a proposal of marriage into an insult. As if it had been consolation, for forgetting the film.

On impulse, she decided to look in on the college bar and see if there was anyone worth going with. It was nearly empty. Crispin Thorpe was reading a notice near the door. She had an idea he had just been cleared of some rather sordid allegation. And he was damned good-looking.

He looked up, caught her eye and made her mind up for her. "Fancy the cinema?" she said breezily and mentioned the film. "I've got a spare ticket." He raised an eyebrow, and she received the impression it was this information that interested him, more than the film.

"How long have I got?"

"About half a second to decide. Rather longer till the film."

"I need to deliver something to a room. Shall I meet you in the P'lodge in five?"

Clare waited outside the porters' lodge, thinking how much she disliked the affectation of referring to five minutes as 'five'. She wondered why she hadn't simply gone back to her room, changed into something comfortable and sold the tickets.

"Dinner?" he said, swooping her out of the college with an arm lightly around her waist. It was presumptuous, but she was in the mood for it. "How about Brown's?"

They nearly didn't make it to the film. Clare found herself enjoying being with a man several years older. Urbane, charming, sophisticated. For all she knew, with a partner.

He ordered champagne and suggested he chose for both of them. As they chinked glasses, their fingers touched. His smile was almost tactile.

"So," he said eventually. "You are tactfully not asking what I'm celebrating, and I am tactfully not asking why you have a spare ticket."

It was her turn to smile.

The next time she put her glass down, he stretched out and lightly stroked the back of her hand with a finger.

"I'm being careful, as you see. Though I don't think you're like that."

"Like what?" she asked, not moving her hand.

"Prick-tease."

"You don't waste much time, do you?"

"I don't suppose you do either. You look as if you're in a hurry. To the top." Curiously, she found this more enticing than anything else he had said.

Oysters arrived.

"I'm not sure I've eaten oysters before."

"May I?" And he moved his chair next to hers.

By the steak he was touching rather more than the back of her hand. Eating red meat, after Kathryn's pescatarianism, felt like a harmless and satisfying revenge.

The physical magnetism was even greater than it had been with Kathryn. She began to assume they would give the film a miss, until he suddenly called the waiter and said they had to be gone in two minutes. They were in a cab in less and at the cinema in perfect time. After such a sensual meal she was intrigued that he spent the film in rapt concentration.

As they emerged into the street he called another cab and said, "My place," but it no longer sounded like a question.

"Let me show you round," he said, unlocking the front door. "This is Simon," and he nodded to a young man in the kitchen.

"Hi."

"This is my room," and he ushered her upstairs into a room with a large bed, overlooking the garden. "Brandy?"

"Thank you."

He returned with two balloon glasses and an unopened bottle. He was a smooth operator. All would have gone according to plan, but that he happened to drop into the ear he was touching so exquisitely, as he twisted her hair between his fingers, "I don't quite get the beauty and the geek thing."

"Mmm?" She pulled her face away to look at him.

"You and the nerd. What's that about?"

In that moment, Clare saw him. In his socks, hair all over the place, confused about his locked door. Will you marry me? The only time anyone had asked her. It was gauche, it was clumsy and extremely badly done. But with the best heart in the world; even she could see that.

"I'm sorry," she said, rolling away.

"I assumed you're not committed."

"I'm not." She stared at the flame in the scented candle. "No, we're not."

"Come here then." He tried to pull her towards him.

"You're right." She sat up, her back to him. "But I ought to finish that before starting this."

"Sweetheart, we're not starting anything. We're just enjoying ourselves."

"I'm really sorry." She fumbled for her bra.

"Right."

"I'd love to resume this another time."

"Dream on. There's not going to be another time."

She remembered with a shock that she was in the presence of someone who had just been tried for sexual assault; possibly attempted rape. She had heard him lock the bedroom door when he came back in. It would be her own bloody silly fault if he decided he hadn't heard, No. And there would be FA she could do about it.

"You don't need to look at me like that. After the experience I've just had? You're all bitches. The key's in the lock. I'll call you a cab."

"Thank you. I'll walk."

"Dressed like that? You're asking for it. But we know that, now, don't we?"

"I'm sorry," she said again. "This has been entirely my fault. I had a difficult ..."

"Spare me the sobs. We've all had a difficult."

"Thank you for dinner. You want me to go halves?"

"I wasn't buying you."

She let herself out, furiously postponing the tears. She desperately wanted a cab: her high-heeled shoes would be vices, within minutes.

By the time she reached King's Parade her feet were howling and she was extremely cold. She didn't turn towards the market for her room, but let herself into college. Perhaps Theo's room would still be locked. In which case, perhaps she would accept his offer to be lifted through the window. Or simply go back to hers, run a hot bath and have a very large drink.

It wasn't. She looked into his bedroom and sensed him asleep. She took off her clothes and got in beside him, chilled and aching.

"Sorry," she whispered.

He didn't really hear her. But his body responded as any man's might.

Chapter Thirty

SECOND WEEK OF ADVENT

Charlotte couldn't identify what it was about Advent that was so different. The manic fullness of term had ended: lectures, supervisions, practices and orchestras; the gusts of a wild schedule which had buffeted and swirled her through the autumn had died away.

But Cambridge had not slowed much. Members of her own year were drifting off, like the yellow leaves which lifted their heads in the breeze and shifted into gutters to be kicked up by exuberant choristers on their way back from Evensong or grabbed in handfuls by undergraduates as if they were snowballs.

A few Third Years, mindful of the final reckoning in May, were studying by day but still raucous by night. Charlotte could hear them from her room. Suki had told her that the noise from a bar in Trinity Street had kept her awake the previous term. When she mentioned it to a porter he said, "You should have told us, miss. Trinity owns all the property along there."

Charlotte said she thought Trinity owned half East Anglia . . . if not half of England.

Don't be silly, Suki said.

Theo noticed the security measures with relieved satisfaction.

He had learnt, in early childhood, not to be anxious about something he couldn't influence. He had played his part. If the Chapel were now lost – even if he himself was – it was not his responsibility any more.

Ann had told him he must never take his own life. He understood straight away; just as he did when Alan taught him the rules of chess when he was five or what a dotted minim was when he was three. The option was ruled out as a mathematical solution might be, so you move on to the next idea. It is a waste of time to revisit it.

But she did not tell him he had to stay alive. If he took up some insanely dangerous sport or joined the Army, that was fine. If he was in Chapel and the building collapsed on him, he would not be to blame.

So he was able to observe with a calm and detached interest as cordons were put up and dogs brought in. He would have liked to watch them: going systematically from vestry to side-chapel, stall to pew, ballooning out the altar-cloth with their busy tails, streaming up to the organ loft and sniffing out the pedals, examining the stops. Presumably if anything obstructed the pipes the organist would know. Theo had seen a Victorian engraving showing dogs playing in the ante-Chapel: perhaps dogs were once commonplace in college.

What about the inner roof? Up the stone spiral staircase they would go, through the dark spot where you can only progress by feeling; perhaps skitting on their nimble feet on the inner boat-crafted stone skeleton. Sniffing at the holes looking down on the crowds below. There was nowhere to hide anything there. They would be taken up onto the outer roof, the wind flapping their ears and ruffling their fur, the drop perilously sheer to where tourists walked below.

"Don't give it too much thought, Theo," the Dean said, hardly pausing as he passed. This centenary service would be John's first overseeing the Nine Lessons. Would he mind if the service was cancelled? Presumably lots of people would.

What Theo didn't see were the seemingly interminable meetings in Peter and Caroline's house. Every day, suited and serious officials met in the Provost's lodge: representatives of college, university, police, BBC and trickiest of all, the Palace. Each needing to be true to his or her particular training and professionalism.

Caroline sat at her pock-marked desk overlooking the vast and ancient lawn, trying to meet her self-imposed Christmas deadline. Her home had been turned into a police HQ. If the cause hadn't been so dreadful she would have relished the first-hand material. But from her study window she could see the West End of the Chapel and shuddered at the daring. It couldn't happen, of course. Except it did . . . to the Twin Towers and the Buddhas of Bamiyan and untold priceless monuments in Iraq.

She gazed at its serene and majestic permanence, soaring into the Fenland sky ever since Cambridge herself could remember and, writer though she was, couldn't begin to imagine it shivering to nothing in the shattering of a second.

Pete didn't want college staff even knowing the meetings were happening, so it was often Caroline herself who took refreshments into their drawing room, hearing enough snippets to consider crime fiction as her next project. That evening Pete would fill her in on the more gossipy, less sensitive details.

As far as the Palace was concerned, all the cathedrals and monuments in the world could be blown to bits as long as not one of the impossibly long hairs of the Duchess's lovely head was harmed. At the other end of the spectrum were the Dean and the beleaguered BBC producer, both of whom managed to claim a dubious high ground by implying a contempt for their own personal safety. At one point, when a meeting had gone on long after nerves were frayed beyond bearing, the gentle Dean exploded in a fluster of rage that anyone should bully him out of caring for his flock. There was a moment of tired silence, before the producer came unexpectedly to his aid and said he felt just the same. What he didn't add was that he had already had more than one nightmare, waking his usually unflappable cat peacefully asleep on his duvet, having seen the Chapel dissolve into biscuity crumbs . . . and failing to catch the moment on camera.

The police, of course, had the final say. On everything. Pete told Caroline over a much needed beer in the kitchen that it felt as if the college was the least significant player. "We're hosting the damn thing. The Duchess is a guest: it's not her own personal showcase. As is the bloody Beeb. It's supposed to be a service of divine worship" – ironic, Caroline thought, coming from an avowed agnostic – "for members of the college. Not . . ." He downed half his glass in one draught.

"What?"

"Oh, you know. 'Don't cough during the organ voluntary because of all those listening at home.' Sorry," he smiled, relaxing as the Old Peculier hit the spot. "I know there are millions listening in and they matter too. But I do sometimes wonder why I took this job on. Any serious research seems a very long time ago."

"Of course it is." Caroline came round and put her arms around him. "You don't imagine the Archbishop of Canterbury has time for parish visiting? Talking of research, what happened over that dubious funding business?"

Pete groaned. "Crispin Thorpe?" He must be tired. He wouldn't normally let slip a name. "Arsehole. He certainly did it: God knows why. I was hoping the court case could save us some vile publicity. Now he's been found not guilty we'll have to confront it. Could easily cost us a third of a million in legal fees. It'll have to wait till next term: sixteen hundred people being blown to bits is a bit more serious than bribed research."

"Will the service really be cancelled?"

"At the moment, the chance of its going ahead seems very slim indeed. And all that idiot of a producer seems concerned about is his programming schedule. I mean, honestly. They can shove on last year's service, for goodness' sake. Or an Agatha Christie."

"You know they can't. Do you really want that second beer? Count to ten before you open it," she reminded him of their pact.

"Yes I bloody do." He was prising the top off. "But honestly, it's not life or death is it? I mean, it *is* life or death. But whether we have a broadcast on Christmas Eve isn't."

"No, but then most people's jobs aren't, are they? Most Nobel Prize-winning research isn't life or death. Some of it is: not much. If people didn't behave as if it was they wouldn't get anywhere. If organists didn't genuinely believe a top A more important than nuclear disarmament, they wouldn't be first rate organists."

"There are some impressive achievers," Pete said, drinking directly from the bottle, "who still retain a sense of humility and modesty."

"Name one."

"Me," he smiled.

"You don't have a vastly inflated idea of your own indispensability," she conceded. "Usually. But – and I can quite see this may have escaped your notice – you don't have a gong. Nor do you have, by any normal definition of the phrase, a household name. Actors on the Archers are better known than you are. Though you are still surprisingly attractive. For your age. To me. Are we going to bed?"

"You know what?"

"What?" She turned back to him encouragingly.

"We really do have the best police force in the world."

"And I thought you were about to tell me how beautiful I am. Or even, just for a moment, clever."

"They are amazing. Completely bloody amazing."

She smiled rather seriously. "Under the circumstances, just as well."

Liz knew it was time to get ready for Christmas. Mark expected her to host a party for his employees. Decorations, tree, food. However much she looked forward to Crispin's homecoming, it wouldn't be a family Christmas. It would be dominated by Selina in her absence, just as it had always been by her presence.

Tirelessly she reiterated, unconvincingly, that she didn't love Selina anymore. She honestly suspected Mark might have achieved this coveted detachment. He had confided in a rare moment of intimacy his biggest fear, that when she did eventually come home, he wouldn't want her any more.

Surely there was something that could put Liz beyond the pain of love. Suppose Selina joined ISIS – the idea was not totally ludicrous – and blew up a primary school? Liz couldn't summon the children up enough to care, or imagine what it would be like to eliminate just one.

Suppose she got Crispin into trouble and destroyed his career? Then Liz wouldn't know what she would live for. The thought seemed worse even than his death.

And yet . . . If Selina ruined Crispin somehow, even as Liz would hate her, she would still feel this terrible, involuntary love. The agony would never go away.

As soon as he said it, George knew it was a mistake. Never brag: that was the rule. In truth he seldom had much to brag about.

In any other school, his mother reassured him, he would be the star pupil. He was going on to the local state school when he left the choir school. "You'll see," she said. "You'll be top of the class there, and leading the orchestra." He wasn't bullied, or anything like that: he just felt ordinary. He didn't even get voted onto the School Council, though it had been his idea.

Now he had something no one else had. And stupidly, he had said so. Nothing stayed secret in the choir for long, but he didn't need to volunteer the information. So of course, when he tried to backtrack he was collared. It wasn't a proper fight: just a ragging. Johnny wrestled him to the ground. The half-frozen winter mud nipped at their skin as they tussled, and chewed at their clothes. Then the bell sounded for the next practice and George thought he had got away with it, but just as he and Johnny were scrambling to their feet Angus reached inside his trouser pocket.

"Holy shit, Hall."

"Give it back. Please," George begged. "It isn't properly mine." He was really worried now. "Well it is, but I have to look after it. Please, Angus."

"I'm just looking." The others had crowded round, shoving and jumping on each other. George might have been pleased, if he hadn't been near tears of fear. The man had impressed on him the value of it, and that it wasn't his until Christmas Day. No way could his parents replace it. "How much pocket money d'you get?"

"There's the second bell," George said. "We'll get wrecked." Fortunately, this was true. Being late for practice meant loss of privileges for a week. For the day pupils there was less than a week of term left, of Latin and football and concerts. For the choristers, the work was just about to start: the Easter service to record; most of the Christmas music to learn. They broke into a run. Last one there was a dur-brain ...

From time to time as they sang George put his hand in his pocket. It was still safe and smooth and expensive-feeling. To his relief, at the end of practice the others seemed to have forgotten. It wasn't until evening, when they had all finished prep and there was a short film in the TV room before showers, that Cory asked him about it when they were alone. Cory didn't have a mobile so when he wasn't borrowing someone else's, he had to linger near the school call box when he was expecting a call.

"Let's see, then."

"See what?" George said carefully.

"What you had in your pocket. I couldn't see before: the others were all in the way." Cory was in the year below George and Johnny and Angus. "C'mon. Don't be a twat."

George felt silly, looking around to ensure they weren't overheard.

"They're all watching the film," Cory said. "It didn't sound that good. Some spy thing."

It was reasonably private by the call box and you could hear anyone coming down the stairs.

Carefully, George pulled it out of his pocket.

"Woah," Cory said. "Sick."

For half a minute the two boys sat in silence, as George demonstrated some of the functions. Suddenly they heard adult footsteps and he slipped it under his thigh.

"Hello boys." The gappy was eighteen, Australian, very blonde and going to uni next year to do Sports Studies. And right now, completely not what they wanted. "Not going to the film?"

"My mum's ringing," Cory explained.

"Okay," and she swung round the corner.

"She does that on purpose," George said.

"What?"

"Shows off her bum."

"Let's see again." Being a year younger than George, he was less interested in the gappy's bum. "Where d'you get it?"

"You know that guy I went to see?"

"When you lied and said your parents were taking you out to tea. You know that's really dangerous, right?"

"What is?"

"Meeting someone off the internet. Don't you remember that shitty film they made us watch? About that kid who got murdered?"

"*The Life and Death of Brock* . . . something. Yeah, yeah. Well, it wasn't dangerous, was it?"

"You're too young for Snapchat anyway," Cory continued rather primly.

"Whatever. Anyway, he gave it to me."

"Why?" Cory was even more suspicious. "They're really expensive. That's the latest model and they're, like, hundreds."

"Yeah."

"What d'you have to do in return?"

"Just take it to the service."

"Which service?"

"Christmas Eve."

"Why?" he said again.

"He was a chorister ages ago. He doesn't want to queue all night and sit miles away up by the altar. And he's made a shit ton in bitcoins, so he's minted. He just wants to hear it." George was repeating the man almost word for word.

"Why doesn't he listen on the radio like everyone else?"

"He wants to feel he's there. In the choir stalls."

"The BBC microphones are right there." Cory, unlike George, had no need to believe the story in order to possess an expensive device.

"He wants to feel part of it. That's why it isn't mine until Christmas Day. I just have to make sure it's turned on, and then it's mine to do anything I like with."

Cory's father was a vicar in an inner city parish. His parents said it was always the person who opened the vicarage door, who was duped. His mum had been conned by a woman in tears whose car had broken down: as soon as his dad came home he rang the police, who confirmed the woman was a well-known crook. But his dad handed over nearly sixty quid for a baby who needed a kidney: his mum said she would never have fallen for that one. He was experiencing the same sensation now. Something was wrong. How could George not realise? They were all drilled in the dangers of paedos, till they were sick of it.

He couldn't dub George in, obviously. So he had to persuade him. At least to tell his parents, if not a teacher.

"I can even sell it," George said. "On eBay, and keep the money."

"George," he said. "Um. This is actually important."

"You're jealous," George said.

"No, I'm not. Yeah, course I am. Anyone would be. But what if . . . Okay. Suppose your life was in danger?"

"How could it be?"

"Just suppose."

"I don't ever have to see him again."

"Maybe it's stolen, or something."

"And?"

"I just have a really bad feeling. What if it's drugs?"

"What if what is?"

"You're my best friend, George." This was news to George. Cory might be the year below, but he was cool. "I don't want to wreck it for you."

"Right."

"Just suppose this could get you really hurt? Or someone else? It wouldn't be worth it, right?"

"Of course not."

"I think you should tell someone."

George said nothing. He knew he wasn't going to. But on the other hand . . . Cory was sensible. That was why he liked him. He was more mature than a lot of boys in George's year. "Okay, if he contacts me again. I promise. Nothing bad can happen if I never see him again, right?"

Cory was about to say, yes, something very bad could still happen. He just didn't know what.

But at that moment the telephone rang. He jumped to answer it. "The choir school," he said. "Hello mum." He turned to say something to George. Like, I won't be long. But George had already got up to give him some privacy, and was going into the TV room.

Where he stayed for the next hour, not laughing with any of the others at the film, which turned out to be quite funny. He sat apart, contemplating everything his friend had said, his hand on the very expensive device in his pocket.

Chapter Thirty-One

MIDWEEK

"I would stake my professional reputation on it." The trainer's words had the more impact for being softly spoken. "There is nothing there."

There was a silence of several minutes.

"Good." The Head Porter was the first to say it. "How sure are you?"

"Those dogs are the best in the country. My team has been over the place with a toothcomb."

Pete winced inwardly at the mismetaphor.

"So it was a hoax?" somebody asked.

"My brief is to find what's there. My dogs can't find anything. In the roof, on the roof, every side-chapel, pews, organ, the offices or whatever they call them. Assuming there's nowhere I haven't been told about. If they can't find it, nobody can."

"With due respect," Tom chipped in, "when I was in the Met, there were some things dogs couldn't smell. Inside an airtight container?"

"So," the Dean ignored him, "the service can go ahead?"

"Not necessarily," the Chief Constable said firmly. "We can't investigate further until we get another lead. It doesn't mean we're sure enough to risk lives."

They seemed to have reached stalemate.

"This may sound naïve," the Provost asked; he had experienced a few terrorist attacks himself. "But perhaps he hasn't put it there yet?"

"Which is why," the Chief Constable explained, "we keep the building sterile from now on. No unauthorised admittance. Anyone going in is searched. Every time."

"Everyone?"

"Everyone."

"The Duchess?"

The Palace representative breathed rather ostentatiously through his nostrils.

"Obviously not the Dean as he processes in. Happily, if he had a device big enough to destroy that building sewn into the hem of his cope or whatever you call it, it would be heavy enough for him to feel it. But yes, if someone has access to the Queen's hats, that bomb is going to go off one Remembrance Sunday whatever we do. There are limits."

"And the choristers?" It was the first meeting the organist had come to. "Are all the boys going to be searched?"

"Gentlemen," Peter said. "And ladies." He made a courteous nod in the direction of the dog handler, completely forgetting the other Palace official. "I'm sorry but I have to be at a meeting in London this afternoon. Can I just be clear in my own mind?" He looked round the room. "The present position is that we have eliminated every possible place for an incendiary device in the Chapel?"

The Chief Constable looked at the dog handler, who nodded.

"So we are back with a chance of the service going ahead?"

There are numerous cares resting on the shoulders of the head of an academic house. Multi-million pound deficits; press accusations of elitism; abstruse aspects of human rights: all serve to whiten the hairs within the Master's, Principal's, Dean's, Mistress's or Provost's Lodge.

Pete gazed out at the ghost of his own reflection speeding through the dreary winter countryside, gazing dimly back into the carriage. Everyone else, going for Christmas shopping or the lights in Oxford Street or some networking Christmas party, seemed carefree and blithe.

Contemporaries from his student days who had gone on to manage billion pound hedge funds or command the Navy surely had nothing to compare with this. Not even in the modern military was a man weighing up the lives of sixteen hundred people in one afternoon. And for what? For a service of divine worship on the radio.

If it was cancelled the ramifications would rumble through the rest of his tenure. The year there was silence on the airwaves when there should have been the exquisite pinprick of silver sound and a child's timely reminder of what happened once in King David's royal city. Perhaps the BBC would start broadcasting the service from different churches and cathedrals, like Radio 4's Sunday Worship. Which might be more appropriate. But it would hardly make Peter revered in the retirement he was suddenly looking forward to.

The alternative was very much worse.

To his surprise he saw people packing away laptops and stretching over heads to reach hats and umbrellas. They were pulling into King's Cross.

When his taxi deposited him back at college it was after 10 o'clock. He normally took his bicycle to the station, but it had been raining with a steady and dismal determination, and his expenses would be covered. Now, surprisingly, it was a bright, clear night, stars wide-eyed overhead.

In the nearly-deserted street he heard someone running up behind him. Momentarily wondering if he might not live until whatever happened on Christmas Eve, he turned. It was Theo Wedderburn, out of breath, clothes and hair strongly suggesting he had recently been tousled through a particularly vindictive hedge.

"Can you let me in?"

"Lost your key?"

"Don't think so. It's probably in my room. Or perhaps it's been handed in: that sometimes happens when someone else finds it before I do."

Pete opened the eye of the needle.

"After you," Theo insisted.

As they walked through college, Peter suddenly said, "Want a beer?"

"Yes, please."

"That was quick."

"I worked that out some time ago. Beer; tea: yes. Toast: no. It's not a hundred per cent accurate, but it's a workable hypothesis. It used to exasperate my grandfather if he asked me what I wanted for breakfast and I had to work it out from first principles. You have to consider how well or otherwise he makes toast; whether my grandmother will put too much marmalade on; hardest of all how hungry you are, which I still haven't worked out how to measure."

"Hoegaarden all right?" Peter said, opening the fridge to Caroline's favourite.

"Yes. Unless you have anything else?"

"We haven't."

"Good."

Peter took down two half pint goblets in green glass which had been a Christmas present from an aunt many decades ago and had miraculously survived. Had Caroline just found these, too?

"Kitchen or sitting room?" Pete asked.

"The difficulty," Theo continued, "is when you're offered an apple. That is sometimes yes and sometimes no, so it's more confusing. Er, what?"

"I wondered where you'd like to sit."

"That's not on my formula either, sorry. I don't think I've seen your sitting room, have I?"

"It's quite cosy: small family room. But then so is this, and the fire won't be lit. Sit down."

"I like this room."

For a minute or two they drank in companionable silence. "This plan you uncovered," Peter said. "To detonate the Chapel. Are you worried?"

"No."

"Not at all?"

"No."

Peter nodded, satisfied. "So you think it's not going to happen."

"No."

When Caroline came in to get milk, she was surprised to find them sitting together, not speaking. Pete normally went straight to bed after London. She was just going out again when Pete explained. "I was just asking Theo about the, um, danger. He doesn't think anything is going to happen. I don't think anyone does now. I expect the service will go ahead."

"Oh, no, the opposite," Theo corrected him.

"Sorry?"

"I think something *is* going to happen."

"I thought you said you aren't worried about it."

"I'm not worried about death. Nor global warming, and that's happening already. I might be very sad," he added for further clarification, "as when my grandmother died. In fact I'll probably be a lot more sad when the Chapel is blown up because my grandmother was going to die anyway."

Caroline left the room, shaking her head imperceptibly. "You believe it will?" Pete found it strangely hard to say. 'You think the Chapel will be destroyed?'

"Probably. But obviously the police know far more than I do. So they're more likely to be right. I'm planning to go to the service."

"So am I."

"My grandmother once asked me if it's possible that I know more than I realise. I thought it an irrational question at first, and it upset me. But then she explained that sometimes in detective stories, people see things they don't know the significance of."

"You think you do?"

"Not exactly. I think I know something which nobody else knows. Only I don't know what it is."

"I think we need another beer. No need to mention it to my wife."

"I didn't realise I was supposed to anyway."

A wooden cuckoo burst in on their companionable silence, lurching out of its den with a hideous screech and insisting eleven times who it was. If he'd had the energy, Peter would have thrown something at it.

"Do you know him?"

Theo considered. For a while. "You mean, did I know him before this term?"

Suddenly Pete felt very tired. In five minutes, he would go to bed. He would hold Caroline to himself, and be asleep almost instantly. Even if he did wake up again in a few hours, in a cold sweat.

"What nobody knows," Pete said, "is where it could be. The bomb. The dogs can't find it, and apparently they can find everything."

"Yes, but he would know that," Theo pointed out.

"Why?"

"Didn't he work with animals?"

Peter examined him sharply. "How do you know that?"

The silence was so long Peter thought perhaps Theo hadn't heard him. There was a distant shout in the street: staff going home after closing, perhaps. A loo flushed upstairs. Theo finished his drink, put his glass on the table and looked Peter steadily in the face. His eyes were a clear hazel green. Strange, with the dark colouring of his hair.

"I don't know," he said. "That's interesting, isn't it?"

The rain came down in a relentless grey wash. Charlotte thought of the crackling fire at home, Folly lying with her face on her paws, steaming bowls of her mother's homemade soup, a half-read Woolf or Josephine Tey on the coffee table and Bach or Mozart on Spotify. The windows streaming. Wellies needed just to let the hens out. Her stepfather bringing in a fresh basket of wood.

Her college radiator wasn't working. She could report it to the P'lodge, if she could be bothered. Her mother had told her of the gas fire her father had as a student; of hanging slices of bread on paperclips wound round the cage to make toast; even throwing them at the fire to see who could get them to stick first time.

There was no work she had to do. She picked up her second-best violin. Then changed her mind. She wound a scarf around her head to keep the rain off her hair, and ran down to Theo's room by the river.

A sudden flash as she dashed into his staircase had rumbled into thunder before she reached his door.

"Tea?" she said.

"Good idea. The kettle is . . ."

". . . in your bedroom. The tap is upstairs. The screwdriver is on the table with the kettle. The milk is hanging out of your window."

"What was I doing?"

She had never seen him on his piano stool before. "Playing the piano?"

"What were you doing?"

"Funnily enough, playing the violin. Or rather, not. That's why I came. I need my Vuillaume."

He went into his bedroom and she heard a rather old-fashioned scraping of furniture. "Here," he said, bringing it out, case a bit dusty. "I have a loose plank which no one knows about, under a leg of the bed."

She opened it up and smiled at her new friend. Carefully fixed inside the lid was her full name, in Guy's handwriting.

"I was playing this," he said, as she tuned it. "You take the melody. Then I won't need to sing it."

There can be few activities more conducive to friendship than making music together. With just skill enough to read notes and musicianship enough to give feeling, a couple of semi-competent amateurs will find as much companionship as consummate professionals. Perhaps more.

Within minutes all Charlotte's thoughts of home were forgotten.

Theo's collection of music was catholic and mostly easily playable. Irish folk songs. Beatles. Vaughan Williams.

She took the tune while he romped through the accompaniment. She was a much better musician: or rather, more accomplished, playing far more of the right notes. But his ear was sound, and he was a performer. Even though he skipped and leapt across many chords and approximated the rest, he made the music sparkle and dance.

"Oh, this is great!" Charlotte said with unfettered joy, as he tossed another page of music over his shoulder, never letting the bass waver with his left hand. She almost wished her mother and brother could be in the background, doing something else while the music gave texture to the afternoon. "This is so what Cambridge should be."

"Should be?"

"You know what I mean."

"No idea. *Les Mis*. Played this before?"

"My godmother took me, when I was twelve."

"Then you know it better than I do," and he started the opening chords of *Bring Him Home*. "How on earth did I come by this? Easier for me than you, I think."

"Wait!" she cried. It was one of those pieces which was simpler to read than to perform. "Start again," she said half way through. "I've got the idea now."

Despite many dropped notes he proved a surprisingly sensitive accompanist, following her lead and giving her limelight. She milked it for the sentiment. Towards the end, she was able to exploit the tune and soared to the final top notes near the bridge, holding them as long as possible while the piano faded away beneath her.

The notes hung in the silence.

"Theo!" she laughed, astonished. "You're crying."

"No I'm not," he said, fishing in his pocket for a handkerchief. "Just my eyes are. Ann played that to me once, when I was at school. Or rather, very much not at school. Silly, really, because I was home."

"I'm sorry: I shouldn't have laughed."

"It was absolutely the right thing to do. The only possible response," wiping his eyes, "to the potency of cheap music. The Mendelssohn is much better, anyway."

"Mendelssohn?"

"'*Hear my prayer.*'"

"Ah, yes. It is, really," she conceded.

"I sang that for my voice trial, when I was seven. Ahah! Here. You are the Nightingale, obviously."

He handed her photocopied sheets, sellotaped together: '*The Dicky Bird and the Owl*, Sir Arthur Sullivan', and started to play the introduction.

"I don't sing in front of people," she objected.

"Don't be silly," he didn't stop. "There aren't any people. Your entrance is coming up."

"What nightingale?"

"'A dicky bird sat . . .' I'll singalong till you get the hang . . . 'and warbled by . . .' You'll get lost if you don't start!"

Charlotte plunged in, trying to keep up, soon laughing even more at his low baritone 'Tweedle-eedle-ee's than at his outrageous falsetto 'an opera star I will be's. Half way through, any attempt to hold it together disintegrated. "Please, stop!" she begged. "I really can't sing and laugh at the same time."

Without warning, Theo turned on his piano stool. "Disaster!" he exclaimed, clapping his hands.

"What?" She was genuinely concerned. "Have you forgotten an appointment?"

"Yes. Teatime. We've forgotten cake."

"I thought of going via Fitzbillies. But it was chucking it down and I didn't know if you'd be in. Shall I go now?"

"Certainly not. It's still chucking down. We can have tea and cake without the cake."

So they did, sitting either side of his college-issue coffee table, with his latest experiment, Advent Tea. Like Christmas Tea without the cloves and cinnamon.

"I loved that bit where you played a twiddle," he said. "What do you call it?"

"Acciaccatura?" she said. "Or appoggiatura, perhaps."

"I once knew a man who knew the difference. Also said his father was John Lennon and he understood post-post-Modernism."

"I do, actually. Know the difference." She picked up her violin again. "Hang on. I should have done this hours ago." And she took off her dangly earrings and laid them on the table, to stop the left one hitting the chin rest.

She started to play an acciaccatura, before realising Theo was staring.

"You wore those before."

"Well, I . . . often wear them. They're my winter colours. Ice, snow, sky. I like . . ."

"Shh."

She lowered her violin.

"Yes." He said eventually.

"Can I help? You don't seem . . . very happy."

"No. Thank you." He continued to sit very still. "I might break."

As quietly as she could, she put her violin in its case.

"I didn't want to remember."

He stood up and flung open the window. The rain beat down. He put his head into it, and let it run down him for a while. Then came back in, shut the window and sat.

"Harold. Shroud. He was strange, but you don't know that as a child. Expelled. He tried to kill me, I think. Possibly more than once. He still hates me. I knew all along. I just didn't know I knew, because it hurt too much."

He took the fresh hot mug of tea she offered, and looked up. "Thank you."

She handed him a towel. "You might want to dry your hair."

"I know where it is. And why the dogs couldn't find it." He looked at the towel, puzzled. Then put his tea down and started to dry his hair very slowly, as if every movement hurt. "I suppose this is urgent. Which means it's very important we don't rush it. Bring your coat. Do you have a hat or anything? I have an umbrella. Somewhere."

"Here," Charlotte found it behind his wardrobe.

"Money," he said, putting his wallet in his coat pocket. "Telephone. Gloves. Scarf. Knitting? No. New Testament? Toothbrush? I don't think so. Perhaps that's it."

As they started to shut the door he paused. "I have keys somewhere," he said. "Your fiddle." And he went back into the room, found his keys, latched the window securely, came out and locked the door.

Charlotte followed him to the porters' lodge.

"There was someone working here. Fifteen years ago. Twenty perhaps."

"Before my time," the porter replied.

"Before anyone's time," the second porter chipped in. "None of us were here then."

"A Fellow," Theo went on. "Ancient History, or . . . Arch 'n' Anth perhaps. He had a name."

"I should think so."

"Schubert. Schumann. Schoenberg. He left. There was some unpleasantness."

A Senior Fellow had come in, and was waiting.

"I must find him," Theo continued. "I mean, this evening."

"Don't see how we can help you, if you don't know the gentleman's name."

"Of course you can," Theo said angrily. "You just tell the computer to look him up under the information I've given you."

Charlotte put a hand on his sleeve. He looked at her, and then back at the porter. "I'm sorry. Mr Foulger will have gone home now, I suppose."

286

"He will indeed."

"Please, give him a ring on his home number, or mobile, or whatever you have for a serious emergency, and tell him I need to talk to him. That I've remembered something, and it's urgent. He'll speak to me."

Somewhat to the porter's surprise, Theo was right: within a few minutes he was talking to Tom. A minute or two later, armed with a security password, he was ushered in to use the lodge computer.

The porter nodded Charlotte permission to come in and stand behind his shoulder.

"Baldock," Theo said after a few minutes. He closed the programme carefully so the information would be no more accessible than it had been before. "Thank you," he said, turning as they left the lodge. "I'm sorry I was rude. I'm . . . er. Yes."

They stood on the Cobbles. "Taxi or bicycle? Bicycle is usually quicker, but – oh, taxi!" he hailed. "There is a train in nine minutes. Five pounds extra if you get us to the station in time."

"This is England not bloody Turkey," the cabbie said. "If I can get you there, I will."

Theo bought two return tickets while in the taxi and they caught it by half a minute.

"Now," he said, as they settled in the train facing the direction of travel, at a table, in true childhood fashion. "The question is this. Do we want more tea, or a whiskey?"

Charlotte thought she might be given some kind of explanation. Instead, the journey was spent hearing about his time a chorister, and when he was asked to turn the pages for the organ scholar for a concert. He stepped up to the console, in an ornate baroque church packed with several hundred people, and was confronted, not with notes, but with nothing but numbers. If they'd told him in advance he would have found out how to read figured bass beforehand. If he'd been told a minute earlier, he would have counted carefully using the time signature. His father would have told him what to do. If he had been alive. Fortunately, it all made sense and before he got to the end of the page he had more or less got the hang of it.

He was an entertaining raconteur. Charlotte asked him if he'd done any acting at school.

"I turned up on the wrong day for my audition," he said, looking out of the window. "Which is why I always answer my telephone."

They had arrived at Baldock. Fifteen minutes later they stood in front of a small, redbrick suburban semi with a carefully tidy garden, winter-bare. Theo rang the bell.

A small woman, probably aged over eighty and with an apron on over her clothes, opened the door slightly. She had left the chain on, and her eyes were wary.

"I've come to see Professor Strauss," Theo explained. "I'm sorry not to have telephoned first, but it's a little urgent. He was kind to me when I was a boy. My name is Theophilus Ambrose Fitzwilliam Wedderburn and this is my friend, Charlotte Sebastian. I'm afraid I don't know her other names."

"Did you say Wedderburn?"

"My father was Alan, the organist."

"And you are little Theo?"

"I suppose so. Are you Mrs Strauss?"

The door shut.

Eventually it opened again, without the chain. Charlotte thought her eyes looked a little redder.

"Come in Theo. And Miss Sebastian. Please."

She showed them into a neat, rather small sitting room. Despite a gas fire being on low, Charlotte decided to keep her coat on.

"I have a little sherry," Mrs Strauss said, fetching three tiny glasses from a cupboard. "I suppose you don't know what happened?" She poured them each a drink and sat down. "To my husband?"

Chapter Thirty-Two

NIGHT AND MORNING

"Twenty years ago next March," she said, gazing at her own barely filled glass. "Henry – Heinrich, they all called him in College – was planning to retire soon anyway. He thought of stepping down the previous summer, when he was sixty-five, but you know how academics are. How different things would have been . . ."

The fire breathed noisily. Charlotte took a sip of her sherry.

"You must have been . . . how old? A little boy. Nine or ten I suppose. But you may prefer to tell your side of the story?"

Theo said nothing.

"He was very distressed by the time he told me. I heard it from the police first, would you believe." She pinched the bridge of her nose. "Their version was very garbled and I naturally waited to hear it from him. He was always so clear and precise. That was something his students loved about him: do you remember? But I'm forgetting: you were a schoolboy, not an undergraduate. Would you like some more sherry?"

The decanter was empty.

"Please don't worry," Charlotte said.

Mrs Strauss resumed. "Heinrich knew more than anyone about the history of the Chapel. There was Hilary, of course, who wrote that beautiful book about the windows. And others knew the musical history, or the politics. But Heinrich knew the Chapel. He was going to write his book in retirement. Someone came here wanting his notes; to write it posthumously, with Heinrich's name on the cover. I suppose I should have gone along with it. Are you warm enough?"

They nodded, somewhat untruthfully.

"He was almost the only person who knew about it. The only one who'd been down there. I found it hard to believe. I mean, surely the porters or . . . I don't know. Not the Provost: what interest would he have in it, necessarily?" Charlotte noticed that she pronounced the word correctly, with the stress on the first syllable not the third. "He'd been down there twenty-five or thirty years earlier. The strange thing is, hundreds walk over it every day, and never notice it."

Charlotte was trying to remember where they had been, coming out of the Advent service. She envisaged her earring, nesting in the stone.

"Because you were Alan's boy . . . We were so sad for you, Theo. And your beautiful mother. They never caught him, did they?"

"Not exactly," Theo said.

"Heinrich was really taken with you. Not just for your father's sake. Said you were the cleverest child he ever met. So considerate and gentle, too."

"I remember him. Now. I had forgotten for a while. I don't remember . . . things in my childhood."

"I'm not surprised," she said kindly.

"Or yesterday, actually," he admitted.

"I miss him so much," she said. "After all he'd put up with, in Germany. They were dreadful times, after the war. Sorry: this is not of interest to you. Lots of old people are lonely. I was lucky to have him for so long."

"It's very interesting," Charlotte assured her. "All of it."

"He invited you, as a treat. The rest was my fault. He'd be here now if it hadn't been for my stupidity, interfering. That's what I have to live with. I said, 'Heinrich, he's a little boy. Let him bring a friend. It would be more fun for him.'"

Without warning the tears streamed. Theo was already on his feet, then sitting on the arm of her chair, holding her as if he were her grandson.

He took a clean handkerchief from his pocket. "I'm sorry," he said. "I think it's the wrong day. Unless it's Friday today."

"You haven't changed a bit," she said. "I barely knew you, but from Heinrich's description. Did your mother give you these?"

"Yes," he said. "Please keep it."

"I couldn't possibly. It must be part of a set. I'll launder it and send it back to you. I'm afraid it might not reach you before Christmas, now."

"My mother can tell me which day it is."

"Anyway, you brought that . . . I'm sorry to be uncharitable, but that nasty piece of work. Stroud, wasn't it?"

"I didn't bring him. I remember that, now. He was in the year above. He found out. I don't know how. I didn't tell him, and I don't suppose your husband did. I thought it was all right because I could say that I had been invited on my own. But when your husband said I could take a friend . . . I didn't know that you're allowed to lie, sometimes. My mother hadn't taught me that yet."

"I'm so sorry, Theo. More sorry than you will ever know. What happened next . . . Basically Stroud tricked him. Heinrich could hardly believe a boy could be so devious. So wicked, really. He never believed the worst of anybody. Stroud asked to see the writing on the wall; that medieval graffiti, up by the East End. A long way from where you were. And he didn't notice . . . You must remember all this."

"Actually," Theo said, "I don't really. I remember a fear. Quite a serious fear. The darkness was all right: darkness, in itself, isn't dangerous. The cold wasn't too bad, because I thought I could probably endure that for several hours. And of course I wasn't frightened of dead people because they were dead. People asked me afterwards and that was just silly. What frightened me was knowing it was on purpose."

"That was very disturbing. This boy Stroud," she turned to Charlotte, "shut Theo in. He pulled the stone trap door up over the opening and dropped it shut. Apparently it's much easier to shut than open. Still, not something you could do by mistake. It had been opened to show the boys, and Stroud shut it when Heinrich was already walking towards the East End. Knowing Theo was down there. I dread to think how long it was. Probably half an hour by the time Heinrich realised he was missing and ran to the porters for help. Obviously Theo couldn't get himself out. He was a little boy."

There was a silence for some minutes.

"Mrs Strauss," Charlotte began.

"Helena, please. Call me Helena."

"I knew I couldn't," Theo explained, "so there was no point wasting oxygen trying. Nor calling. So it was simple really. I just had to wait, and assume someone would work it out. Before I ran out of air or body heat. It's surprising I was frightened at all, as there wasn't any point. But I realised, if he could do that, he could do other things. Suppose he did something to Professor Strauss. Perhaps no one would know where I was until it was too late."

"Helena, Theo," Charlotte said. "This must be upsetting both of you. I'll make some tea, if you don't mind me using your kitchen?" Neither objected. While the kettle boiled she found a teapot; a small jug; three delicate bone china cups and saucers.

"Thank you, dear. We took a little pause while you were gone, and I asked Theo about his mother. Anyway, Theo knows all this already. What I hope he was too young to be told was that Harold Stroud then accused my husband of interfering with him. He claimed Henry had shut you in on purpose, and then abused him, up by the altar. He must have read a story somewhere, I suppose. Everybody knew the boy's character, but that wasn't enough to clear Heinrich. It was enough for his colleagues, and the college, and all the people we loved and cared about who knew it was outrageous. But it wasn't enough for the tabloids. It went on and on. We couldn't escape anywhere. We went on holiday, and were accused of 'running away'. He had to step down immediately. It wasn't fair on the college. If he'd been a young man, with his career ahead of him, I suppose we would have braved it out."

"How did you get out, in the end?" Charlotte asked. "Sorry. Stupid question."

"Poor boy," Helena said.

"They kept asking me," Theo said, "who shut me in. Obviously it was Harry. But if they couldn't work that out, how could I help? I hadn't seen him do it."

"What did you want to know?" Helena Strauss asked.

"I needed my memory back. To know where it is."

"You know now?" she asked. "You don't need me to come back to Cambridge?"

"No. I knew all along, but I needed you to tell me. He's put something in there again."

"He's very clever. That's why your father wanted to give him a chance. Now," she changed her tone. "You've been travelling. Can I give you some supper?"

They both reassured her they wouldn't take up any more of her time.

"Mrs Strauss," Charlotte said. "Helena. I hope you don't mind my asking, but how did your husband die? Was it connected?"

"They said it wasn't. It's hard to imagine, till you've been through it. He could hardly bear to walk down the street. And of course, that crime is hated more than any other. Horrible letters. Things posted through our front door. Disgusting. He stuck it out for nearly a year. Then he had two heart attacks, one after the other. And do you know what?"

Charlotte waited.

"I was glad for him."

In the train afterwards, Charlotte asked, "Do you think we should have stayed and had supper with her?"

"I don't know."

"She must be so lonely. I wish we had."

"Let's go back and do it next term. After all this."

"Yes, let's," she agreed enthusiastically. "But really. Not like most people, when they say they'll do something and never do."

"Though 'next term' is making an assumption."

The night rushed past, scattered with lights promising warm homes and other people's Christmas preparations. There were very few people in the carriage, and none near enough to overhear.

"Theo. Is it a crypt, or what?"

"Yes."

"How is it possible so few people know about it?"

"It's not a secret, as far as I know. I've read histories of the Chapel, and never seen it mentioned. Why would anyone think of it? Presumably the police asked for a map. It's probably not on any. Professor Strauss told us he was the only person who'd ever been down there, twenty years ago, and the Provost and Head Porter are both new. They've probably never heard of it. Professor Strauss wouldn't have wanted to talk about it, would he? He never wrote his book. It is . . ." He waited for the right word. "Wicked."

"That's why you were upset? When my earring fell."

"The dogs wouldn't smell anything through the stone. People are buried there. A painter. One of the Bloomsburies. In an urn or something. Fry. I didn't know who he was, but I thought the name was interesting. And Keynes. I was a child, and assumed it was spelt like . . . garden canes. Like the things adults used to hit boys with."

"People must know where Roger Fry is buried! How could that be a secret?"

"Perhaps it's even on Wikipedia. That doesn't mean the police would know, if no one in college told them." The train shuddered to a halt. "Oh, here we are. I'd rather walk, but I suppose we're in a hurry. Bother."

"You haven't got your gloves or scarf or umbrella." She grabbed them off the rack as he headed for the exit. "I don't think we're in that much of a hurry. Ten minutes isn't going to make much difference."

As they walked back, with drunken young men three abreast pushing them off the pavement and girls in impossibly short skirts tottering on high heels, Charlotte said, "I'm not sure I've understood why we needed to see her. You knew everything already, didn't you?"

They turned by the towering-spired Roman Catholic church, said to be the last point to disappear from the city in the event of a Biblical flood. Theo didn't answer until they were nearly at the Fitzwilliam Museum.

"I wasn't quite ready," he said. They had reached King's Parade. "To remember."

It was barely nine thirty when they let themselves back in to college.

"Provost," Theo said.

"Would you prefer to go alone?"

"Not 'specially. You know about it, because of your earrings."

"I'm not sure I do, really. Just that something's going on, and the Crypt has something in it."

"Ah," said Theo. "Do you know the Sally-Anne test?"

"No."

"Two dolls: Sally and Anne. Sally puts a marble in her basket, then leaves the room. Anne takes Sally's marble and puts it in her own basket. Sally comes back in. Where does Sally look for the marble?"

"Why are they dolls?" Charlotte asked.

"That," Theo said, "is a very good question. Autistic children think Sally looks in Anne's basket because they can't understand her not knowing it's there if they know it themselves. I wonder if they can hear this bell." They were standing at the official front door which faced the vast lawn. "I don't know why I came to this door: I've never used it before." They went to the side door.

"You sure you want me to come?"

"Hello, Catherine."

"Give me a moment, Theo," Caroline said. "Someone's just rung the front door."

"That was me."

"Sorry?"

"Is Pete in?"

"He's at a concert. Do you want to come back tomorrow?"

"No, thank you," Theo said. "This is Charlotte Sebastian."

"Good evening, Charlotte." Caroline was used to fobbing people off. "Do you mind my asking what it's about?"

"Not at all," he said, taking off his gloves and scarf. "Does he keep his telephone on in a concert?"

"Not usually." She paused. "Though he is keeping it on at the moment."

"Good," Theo said.

"Is it very important?"

"Yes."

She gave up, and dialled her husband. "Will he know what it's about? Ah, Peter."

Theo turned to Charlotte. "We're back to Sally-Anne again. How can I know whether he knows?"

"We'll see you in a few minutes, then." She hung up.

While they waited Theo asked Caroline about their Christmas plans, whether her parents were visiting, would they be going away? Caroline wondered about Charlotte. Wasn't Theo's girlfriend Clare Savage? They must be old friends: they seemed very easy together.

It was nearly a quarter of an hour before Peter came in, flushed from the cold, pulling off his coat and puffing the December night into his warm kitchen.

"Hello Theo!" His memory struggled for a moment. "Charlotte Sebastian, isn't it? Shall we go into my study, Theo?"

"It's in the Crypt," he said. "I'm sorry to have been so long working it out. I presume it's not too late or everyone would know by now. Or not know, perhaps. Which would be worse, obviously."

Peter glanced at Charlotte.

"She doesn't know," Theo explained. "Though she knows it's in the Crypt because she dropped her earring on it."

"I see," Peter said. "Thank you, Theo."

"Right," Theo said. "I suppose that's all you need to know. We'll be off then."

"We may need more," he said. "I'm sure the police will want to speak to you."

"Okay," Theo nodded.

"The Crypt, you said?"

"In the Chapel. Or rather, antechapel. Obvious really. Do you mind if we go now? I need food, sorry. Can't stay."

"I've got your number, Theo. Keep it on. Stay within easy reach. Thank you."

They were already out in the night-bright cold. "And sleep, I think," Theo added.

"I've got cheese and apples in my room," Charlotte offered. "I could get a takeaway?"

"Don't care. Anything."

The nearest place she could think of, out of term, was Gardies. The queue would be half-way along Rose Crescent. Cheese and apples were obviously not enough.

"Wait," she said, and ran back to the Lodge before she could change her mind. "Mrs Langdon Murray, I'm so sorry." She realised, to her shame, that she was near tears. "It's been a rather harrowing evening. I'm not sure Theo is quite well. Is there any way . . . I don't know . . . an omelette or something? I'm sorry: it's an awful imposition."

"I'm so glad you've come back," Caroline said warmly. "Bring him in. We'll feed you both. Pete's on the telephone already."

He was already taut as a garrotting wire. Every particle in his body strained towards Christmas Eve. Each night he lay on his bed but barely slept.

Within seconds, his alarm told him it had been found. At first the change in the signal was so slight, it could have been down to error. And then he saw it: the movement of the red dot on his screen. It had been discovered. There was no doubt now.

Fuck.

I have allowed for this. Not just one, but two fall-back plans. I will succeed.

He made himself a strong instant coffee. The dot would soon disappear, as it was dismantled and the GPS chip disabled – presumably examined to see if it could lead to him.

The sooner he moved on to Plan B the better. Everything was in place. There was nothing he could do now, in the small hours of the morning.

And Plan C.

The puzzle was why now, after it had gone undetected by the dogs.

That fucker Wedderburn. With fierce violence, he jerked on his tap and threw the rest of his coffee down the sink. The college had not remembered about the Crypt, exactly as he had gambled: it was not known about, much, even then, which was why it was such a 'treat'. Wedderburn had sneaked on him again, probably telling lies about that ghastly old creep with the German name who had abused him. As good as, anyway.

He would make Wedderburn pay. He had several hours before daylight, to plan his next move with the meticulous detail that was his hallmark.

The next day Theo woke up feeling as if he'd been there before. He had a memory of distress, but also of something comforting underlying it all.

If he could get back to work, nothing would matter. Even his doctorate didn't matter, in the face of his exciting finding. Surely he wouldn't be interrupted any more, before Christmas. He'd had the most exciting breakthrough, in mathematics, since he was a boy. Since 24th October 1994.

He spread out his papers.

It was at that point that his door was rapped with a particularly forceful knock. He wondered why policemen always look so much bigger than everyone else. Presumably it's all the paraphernalia they carry around. Like a toddler in a spacesuit.

"Hello."

"May we come in, sir?"

"Out of interest, what would you say if I said no?"

"It's your room, Mr Wedderburn. We won't come in without an invitation. It is Mr Wedderburn? DC Sean Southern."

"Probably." It was too late: they had interrupted him now. "I suppose you'd like tea or something. Or do you drink coffee?"

"Tea for me. Coffee for my colleague here, PC Johnson."

"I ought to warn you coffee is a lot more complicated."

"Whatever you're having will be fine," PC Johnson assured him.

Theo preferred not to remember the rest of that morning. He had to go through the events again and again. How everything changed after his father's death. How Harry Stroud – as everyone called him: Shroud was much more accurate – had tried to kill him. Twice. When he felt he could no longer bear any more, it was his turn to ask.

"Have you found it?"

"Have we found what, sir?"

"What you were looking for? The bomb that could have destroyed the Chapel and killed sixteen hundred people? Was it in the Crypt?"

"We found the Crypt, sir. We are very grateful to you."

"Did you find it?"

"Everyone is safe now, sir. Thank you. You have helped save a very important heritage site."

"Thank God."

The two Policemen waited. Eventually one of them coughed.

"It was worth it, sir. However painful all that was."

Theo wiped his face. "Thank you. That's all I needed to know. Excuse me." He blew his nose.

"There is no danger now, sir."

From: pml19@cam.ac.uk
To: tom.foulger@kings.cam.ac.uk
Subject:
On: 15 12 18 at 12.32.15

hi tom,

caroline gave me your message. trust i understood correctly. much celebration if so.

pml

From: tom.foulger@kings.cam.ac.uk
To: pml19@cam.ac.uk
Subject:
On: 15 12 18 at 12.47.38

Dear Pete

You probably did. I'll pop over shortly and confirm. The Dean will be happy (and the Beeb delirious).

Tom

From: robyn.mclarty@cambridgeshire.pnn.police.uk
To: alice.cannington@royal.gsx.gov.uk
Subject: Update
On: 15 12 18 at 13.21.52

Incendiary device located and disabled. Area will be kept sterile till 1200 24.12.18 and high alert anti-terrorist measures kept in place. Chapel now deemed safe for public use.

Yours,
Robyn McLarty,
3019, Cambridgeshire Police

Please think about the impact on the environment before printing this email - is it necessary to do so?

From: alice.cannington@royal.gsx.gov.uk
To: robyn.mclarty@cambridgeshire.pnn.police.uk
Subject: Update
On: 15 12 18 at 15.15.04

Dear Ms McLarty

Thank you for your email. Please be assured that I will forward this on immediately to Miss Olivia Humbery-StJohn, Assistant Private Secretary to HRH the Duchess of Cambridge for her security team's consideration.

Yours sincerely,
Alice Cannington.
Miss Alice Cannington

Secretary to the Private Secretary to HRH The Duchess of Cambridge
Household Office of The Duke and Duchess of Cambridge
Kensington Palace, London, W8 4PU
www.royal.uk

Note, delivered by hand, in Miss Humbery-StJohn's handwriting:

Your Royal Highness,

Provisionally, it is now looking possible that the visit to Cambridge University on Christmas Eve may go ahead. We'll keep an eye on it.

Olivia x

Chapter Thirty-Three

THIRD WEEK OF ADVENT

Ever since Advent Sunday the school term had tumbled over itself faster than ever. Hui was the only chorister whose family wouldn't be coming for Christmas. Even his grandparents in England, usually so scrupulous, couldn't be there: his great-grandfather was in hospital, Hui assumed probably dying as he was so very old.

He had been invited to go home with Cory after the Christmas services were over, as he couldn't fly home until Boxing Day. He alone would get *three* Christmases. Hearing of Cory's family filling their vicarage he almost envied English children, with their numerous brothers and sisters and cousins.

He had heard grown-ups say that the worst thing about the One Child Policy was the expectations. His parents, grandparents, even his uncle had no one else. They would all be watching him on the television; then waiting up to hear him, live, on the radio. The other choristers' families would be listening too. But not with the same undiluted dedication.

Another week of chorister 'Slack'. It wasn't 'slack' at all, but it was still called that, maybe from forever ago when choristers had time to go skating and play chess and read books, after all the other children had left.

He would have liked Dr Wedderburn to accompany him home again. During the flight last summer, Dr Wedderburn had taught him far more interesting maths than any of his teachers ever had. And he had treated him differently. Like a grown-up. As if Hui could understand much more difficult concepts than in fact he could.

Yes, he liked Dr Wedderburn very much indeed. He hoped he would meet him again.

His expensive barrister, Crispin felt, had had rather an easy job of it in the end. The press had been highly sympathetic: his friends even more so. It was he who emerged the victim – of a malicious and unfounded accusation.

Which left him free to worry about something far more serious. Being found not guilty of one allegation had, illogically, made him feel more confident about the other. The Provost had stopped him in college near the beginning of term, and said he'd like an opportunity to talk to him. When nothing had come of it he assumed – at first – that he might be in the clear. With a flushed feeling of needing to extricate himself as soon as he could, he thought he might just have got away with it.

He had been insane to get involved. It had happened so subtly, so slowly, that he was caught up in it before he realised how compromised he was. Academics accept funding all the time. Research can't happen without it. Surely, in the early days he hadn't even known he was doing anything underhand. Weren't others compromised far more?

He had spent the intervening weeks since Peter's comment discovering some pretty shocking cover-ups. Grants merging into conflicts-of-interest merging into outright fraud.

Hushed up by authorities.

Professor Richard Eastell of Sheffield University, for instance, simply appeared on Wikipedia as having been the subject of various 'controversies'; at his eventual hearing by the GMC, the brief paragraph continued, he was found 'not guilty of misconduct' because he hadn't 'deliberately set out to mislead'. But Crispin knew which colleagues to ask. It didn't take long to discover that Eastell's department had been in receipt of around four million a year from Proctor & Gamble . . . coincidentally employing someone who wrote a paper claiming results for a drug they happened to produce. Which paper Eastell put his name to. Without even seeing the data.

Or the infamous surgeon Dr Anjan Bannerjee, found guilty of serious professional misconduct for falsifying research, who later received an MBE despite further scandals surrounding his name. True, he was stripped of it again. But the very fact that he was nominated demonstrated that his colleagues thought highly enough of him – or more likely of themselves – to ignore allegations of 'financial irregularity' in the light of his achievements.

Men who attend the same universities, share the same qualifications or work on the same teams. Who close ranks...

Perhaps even more shocking, Banerjee's research supervisor at KCL, Professor Timothy Peters, covered up for his protégé and put his own name to a paper which several colleagues knew was fraudulent. He received his reprimand ... and kept his A+ merit award, worth around £75k on top of his salary. Annually.

Surely all this, committed by such eminent men, was far worse? Crispin hadn't falsified anything. Yet. Provably. There was no evidence against him, even if Peter had somehow learnt what Crispin was in receipt of. And how could he? Cryptocurrency can't be traced: every schoolboy knows that. Peter must have been wanting to talk to him about something else altogether. Or perhaps was giving him a veiled warning, and a chance to regularise matters ... even pay the money back? As if he could, now.

In his heart, Crispin knew the truth. The Provost had been waiting to see what would happen. If he, Crispin, had been found guilty of an unrelated criminal offence it would have saved the college having to challenge him over his academic integrity. His career would have been over anyway.

Clever. Cowardly. And a very great deal cheaper.

Now he had been cleared – of an accusation which, he knew, not a man in the world doesn't fear – he would face a far worse charge, with far less sympathy.

He must construct a defence.

His lodger, Simon, worked in the University Chemistry Lab, part of a team in receipt of a grant from Glaxo Smith Klein awarded the previous term: Simon had come home, after celebrating at his supervisor's house, long after midnight, having mislaid his front door key (yet again) and needing Crispin to let him in.

Crispin remembered the sum being in seven figures ... not that the amount changed the principle. And that was perfectly above board and transparent. Apparently.

His disgust at the time had been genuine. He had chosen psychology because of ideologically held convictions as well as academic aptitude. He knew plenty of psychiatrists who prescribed – perfectly legal, supposedly objectively researched – drugs which could wreck patients' lives. Lorazepam, which not only caused decades-long addictions but also prevented proper therapy which could cure rather than simply masking the pain. SSRIs given to adolescents, despite universal ignorance as to the effect on the developing brain because testing on minors would be 'unethical ...' But it was not unethical to experiment on adolescent patients, apparently.

It had happened to his own sister, for God's sake.

Why did these esteemed professors and doctors of psychiatry dish out dangerous and addictive pills as if they were smarties, if not because of financial interest? They might not be in receipt of crude brown envelopes. But they accepted the luxurious conferences in Barbados or Venice; the fat consultancies and speaking fees; even (he picked up these threads too) the opportunity to buy shares in the big pharma companies.

He needed to know more; much more. His professional survival was on the line. Whatever Selina said, he wouldn't even get a job in business if he cocked this one up.

Clare was not entirely sure why she had come back to Cambridge. Nor, more curiously, why she hadn't told Theo.

She had gone home to her parents' for a night and found it so claustrophobic that three weeks of it would have driven her nuts. Paradoxically, she probably got more work done at home. Meals were shopped, cooked and washed up for her. Her father put a little desk in her bedroom overlooking the fields. Perhaps it was because everything reminded her too much of the summer and Kathryn: the last time she'd been home, it had been as half of a couple. So the next day she lied, told her mother she had been recalled to

Cambridge to go over something with a senior colleague and she would be back for Christmas.

As to why she hadn't told Theo, there seemed no immediate need. If she bumped into him she would say that she hadn't realised she would be coming back and hadn't got round to telling him.

Thus she stayed in her room, working steadily and quite efficiently, only going out for provisions.

When she woke, that morning just before Christmas which was to become so memorable, it was to a dawn of such silver low-lit crispness as only an English winter boasts. A small stripe of washed sunlight spread itself on her pillow, just missing her face. She felt better than she had in months. Below, the market was already bustling. The Sainsbury's in Sydney Street presumably opened at seven.

Drinking two coffees one after another she washed her face, cleaned her teeth, put on the same jeans, T-shirt and hoodie she had been wearing for several days and didn't bother with makeup. She wouldn't see anyone she knew.

She shoved her credit card into her back pocket along with her iPhone and key-card, and slipped out into the morning.

It was a split second decision.

She was to agonise over it for years: what would have happened if she had jumped in the other direction; how many people's lives would have been different.

How different history might have been.

At first, she couldn't quite process it. A man had his arm around her, as if they were a couple, and was steering her in the opposite direction from the one she had intended.

She felt something sharp in her ribs. "Don't say anything. Keep walking. Yes, this is a gun. Yes it's loaded. You won't be hurt if you do exactly as I say."

They had reached King's Parade.

"It's not you I'm interested in. Don't say anything, act as if you're my girlfriend and you'll be unharmed."

She didn't have time to do anything except believe.

"If you do anything I haven't told you to, I'll kill you. Don't think being caught will deter me. I'm on a suicide mission anyway."

He moved his hand to her back pocket and removed her telephone, card and key.

He steered her towards a taxi. "Get in, hand this to the driver and tell him to keep the change. Don't say anything else. At all. If he chats, ignore him."

He gave her a piece of paper with an address, and a ten pound note.

She did exactly as he'd told her. Got in, waited for him to follow then leant forward, handed the note and paper to the driver and said rather squeakily, "Keep the change."

"Thank you miss." He turned. "Most generous, thank you." Her companion had a scarf over his face, as if against the cold, and a woolly hat. Surely we look mismatched? Then she remembered her lack of makeup and sloppy clothes and realised there was nothing incongruous to arouse suspicion.

"Late party?" The driver looked into his mirror. They didn't respond.

This might be her only chance. The conflicting risks boxed in her brain. She wasn't the person he wanted. Her life wasn't interesting enough. If he simply wanted to rape someone he had chosen a heavy-handed method. Perhaps he would dispose of her afterwards?

She was so terrified – and confused – it was easier to make no decision and do nothing.

There was very little traffic. Too early in the day for Christmas shopping. The university was long out of term. Within minutes they had left King's Parade, entered Trumpington Street and were in an area of Cambridge Clare barely knew. She wished she had dared read the address. To her dismay the traffic lights were in their favour, and they swung into a tree-lined, expensive-looking street. She noted the huge Victorian dwellings set back from the road behind sweeping gravel drives and wondered if any were still privately owned.

A tiled roof; a monkey puzzle tree; a conspicuous house number on a gatepost. Anything might help ...

They stopped outside a house at the very bottom of the road, and he indicated that she should get out first. He followed close behind and the taxi turned and drove off.

There was no one in sight. She wondered if anyone might be

looking out of a window. She didn't dare stumble, or indicate anything amiss.

He pushed her towards a quiet lane alongside the last house.

"Across that field. Don't look suspicious. I've got you covered all the way."

Her trainers were woefully inadequate. They were almost immediately clogged with ploughed earth and she struggled not to fall. Her clothes desperately deficient. For a five minute nip to Sainsbury's it wouldn't have mattered. When would she be back in the warmth of her room? Within the hour? The day, even?

The field seemed to go on and on.

"Please," she said quietly. "Can I scrape the mud off my shoes?"

He ignored her.

In his father's foots he trod, now the ground was eeeven. No, that was wrong. In the liege's feets . . . No. In his footsteps glad he trod. Crisp and white and even. Anything. She must think about anything, to keep herself steady. The trees on the horizon were no nearer. She shuddered violently, though whether with fear or cold she didn't know.

She tried to turn but he snapped, "Keep walking. Don't stop."

A rapport. Munchausen's Syndrome. Don't be stupid, Stockhausen's Syndrome. Important to establish Stockholm's Syndrome. And very, very important not to be stupid, keep thinking, a clear head.

They had reached the line of trees. Instead of being relieved, she was even colder and they were further from the houses, almost invisible and surely out of shouting distance.

"Stand with your face against that tree. Hands behind your back. I've still got you covered and no one will hear anything."

She heard a terrible rip, loud as a gunshot, and started shaking.

Then felt something harsh and sticky on her wrists. Duct tape. She wanted to cry with relief. He had put the gun down then. Could she make a run for it? Of course not: she would only manage a few steps. Even without a gun he would be far faster on his feet. If she had been able to see him . . . if she had known he would be unarmed for a split second . . .

The movement over her head was so unexpected she flinched and the tape went over her nostrils. She panicked. She would suffocate!

He had to know she would suffocate . . .

"You stupid fucking bitch. Keep still and I'll redo it. Anything funny and I'll shoot you."

She stood as still as possible, shaking as she was. He tore the tape off her face, taking swathes of her hair with it. She heard more ripping. Keep absolutely still.

Quickly, she said, "I won't make a sound. No one will hear me from here. Please let me breathe."

He ignored her and the tape went over her mouth.

"Turn and sit."

The ground was surely wet. How much colder would she get if she sat down?

"Suit yourself. I'm taping your feet either way."

It was safer to comply. She put her back to the tree and lowered herself down, wondering whether it would be possible to tear the tape on the rough bark of the tree.

"Don't."

Her eyes raised a question.

"I know what I'm doing. Don't think I'm a fucking moron either."

She must even think the right thoughts if she was to be safe.

"Feet out." As well as being wet the ground was uneven, she was sitting on a root and she couldn't lean back because of her hands being behind her. He started to pull off her trainers.

"You can keep your socks on. Don't say I didn't look after you."

She nodded, trying to look thanks.

Her eye caught a sawn-off walking stick: the 'gun' which had silenced her in the taxi. "Yeah, and it did the job."

How easily she could have got help! He could have been arrested by now . . .

"Aren't you glad I wasn't pointing a loaded gun at you. I don't do unnecessary. You behave, you might get out of this alive."

He picked up her trainers. "Not that you can, but don't move. There's no one within shouting distance, you won't get anywhere and I'll be bloody annoyed. And I don't like annoyed."

She watched him go, straining eyes and ears for any clue. She saw a glimpse of him between the trees. After a count of just over twenty she heard a faint splash. Then another.

They were near water; presumably the Cam. Water conveys sound. But how far, how she would reach it, where the nearest dwelling might be on the other side . . .

With a pang of irony she realised Theo would know. He was on friendly terms with every inch of the river, from the Weir right up to Grantchester as well as the Backs.

The thought came to her, unwelcome and unexpected. Was this something to do with him? Her father still believed being involved with cryptocurrency was dubious. She told him this was rubbish, and when she relayed his comment to Theo he had sighed with exasperation. She knew Theo was right, really. But she wouldn't put it past him to be led astray by something daft or dangerous.

She was already wishing she hadn't drunk two mugs of coffee.

The cold was biting her bones, aching into her wet thighs and prodding her back. She tried to shift her weight and made it worse.

"Cold?" he asked, without looking up.

She nodded.

"Pity. Need my coat myself."

Her face itched unbearably.

The trembling began in a small way. At first she didn't attempt to resist. Perhaps it would warm her. It would tell him how wretched she was. As it grew it became more violent, till she wasn't sure if she could control it. Her teeth were knocking so loudly she could hear nothing else. Her body spasmed.

For a long time he didn't react. Then, without looking, "Bloody annoying, that."

Stop it. Stop the shaking. He must not get annoyed.

She tensed her muscles as hard as she could. Could it end in death? Or mutilation?

Not rape, surely. But of course it could. Because he was angry or to threaten or simply because he was bored.

What did he want? Might he start cutting off bits of her body for ransom? What difference would it make to know? She couldn't negotiate or build rapport.

The unfriendly sun had hardly moved. From time to time she struggled to breathe, and this really frightened her.

She realised with an indifferent humiliation that warmth was spreading into her trouser seat.

It would not stay warm for long.

Chapter Thirty-Four

DAY

Straight after he dropped the weird couple off in Latham Road, Andrius – Andy, as he had become since moving to the UK – had been flagged down by a couple of older ladies, wanting the Grafton Centre for 'last minute' Christmas shopping. He hadn't started his own yet. His wife had lots of presents under their new little plastic tree. "Daug gražiau, Andriau, ir nereikės šluoti spyglių." (Much nicer, Andrius, and we won't have to sweep the needles.)

After them a gentleman needed to catch a train . . . and so it had gone on for most of the morning without even a pause for the sandwiches his wife had made for him.

Just when he thought he'd earned a breather, a pair of out-of-season tourists asked to be taken to 'the university.' He had made the same mistake himself on arrival, until another driver told him how Cambridge worked and where all the different colleges were scattered. "When they want 'the university,' mate, take them to King's, Trinity, John's, any of the posh ones. They just want to see some old buildings and a few punts, and they'll be fine." He could have made double-money: he knew plenty of other Lithuanians who would have fiddled with the clock when unwary foreigners got in. He took them to King's Parade.

"Where do we go?" the man asked in what Andrius thought was an American accent.

"Anywhere you like. University all around. You must pay for some colleges, but all friendly. Happy Christmas."

"Happy Christmas to you," his wife said, "and have a nice day now."

It was time to take a few days off. His wife's family was coming to stay, to their terraced house off Mill Road. They would bring herring with them, and Kūčiukai, with poppy water. Twelve dishes on the table on Christmas Eve.

As he ate his sandwich he stared out of the car window, not really seeing the elderly academic on his bicycle or the young girl glued to her 'phone. He was looking at the spot where he had picked up his first fare of the day. Courting couples don't take cabs at seven o'clock in the morning.

Not talking. A couple newly in love generally sink into each other in the back of the car, wanting the drive to last. That couple had sat next to each other, but with no affection. He had caught the woman's eyes and would have said she was fearful, but she looked down again straight away.

And such an odd place to be dropped off. As he'd driven away he had looked in his mirror and they weren't approaching the house.

He liked the British police and realised they were generally benign, but had such an ingrained fear of authority from his childhood that it would have taken a lot more than his current vague unease for him to approach them.

"Addenbrooke's please." The man opening the back door of his car was perhaps a surgeon, or somebody important.

"Of course, sir." He put the half-eaten sandwich back in its bag.

Ann was wrapping presents.

Theo was both the hardest and easiest to shop for. Easiest, because he genuinely didn't mind if he didn't receive anything. And hardest, because that was the issue: finding anything. Nevertheless she enjoyed giving to him best. She could give him a pencil shaped like a tenor saxophone, or a pair of cufflinks with a tiny working pencil on one wrist and a sharpener on the other, just because they made her laugh.

Already the chestnuts had been peeled, scorching her fingertips but tasting so much better than vacuum-packed ones. The parsnips were par-boiled, dusted with parmesan and mustard powder and open-frozen. Both stuffings were made. The brandy butter crusted with nutmeg, the cranberry sauce rich with port and cinnamon bark and the bread sauce thick with butter and cream and peppered with cloves.

Brian never quite understood why they didn't put their decorations up at the beginning of the month like everyone else. All Ann could say was that they'd always bought the tree on the twenty-third and decorated it on Christmas Eve . . . to the sound of the Nine Lessons on Radio 4, unless she was attending in person.

Now she sat at the mahogany table which she and Alan had bought in an auction when they were first married, surrounded by wrapping paper: tasteful dull red with raffia string, for Brian; glittery gold with silver ribbon, for Charlie; and for Theo, paper to annoy him like a nail across a blackboard . . . music paper, covered in notes which were completely unplayable: a key signature that didn't exist (three sharps: G, B and A), a time signature which was then not honoured (four four, followed by a minim and two quavers in one bar and then five demi-semis in the next) and in the bottom line (no bass clef) something which wouldn't have harmonised at all. It would serve her right if he insisted on playing it.

What she meant, when she told Brian that was how they'd always done it, was that it was how she and Alan and Theo had when it was the three of them. Brian was not touchy at all. Nevertheless she suspected that her life before must seemed tinselled with a dusting of glamour he knew he could never give her.

How she was looking forward to Theo's being home! Even though he lived barely ten minutes' walk away, she still went weeks without knowing how he was unless she called at his rooms. Theo didn't really do telephone: not just for chatting.

But when he came home he was fully there in a way that neither Charlie nor even Brian truly was. He would fix the internet and order loo paper and change dead light bulbs for energy efficient ones and advise her about interesting things she could do with her life and urge her to apply as violinist to a professional Cambridge chamber group which had recently lost its second fiddle.

Far more important, as soon as he walked in they would be laughing at jokes no one else understood, so all they needed was for one of them to say, 'Goldfish; what goldfish?' or 'Hitler's ball?' and they would be off, Charlie and Brian rolling their eyes.

Theo's theorem was doing what it should. He'd had one or two minor glitches, now smoothed out far more easily than expected. The almost-primes in his sequence were indeed pseudorandom in the strong sense he needed for his new transference principle, for translated multiplicative and additive structure.

And the primes were dense in the almost-primes. Just as it should be . . .

It was beginning to get dark. He looked in his pocket for his handkerchief. His Friday handkerchief seemed to be missing. He wondered why.

"Text message," his watch said politely, in his own clipped tones.

He needed more tea.

The Chapel was safe. The people were safe. The little eight-year-olds and almost adolescent thirteen-year-olds; the members of the town who would queue on Christmas Eve; the parents visiting their chorister children; the Provost and his wife and the other Fellows: all safe.

So why did he still feel sickened? Why did he keep thinking of refugees crossing cruel seas . . . children going to cold, dark graves . . . beautiful and ancient monuments falling in the sand?

In three days he would go home to Ann and Charlie and Ann's husband Brian, and they would eat free-range goose or rack of beef or something equally Ann-ish. Unless Brian cooked, in which case it would be once-frozen turkey with Oxo gravy from Lidl. It didn't matter.

Nothing mattered.

One day it would all collapse into dust and even maths wouldn't matter anymore.

He looked at his watch and saw the first few words of the text. "Theo, this is urgent. Can you . . ." Clare didn't do unpredictable. She did plans, and being on time, and that sort of thing.

He went into the bedroom to top up the teapot. For a minute or two he couldn't find where he had put the milk. It would be Christmas soon. Perhaps Ann would like a present?

He shook his wrist to show the whole message: "Theo, this is urgent. Please come and meet me. Now. I'll explain when you get here. Cx. PS Did I say, it's urgent? Very."

His telephone started to sing the alarm: his tea top-up had brewed.

It was Clare's style. Sort of. She often expressed exasperation at his not doing things more quickly. It wasn't unusual for her to tell him what to do. And the PS was her sense of humour too. If that's what it was.

So he wondered what was bothering him. Other than the deepest wrench of sorrow that yet again, his work would have to wait.

Andrius was back in King's Parade. It would be getting dark soon. His last pick-up had been a couple of schoolgirls, heels like the Eiffel Tower, studs through the most unlikely places in their faces. He was baffled how they stayed warm enough to survive. And yet they seemed more robust than the girl in the sensible jeans and warm college hoodie he'd picked up first thing.

He recognised her hoodie from the colours. He had seen other students with the same purple and white, on a T-shirt or a scarf. He was outside the same college again now. They were friendly in there. When he was new to his job he had pulled in on the Cobbles, not knowing he shouldn't, and one of them had come out to tell him, but he did it in a very nice way and advised him where he could turn round instead. And they had a quick chat about home because the man had recently been on holiday to Palanga and told him he loved the Baltic.

There was a brief lull. Nobody was going to book him in the next five or ten minutes. He cut the engine and went into the college to tell them, in case they were interested.

Clare had never shared her location with him before. He had set their telephones up so she could track him any time: if he was late for some event she wanted him on time for – and she usually did – she could then tell how late he was going to be. And ring him up and tell him how annoyed she was. And he could apologise.

It didn't work the other way around. This made sense. She was always on time. Sensibly, she had done so now because she wanted him to join her.

He knew the place, more or less. Half way to Grantchester. By punt. Beyond Fen Causeway by about a chapter of *Winnie-the-*

Pooh. Before the river turns, with the few small gardens which go down to the bank: where his house would be, one day. She was on the East side of the river, just before Paradise Island.

The most obvious way to get there was by river. It would take at least an hour, and he'd have to haul a punt up the rollers, beyond the Mill Pond at the Weir.

River transport didn't usually fit Clare's idea of urgent. Indeed, rivers didn't really go with Clare's lifestyle at all.

Bicycle would be faster, but wouldn't get him all the way. He could bike to the corner of Lammas Land and walk the last stone's throw. It was impossible to tell from Google what the terrain would be like. There could be tributaries, not in flow when the photograph was taken in high summer. Or barbed wire. Or a ditch full of nettles and an old bike. The most likely hazard was that he would find himself in somebody's garden.

Wrapped in his grandfather's heavy wool coat, a knitted scarf and his leather-and-tweed gloves, he was just nearing the P'lodge when his telephone flashed 'low battery'.

Drat. He hadn't plugged it in while he was working.

"Afternoon," Stefan, the porter on duty, looked up. Seeing Theo's telephone he said, "You want to plug it in again?"

"Please," Theo said. "I wasn't expecting to go out."

"Assignation, eh?" Stefan said.

"Yes. On the river, half way to Grantchester."

"Bit cold, this time of year. Hope she's worth it." And he winked.

"Yes. Thank you."

"Any idea when you'll be back? I'm off at five."

"No."

"Enjoy yourself."

Theo went out into the cold and unlocked his bike.

"Now sir," Stefan turned back to the slightly-built man with the Eastern European accent. "Run that past me again?"

Theo was glad of his scarf and gloves. The sky frowned low over Cambridge. The Swiss blue of the morning had slurred into dishcloth grey. Few were outside and those mostly bent, lashed by a stinging sleet. Theo found the wind against him, his spectacles blurred with slushy rain, and as he turned at the roundabout into Fen Causeway his eyes were momentarily blinded and he wondered whether the lorry shuddering beside him had seen him.

A couple of miserable ponies on the common stared at the sodden ground through their plastered fringes. A bedraggled mother tugged her wailing child and jabbed at the pelican crossing, screaming at her offspring to be quiet.

Even the lights which were beginning to come on behind a few windows seemed unenthusiastic and smeary.

When Theo reached the corner of Lammas Land, he dismounted and considered. Grantchester Street was ahead, with its small back-to-back terraced houses, now priced way out of the average academic's range. He put his hand in his pocket to consult the map on his telephone, then remembered. Never mind: he'd memorised it.

Clare thought she could have endured anything, were it not for the cold. The wet, and the cold.

She had clamped her mind onto the image of a bath: taps steaming; bubbles winking; a hot drink; her mother with a warm towel. It would happen. One day. If she fixed on that, she would survive.

The rattling of her teeth filled the dripping, dank glade with clattering. She had got through this before, she told herself. When she was a child, her mother hadn't collected her on time from a riding lesson and she had waited, in a barn, as cold as this.

Rape. He would not rape her. No one would rape her stinking of urine. Hair slapped to her head, face shaking with cold. Rape is an act of war, not lust. He might rape her just for the terror of it. Rape is just a physical act. Everyone has bad sex sometimes. She would go to a police station and get checked over, all the advantages of modern medicine to protect her.

One day she would be warm again. Today, perhaps tonight. It must be. She could not survive a night like this. Not another hour.

Don't think how long it will be. It will come to an end and you will be warm.

Some people don't survive. He is mad enough to kill you. And then you will never see your mum to say goodbye and Kathryn will never know how much you love her and that you still love her and everyone will think it was Theo and you are straight and it is Theo you love.

This is his fault. Nothing is Theo's fault. He is a bloody fool and innocents can do a hell of a lot of damage. Will Theo help me? Will anyone?

My wrists. My mouth. The tape cuts. Cheeks, wrists, ankles. Sitting on a root. Cutting my bum, my coccyx, digging. Would be okay if it was summer. And no tape. Then I could talk to him, and negotiate, and he wouldn't hurt me.

Sleet. Tears. Freezing. Bloody Theo.

Theo was finding it hard going, but then he had expected to. He had locked his bike to a lamppost by Owlstone House, once presumably a gentleman's residence and now postgraduate accommodation, and gone through the rather overgrown garden. No one was about, which wasn't surprising given the time of year and day, and he reached into his pocket for a torch to light his way. Ah yes: charging up in the P'lodge.

The grass reached his knees, heavy and clinging as wet rags. He met a broken down fence, fairly easy to climb over, then more inscrutable undergrowth. His shoes had sunk into soggy marsh and the mud was well over his ankles. His thick brogues were stout, but gumboots would have been more suitable.

The sort of place, he thought, where Eeyore pitched his home. Thistles and swamp.

If his bearings were correct, which they usually were, and he didn't hit any major obstacles such as streams or electric fences, he should be at Clare's location within about fifteen minutes.

Rather unlike Clare, this. Theo found people endlessly interesting, and he was intrigued to incorporate this new data into what he knew of Clare.

Stefan would have dismissed the pale-faced, worried cabbie if his boss hadn't happened to walk into the lodge while they were talking. It seemed rather a non-story. A couple of kids had got into his car early in the morning, one of them wearing a college hoodie and seeming out of sorts. Well, yeah. Sometimes students were out of sorts first thing in the morning. He would perhaps have made a few notes for form's sake, taken the guy's telephone number.

Tom made him tell the story all over again. Then he opened up all the students' IDs and asked if Andrius would recognise the girl in the hoodie. The cabbie said he thought so, but not the man: he had a scarf over his face.

"See who is up, will you?" Tom asked.

"Not many," Stefan said, "except the choir. And anyone helping on Christmas Eve."

"We can eliminate the choir, obviously, as this was a female."

There were very few undergraduates still in college. Andrius was shown the unflattering passport photograph of a girl with short blonde hair. "No," he said. "Dark." The next was rather mousy, and he shook his head.

"Charlotte Sebastian?" Tom asked. "First year. She's still here: I saw her this morning."

"Pretty," Andrius said, of the girl with the sweet face and long chestnut hair smiling from the postage stamp photo. He had become much more voluble since moving to England: when he went home and chatted in the street, they thought him odd. "But not her. This one had short, straight hair. Sharp face."

"Couldn't be a post-grad, could it?" Tom wondered. "Clare Savage, perhaps?"

"She went down ten days ago," Stefan replied. "I saw her go."

"Look her up."

"That's odd. She signed back in twenty-four hours later." He showed the driver.

"That's her."

"You sure?" Tom asked.

"Yes. I sure."

"Was she with this gentleman?" Tom continued, scrolling through. "She's currently an item with Theo, isn't she? Here."

"Don't think so." Andrius shook his head.

"Theo went to meet a girl an hour ago," Stefan chipped in. "He seemed a bit baffled. But then he usually does. Left his telephone here for charging."

"Show me." Tom swiped it open. On the screen was a map showing Clare's location, upriver half way to Grantchester.

"Where did you drop them off?" Tom asked.

"Latham Road."

"What time?"

"Just after half past seven this morning."

Over eight hours ago.

"Thank you for letting us know. We will find the young lady and make sure all is well. Stefan, can you take this gentleman's contact details? We are very grateful to you, sir."

Tom went into his private office to ring the designated police number which would get him straight through.

Chapter Thirty-Five

DUSK

Theo's clothes were well designed. His grandfather's coat repelled the clutches of the grasping branches. His gloves – which he had considered an extravagance even half-price in the sale – were appropriate for breaking twigs and bending barbed wire. His jeans were soaked below the knee and his socks would need a good wash, but his shoes would dry out stuffed with newspaper. Ann was adept at rescuing items of his wardrobe.

It was interesting not to have a telephone. He estimated he was within a furlong of Clare's location.

He wasn't sure what he was supposed to do now. It had only just occurred to him that he had no way of crossing the Cam. He had not factored in that it was winter. In summer, a passing punt would appear within half an hour or so, and give him a lift to the other side – provided the passengers understood English, or sign-language, and how to steer.

He had more or less reached the bank. As is so often the case with that kind of Expotition, the last few feet were the hardest, with impenetrable bushes and the large branch of a fallen tree in front of him. He could glimpse the mud-green river through the murk ahead edging its sinewy course towards Cambridge, back the way he had come.

"Clare!"

The falling night hugged her name to itself, offering no echo.

He pressed on, climbing over a tree trunk. He turned upstream. It was slow going and the light was failing, but there wasn't much that could turn Theo back and thick vegetation, soggy earth and the occasional tributary in the gloaming certainly wasn't it.

"Clare," he called two or three times more. "I'm here!"

Until eventually he heard a voice he wasn't expecting. "Wedderburn."

Theo had trained himself, since he was a boy, to recognise his feelings. Nevertheless, he wasn't sure whether this sudden heavy pain, like a dank sense of danger opening beneath his ribs, was fear or anger. It was memory. A memory he had long ago put away. A memory, amongst other things, of drowning.

"Clare is here."

The voice was the other side, further up. His progress was blocked by a small bushy tree, so he had to go inland.

"And you can fucking hurry up, Wedderburn. Still late for everything."

"I can't, actually," Theo called back. "It's quite tricky."

"Well you'd better get here faster than your usual."

Theo no longer reached automatically into his pocket for his telephone. He envisaged it, plugged in, back in the P'lodge. Probably fully charged now.

He knew no way of hurrying. He only knew how to press on, doggedly. There was no need to be anxious: he was doing the best he could. If Clare paid the price, it would make him very sad but he was doing all that was possible. So he didn't understand why there was a grip of dark hollowness at the centre of his being.

"Where the hell are you?"

"You sound a lot nearer now so I must be nearly opposite."

And then Theo saw him. More to the point, he saw Clare. At least, he assumed it was Clare. Her mouth was covered with what looked like a dark letter box. Her arms were behind her back, presumably tied – or perhaps more likely taped, as was her mouth, he now realised. And her feet were taped as well, together. She was lying on the bank, and at that moment, Harry picked her up as if she weighed hardly more than a doll.

It didn't matter who it was. It was a human being.

"What are you going to do?"

"Drop her in. It's all down to you now, Wedderburn."

"I can't really swim."

"I remember. I expect you do too. So what are you going to do? Watch her drown?"

"It wouldn't help her if I were to drown too, would it?"

"Nice logic. And absolutely fucking typical. Let's see how much you love her, shall we?"

Theo didn't wait to hear Clare hitting the water but dived too fast to think, shallow and hard. He barely knew what he did, finding himself in a confusion of dark, thrashing river, but now he was near the other side, with Clare's – or someone's – body in front of him, pushing her towards the bank. With his hands he grabbed something thick and earthy, with his feet he pushed against a slimy slope. The other man took her and pulled her out, and then took a knife from out of his pocket.

"You can bugger off now, bitch."

She was staggering, between knees and feet. He must have cut them free.

"And you can hurry all you like. If you care enough. We're a good half hour from the nearest house and he won't be around by then. I don't know if you worked out this equation, Wedderburn," he turned with a sneer, "but your tart was shagging someone else. And you've just given your life for hers."

Theo could barely breathe with the cold, still in the water as he was, his body gasping violently and coughing the Cam out of his lungs. He heaved air in, trying to control the ferocious spasms.

"What d'you want?"

He was kicked lightly in the face and lost his grip, sinking back into the whirling darkness. For a moment he thought he might not make it back up, but his hands found a root and he managed to reach the air. His coat and the rest of his clothes – particularly his shoes – were heavy. He hadn't got long. And the cold was shaking him like a rag.

"Just want to tell you something, Wedderburn. And then you can say goodbye."

Clare was scrambling away. Theo judged the other was right. There wasn't much she could do for him.

He was still convulsing ferociously and struggling to keep a grip on the bank. He had minutes, perhaps. He didn't rate his chances of reaching the bank behind him, with his heavy clothing and his poor performance at swimming. Not since Stroud – he knew him now, with razor certainty: Harry Stroud, one year above him in the choir – had nearly drowned him in the school swimming pool almost two decades earlier. He knew the river bed was too deep to help him, having measured out the journey to Grantchester with punt poles on many summers' afternoons. Nevertheless it was his only chance. He had swum well until he was nine: until that trauma. His body wouldn't have forgotten.

He must normalise his breathing first.

"Listening?"

"Yup."

"Good. This won't take long. I've got a plan I've been working on for a long time, and you're trying to bugger it up, right?"

"Yup."

"Thought so. Smarmy bastard. You put them onto the Crypt, didn't you?"

"Yup."

"Right. Well you're not going to put them onto this. 'Cos you ain't gonna be there. And even if you did, you couldn't stop it. Nobody could. That Chapel goes up, or rather comes down, at twenty past three on Christmas Eve. Full of divine worshippers. Or not. No matter what anybody does."

"Yup."

"Stop saying, Yup, like a fucking puppy. You know what an escrow is."

"Yes."

"Because you told me. The Marigolds are perfect for it. And I've set it up. There is going to be a bomb in that Chapel which they're not going to find. And it's going to be detonated by a person they're not going to find. Because I've set up an escrow that they're not going to find, in a currency they're not going to find. All thanks to you. If they arrest me after I've killed you, I'm not going to care. I don't care what happens to me, or you, or anybody. Because I'm going to achieve the one thing I've wanted all my life, and make a difference."

"Obviously," Theo heaved. "You care. Wouldn't have gone. All this trouble. Get me here. Otherwise."

"Right."

He was beginning to master the breath. "Not an escrow. Strictly. Delayed payment. Quite smart."

"Not so stupid now, am I?"

His breath was as regular as it was going to be. It had to be now, before he got colder. He was sinking in the water as it was, and his shoes were beginning to stick in the mud of the sloping bank.

"Why telling me?" he asked, still wanting a little more time, knowing the answer full well.

"Because I wanted . . . you fucker!"

Theo had barely gone one unsatisfactory stroke – pushing himself off the bank with his feet as hard as he could – when he was punched, hard, in the back. He turned and grabbed whatever had hit him, and found himself gripping a stout stick. Harry must have had it ready to push him under. He twisted it hard and swung it to one side. It can't have taken much to push Harry off balance: he didn't have much to give. Harry half fell, half stepped into the water, and lunged at Theo with all the force of his fury. Theo pushed his hand into his face, and for a moment had the advantage, shoving against him to head for the opposite bank again.

But Harry was too strong for him, and too good a swimmer. He grabbed hold of Theo's leg and pulled it up, so that Theo's face went under the water. Twice, he managed to come up, and gulp air. The second time, he barely managed to take any in before being pulled under again.

He knew, with his chorister's training, that he could hold his own under water for longer than most. But so could Harry.

He could only come up once more.

His coat was dragging him under. Harry was pressing him down. His struggle was less than it had been. For Ann, he thought.

I promised Ann.

I must make it for Ann.

He made one last effort to reach the sky, shoving with everything he could summon against the greedy water. He nearly reached the surface, before he was thrust again from above.

He couldn't do it.

He sank, knowing he had kept his promise. All his life long, he had kept it. He had not killed himself. He let go, and gave himself up to the water's stern embrace.

The loss of consciousness was quick and painless.

Charlotte felt an unaccustomed listlessness. She had planned to do lots of reading before Christmas, so that when she got home she could take a complete break. In truth, she thought she might do a couple of hours every day at home too. She loved her studies.

But she couldn't settle, the last few days had been so strange and disruptive. For the first time, Oedipus's agonised ignorance and Kreon's righteous anger and the Chorus's annoyingly calm and placid commentary no longer seemed the most interesting thing she could immerse herself in.

She felt acutely homesick. She almost wished she hadn't volunteered for the Nine Lessons. She remembered with longing helping her mother in the kitchen and going with her stepfather and brother to choose a tree from the farm; even going to dreary drinks parties at the neighbours' and having soggy canapés and cloyingly sweet mince pies and mulled wine tasting too much of cloves, before getting home to their own Aga and a welcome mug of tea.

But then she and Theo wouldn't have gone to meet Mrs Strauss and heard her story. Not that her rôle in it had mattered. But Theo's had.

Charlotte pushed her books aside and got up to close the curtains. Then decided to get some fresh air.

She walked down to River Court and the gnarled old tree in the courtyard by the steps leading down to the water. The river looked lazy and indifferent in the dusk, with dark little eddies brushing the surface and swirling gloomily in pointless circles. How dreadful it would be to drown; to be pulled in, and sucked away from everything warm and vibrant and full of life's enveloping complications.

She shivered a little and turned, unable to resist glancing at Theo's rooms. There was a dim light burning within. That meant he must be in: never even left an unused socket switched on. The last thing she wanted was for him to think she was watching or pursuing him in any way. Not, she reflected, that Theo would think that anyway. He would just wave, and say hello, and offer her a cup of tea.

She was tempted to glance in, just to see his head bowed over his desk, engrossed in some task; his mind fully engaged and oblivious to everything else. But perhaps he would suddenly look out of the window for inspiration, or get up to put the kettle on or draw the curtains . . . She would leave him alone to get on with his work. She must get back to hers. It would be Christmas Day in three days' time. She would be home soon enough.

And then just as suddenly, she didn't want to leave Cambridge after all.

With twenty-five years of police training it didn't take Tom long to join the dots. Theo's involvement clinched it. He didn't need to understand the connection.

By the time the police reached the lodge Tom had located the exact spot on the river, half way between Newnham and Grantchester, indicating Savage's location. This was the last thing Theo had looked at on his 'phone and it was a reasonable guess that's where he was headed. It looked pretty inaccessible. Presumably he would cycle to Chaucer or Latham Road, and then walk across the fields.

"You won't get all the way by car," he told the officers. "What resources have you got?"

They could send a chopper up the river to land within fifty or a hundred meters of the spot. And the Fire Service might have something.

Tom went with them in the marked car, telling Stefan to call back-up for the lodge and ring him immediately if anything happened. As they swung away from the Cobbles he put in a call to the Provost's Lodge.

It was just on four. Nearly dark.

Clare had never known real, searing fear. Such as men, and women too now, must feel in the heat of battle, life and death in the balance.

Theo's. She had no doubt whatsoever that her kidnapper meant exactly what he said. He intended to kill. He had said there was nothing she could do and she believed it. But she had to try.

She blundered through the trees, hoping she was heading in the right direction in the darkness. Barefoot, wet through, every pain sharpened by crushing cold so that each wrong step stabbed halting pains up her legs. She fell over, unable to balance with hands still behind her back and her mouth taped.

After stumbling for minutes – or hours? – she found a tree with a stick jutting out of the trunk and thrust her wrists at the sharp point over and over, jabbing at her flesh. Crying with frustration, she urged herself on, or Theo would die. What difference would hands make? She had no telephone. Even if she could shout, there was no one to hear.

It was then that she heard the helicopter, pummelling the air and deafening the winter solitude. Wild with desperation she shouted inside her gag, as in a nightmare, making no sound. Staggering, she fell scrambling towards the edge of the trees. She didn't see the barbed wire fence until she was up against it. Yanking the wires apart with her legs, she pushed herself through, tearing clothes and skin.

And there she stood, her feet freezing to the soil, the helicopter buzzing into the lowering sky as it droned into the distance.

"Bloody cold."

The two burly firemen looked as if they would dwarf the bobbing dinghy. They were putting in just above the Weir, by the rollers which athletic male undergraduates drag heavy punts over in summer for the Upper River while girls stand chatting on the long-grassed bank. Now a couple of moorhens swerved to make way for the lone boat in sharp-cold water.

A woman walking beneath the Anchor pub with a bicycle and a small black dog leant on the Weir bridge to watch. The dog yapped as the men clambered in and pulled the string on the motor.

"Luther!" she called without conviction. Satisfied that he had seen them off, he trotted back to her now that he had nothing more pressing to do. But he was distracted by a clump in the grass and marked it, kicking the earth up behind him.

On a whim she decided to bike along the bank instead of turning home for Newnham. Undergraduates seem so much younger and more vulnerable these days, not enjoying themselves as they did forty years ago, working harder and achieving far less.

By the time she went under Fen Causeway the dinghy was long out of sight. She could hear it for a while but she had lost interest, and turned for home.

The men didn't talk much as they steered through the darkening digits of the branches. The boat was nippy, but visibility was poor and they couldn't go as fast as they wanted: it wouldn't help anyone if they capsized. A few ducks woke reluctantly and clattered out of the water with a grumble. Sleet threatened. They could hear the chopper muttering.

As they turned a corner the lookout in the prow indicated with an outstretched hand that his colleague should slow the motor. Then he clicked his fingers for him to cut it.

The helicopter deafened, landing to their left in front.

There was a raw shout from somewhere along the river. The splash of breaking water and someone thrashing.

It was the dark bobbing midstream that had caught his eye. The momentum carried them against the sluggish current till they came alongside. It was as he'd thought.

The surface swell of a human body.

Chapter Thirty-Six

EVENING

Charlotte still had a few presents to get. She had spent too much on Guy (because she never knew what to get him): a yellow silk paisley cravat from the market. A glass-guarded silver-plated candle holder for her mother, for summer evenings in the garden. For Michael, a battered hardback signed early Terry Pratchett which she was very pleased with. A revolting doggy stocking for Folly, containing pig's ears. And a "Souvenir of Cambridge" paperweight for Anika, their cleaner, who had been so proud when Charlotte received her offer. Now there were just a few school friends to buy for.

She dashed into a shop she hadn't really wanted, to escape the explosion of hailstones spitting in her face. She was surrounded by canned heat and canned carols, shook her hair like a dog and earned a telling off from a shop assistant.

Half an hour and some unsatisfactory chocolates and a viscose scarf later (she wanted the silk, but was at the end of her budget) she ran back to college through the worsening sleet.

There was a police car on the Cobbles.

"What's happened?" she asked a porter whose name she couldn't remember.

"Hello miss," he said, not remembering hers. "Incident upriver."

"Not serious?"

"Lethal that water." He was half-busy, as porters often are, logging something into a book.

"Someone hurt?" It couldn't be. Nothing awful could happen this golden Christmas.

He looked up, neither denying nor acquiescing. Suddenly, having no idea why she did so – hadn't she just seen a light in his room? – she blurted out, "Theo?"

"Pardon miss?" She had his full attention now.

"It's Theo! Wedderburn."

There was a moment before he said, "What do you know?"

"I don't. I just . . ."

"I think you'd better come this way, miss." He opened the counter just as the Head Porter appeared.

A few minutes was all it took to tell Tom that she knew nothing. Though it also told him much, of no consequence to his enquiries, that she hadn't intended anyone to know.

She emerged into the Front Court still clutching her pointless Christmas purchases. She looked around for a bin to drop them in. There wasn't one. Of course not. Terrorist threats.

The cold sky wept onto her face. She began to walk, she had no idea where. She went blindly past the eighteenth century building, with its stately white-grey stone dominating the centre of college, towards the bridge.

As she got nearer she started running, slipping on the wet paving and sprawling on the path, crushing her shopping. She scrabbled up and on, not bothering to wipe off mud which now clung to her knees and coat.

"Theo?" She banged on his door, knowing he wouldn't answer. "Theo, please!" He never locked his door. Her wet hands struggled with the knob before she admitted defeat. She went outside, flung open his window and saw the lamp, casting a pool of light on some uncompleted work in his beautiful, looped writing in black fountain pen.

He never wasted electricity. She had only known him for a few months but already she knew this with absolute certainty.

She dropped her bags and clambered through, careless of her clothes and her person. She sat down at his desk and lifted the paper up to her face. What had she hoped? It smelt only of dry paper.

Her tears splashed onto the ink of his calculations as she sobbed uncontrollably.

When they handcuffed him and put him in the back of the four-by-four all he could think about was how fucking freezing he was and when he might be able to change his clothes.

He was angry. So angry he felt his teeth grinding in his cheekbones.

He strained to see them buggering about in the water but some arse of a copper forced him front-facing again. All about power, just like fucking prep school. As they bumped down the rutted lane in the direction of Grantchester, he remembered how tidy the lush trees had looked when he researched the spot on Google Earth, laid out in a grid, clad in their pale green lingerie from when they'd been photographed in summer.

So that's what the sound was. Chopper coming down. In the thickening darkness he could make out the bottle green of its body and yellow cap. Cop-copter then, not medical. Come to fish Wedderburn's body out of the water. Good luck to them. There had been a gratifying crunch when he jumped on him. One mission completed. He'd done for Theophilus Ambrose Fucking Wedderburn.

Three-cornered stool. First leg, kidnap and lure, pretty damn near according to plan. Two more to go. And they couldn't torture it out of him: beautiful, democratic Britain. Three more days, and it would be rubble, his own Ground Zero. If he spent the rest of his life behind bars, he would never be wiped out. And after he brought down that fan vaulting on two thousand people, they would never let him out.

Even if the kid buggered up and the iPhone was confiscated, there would still be destruction in the building, chaos and world-wide news. But the boy was smart. He had very much wanted that iPhone. And was terrified that if he failed and was caught, he could be slung out of the choir school, too. So he would find a way to do as he'd been told. Smuggle it in. Turn it on. And reap the results himself. Right on the bullseye. That was the beauty of it.

He liked the symmetry. The centre of music and childhood and excellence would be the centre of his plan. It would stun the world. Far more than terrors in crowded concerts, which killed children incidentally. This would target them, specifically . . . and the most gifted children too.

Suppose they evacuated the building? If they had any suspicions, the service would not go ahead. But he would still succeed. Fewer deaths. But the BBC schedule turned on its head; the Chapel destroyed; websites written about him. Silver-lining was, if it happened that way he'd be rehabilitated and, out of prison one day.

Any case, they could never take today away from him. Whatever did or didn't happen – and it would: children, building, all; he was on a roll – he had done for that bastard at last.

Christ, he was cold.

But Wedderburn was colder.

Three days till Christmas Eve.

George's family was coming tomorrow, and taking him to Pizza Express if they arrived in time. Then he would hardly see them till tea on Christmas Eve, after the service. His last Christmas. The opening soloist would be chosen from the top year, so it would be Johnny or Angus. Robert was still head chorister, but his voice had started to break. Lousy luck, two terms before he was due to leave. He'd been told to mouth on Christmas Eve, and not sing any high notes. They wouldn't know who was doing the solo until five minutes beforehand. It depended on who was in good voice. Which, given the time of year and hectic schedule, was impossible to tell beforehand.

A few weeks ago a man, a hundred and one years old, had come to talk to them. He had sung in the first broadcast, as a chorister, in 1928. Then he had become a choral scholar of the college, and then Head Master of the school. He was very funny. When they'd asked him whether he'd sung the Once in Royal he couldn't remember! He said it wasn't anything special then: all the boys sang lots of solos, so why would he remember that one? Though he did remember lots of other things, like what bedtime stories the head's wife had read to them in her drawing room. And the first BBC man who came to record the service all on his own: Mr Anderson and his 'box of tricks' in a suitcase.

It would be tea in fifteen minutes. Then film, cocoa, bed. There was no one around. He went to his locker and took out the iPhone. It was worth hundreds. All he had to do was turn it on during the service, and then it was his. He shouldn't have told the others. He would show it to his brother Nick on Christmas Day. He had an idea that his parents, his mother, would take a dim view of him accepting such an expensive gift in exchange for doing something he wasn't supposed to do. That's why he'd promised not to tell.

It wasn't like a promise to a paedo. If a creepy old man puts his hand down your trousers and makes you promise, you go straight to a teacher. It's not the same if a grown-up gives you a present and tells you to keep it secret till Christmas Day. Because: one, you can tell eventually; and two, presents are often secrets.

And, three, you're not going to get hurt, are you?

Cory said that stuff because his dad's a vicar. Vicars think you shouldn't wank, and that doesn't hurt anyone, does it? Of course, there would be extra security because of the princess (they weren't supposed to know, yeah right) but the choir wouldn't be individually searched: there wasn't time.

And the moment the red BBC 'recording' light went off at half past four, he could do anything he liked with it. The fact that the man had known what happens in the service made it more convincing. He really had been a chorister.

Cory was wrong.

When Crispin got to his house he saw a taxi waiting outside and the door on the latch. Simon was leaving for Christmas. The hall was full of his stuff. Christ, he was messy! He had presumably nipped out, and left the door open because he would be back in a minute.

Simon's keys were on the hall table. His old-fashioned Yale for Crispin's front door; a different backdoor key; another that must be for his bike; and his university key-cards. One for his college, and another for the Chemistry Lab.

Without stopping to think, Crispin put this last in his pocket. Then, breathing faster than usual, he left the house, walking quickly past the still throbbing cab. He didn't stop until he reached a coffee shop, ordered something at random and sat at a small table far inside and well concealed. Not until then did he ask himself why.

Simon was unlikely to miss his key until next term. Even if he did, he wouldn't want to look for it and risk missing his train: the taxi was presumably taking him to the station. He would report it lost at the beginning of the Lent Term and get another. Though by then Crispin could 'find' it somewhere, and put it in his bedroom.

A more difficult question was what Crispin could gain by it. He wasn't sure, quite. He needed to know far more about other people's research funding, in different disciplines. Chemistry is surely the most compromised, morally. How can pharmaceutical findings be independent if they are bank-rolled by the very companies which make money out of them?

He would just look around the lab. He had no idea what he would find, but it wouldn't hurt to snoop a little, would it? He would do nothing until it was shut for Christmas. Then he would just take a look. Nobody would see him. If they did, he would say his lodger had borrowed something of his – a book; anything – and left it on his desk in the lab.

He waited nearly an hour before going back and letting himself into his empty house.

Crying is supposed to make you feel better but Charlotte felt a lot worse. When the tears were gone, the loss would still be there, always and for the rest of her life. She hadn't believed their friendship would ever be more than that. But she had thought he would be there, for ever.

Her telephone had a ring tone which made her laugh – Michael telling a joke, really badly – but it didn't. The reflex to answer was automatic.

"Hello."

"Darling, whatever's the matter?"

"What?"

"You sound awful."

Faced with her mother's flawless perception, she sobbed afresh so incoherently that her mother couldn't make anything out at all.

"Stop. Take a deep breath. Have you got a hankie? Don't answer. Just blow your nose."

She hadn't. On the table was one saying, 'Saturday'.

"Mummy?" she said eventually.

"I'm here."

There was a rather filled silence. "You still there?"

"Of course. Now, start again. Can you tell me what's happened? If not, it doesn't matter. I can wait."

"Someone in college has drowned. In the Cam. He fell in," she added unnecessarily.

"Oh darling, my goodness! I'm so, so sorry. How awful." There was more wordlessness between them for a while, before her mother asked quietly, "Not your friend with your violin?"

Charlotte burst into tears again.

"I'm coming to see you. On second thoughts, you come home."

"I'm supposed to be helping . . ."

"Doesn't matter. We can discuss it when I come to pick you up."

"Oh, Mum, will you?"

"Let me think. Michael's singing a solo in church this evening. The *Once in Royal*."

"Oh, no, you mustn't," Charlotte agreed.

"I could come afterwards. Tell you what. Promise me you'll have an early night and we'll come in the morning. Will you be okay?"

"Yes. Of course. I didn't even know him well. It's just such a shock. I spent all Thursday with him. It doesn't seem . . . real. I mean, possible."

"No," her mother agreed. "It never does," she said, wondering about the all-day-Thursday. "The whole college will be in shock. We'll be there first thing tomorrow morning. If necessary, your father can skip Michael's . . ."

"No. Please don't miss it." Her father. She had never said that before. "Tomorrow morning will be fine."

"Sure?"

"Yes. Thank you."

"Is there anyone to look after you tonight? A nurse, or someone? Chaplain?"

"I'll be fine. Really."

Tonight, perhaps she would be. And never again.

Ann was alone when she got the call.

Unusually, Brian was out with colleagues. The most junior in the team had resigned over a point of principle. They all agreed with him, though none had done the same. Charlie was out with mates. He usually was.

With dull resignation, dry of tears, she unhooked her coat from the rack by the loo. She nipped in for a few squares of paper to blow her nose and caught herself in the glass, looking haggard. Same loo, same glass which had had such fatal effect before.

Theo.

How much weeping and heartache had he caused her since he entered the world twenty-nine years ago, never any of it his fault? She didn't weep now. She flushed the tissue away and did up her coat.

She turned off the oven. She had no idea how long she would be.

Clare was so tired, she couldn't lift her head.

Already, she couldn't remember how cold she had been. She was in a deep, white bed. She had a vague memory of questions, and being examined – only marginally worse than a smear test, really – and of saying she didn't think she'd been sexually assaulted but didn't really care.

If anyone had said to her . . . if Kathryn had said – the sort of provocative comment she loved about her – that rape didn't matter when it came to staying alive . . . She didn't have the energy to remember anger . . . what was the word? Ironic.

There was something white and fluttery, where the window should be. They had injected her. And given her something silly and hospitally to wear but oh, it was dry! Her parents were coming to see her.

Where was Kathryn?

She had an idea there was someone else. She couldn't remember who.

Chapter Thirty-Seven

Fourth Sunday in Advent

In the same hospital someone else woke up. Or rather, opened his eyes. He wasn't sure whether he was awake.

The first thing he saw was Ann.

"Presumably this means if I'm dead, you are too."

She smiled. "Presumably."

"That would be quite a coincidence. So it's more likely I'm not."

"I hope Heaven is going to be a bit more exciting than Addenbrooke's Hospital."

"You'd think. On the other hand, you know Wisclos? Dreary play. French chap. Probably pronounced it, 'Wee Clow.'"

"Huis Clos? Sâtre? I do, yes." She sat on his bed. "I'm very surprised you do."

"Had a friend in it last term. Studio production. If indeed this isn't the New Creation, and we still have terms and time."

"Safe to assume."

"It was very like a hospital ward, that play. Only worse. Low on plot-line. And jokes, custard pies and singalongs. Probably lost in translation. I'm wondering," he tried to sit up, "whether I'm having one of those tacky near-death experiences, when you see all your loved ones looming out of the nothingness as you drift towards a schmaltzy light, and then suddenly get yanked clumsily back to life and write an awful best-seller which not very clever people use to argue for the evidence for Christianity."

"Please don't," she said. "Unless you do it under a pen name and sell enough copies to buy me a sweet little pebble-flint cottage in Cley-next-the-Sea." She held his hand. "You're loquacious suddenly.

Perhaps you've died and come back as an anthropologist. I'm glad you're here. Though possibly with another of your remaining lives gone, and a good ten years off mine."

"So I'm alive? In that case can I have some tea?"

"Brian and Charlie went to get some. I'll give you mine when they come back."

"Is it teatime?"

"About half past two in the morning. Does that count?"

"Mmm," he said, shutting his eyes and falling asleep again.

So often, she had worried about Theo. Seldom had her worry been so quickly resolved. Extremely welcome though the surprise had been, she found herself almost as exhausted by the relief as the fear.

The next time he woke it was four am. He opened his eyes again, said, "Teatime," and then, "I've got to go. He told me something. It's really important," and tried to get out of bed.

"Theo, for goodness' sake," Charlie said.

"Get back into bed," Ann said. "You nearly died. If it hadn't been so cold that your body shut down, you would have had irreversible brain damage. The hospital isn't convinced you haven't."

"Cryonics!" he cried, delighted. "That is very exciting." He considered this for a moment, before – most uncharacteristically – remembering something else was more urgent. "But I do need to talk to the police."

"Brian has gone to get them. Stay in bed and shut up, do. Or you won't get any tea. Charlie, get him what passes for tea from that revolting machine."

"So my organs actually shut down? One of those scientific theories, so elegant in design and so rarely working in school lab experiments. There was a toddler who was face down in a freezing pond for about forty minutes, who didn't have any brain damage. Now me."

"I'm sorry to disappoint you," Ann said, "but it was only a few minutes. You are not a medical miracle. Any more than you were already."

"I did think I was dead, though. Obviously, I didn't think I was already dead. But in the way that Hebrew only has two tenses, you know: finished or not finished. I thought I was in the completed tense. Rather disappointingly, I didn't have a cinematic flashback, seeing all my life in reverse, with you getting younger and Alan alive again. Nor angels singing me to my rest. Nor a white glowing core of divine beauty which I was loth to tear myself away from. I don't actually remember anything, after conking out."

"Thank goodness for that," said Ann. "You probably would have woken up neurotypical, gone native, married a trainee doctor and settled down in Guildford as a language teacher specialising in Welsh and Old Norse."

"Why a language teacher?"

"You wouldn't be a freak any more or understand computers."

"Horrible. Particularly the doctor in Guildford. I do still seem to be myself, however."

"You do."

"So I need *tea*. And to talk to the police. Possibly urgently. Not a word I use often. What happened to that . . . boy I used to know? The rather unpleasant one. Who tried to drown me. Twice. Who ought to be called Shroud."

"Under arrest. Kidnap, assault, attempted murder."

"Ah, tea!"

The tea and the representative of the police, ushered in by his brother and stepfather respectively, arrived at the same moment.

"Thanks bro." He gazed into the polystyrene cup at the colour of a wet winter sky in Margate. "Unfortunately however, this isn't tea. It is almost, but not quite, entirely unlike tea."

"It came under the label of tea. Is that original? It sounds familiar."

"Almost. Did it specify whether it was Oolong, Keemun or Vithanakanda Estate Ceylon?"

"'Fraid not.'"

"This, however," Brian said, "is a policeman."

"PC Hasling, badge number one oh one," said PC Hasling.

"Seriously?" asked Charlie, who had only recently discovered Orwell.

PC Hasling badge number 101 must have been used to this question, particularly in Cambridge, and didn't rise to it.

Theo would have preferred a more senior police officer, but he gave him all the information he could.

The notes taken and PC Hasling (badge no. 101) having retired, Brian said, "You mind if we go home to bed, old man? You need sleep, I've got work to do before Christmas, your mother's been up all night and Charlie was on the razzle before we got here."

"I'll stay," volunteered Charlie.

"Have I any clothes?" Theo asked.

Ann indicated a folded pile on a chair by the window, and a large black sack she was taking with her. "I'll try and rescue these."

She came over to his bed and gave him a hug. "Thank you," she said when she could command her voice.

"What for?"

"Staying alive."

"Adults never cease to amaze me. Apportioning praise or blame for something you couldn't help."

"You're wrong," she said, releasing the hug and looking at him, still not quite able to control her face. "You're alive because you decided to be."

"I suppose you think I wanted to finish my thesis? Or couldn't bear to miss your Christmas cooking? Or decided to do my duty. The truth, I deduce, is that someone found me by a fluke and fished me out by a whisker."

"You're alive," she said, "because you left very clear information in your porters' lodge as to where you were going, and then fought very hard against the maniacal murderer who was determined to kill you."

"Ahhh!" Theo realised joyously, throwing his head back and laughing long and gleefully. "Very neat . . . And you credit me with leaving my telephone charging in the P'lodge on purpose? Having let it run out of battery on purpose, before I even knew I was leaving my room."

"Of course."

"Neurotypicals are completely illogical."

"Superficially only. Beneath our illogic there is a Deeper Logic, like in Narnia. You forget, I have done a course in counselling, and can spout all sorts of infuriating and unprovable assertions about the power of the unconscious. Love you. See you at Christmas."

The brothers nodded them out, and then waited a few minutes.

"Right," said Theo. "Shall we get breakfast?"

"Aren't you supposed to be staying put?" said Charlie, shocked and delighted.

"What for?"

"Tests? I dunno."

"I'm obviously alive. I can feel a lousy cold coming on and one of my legs is very sore, but I'm not going to die, am I? Not now."

"Aren't you needed by the police?"

"I don't mean fleeing the country. In my rooms we can have a decent pot of tea, then beer, then it will be time for college breakfast. I won't recommend a swim first, though: I've tried it and it's overrated."

Charlie was already tossing items of clothing for him to put on.

"Simpler if you don't let the nurses see," Theo observed, wincing and glancing through the window in the door. Too late: a very pretty, young blonde in uniform came in.

"Can I help?"

"No, thank you," said Theo.

"What are you doing?"

"Discharging myself."

"I'm not sure you can." She looked worried.

"I'm not sure you can stop me."

"The consultant wants to see you in the morning."

"I'm sorry," Theo said kindly, "but I need a proper cup of tea, and I'm a bit busy. I quite see it's not very fair on you, so why don't you tell your superior that I seem to be leaving, and you can't stop me. If you can give us a sporting start of five minutes, it would be kind."

She hesitated. Then said, "Okay," and flashed him a beautiful smile on her way out.

"Bloody hell," Charlie said, "do you have that effect on all of them?"

"I don't know any other nurses."

"I don't mean nurses. I mean women."

"What effect?"

"You really are dim, aren't you?"

They took the stairs three at a time – Theo hopping alarmingly whilst holding the nearside bannister – before anyone else could appear.

Charlotte wasn't sure why she had bothered with college breakfast. Except that her mother had told her to. There was almost no one there, and just cold toast and cereals.

She thought over Guy's shocking phrase when her parents rang after Michael's service: that she hadn't 'lost a limb or anything.' But he had. Lost everything. Brilliant, kind, unique Theo.

She pushed away the soggy cornflakes and lukewarm tea she'd paid for, sloshing it on the tray. She couldn't remember ever eating cornflakes, other than to realise how pointless they were.

It didn't particularly shock her, when she looked over to the other side of the nearly empty Tudor hall at two men talking together, that one of them looked like Theo. A younger, fairer version, and not really mistakable for him. Grief plays tricks on the mind and she had thought of nothing else all night.

She stared. His companion had turned her way. It *was* Theo. The absolute image of him. She could honestly almost believe it really was. Not in clothes she had ever seen him wear. But his mannerisms, his hair . . .

She turned away.

I mustn't believe it. I will end up insane. She wondered if this was what it felt like when people thought that their Lottery numbers matched up.

Theirs was supposed to be the most haunted college in Cambridge. She fixed her eyes on the blond oak panelled wall in front of her.

"Hello," said a familiar voice. "I thought it was you. Vile breakfast. This is my brother, Charlie. Charlie, this is . . ." She didn't care that he'd forgotten what her name was. He was here and he was real. "They call her Charlie too, but I'm not sure she likes it."

"Oh." She held her hand over her mouth. I mustn't cry. I just mustn't. It's too ridiculous for words.

"I say. Are you okay? Do you want a hug? Women often do."

And he sat down next to her, enveloping her in a warm, friendly hug while Charlie stared at the most ravishing girl he had ever seen before rolling his eyes to the ceiling for nobody to see.

By the time the Provost's PA knocked on Theo Wedderburn's door she was almost at the end of her tether.

Normally cool as a summer cocktail, Helen Jamieson coped with anything. Her children said so, her husband said so and above all the Provost's wife said so. But this year the accumulated chaos of the Royal Visit and the terrorist threat coming on top of the usual BBC disruption, not to mention one member of the college who had just been cleared of sexual assault now being apparently guilty of bribed research, and another almost drowning, meant that for the first time she hadn't got her own family's Christmas ready.

She seldom worked at weekends, and never on a Sunday. Before today. Which was rapidly becoming the worst working day of her life. That morning even the Provost had snapped at her which had really shaken her, though he had apologised immediately afterwards and asked Caroline to make a cup of Helen's favourite coffee. She only ever drank herbal tea.

This latest intelligence had put them all on Red Alert again. Privately, she thought the service should never have been reinstated. The last straw was that Theo Wedderburn, the source of the information, had now disappeared. She knew – none better – that academics were sometimes pretty low on common sense, but this took the biscuit. He had been wanted for some time before Helen asked if anyone had actually looked in his room.

She was an efficient woman. She had never previously, in the course of her duties, had to drag a Junior Research Fellow out of bed. Nevertheless she did it with the minimum of fuss and not much more than twenty minutes later – which was about fifteen more than she considered necessary – she delivered a groggy but more or less dressed Theo Wedderburn to the Provost's Lodge and two waiting police officers.

The next time she went in she heard someone say, "It's at moments like this that one almost wishes one had recourse to torture."

Theo was back in his room. He needed food. He also probably needed about thirty hours' sleep.

He wondered why he was breaking the habit of his life, and worrying about something that was not his responsibility. He had reported everything Stroud had told him.

He had told the Detective Constable about their time at school together: how Stroud had tried to drown him in the crowded school swimming pool, holding him under until someone spotted and hauled him out to cough water out of his lungs. He didn't bother to say that he had known he could die, that no one acknowledged the attempted murder and that it had given him a terror of drowning ever since.

He had also explained how Marigolds have several innate advantages, one of which is the facility to make a delayed payment. With characteristic patience, he had explained how cryptocurrency works in general, some of the differences between bitcoins and other currencies and most specifically, why Stroud would have chosen this one in order to pay an accessory.

"He has transferred the money already, and can't now get it back. An accomplice will know this, so he will trust the payment."

"You mean the accomplice has already been paid."

"No," he said, for what must have been the third time. "Like putting it in a bank. But a bank he can't now get it out of. A trusted third party."

When the policeman had been introduced, Theo had understood him to be relatively senior. But he was slower than the dimmest undergraduate Theo had ever tried to teach. He turned to the woman officer.

"You understand, don't you?"

"I think so," she nodded.

"His accomplice will be paid when he's done whatever it is Stroud has commissioned him to do. It's a very secure form of payment."

"In, what is it, sort of virtual money?" asked the more senior DC.

"No." Theo said again, and counted to eleven. In binary. "Not unless you consider the ten pound note in your pocket to be virtual money. It is money-money. It represents . . . whatever money represents. Houses. Silly cars. Beautiful women."

The woman officer looked up from her notebook and raised an eyebrow.

"Sweeties," Theo continued. "You know how money works. So it doesn't matter that he's in custody. You can't intercept the payment. You can only intercept the bomb or whatever it is."

The DC assured Theo that the incendiary device had already been intercepted and disabled. The Chapel was sterile, there was security at the South Door – and no other doors in use – so nothing dangerous could be re-introduced. Harold Stroud's threats to him were bravado. This fitted his psychological profile. And it fitted the circumstances: his plan had been thwarted, he was extremely angry with Theo and it made sense that before killing him, he would taunt him.

They both thanked him very much for his time. "You can forget all about it now, sir, and enjoy Christmas. Will you be going home to your family?"

So why couldn't he? What was it that he knew, which the police – the college, the Palace, the Home Office – didn't know? They were anti-terrorist professionals. Adults. He was only a child, trying to tell the teachers in the staff room . . .

Judging by the gathering gloom, the service would be going ahead in not much more than twenty-four hours. Theo hated, perhaps more than anything except deliberate cruelty, the pressure of time.

He couldn't think if he was flustered. Or upset, anxious, tired – or hungry. He went upstairs to the kitchenette on the half landing. When he opened the fridge he thought he must be on the wrong college staircase. He couldn't see anything familiar. He shut the fridge and went back out onto the staircase and looked at the names above the doors. His name was there. The staircase appeared to be the correct one. He went back into the kitchen and opened the cupboard and saw his own mug, cleaned and put away.

He opened the fridge again. It was empty. His sliced wholewheat bread, with his name on the package written with a laundry pen, gone. His named mayonnaise, gone. His milk. His sliced cheese and quorn – like the lost horn in Flanders and Swann – gorn.

The world had gone mad. How was he to solve the hardest problem of his career – no, not the hardest; but surely the most important – without a sandwich? It almost seemed an act of terrorist sabotage in itself.

A cleaner whom he didn't recognise was coming down the stairs. "Excuse me. Do you know where Dorothy is?"

"Off, isn't it," she said cheerfully. "I'm her substitute."

"Hello," Theo said. "I'm Theo. Wedderburn." She didn't look likely to stop so he went on. "I can't find anything in the fridge."

"Clear-out, di'n' I. All past its sell-by date. Lovely and clean now, ready for Christmas and next term."

"You stupid woman," Theo said, surprisingly vehemently. "That was all perfectly good food."

"Oi," she turned. "Don't you talk to me like that! I'll report you to the Dean."

"You don't mean the Dean. In this college, the Dean is responsible for worship, not discipline."

He was so angry he couldn't trust himself to say more. The waste of the food alone was bad enough. But the time and energy to buy more . . . How could he go shopping, hungry as he was, and find time to think as well?

"Cheeky monkey," she said, flouncing out.

He went back to his room, defeated. He didn't even have milk to make tea. Presumably she had poured that down the sink. He sat at his desk staring at the wall, utterly devoid of ideas.

He didn't hear the knock on the door.

"Sorry," said a comfortable voice. "You're probably busy. I just wanted to check you're okay?"

He turned. He looked weary, but smiled a little. "Hello."

"Sorry."

"Aren't you at home?"

"I cancelled my mother coming. As the service is now going ahead . . ."

"It mustn't. It really mustn't. Horribly, I think it is."

"Can I help?"

"Yes."

Charlotte waited.

After half a minute or so, Theo took a piece of paper covered in mathematical scribblings and read it through. Then he turned it over, to its blank side. Then he looked over and under various items on his desk until he found his fountain pen. Then he wrote a list.

"Please," he said, "could you buy these for me? Wait." He looked around the room. "Where are my trousers?"

She refrained from reassuring him that he was wearing some. "I can use my money, if that helps?" she offered.

"Ann took it out. She's clever like that. Of my pocket."

After a few more minutes he came back from his bedroom with a very wet leather wallet, took out a few twenty pound notes and wrung them like washed socks. He spread these out carefully and extracted his card.

"Here you are."

"Please don't give me an algorithm. I'm a classicist."

He stopped, confused. "This has never happened to me before. I change it every few days, to keep me on my toes. I can't remember what I've changed it to. Or why."

"To keep on your toes?"

"Why, mathematically. What's the time in mid-America?"

"The middle of the night, probably. Will that tell you?"

"It will tell me when I can ring Evan. He might be able to save the Chapel. Perhaps I should ring him anyway."

"Yes, you should. I'll use my money."

"Thank you." He wasn't listening. "I can't think, if I'm hungry."

Charlotte went to Sainsbury's for everything on the list then back to college via Gardies. She waited an agonising fifteen minutes for a greasy rôtisserie chicken spattered with herbs, with cheesy chips, which all smelt exactly as it should. She would have liked to get him a pint of ale to cheer him up, but didn't think it would help.

When she got back he was just emerging from the bathroom upstairs, his hair clean and tousled.

"I got this for you," she said, putting it on his desk.

"Oh," he said. "I see. That was clever. Did you go to the Gardenia? I don't suppose you could afford this. I'll choose a suitable PIN for you sometime."

"It had better be easy. I can just about manage the Today Programme puzzle at ten to seven. Occasionally."

"In the meantime do you mind having wet notes?"

Chapter Thirty-Eight

EVENING AND NIGHT

Charlotte probably should have left hours ago. She could find no justification for staying. But even less reason to leave: it was 23rd December; she wouldn't do any more work before Christmas; all her presents were bought; nobody knew where she was. And Theo seemed content for her to exist there, as if she were familiar college furniture.

Messages left too much trace, he explained when he stopped for more tea. Not that leaving a trace mattered. Only Microsoft would be able to hack in, they were up against a lone lunatic not the White House and Harry was in custody. Besides, speaking is faster than typing.

She didn't need to know any of this, but thought telling him so would take longer than hearing him out.

Thus Theo and Evan had been on a Skype video call for several hours, much of it silently. Meanwhile, Charlotte worked her way through his bookshelves. CS Lewis, theology and fiction. Several Terry Pratchetts – not (she noted with satisfaction) the one she had just bought Michael. Box-set Lewis Carroll. A few random novels. *A Thousand Years of Annoying the French*, with a book mark indicating he was part way through. Some serious biblical commentaries, looking unread.

She picked up the beautifully illustrated facsimile of *Alice's Adventures under Ground* and entered its chaotic world. By the time she returned the book to its place, it was seriously dark outside.

"Shall I get some food?"

The Skype connection was so poor that Evan's image was frozen on the screen.

"I agree," Theo said.

She took one of the still-damp twenties and let herself out. Twenty minutes later she was back, from the Van of Death, with a couple of warm kebabs and a box of extra salad.

He tucked in as if he hadn't eaten for a week. "Salad. Good."

"Tea?"

"Dunno." Then, "Did you say tea? Isn't that always yes? Or is that toast?"

"Toast is a no," she said. "Tea is usually yes, but perhaps today is different?"

"Don't let today be different," he said. "Please."

As the tea brewed she said, "Does it help to talk about it?" She had set the alarm on her telephone for three minutes. The tea was poured and drunk before he spoke.

"There is only one way to do this."

She waited several more minutes.

"It may not work. But there's nothing else. Evan came up with the same."

"I can't quite remember how it goes," she said. "'When you have eliminated the impossible ...'"

"'... whatever remains, however improbable, must be the truth.' Exactly. Or in this case, the method." He held his mug out for more.

"When I was in China," he continued eventually, "I visited a factory which made miners for Marigolds. Like bitcoins but less well known."

"Clever name."

"And noticed an anomaly. Something which shouldn't have been there. Fairly innocuous. But unethical. They had installed something called Trojans."

Charlotte's mind went straight to Æneas and his companions, Achates and Misenus. She had been reading Virgil's *Æneid Book VI* in the last week of term. She pictured the fall overboard, the cruel murder and glorious burial of Palinurus. Around line three fifty and following, she thought.

"Short for horse, obviously," he explained. Of course. Treacherous wooden cuckoo in the nest of the doomed city. "A Trojan is a program inserted into someone else's computer, which enables you to control it from a distance. Sometimes called a 'back door'. It doesn't have a mind or mission of its own. It enables you to do things inside someone else's computer which you wouldn't normally be able to because of the computer's security system."

"Why . . ."

"Why did they do that? I don't know. I have no reason to believe their intent was sinister. Of course, you *could* do something sinister with it. For instance," he considered. "Suppose you want to disrupt a rival's website. A computer with a Trojan is called a Zombie. A network of Zombies is a Bot Net. Now, if you tell your computer to make two hundred thousand hits per second on your rival's website, it will immediately be noticed and blocked. If you set up a Bot Net to make two hundred thousand hits a second, it will look like two hundred thousand different computers all hitting the website. Because that's exactly what it is."

"So what would happen?"

"The website would crash."

"Do you think that's what they wanted to do?" Charlotte asked.

"Why would they want to do that?"

"I don't know." She was only a term into her course, and already anything after around AD 50 felt slightly irrelevant to her.

"They might," he continued, "have set it up to mine free Marigolds. Which would still be immoral, though harmless. They could cream off two percent of all their clients' productivity, and then own all that currency for nothing. But they can make unlimited mining machines anyway and generate all the currency they want. All they'd be gaining would be free electricity. I don't think the PR risk would be worth it. If anyone discovers they've inserted Trojans into their machines the company's reputation will be ruined. I suspect the reason was more idealistic."

"In what way?"

He thought again. "Consider a fork."

"Like, a knife and fork?"

"Generally, a block of coins has to be added to another block in a linear fashion. The word 'block' is just jargon for a line of currency. Sometimes the line, the currency, splits into a fork by mistake. Like lightning. Two miners come up with a block at around the same time. That doesn't matter because they sort it out between them, so you can ignore that. Except to understand what a fork is."

"A branching?"

"Exactly. Theoretically you can get two lines, both claiming to be legitimate. That's not quite the right analogy for you, is it? Like the Tudors. Lady Jane Grey and Bloody Mary. You have to choose one or other: you can't have both. One line is the true one. And it doesn't much matter which it is."

"It does if you're Protestant," she objected. "Or Catholic."

"Obviously to the individuals it matters very much. If you've got coins in your pocket: numbers locked away in your safe. But to the principle of the thing, the continuing of monarchy as a form of government, it doesn't matter. This actually happened, historically."

"Well, I know. Lady Jane Grey is one of my heroes."

"In 2013."

"Oh, I see."

"A split was created unintentionally, when half of the miners had a bug in them, incompatible with the other half. Obviously you have to choose one line as legitimate and destroy the other which threatens it. Last year, humans started splitting the currency on purpose. Creating 'Bitcoin Cash' and 'Bitcoin Gold Hard Fork', and so on. It's not that unusual for humans to interfere. Remember when Amazon deleted all the copies of *1984* on Kindle which had been downloaded without copyright?"

"Um..."

"They could have put the Trojans in for that sort of reason. It would be underhand, but it wouldn't be malicious."

"So... it's quite a good idea?"

"It's a terrible idea," he said passionately. "All the students who had made notes on their Kindle copies lost their work. You couldn't do that with a paperback, so why should you with a download? It undermines the entire credibility of an online library. The thing about cryptocurrency is that it is the first truly democratic form of money. No Bank of England. No Queen's head on the coin. Only people, and computers. And algorithms. That's why it was invented, and why it will survive. No hierarchy making decisions: the purest form of currency there is. The person who did this, who put Trojans into miners, could play God. Like the monarch, before *Magna Carta*. If you have control of half the Marigolds in the world, you can do anything with it. The currency only works because you assume other people can't do that, and you trust it."

"So why haven't they? You trusted them enough to convert your bitcoins to Marigolds."

"They're computer nerds. Nerds aren't anti-social. Look at Wikipedia: millions of people working for nothing. They have different kinds of social networks, but they don't want to destroy the world. Why would they?"

She swirled her tea, contemplating this momentous claim. Was it his own innate goodness which made him assume so? "Why didn't you report it? Are you going to? What difference will it make?"

"I get confused," he said at last, "by more than one question at a time."

"Sorry," she said. "I'm confused too. How can I help?"

"There was no reason to. I think so. I'm not sure. You are already." He rubbed his face. "I need to wash."

While he was out of the room Charlotte cleared the finished meal. She went upstairs for a cloth. He hadn't shut the bathroom door. His head was in the basin, the taps pouring over it.

Ten minutes later he came back looking like a storm at sea. "Do you mind if I go on explaining to you?"

"I find it very interesting. What I really want to know ..."

"Don't. Please." He held his hands up to silence her. "Let's assume the Chapel is to be destroyed tomorrow. By a device which the police can't find. Triggered by a delayed payment."

"In Marigolds?" She thought she was beginning to follow him. She felt very stupid, that it had taken her so long.

"Exactly."

"The same currency as the miners in China." Her eyes widened with understanding.

"Yes."

"Which have the Trojans?"

"Yes."

"So the people you met in China can destroy the currency?"

"I believe so."

"No payment triggered?"

"An utterly worthless one, anyway."

"No accomplice paid?"

He nodded.

"Ergo, no device detonated. So easy!" She clapped her hands.

"No."

Obviously.

"As always," he resumed, "the weak links are the humans. If they deliberately undermine the currency, using devices which they have inserted immorally into their own miners, it will be the end of everything they've worked for. Their professional credibility. Their business ruined. Why would they do it?"

"Well, because . . ."

It was obvious to her – to them, on their side of the world – that everything possible must be done to prevent this attempt on the lives of sixteen hundred innocent civilians. Even with the service cancelled there would still be the loss of one of the world's most iconic cultural creations. Perhaps with some attendant risk to life. What did a small family business matter?

But Charlotte wasn't sure how much she herself would care for something she'd never seen. If someone asked her to ruin her family for the sake of some artefact on the other side of the world, which she knew nothing of . . . For all she knew, they had hardly heard of Cambridge, let alone the Chapel.

"So what will you do?"

"Presumably the Foreign Office has ways of persuading people to do things they don't want to do. I must go and see the Provost. He'll tell the right people."

At the door he hesitated. "Will you still be here?"

"Would you like me to be?"

"It wouldn't inconvenience you?"

She smiled. "Not at all."

She pushed off her shoes, curled up in his armchair and started on *Alice Through the Looking Glass*.

She woke to find him back in the room and the book on the floor. She had no idea what time it was, nor for a moment why on earth she was there. She pushed her fingers through her hair. "All done?" He nodded. "You'd better get some rest. Me too I suppose."

"I can't."

"You told the Provost?"

"And the police. The Provost rang the Home Office. Obviously, they understood on one level: they are highly intelligent people. Who aren't obliged to tell me what they plan to do. But they didn't . . ." He sighed. "Students can be writing notes, nodding agreement, performing all the right mathematical functions. But it's not until something lights up in their eyes that you know they've got it. The police, the security people . . . they don't feel it, as I do."

She waited.

"I would be able to tell the factory in China what to do. But I can't persuade the Home Office to make them do it. Funnily enough, I suspect Pete believes me. But he has to trust people to do their job." He looked at her. "What did you say? Or didn't you? You're neurotypical, right?"

"Am I?"

"You instinctively feel certain things, without needing to be taught. When you were a baby, your mother smiled and you knew she was pleased. Or cried, and you knew she wasn't. There was no deliberate process of learning: you just knew."

So far, so clear.

"I had to learn it, consciously. Not that particularly, because I'm not very autistic so I got the more obvious things: smiles and tears, shouting or cuddling. But more subtle emotions were alien. That a teacher was getting irritated. That a girl didn't fancy me. It was like a foreign language: accessible but not instinctive. What I knew instinctively was a computer's emotions. When I was introduced to my first computer, as a child, I knew effortlessly when it was unhappy, or excited, or hot and bothered. My teacher knew a lot more maths, because he was older. But he didn't have this instinct. Fortunately, he could see that I empathised with the computer in a way that he didn't."

Charlotte didn't dare interject.

"So he trusted me and he gave me one and that was very important to me. I now know instinctively, deep in my soul, that the Chapel is not safe. That the Marigolds have been set up to destroy it. And that we must . . ." Again, he ran out of words. "Wreck the currency. Stop the payment. To prevent this terrible thing that will otherwise happen tomorrow. The Provost listened to me: of course. But the others don't feel it, as I do. They don't understand how digital money works. How nerds work. They aren't autistic enough. And there isn't time to teach them."

For a minute or two neither of them said anything.

"Harry and I understand each other. We think the same way. Like. Lovers."

He needed to keep his concentration going for long enough.

"That money must be destroyed. Or so badly disrupted, for twenty-four hours, that it becomes meaningless."

After a long time she asked irrelevantly. "What's five and a half centuries divided by five years times sixteen choristers?"

"It might be restored again afterwards," he went on. "Possibly. I don't do arithmetic. I'm a mathematician."

"Under two thousand, isn't it?" she suggested just as he said, "Probably just over eighteen hundred. A little more than the congregation tomorrow afternoon."

"Do mathematicians not do arithmetic?"

"We do elegant solutions."

"What do you suppose it was like," she was asking herself more than him, "being a chorister in the mid-fifteenth century?"

"Scratchy woolly leggings. Cold winter mornings. Exciting. Rough. Bad teeth. Boxed ears. Latin and Greek. Perhaps a bit like being an African child, the first to go to school, having to support all the family because you're the lucky one?"

"Can you imagine," she said, "if there are no more choristers in the future? After . . . tomorrow afternoon."

"That's a bit like asking, can I imagine my legs being sawn off. Why would I want to? Unless it's necessary, to prevent it."

"An elegant solution . . ." She was still hunched in his armchair, hugging her knees. He sat down opposite her, searching her face as if suddenly reading the answer.

"That's it," he said slowly.

She thought back over everything she'd just said. "Theo, how do you know the owners of the Chinese factory? Who introduced you? Wasn't it . . . isn't there . . . a boy in the choir?"

"Li's nephew. The solution." He stopped again. "It may be elegant. In the mathematical sense. But it's not entirely honest, is it?"

"What isn't?"

"If there is a genuine risk to life, Hui will not be in the Chapel."

"You are assuming the police are right."

"They're a lot more competent to judge than I am. Nevertheless . . ." He touched the tips of her fingers in his excitement.

Into the stillness which followed, Charlotte heard a drip of rain somewhere outside.

"Are you aware . . ." He let go.

She breathed again. She hoped the heat in her face didn't show.

". . . that people with Asperger's syndrome can't lie?"

"I've read *The Curious Incident*."

"Conglomerate of clichés. Doesn't matter. It's a good story. The reason I can't lie is not because I have a moral problem with it. I mean, obviously, everyone has. It's because, once you tell one, you don't know where it will end. Two and two make four; the world has gravity; I am twenty-eight – or nine, is it? But if I start telling you my birthday is in November, or I have a sister called Lucy, I have no idea where that will take me. Where did Lucy go to school? How old is she now? Does she like the colour red? It's too complicated."

"Is this by way of telling me you think this is a legitimate lie? To say Hui's life is in danger?"

"I'm not very practised at it."

"You think I'm an experienced liar?"

"What do you tell your grandmother when she gives you a Christmas present you don't like?"

"Thank you for the lovely present, Granny."

"Exactly," Theo said. "You have practice. Everyone has. Except autists. If the service goes ahead, Hui could be killed. And fifteen hundred and ninety-nine others. Obviously that's ridiculous and the police know what they're doing: they'd never let the service go ahead. But we have to assume they might and it could and it isn't. Just in case. In case they've made a mistake. In case there is the tiniest risk."

She had mostly only seen Theo calm and detached. He was rather exciting like this.

"By agreeing to what I have to ask him, Li and his two colleagues would ruin everything they've ever worked for. Like trying to persuade Michelangelo to smash David into shingle. And as wicked. But not quite as wicked as the alternative."

"What do you want me to do?"

"They have to believe Hui's life is in danger. Definitely and urgently. Any doubt in Li's mind, and he's not going to demolish what he's spent a lifetime building up." For all his integrity and honesty, he needed this small wrong in order to achieve a great right. "And I can't lie."

"Right," she said rather too confidently.

"Not well enough for something so important. What time is it in China?"

"I don't even know what time it is in England," she said. "And whereabouts in China? China is huge. Where's the factory?"

"I can't remember. I was driven in a car."

"Never mind. We'll ring them anyway. You're not going to believe this . . ."

"Mid-morning in Shanghai." He was already dialling. He listened for a moment then hung up. "I only have the number for the factory landline. Presumably closed for Christmas. I couldn't understand the voicemail."

". . . but I learnt a little Mandarin at school. Only for a year, I was never much good and I've forgotten most of it."

"Let's hope you know enough for this then, because it could take hours to find a Chinese speaker at this time of night, out of term."

He dialled again, on speakerphone. After twenty rings it cut to a rapid foreign voice. She gestured for something to write with.

"Again please." She scribbled something. "It's a telephone number to ring out of hours."

She needed to listen many times, each time adding a digit or two, occasionally correcting. She wrote with Western lettering. Bā. Líng. Sān.

"Numbers were the first thing we learnt. That summer, I injured my thumb and had to do physiotherapy, because of my violin. Each exercise had to be repeated twenty times, so I counted them in Mandarin. I think that's correct, now. Ninety-nine percent."

"It can't be."

"What?"

"Ninety-nine percent correct. There are only fourteen digits."

She laughed. "Expression of my brother's. Meaning, I'm ninety-nine percent confident that's correct. You need the code for China."

He looked it up.

"Theo, wait."

It was not often that this was said to him. He couldn't remember anyone, even in his distant childhood lost in its fog of pain, telling him to take longer over something.

"What are we going to say? There is quite a lot at stake."

"Yes."

Suddenly she couldn't think of anything. Perhaps it was like grabbing a child out of a fire: you just had to do it. "Maybe I can't prepare after all. Like a really important exam: there comes a point when extra time won't help."

"I wouldn't know. I never have enough time."

"Can I ask an intrusive question?"

"Yes."

"This is going to sound silly. Do you ever pray?"

"Yes."

"In that case, can we pray first?"

"God, we think this is a good idea. Or rather, it's the only one we've got. We hope you do too. Or that you have a better one."

And he dialled.

Chapter Thirty-Nine

THE DARKEST HOUR BEFORE DAWN

Yuri knew it would be better to sleep, but it was out of the question. In not much more than twelve hours, he would be very wealthy indeed. Curiously, it did not occur to him that he was being over-paid. He had always believed life owed him. Now it was just a few buttons away.

For the umpteenth time, he checked the exchange rate on the weird digital currency he was being paid in. It was called 'Marigold'. He had discovered these were a kind of plastic yellow glove used for menial domestic work. He smiled: apt maybe. His 'Marigolds' had already been deposited. Thirteen thousand, six hundred and sixty-six (point thirteen). A strangely precise number.

He preferred to check it out in sterling, as the fluctuations weren't so nerve-racking. The value of Marigolds had gone up since the agreement. Because of this, he had assumed the man would try to bargain him down. Instead, he had given Yuri a few coins as a taster and told him how to sell them. Thus Yuri had bought himself new trainers, a good suit and a very expensive meal.

Before the end of Christmas Eve, he would be a multi-millionaire. In British. Or American. In roubles it was over two hundred million. He had spent the money so often in his head that he should have got used to it, but the amount still made him giddy.

It would be transferred to his account the moment his job was done. Before it was even dark again. He checked the currency as obsessively as a man with a loose tooth runs his tongue repeatedly over it. If at any point the exchange rate plummeted, he could just pull out. No danger. No one would even know.

He only had to stay in the room for one night. He had thought of bringing a sleeping bag and small bottle of vodka, but didn't want to take any risks.

The evening before, he had let himself in discreetly, with the Yale key provided, through the small door alongside the boutique. Up several flights of dark, musty-smelling stairs which reminded him unpleasantly of home.

When he had glanced surreptitiously out of the window, no one had looked up from the street below. There were groups of people laughing, joking, drinking wine; as if planning to stay out all night.

He had found the drone – or UAV, as he, more accurately, referred to it – waiting for him, as promised. Loaded up and ready.

He had practised with one identical every day for weeks, in a different location each time. At this time of year there are few people about in the fields, except occasional dog-walkers. He always stopped if he saw anyone coming.

He could now fly it with expertise. Aim at targets: time it precisely. No more practice now. He would not touch it until the hour.

'Seventeen minutes past three.' Less than a dozen hours from now. Afterwards, the distraction (or was it 'destruction'?) would give him plenty of time to evacuate, leaving no trace. He was to wipe the key and post it through the letter box. And dispose of the control panel. It was in his interest to do both thoroughly.

And then, almost immediately, start selling his 'Marigolds'.

That night, Charlotte discovered she could never work in the City. Nor as a surgeon or barrister or anyone who gambled with high stakes.

Being a concert violinist – standing alone on an empty stage, every eye upon her – would, by comparison, be exhilarating rather than terrifying: she enjoyed performing. But if she had ever thought herself incapable of nerves, she didn't now. The nauseous rack-tautness in the knot of her stomach, the vice which gripped her head in a band of tension, were so intense it was almost unendurable.

To begin with, they couldn't get through at all. Theo dialled the number several times and each time received the unobtainable tone. So Charlotte asked him to play back the original message, and suggested a six instead of a nine.

"Liù. Jiǔ. They sound so similar. And they speak so fast."

Theo reversed the numbers, and received the same tone.

"Perhaps you should find a better Mandarin speaker." She clenched her resolution not to cry. "Yī, Èr and Sì all sound a bit confusable too. None of it resembles how we pronounced it at school. I'm sorry, Theo."

"Which of these do you think it is?"

"The first I gave you. Nine, not six. It sounds like Jiǔ to me."

"In that case something else is wrong." Theo checked the code again. "Bad websites make me so angry." He tried a different area number. "Good. Different tone."

Charlotte felt the sweat starting from under her hair. Paradoxically, she shivered.

The tone ran on until it cut out. Theo put more instructions into his telephone and received the same tone. "Dialling. No one there to answer. Not your fault."

"What do we do now?"

"Keep trying. What else?"

When they had done so more times than seemed profitable, Theo put his iPhone down.

"Shall I do something?" Charlotte asked.

"Like what?"

"Update the Provost. Ring the police?"

"The police know. Or should that be, knows?"

"I think it should be know, but . . ." She was about to say, perhaps it didn't matter. But it did. Everything important mattered to Theo. Language. Numbers. A bad website with a misleading code. Even only a few hours away from several hundred people being blown to their deaths, these things mattered. Perhaps that was why. Because safety and democracy and a decent police force and the freedom to enjoy centuries of their college's heritage were all of a parcel with the accuracy of language and thought which Theo cared about.

"I think so too. Let's persevere. You could make more tea. But don't do anything else, please, because I could get distracted."

In the half-landing kitchenette she shook so much she spilt more water than she put in the kettle. She brought back an unopened packet of chocolate biscuits.

"I don't know how these escaped your avenging new bedder."

"Probably hers." Theo put three in his mouth.

He dialled again. The tone was different. He spat the biscuits into his waste bin.

"That was stupid," he said.

"What was?"

"Wasting those biscuits. Engaged tone. Idiotic reaction. Could be someone else ringing and engaging the line. But somebody is awake in that part of the world."

He rang a few more times, barely waiting inbetween each attempt. On the third try, on the second ring, the telephone was answered by a Chinese voice, speaking too fast for Charlotte to understand.

"It is Theophilus Ambrose Fitzwilliam Wedderburn here."

"Ah, Doctor Theo," said a pleased voice. "Happy Christmas. Is Li here."

"I am ringing you about something rather important," Theo said. "And urgent. Please may I speak to your wife?"

"My wife?"

"Ah Lam?"

"My wife no speak English. What you want say her?"

"I have a friend here who speaks Mandarin. Please may we talk to her?"

"I no' understan' why you talk my wife."

"I know," Theo said patiently.

"Okay. I no sad but she no understand."

Theo handed his telephone to Charlotte. There was a wait of some minutes. She could hear negotiations: a man's voice, insistent with possibly a tinge of anger. A woman's, compliant.

Eventually the woman's voice in her ear, saying something like, "Ehahh?"

Charlotte had jotted a few words down in Pinyin. She didn't need the paper but kept it in front of her anyway. Singing children. Sister's son. (She couldn't remember the word for nephew. Or, unfortunately, brother.) Fire. Help.

Theo understood nothing, but recognised sounds as Charlotte repeated herself, patiently. Down the line, hysterical babbling. Eventually silence, of a sort.

"I think I've failed, Theo. I am so sorry. I can't speak the language well enough. And she's only his aunt after all. If she were his mother," She proffered his telephone back. "Or if his mother were English . . ."

"Don't hang up!" Theo said suddenly, urgently. "She is." He gave her the paper and pen again. "Ask for Monica's number. Mrs Zhang. Her . . . sister-in-law-in-law. Hui's mother."

Afterwards Charlotte had no idea how the words came to her, in a complete sentence. "Ni neng gei wo Hui ma ma mo ni ka de dian hua hao ma ma?" Having said it once, she said it again, several times. She had no idea whether it was right, but she hoped it made enough sense.

It felt like a miracle. Mrs Li gave her a number – presumably to get rid of her – which she read back to her several times.

"Mrs Zhang?" Theo said a few minutes later. "I'm so sorry to ring you in the middle of whatever it is. It seems to be night here, so perhaps it isn't there. I came to stay with you in the summer. July, I think. Theophilus Ambrose Fitzwilliam . . . yes, that's right."

Charlotte was biting pieces of skin from around her nails, for the first time since she was five.

"Have you read the book, *The Curious Incident of the Dog in the Night-time*? Or perhaps seen the play? Funnily enough, I don't think it's very accurate, myself. But perhaps this isn't the time to discuss that. Do you remember Mark Haddon, or perhaps his character, whose name I can't quite remember at the moment but that doesn't matter either, claiming that people with autism, or Asperger's syndrome, whichever he calls it, can't lie? I don't know whether I told you, when I was with you in Shanghai, that I'm probably on the spectrum myself. Not sure exactly where: I've got friends who are a lot more autistic, but then they're probably better at maths. Anyway, the point is, I'm not very good at lying either. I wanted to say that, because it's rather important that you believe what I'm about to say."

Charlotte went up to the half-landing and was sick into the loo. Then she put the lid down and sat on it, trembling like a rag doll. When she had sobbed all her energy out she dried her eyes, rather too roughly. She looked horribly red and blotchy. She went back downstairs.

Theo was still on the telephone. Would she regret, perhaps for the rest of her life, not hearing how he had persuaded Mrs Zhang? ". . . So if you could ensure Li rings me as soon as possible, I will tell him what to do. If I haven't heard anything within a few minutes I'll ring again."

He hung up.

"Well done. You are going to instruct him how to activate the Trojans?"

"Yes."

They looked at each other. Time stilled. Charlotte thought of Beatrice in *Much Ado*, realising something of critical personal importance at the precise moment of someone else's crisis.

Theo seemed about to say something, when the telephone rang and the night resumed.

For a long time afterwards he was giving technical instructions, scrupulously calmly, to an agitated voice the other end. She slipped off her shoes and went to curl up on his bed, shivering rather wildly.

How could it work? Theo, against a lunatic. One who had outwitted the police, the university, even the Home Office. She thought of a hijacked plane hurtling towards Washington DC. Would she be brave enough to "Roll!"?

She woke to see Theo's outline against the next room, a mug of tea in each hand. Her eyes smarted.

"Is it morning?"

"No."

"What's happened?"

He sipped his tea in the darkness.

"You don't need to tell me if you're too tired."

"Do you know what a block chain is?"

"I think you may have told me."

"The block chain is the ledger. The consensus as to which transactions have taken place."

He was working out how to make the process simple enough. For a classicist.

"A fork happens when there is a split in the consensus. Half the miners believe one thing, and half another. It's very rare to get a fork lasting for more than about ten minutes: one side will give in. If a fork lasts for several hours, the currency is unusable."

She tried to convey a sense of understanding.

"Li's company had put in a way to control, remotely, the beliefs of the miners they have manufactured. Presumably as a secret defence against a maliciously-induced catastrophic fork, because I can't think of any other reason. Obviously, they can also use it to maliciously induce a fork. Destabilising the currency. And ruining their business. Nobody will trust them again."

There was silence.

"And they'll do it?"

"That rather depends."

"On?"

"Calpurnia couldn't keep Cæsar from the Capitol. Nor Pilate's wife prevent her husband from passing judgement. Nor Sarah stop Abraham from taking Isaac on a murderous voyage. It's always puzzled me, that. I'm sorry I split my infinitive. Perhaps I've been a bit stressed."

"Anything the French can't do..." She wrapped her fingers around her tea. "Do you think she knew? What Abraham was planning?"

"Doesn't matter whether she did or not. How was he expecting to explain it when he got home? 'Hello, my dear. I realise this is going to sound strange. You see, I heard a voice from God...'"

Despite the strain they had endured for so long – perhaps entirely because of it – Charlotte started to laugh. The Fagin accent was terrible.

"'You what? You did what, you dreadful man?'" he said shrilly, like Judy berating Punch. Then just as suddenly, he put his mug on the floor and sank his head in his hands and let out a desperate cry.

"Is it over now?" she asked gently.

It was his turn to sob like a child. She longed to put her arms a round him. After a minute, far less time than she'd taken upstairs, he too seemed to cry himself out, wiped his eyes, shook his head like a dog shaking off water, and looked at his handkerchief. Its embroidery said 'Sunday'. "Is it?" He looked up.

"I think it counts, if you haven't gone to bed yet. You're still in yesterday's clothes."

She remembered her grandfather telling her how important it was, in the war, to continue shaving and polishing boots and saying one's daily prayers.

"Of course it isn't over. The doing is, though. My part. All we can do is wait for it to kick in. It shouldn't take long. I should have got rid of my Marigolds, really, shouldn't I?"

"Did you have much?"

"I didn't make nearly as much as Harry did, but about a decade's income. I was going to buy a house. I was waiting for it to come up for sale. I saw a kingfisher flash through its garden once. From a punt."

"Will you have lost it all?"

"I hope so. Otherwise it won't work, will it? The currency has to become completely worthless long before breakfast. Shall we play Happy Families? I've got a game my grandmother gave me."

She followed him back into his sitting room. He took an old pack from a drawer and started putting the cards on his coffee table. Miss Bones the Butcher's Daughter. Master Snip the Barber's Son. The dog-eared old cards seemed to summon up a comforting world, though Charlotte couldn't see why. She wouldn't want to be defined by Guy's work.

"Will you get any of it back?"

"What?"

"Your money?"

"It may recover a bit. Eventually. Will we care, as long as the Chapel is saved?"

"No," she said.

"And two rows of little boys."

Theo had not expected his Chinese counterparts to see it that way. "Presumably Li's family may be a bit upset?"

He swooped up the cards. "We've lost them their livelihood. I hope they think it's worth it."

"You realise the significance of the name? Marigold?"

"They make me think of Norfolk. Bright discs of golden sunshine on a summer's day. Or is that geraniums and sunsets?"

"The daughter of King Midas. Turned to gold because of his greed."

He nodded slowly, then dropped the pack and went to his laptop. "Yes. Ah, yes!"

"What?"

"I think we've done it!" He looked as an Olympic medallist might have done a hundred years ago, when restraint was the fashion. "All over Twitter. Marigolds in free-fall."

"Will Harry's accomplice realise?"

"Who knows? We can't tell him, can we? But we've done what we could. If anything happens now, it is . . ." he spoke slowly . . . "Not. My. Fault." He clasped his hands as if in prayer. "I've done what He made me to do." He was still reading his screen. "By morning they should be useless."

Eventually, Charlotte said, "What time is it?"

"Tired o'clock."

They both sighed.

"Do we need to do anything else? Tell anybody?"

"What's the point? The police, the Home Office, didn't believe me."

"The Provost?"

"I think he did. Some instinct. Good idea."

> **From:** tafw@cam.ac.uk
> **To:** pml19@cam.ac.uk
> **Subject:** Chapel
> **on:** 24 12 18 at 05.13.19.
>
> Payment to accomplice should be worthless by breakfast.
>
> Theophilus Ambrose Fitzwilliam Wedderburn.
> PS Neurotypical breakfast.

"Did we finish?" His face looked grey in the exhausted light. "Happy Families?"

"Do you think it's time to get some sleep?"

"Ah, that one. What day is it?"

"Christmas Eve. Monday."

"Isn't something happening today?"

"I think we're rather hoping not."

"I don't want to sleep through Christmas. Like Scrooge. Please will you wake me?"

"What time?"

"Christmas Eve. Ann would mind if I missed Christmas. I expect she'd come and get me but the college might be locked up. And she'd probably prefer me to remember."

"I'll wake you, Theo. Goodnight." The need for physical contact stretched like a cord between them. She showed herself out.

She would be awake for hours: reiterating the events of the day: dreading failure; determined not to let Theo down.

She was asleep before she was quite lying down.

It was unlike Pete to be tetchy.

In his defence, he had had very little sleep for some time. That night, 23rd to 24th December, he had not intended to sleep at all. He had been conferring with senior police, Palace and BBC staff for most of the evening. Then had Theo's visit at around 2am. When he finally went upstairs he was aware that a burly constable remained on duty in his kitchen. He kissed Caroline in her sleep, slipped off his shoes and lay down for a few minutes to allow his brain to recover. Three hours later he awoke with a start and turned on his radio for the beginning of the Today Programme.

A lorry had veered off a road in France. Last-minute Christmas sales were predicted at an all-time high – or low: he wasn't listening. The Downing Street cat had turned up. If only, he found himself almost praying, the college is not in the news tomorrow. Ah, but there won't be a Today Programme tomorrow: it will be Christmas Day.

Besides, there was bound to be something about the Duchess; the centenary of the Nine Lessons and Carols; ninety years since the first BBC Broadcast.

He clicked on his iPhone for an update and saw Theo's email.

"Why am I surrounded by such morons! Isn't this supposed to be one of the top universities in the world?"

By now Caroline was fully awake. She knew better than to quiz him. He would calm down in a minute.

"Don't know why I should be surprised. There are enough Senior Fellows without any sense. Sends me an email at five in the morning. How far away is his room? Twenty seconds? Why the hell couldn't he bang on the door?"

Any answer she might give, Pete could work out for himself.

He dialled. "I think we have a breakthrough. Yes, I know. Officially. I never quite believed it myself. Now it should be. Safe. Of course."

Caroline imagined the other side.

"I'll forward. Very smart young man. I don't say that lightly. This college is fortunate to have him. One of the best mathematicians in the university."

Caroline swung her feet out of bed to make them both a cup of tea.

"If not quite the daftest," he muttered after he'd hung up.

It would be dawn in a couple of hours. Less perhaps.

Yuri risked opening the window slightly. The night was feeble and half-hearted, like the English winter: nothing was ever properly cold or dark here. Within hours the pavements would bustle with disorganised shoppers. The few dozen people who had been there all night had now grown to many more, grouping and gathering way out of sight, as if waiting for something to happen.

Soon it would be mid-morning. Then midday.

By three o'clock the afternoon would be just starting to feel dark again. At around ten past three – not before, in case he attracted attention – he would open the window properly, to give him an unimpeded view. Under his guidance the UAV would rise, trembling, from the unswept floor. Hover, perhaps uncertainly to begin with. Hesitate at the open window. Then lurch through, gaining confidence and speed over the unseeing street, aiming straight at the huge stained-glass window opposite.

Avoiding the stone pillars: that was the important part. But not difficult, with the skills he had honed. It would smash through the lead struts, scattering a hole in the glass, and keep going. The congregation would start, look around, wonder what was happening.

At that point Yuri was to let go of the controls.

It would home in on its target without him. There must be some device, inside the huge church. He hadn't been told what, but he wasn't stupid. Some iPad or iPhone or similar, planted at a strategic point for maximum effect, would be turned on inside. That was crucial: otherwise it wouldn't know what to aim for. He had no idea how it had been smuggled in – there were police swarming everywhere – but that wasn't his problem.

Then he was to count seven seconds exactly.

And then he was to detonate.

He only had a few more hours to kill.

He shut the window. The value of the 'Marigolds' had been going up for weeks, with only minor fluctuations. The previous evening there had been a very slight dip but the last time he checked, the currency had rallied again, and more. The value was still climbing. It would be bad luck to keep checking them today. He could wait, now, until the job was done.

His wealth was assured.

He did not need to keep looking them up.

Christmas

Chapter Forty

ALMOST DAY

"Oh Ron, stop teasing him."

The Stott family had been camping out for two nights.

The previous year, the college had changed the Christmas Eve tradition of decades. For reasons of security and the threat of terrorism, there had been no queuing in the Front Court. Instead, clusters had formed in the street outside, to be given tickets from 7 am. Fortunately, in 2017 the determined had been few, the overnight blight of camp stools and sleeping bags on King's Parade negligible. Most turned up from the small hours on the day itself.

This year was different. The centenary. A hundred years since the first service of Nine Lessons and Carols. Introduced by the Dean, Eric Milner-White, in the wake of the war to end war itself.

Ninety years since one lone BBC technician, Mr Anderson, turned up to the delight of the young choristers, with a suitcase of equipment which he fiddled about with like an eccentric don. Since then the vans and microphones, lights and crews had become so complicated and ubiquitous that it felt to some members as if the college had become an outpost of Broadcasting House and not a seat of learning at all.

And since the rumours of the Duchess had seeped out, as they inevitably had like wine from an old wineskin, the price of a place had become worth several nights' vigil on the pavement.

It had been Dylan's idea. Since he joined his church choir a couple of years earlier, aged ten, his enthusiasm had grown exponentially. He had announced at the beginning of December that he wanted to camp on the pavement for half a week to secure his place. His sensible mother, Sue, said the whole family would join him, apart from his seven year old sister Becky, safe and warm at home with Grandma Jane. Teenaged Jasmine had been engrossed in *Game of Thrones* on her 'phone for most of the previous day. While Ron seemed to have whiled away much of the time knocking off his son's bobble hat and quizzing him about musical trivia.

"Who is the commissioned carol by this year?" he had asked more times than Sue could remember.

"Chilcott," Dylan had surely told him just as often.

"Is he famous?"

"Bob Chilcott? Everyone's heard of him!"

Dylan had sung his first Chilcott carol ten days earlier, and since then had Googled everything he'd ever written.

It had proved a lot colder than Sue had expected. She had wrapped them all up as warmly as she could, but they had emptied the various thermoses of soup and finished the bacon butties and sandwiches long ago.

Members of the college had come and gone all the day before: dons with grey hair and intelligent faces; a woman, perhaps a secretary, in a brisk suit; an energetic man in young middle age, in jeans and a well-worn jumper, jumping off a bicycle before pushing it into the college.

She and Ron hadn't had much in the way of higher education. Sue had gone straight to work from school, and Ron had done an apprenticeship.

"That's the Dean." Dylan had indicated a man coming through the big wooden portal.

"How do you know?"

"Or perhaps the Master. One of them anyway."

Grandma Jane had sent umpteen pictures of a cosy kitchen spattered with sugary snow and misshapen mince pies. Sue had spent the time cold, bored and longing to be home with no work until the New Year. Except cooking, clearing up, cooking again, tidying wrapping paper, emptying the dishwasher, taking empties to the recycling, cooking...

Perhaps one day there would be a Professor Dylan David Stott, Musicologist, at this very college. Then it would all be worth it.

When their second night eventually dragged itself into a somewhat dismal dawn, it didn't feel much like Christmas Eve. The Stott family rubbed grit from their faces and took it in turns to go in search of public toilets.

There were hundreds behind them now, several deep in the dwindling dark, stretching as far as the eye could see and mostly too freshly arrived to be exhausted yet by the sparkling cold. Chattering, stomping, speculating with scattered snatches of conversation as to whether the 'specially commissioned carol this year would be as unusual as last's.

The door in the vast college gate was opened. Someone, perhaps a porter, looked out as if assessing the queue. Maybe this was it.

"Quick!" Sue said. "Pack up!"

There were still many hours till the service.

They had been told they would be given tickets at the start of the day, and could then go away and come back later. Having shed their baggage, which was strictly forbidden.

Dylan said confidently they were near enough the front to be seated in the Choir, for sure.

Whatever that meant.

Charlotte generally woke with the sun and never later than about half past seven.

So she was confused by the angle of light. It must now be Christmas Eve proper, rather than the previous night bleeding into the twenty-fourth without really meaning to. She felt a surge of excitement that she was going home and would be seeing Folly, and her brother and mother and stepfather, though presumably not quite in that order. Guy would build a roaring fire in their farmhouse drawing room; her mother would bring tea or mulled wine. The stockings, one for everyone including the dog, would bulge from the chimneypiece and they would open one present each before leaving the house for Midnight Mass.

The Provost had discreetly asked her to stand down from her cross-bearing duties.

Suddenly she remembered, threw off her duvet and jumped out of bed. Hadn't she set her alarm? What time had Theo wanted waking?

She felt unusually groggy. Twenty to twelve! It was the first thing he had ever asked her to do for him . . . apart from translating a few numbers in Mandarin. Which she had done very badly.

Charlotte usually took some minutes to decide what to wear. Today, she grabbed the clothes she had discarded on the floor, splashed water on her face then took a deep breath and a decision to slow down. She said a quick prayer for the safety of the Chapel as she cleaned her teeth, and then – unusually – locked her door behind her.

When she stepped into the Front Court it took her a moment to work out what was happening. Groups, in twos and threes and more, dozens, hundreds perhaps, waiting patiently to be let into the Chapel. She couldn't see the bank of security checks just inside the South door, worthy of a high-risk airport, with the current threat level set at Critical. But she noticed some of them holding cards – blue, or pink – like tickets, entitling them to entry.

Didn't they realise the service should have been cancelled? Shouldn't it?

She thought of retreating and reaching Theo's room through the underbelly of the College, past the dining hall and through the next courtyard. Instead, she braved the outside, walking briskly down towards the river.

She felt a pang of loss over her first Christmas Eve service. But she couldn't have enjoyed it, wondering all the time whether she might be trapped under an avalanche of tumbling medieval stone. It must be thus when you are terrified of flying: knowing everything is safe, and yet imagining. She remembered Theo's Irish statistic and wondered if he might be happy to go to the service as long as he took his own bomb . . .

She hesitated outside his staircase, shy about waking him. A familiar strain came to her from somewhere, so faint she couldn't identify it: snippets of 'cello – was it from a Brandenburg? – perhaps in Queens'. Surely no one had a window open in this weather?

It was the astonishing cold, in the end, which nudged her indoors to knock on his door, then let herself in. She sensed rather than saw him fast asleep in his darkened bedroom.

"Theo?" she said. "I've brought you tea."

Caroline took most things in her stride. Even she, though, was beginning to wonder how she would manage to salvage Christmas out of the lack of sleep and endless tramp of police boots through her house. She had put a bowl of Covent Garden soup in front of Peter ten minutes ago but he still didn't seem to know it was there. Every time he put his 'phone down to pick up a spoon, a fresh text or email snapped at him.

"Lunch?" she suggested gently.

He nodded, then looked at her as if for the first time in his life.

"Thank you," he said, and tried to smile. Gazing at her hand resting lightly on the table, he raised it slowly to his lips: not a gesture he had ever made before. He looked ten years older than a week ago. "I love you," he said quietly.

"Me too." She smiled encouragingly.

"Like Pooh?"

"What?"

"'"I do love you, bear," said Christopher Robin. "So do I," said Pooh.'"

"I didn't know you were a fan of Milne."

"Neither did I. But someone I was talking to . . . I can't remember." He gave up, hopelessly. "I'm only a poor academic," he said, and looked at her sadly. She wanted to hug him to her like a little boy, and for the first time understood what it might be to be the mother of sons. "I never wanted this job."

"Oh, Pete, you did. You were thrilled."

"I wanted what I thought it was. I aspired to be a Master of our undergraduate days. Teachers and thinkers and writers. I might as well be a civil servant." He ran his hand over his face and looked back at his buzzing telephone.

She contemplated urging him to eat and decided it would only make things worse. "What time do we need to go?"

"Where?"

"To the Chapel," she said incredulously.

"Don't come. Please, don't come."

"Fine." She said instantly. "I thought you'd want me there."

"Do you mind?"

"It will be much easier. I'm so behind with everything. I can listen on the radio while I wrap presents. Like everyone else." She hoped her smile was reassuring.

"Thank you."

It came out inadvertently: "But why, Pete? If it wasn't safe, it wouldn't be going ahead."

"I know," he said. "You know that thing about the Royal Family. Monarch and heir never travelling on the same 'plane together, so if it crashes they don't both go down. Obviously, if the 'plane weren't safe they wouldn't be allowed on. That's all. For the girls. Call it superstition."

He stood up, his soup untouched, and folded her in a tight embrace, his tall frame bending to her slightness. He took her face in his hands and kissed her as he had as a young man.

"Oh yuk!" and "Get a room," chorused from their daughters, bursting in . . . decorated, like trees, with their Christmas shopping.

And thus it was that Peter left her, the love of his life and one he respected above all the Regius Professors and Knights of the Realm, Nobel Prizewinners and Field Medalists, without even a goodbye, and went to take his place in what would surely be one of the most renowned terrorist targets in the world.

Theo and Charlotte set off in the opposite direction, towards the back gate, pausing on the bridge to look towards Queens'. The sky frowned behind naked trees; the river refused to budge. One lone swan drifted, apparently headless, underneath the bridge.

Charlotte shivered. "Perhaps there'll be skating this winter?"

"That would be fun," Theo replied tonelessly.

They moved on.

"Have you got your pass?" A custodian Theo didn't recognise – clipped hair; vivid scar of lipstick – stepped out of the kiosk.

"To be allowed out?"

"To get back in again. We'll be checking everybody."

"You've seen us now," Theo pointed out.

"That won't be enough, on this occasion."

"We won't come back till after the service."

They turned into Queens' Common.

"We won't, will we?" he asked.

"No."

They doubled back along the college ditch until they reached the spot where Theo had hailed their May Ball punt. It all looked very different from the starlit lushness of that midsummer night. Now washed bare, bleak with the deadness of midday; twigs bending wearily underfoot; empty branches dipping and sighing.

Theo wouldn't remember their meeting place, and the gaiety of her first night in Cambridge.

"We need bicycles," he said.

Their bicycles were locked in college. "Why?"

"Can't hitch on a punt," he explained, "at this time of year."

"I'm going to lay the table," Caroline said, "while I listen to the service."

"Bor-*RING*," the younger one said.

"I want to hear the new Chilcott. I'm not going this year: I've got so much to do . . ."

"Oh for goodness' sake Mum!" Their older daughter exclaimed. "Don't give us that crap. Everyone knows." Caroline felt a chill dread. The Home Office had been particular: it was safer if news didn't get out. They mustn't tell even their daughters about any possible danger.

"The place is swarming with cops and there are barriers everywhere," the younger pointed out.

"It was all round my production company before I left London."

"It's a bit mean there isn't room for you. But I mean honestly. There's even speculation about her outfit in *The Metro*."

Fortunately for George, they were all a bit hyped up. TV crews had been crawling everywhere for ten days, the head chorister had his mugshot on the front of today's *Times*, everyone knew about the Royal thing even though no one was supposed to . . . and it was Christmas tomorrow!

He'd been terrified when they turned up for practice that morning and he'd seen the security. Staff were emptying everyone's bags and there were those lollipop scanners you get at airports. Suppose he was accused of theft: could he lose his place in the choir? He had no contact details for the man. Who would believe him?

With wild relief he realised that the choir was not being searched. But perhaps that would happen later . . .

He would just leave the bloody thing in his pocket, and if it was confiscated, it was. If not, he would turn it on, silent, as agreed, and then forget about it.

What mattered was the music.

"I wish I'd brought a book," Theo said. They sat in the Anchor, looking through the window over the weir towards a dreary Coe Fen. Before Charlotte could ask whether he was bored with her company, he continued, "My father said there's no greater pleasure than sitting in a pub with an old friend and a good book. Though of course, the current circumstances wouldn't qualify: I'm not sure I have any old friends. And I doubt it was true, anyway. His greatest love was music."

After a while she said, "It's ten to three."

It seemed unlikely that it could be so threateningly dark, so early. "Shall we listen to the service outside, so we don't disturb anyone?"

The sky was considerably more bleached than it had seemed from within. Charlotte wiped a couple of iron chairs, rather inadequately, with her scarf. It was now savagely cold. And her scarf was wet. Theo took his off with one hand, handing it to her, while finding Radio 4 with the other. He put his iPhone on the small table between them, pulled his collar up against the weather, put on his cheap woollen gloves (substitute for his decent ones which he seemed to have lost), and settled.

One minute to three. After the news (came the announcement) would be the traditional Service of Nine Lessons and Carols from Cambridge. In the presence of Her Royal Highness the Duchess of Cambridge.

Charlotte felt a tightening beneath her ribs.

The three o'clock pips. BBC News, read by Charlotte Green. Threat of terrorism on the other side of the world. Christmas trading up, despite Brexit. Set to be the coldest winter since nineteen fifty-two. Possibility of a white Christmas in the South East and Yorkshire.

Then the hush, and muffled shuffling of the hundreds of worshippers. And one lone cough somewhere.

Whenever she had listened to the service over the years, Charlotte had found that minute to be the most spine-tingling, most precious in the whole anticipation of Christmas. The crystal treble setting the scene: far-away and long ago in the tiny, historically pivotal village; the earthiness of the animals; the vulnerable teenager, younger than Charlotte herself.

And then the child's voice would gather itself for the girl's name. That was the moment, at the top two notes of "Mary", when Charlotte's breath caught and the world held itself for a moment and nothing else existed except the pureness of that double note, only a fifth above the key note but feeling so much higher and more intense . . . Then descending into the gentle ". . . was that mo-ther mild".

They had done it. The congregation, the beautiful Duchess, the kind Provost, the young choristers, the undergraduate back row of men, and all would be well.

"Jesus Christ . . ." the sublime voice of the twelve-year-old soared up to the D again, "her lit-tle . . .

She was never sure whether it was immediately before or just after the word "child".

It startled louder than thunder overhead. It was not the backfiring of a car, nor the bursting of a party balloon, nor any other innocent mistake for terror. It was so loud – the stillness which followed so much more shocking, and absolute, and almost she feared permanent, than anything she had heard before – that the ducks, which had been bobbing on the keenly cold water just beneath them, rose in a flapping cacophony of deafening silence.

It was an explosion.

The sound of death. Of a bomb going off, almost where they sat, it was so close; surely less than half a mile.

Within thirty seconds it would be heard all over the world. In Hertfordshire, where Charlotte's family was listening. In China, by Hui's family. Her grandmother in Shropshire must have heard it before they did, on her analogue radio in the kitchen.

In a moment they would hear it again, on Theo's iPhone.

Except that his iPhone was not playing any more. For the next frame – or agonisingly slow series of frames as she watched – showed Theo's iPhone somersaulting in a silver flash down to the frigid waters of the Cam. She had knocked the table in her horror.

She was shaking too much even to apologise.

For a while they sat, saying nothing. A taxi went over Silver Street bridge as though nothing had happened. Followed by a couple of bicycles. The cows on the common continued to shift slightly, and chew.

After time immeasurable, as if nothing mattered any more, Theo said, "That's it then."

Charlotte nodded, dumb.

The wailing of sirens had begun.

An age later, when they were almost too numb to move, Charlotte said, "Theo. Look."

He turned his face to heaven and removed his glasses.

Out of the darkened sky, in sad sympathy, the snow had begun to fall.

They continued to sit until even their scarves and hats and gloves were covered in the soft downy blanket which had come to comfort the world.

Chapter Forty-One

NIGHT

The eddying afternoon drifted into a dirty white early evening: yellow lights glaring suddenly from windows opposite; tired shoppers chuntering over Silver Street Bridge; the weary snowflakes sinking onto their clothes and Charlotte's eyelashes and Theo's spectacles.

There was very little to say.

Charlotte felt a tedious sorrow, even as she was aware that Theo's loss was far more poignant. All that had gone from her life was the image of a dream; an icon that represented the city she still barely knew although she loved it all. Whereas Theo had lost the nursery of his soul: his own burning bush where he had been called and known by a dearer Father even than the one he lost. It was the destruction of his own Temple of Jerusalem.

Would it be nothing but rubble, like Ground Zero? Would a pinnacled tower or two remain? Perhaps there was merely a gaping gash in one side and a restoration programme would begin, lasting all her undergraduate career and more, the wounded Chapel cobwebbed and shackled with scaffolding for years to come.

And what of the human cost? Was the Senior Common Room decimated, so that they would all be farmed out to other colleges for their supervisions?

She got up from their softly-blanketed table to order a pot of tea. When the waitress brought it out into the still swirling snow she dreaded hearing definite news but the girl was far more concerned to get back inside, and must have thought them deranged to be sitting out.

The pot melted a round scar on the table. Charlotte wished she could have afforded something stronger.

"Irish coffee?"

"What?"

"That's what we need," Theo said. "My mother's Irish. Ann. Her name is Ann," he explained. He rose, and went into the pub.

"Damn," he said savagely a few minutes later, zipping his wallet with reddened, ungloved hands.

"I'm not sure I've heard you swear before."

"They're all talking about it. Explosion. Bomb. I still hoped it wasn't real." She couldn't tell whether they were snowflakes melting on his lashes, behind his fogged glasses.

The waitress came out again, with two steaming wine glasses looking almost like Guinness, the line between the white cream and black coffee as if cut with a knife. Charlotte nodded agreement that she could remove the tea.

"That's the first time," he said, "I've not had seconds of tea. One of many firsts, perhaps."

The coffee scalded their throats through the cold frosting of cream.

"Do you think," he went on, "we will remember this all our lives? The snow on Coe Fen, the lights on the Mill Pond." Seeing the ivory moustache on his upper lip, Charlotte licked hers clean, then drained her glass to the whiskey and sugar crystals.

"I suppose we shouldn't put it off any more?"

"I thought perhaps I would just go home. Ann lives just over there, beyond Selwyn. She's my mother. When do you leave?"

"I'm all packed. My parents will meet my train." Another first. She had never referred to Guy as her parent before. She wondered what it would be like to be invited to Ann's house.

They left their smeared glasses on the table and joined Silver Street, walking against the flow returning from late shopping. How many ambulances would be there? Would King's Parade be cordoned off? Would they even be allowed into college?

And would the skyline be very different? If they had walked out onto the fen they would have been able to see. The Chapel had dominated the horizon for ever, in wintertime with the trees stripped.

Something was eerie.

The snow had stopped falling but was still virgin along Queens' Lane. Already, it had hardened into diamond spatterings in the lamplight. She removed Theo's now sodden scarf and shook off the more recent flakes. They scattered away as if disgusted.

It wasn't until they turned into King's Parade that she realised what it was. There had been no more sirens.

With increasing wonder they walked on, ever nearer to college. Back into a past when disaster hadn't happened. Any time in the previous few centuries. To a water-colour of Edwardian children skating, with the Chapel in the background. To a print of crinolines strolling in King's Parade, in conversation with top hats. To anything before this afternoon. For there, in all her usual glory against the skyline, was . . . not so much the international star of a million hackneyed postcards; but their dear, familiar, own college Chapel.

Just as she had always been, since the fifteenth century. Certainly on her East side, with her great painted glass window, which had been removed for safety during the war, still intact in the darkness.

They increased their pace, still seeing no change, through the porters' lodge. Still the same along her untouched South side. They walked across the lawn onto which Theo, as senior member, was entitled to print the first footsteps in the snow, trying not to run until they reached the West side.

They stared at her usual magnificent face presiding over the river. Unless the North side had been destroyed . . . and by now they knew it hadn't.

There were no cordons. No police in hi-viz jackets. No walkie-talkies or ambulances or blood on the ground and keening. Nothing other than the quietude of a normal Christmas Eve after the BBC has gone home and the congregation meandered back to its own warm houses.

Without warning, without thinking, Charlotte threw her arms around Theo and whooped with joy, while he twirled her round like a child, whirling her onto the great lawn, until they fell and rolled in the snow and jumped up and started pelting each other with snowballs, shouting and laughing. Charlotte threw armfuls of snow into the friendly sky, and then rubbed the coldness of it in her face. A snowball hit her hair and spattered on the ground.

"Enough of that, now!" a stern voice called from the edge of the lawn. They could make out the porter's features only because of the greyness of the sky.

"Sorry." Charlotte scrambled to her feet where she had slipped afresh.

The porter hurrumphed a little for form's sake, then turned to continue his rounds.

"I was invited for drinks in the Provost's Lodge, because I was going to be carrying the cross. We could meet the Duchess! What's the time?"

"I've no idea." He looked up at the sky. "I believe this is happy, isn't it, Lottie? This is what happy is."

"Yes, Theophilus Ambrose Fitzwilliam Wedderburn," she said, tears streaming at last down her face. "This is what happy is."

"George . . ." His mother couldn't resist hugging him.

"Mum!" he said, pretending to squirm.

"Why didn't you tell us?"

"What?"

"That you'd be doing the solo."

"We're not told until just before. Don't you know anything?"

"I thought I'd burst. When I knew it was you. I didn't until Nick told me. He recognised your voice."

"Well, that's great," George said. "How did I get such useless parents?"

"If we're introduced to the Duchess too, I won't need Christmas."

"Well done," his father said, shaking his hand. "Very professional."

That was when George remembered the iPhone was still on, turned to silent in his pocket.

"Where d'you get that?" his brother said.

"Given it," George said dismissively.

"One of your friends?" his mother asked. "That's nice."

"Not likely!" Nick exclaimed. "Buy it off you?"

"Actually," George said, "you can have it, Nick. Christmas present. It's a bit too swanky for school."

"Come on then!" Theo headed for the Provost's Lodge. It was because of custom, not the security presence at the front door, that he went straight to the kitchen entrance. The staff were so busy they barely noticed the doorbell so he and Charlotte joined the direction of the crowd, heading towards the large drawing room.

"Name?" a brisk woman in black asked, checking her iPad.

"Theophilus Ambrose Fitzwilliam Wedderburn," he said. "And Charlotte Louise Sebastian." Charlotte turned, impressed.

"I'm sorry; I don't seem to find you."

Theo started spelling his name.

"I'll go and check," she said, rather rashly disappearing.

Theo entered, Charlotte tucking herself into his slipstream.

"Look!" she whispered. "So thin! How does she cope on those heels all day?"

"The two are connected," Theo said. "The physics is quite simple . . ." And he started explaining inverse proportion.

"You seem to have snow in your hair!" The visitor's face smiled into familiar dimples.

"Yes. Your royalness. High, I mean, ness," Charlotte stumbled, wondering whether she should curtsy.

"Hi," Theo echoed. "Yes, we've just had a snow fight. Ness," he added, helpfully.

"Ooh, I wish I had!" And the dimples flashed again, before she was steered off to work the rest of the room.

"Wow!" Charlotte exclaimed. "She's so . . . ordinary," she added, as the greatest compliment she could think of.

"Who?" Theo asked her.

"The Duchess. Oh, I've met her . . ." Stupidly, she was tearful again. She longed to tell her mother.

"There was a Duchess?"

It is a mistake, Pete knew, to look forward to something too much.

He had told himself too often that once he got through the service (he dared not even think the word 'alive'), he would collapse in their tatty family sitting room with a mug of PG Tips – Caroline busy with the tree, the girls bickering over wrapping paper, the dog farting from too many dropped mince pies – and consider himself the happiest man on earth.

In truth, he knew it would be Boxing Day before he could really start to enjoy Christmas.

After the service there had been a reception in the official drawing room, with all the Royal protocol to be observed: the Duchess introduced to all the right people in all the right order, starting with the Vice Chancellor and finishing with the couple who had worked for the College, husband and wife, for over fifty years. Then he made a point of talking to as many chorister parents as he could, particularly the new ones. When he was a small way into this task the Domestic Bursar came to him worried about offending the Muslim husband of the new Mayor because the Marks and Spencer's mince pies had traces of pork in the suet.

"Isn't M and S a Jewish firm? And why are we buying them anyway?"

"Economy," the Domestic Bursar explained. "We were told to cut the entertaining expenses by fifteen percent. We did a cash flow exercise and someone worked out that buying mince pies was cheaper than making them. So we did a tasting and M and S came out top. A committee meeting..."

"Never mind," Peter sighed.

It was inky as midnight and not quite six when he came back from distributing Christmas bottles and thanking all the staff. Caroline was in the hall, tidying as she went. Seeing her busy he meekly followed her into the kitchen.

"Are you awash with mulled wine?"

"It was a bit sickly, to be honest. I wouldn't mind a proper drink."

"Everything went off all right, then."

"Better than could have been anticipated. Duchess delighted and delightful. Public happy. BBC thrilled."

He sat down facing her across the work-top.

"And you're alive."

"Of course. You didn't think the police would have let it go ahead if there'd been any danger?"

He stuck a finger in the brandy butter carefully prepared for the morrow. "Mmm..."

"You are a pest." Caroline picked up a fork to re-score the top.

"Tell me," he said. "I realise this will sound ridiculous . . ." He reached for the brandy butter again but she was too quick for him. "Was there some kind of bang or noise, just after the service started? I assumed it was my overworked imagination. But then I heard someone else mention it."

"I thought you would have been told."

"What?"

"University Chemistry Lab. Accident. Complete coincidence."

"Must have been some accident, to have been audible from a mile away."

"I imagine, if you make a mistake in a Chemistry Lab, it can be," she said wryly.

"Caroline . . ." He hesitated. "You do know that was no coincidence, don't you?"

"That was the explanation given on the news."

"Well of course. It would be. Because the main explosion never happened. And it's going to stay that way. Don't you remember . . ." It wasn't something they talked of: those dread years when they had to teach the children never to open a package posted through the letter box, and run through a checklist every time they took the car out. The irony was that Pete had always been sympathetic to the animal rights movement, if not their methods. He loved animals. Which was why he had given his life to studying animal behaviour. Until he was promoted to academic bureaucracy.

"Please Pete, I love you to bits but you've already licked that finger. I'll give you a bowl and a spoon if you insist. Though it's not on your diet."

"The police explained it to us that time when the bomb was found under the car."

"Why don't you have one of these instead?" She pushed the fruit bowl optimistically towards him.

"Theo Wedderburn," he mused, ignoring the tired-looking apples. "Our most Junior Research Fellow, almost. One or two members of the SCR thought we shouldn't appoint him. I hope he goes far. Though I'm not sure he will, somehow. We owe him far more than anyone will ever realise. I knew all along, really. D'you know, science still hasn't explained a horse's instinct for a dangerous corner: we're no further on than the ghosts at the gibbet. Or how a dog knows fifteen minutes before its master walks through the door, though it's a different time each day. We'll presumably work it out eventually. Animals' sixth sense. In the meantime . . . Ooh!"

A mince pie, plate and fork had miraculously appeared in front of him. And the brandy butter.

". . . they do. And I'm an animal too. And knew there was danger. We nearly lost our lives. Without Theo . . . No point telling the Common Room. I'd never be able to prove it."

"You don't need to convince me."

"But this does. Decoy explosion. Classic terrorist technique. Draw off the emergency services before hitting the main target."

Caroline shivered slightly. "Why don't you invite him for a drink, to thank him? His room's less than a minute away. And," she smiled, "the girls like him."

"Funnily enough, I did. Sent him an email half an hour ago." Pete tried Theo's number again. "No good," he concluded. "Perhaps he's celebrating somewhere else."

At the bottom of the Cam, in the Mill Pond just under the Anchor pub, Theo's iPhone sank a little further into the mud and settled quietly in its grave.

Lynne would never tell her partner this, but it was her Christmas wish come true: she would have volunteered for duty on Christmas Eve if she'd dared. Getting everything ready for his kids and parents was a thankless task, and one impossible to get right. The children were already glued to the telly, he was opening a beer for his dad and she had been looking out the sickly sherry she had bought for his mum when the call had come through. She would be out till at least ten, she'd told him.

Now she knew they would be there half the night, possibly back at the scene again on Christmas Day.

The mess when they arrived was indescribable. Broken glass, mostly. She had seen footage of the Baltic Exchange IRA attack in 1992, and this looked worse. It was a puzzle how an accident

ANNE ATKINS

could have happened, with the lab shut for Christmas. Just as well, though. You'd be sliced to slivers, standing anywhere near.

This was the reason she had joined policing: this buzz; the energy which kept her going long after she would have zoned out at home. Or more likely, wanted to blow something up herself.

They'd had to stand by for hours, all the evidence being destroyed by water and foam in the meantime. Even the firefighters had to wait for everything to blow up first. It was said to be the only building in the City the Fire Service wasn't allowed into while it was burning.

She saw the ambulance pull up through one of the blasted panes. Lab not quite empty then? "Damn fool," someone said. "Our chemistry teacher said anyone can make a bomb out of over-the-counter ingredients from Boots. If it doesn't take your hand off first."

It was long after midnight, and they were exhausted and grimy-faced, before more information trickled through. Deliberate act. The original explosive hadn't been big. Activated by a timing device. Could have been set days, even weeks, in advance. All the chemicals had done the rest.

Arson? Terrorism? Lynne heard the word "decoy . . ." But no other explosion had followed, so she didn't see how it could have been.

Nothing to do with the poor bugger caught inside, apparently. She had glimpsed a sight of the trolley being wheeled to the ambulance. Not many of the team would be fancying their turkey dinners now. Damn shame. At Christmas, too. Presumably putting in overtime to clear his desk, with the Lab officially shut. She briefly wondered whether he – or she – was young or old. Professor or junior. Perhaps good-looking?

Or had been.

Mark parked in the Addenbrooke's car park. He had turned off the radio when the news came on so most of the journey had been conducted in silence, apart from an explosion of swearing as someone cut across him in the blinding snow. For once, Liz understood it wasn't the driver he was angry with.

It all seemed strangely deserted. Surely just as many people get ill on Christmas Eve as on any other day?

393

After they had been in the waiting room for a few minutes Mark wandered off. He could never sit still, and there was nothing in the pile of *Inspiring Kitchens* and *House and Home* to interest him enough to flick through. He hadn't told her where he was going.

Nor that Selina had returned his call . . .

The glass in the window was dirty, and the sky beyond a sodden grey. Liz had not allowed her imagination to dwell on why they were there. Hospital is a place where you get better. She waited, thinking of nothing, till they could be told that they could take him home.

"Mrs Thorpe?"

A man in a lounge suit stood just inside the doorway. At least he wasn't wearing those ghastly green pyjamas hospital doctors seem to wear nowadays.

"DC Andy McCall," he said, showing her his badge. "I'm so very sorry about your news."

She said nothing for a full half minute. Then, "What news?" as if he had commented on the weather.

"Sit down, Mrs Thorpe. You haven't seen any of the medical staff in charge of your son?"

"We haven't seen anyone. We've been waiting half an hour. When can we see Crispin? What do you mean, news?"

"Are you here with your husband?"

"He was here a minute ago. He gets bored. What news?" She was beginning to sound shrill.

"I'm afraid your son was quite badly injured. It was a big blast. Best wait for the doctors."

"Tell me!"

"Shall we wait for your husband?"

"I hate my husband." Saying it, out loud, suddenly made it real. "Tell me about my son! He is my son, not Mark's. He doesn't care about him, does he?"

"Not mine, eh?" Mark said, coming back with three cups of coffee. A young woman hovered in the corridor, in jogging trousers and a hoodie. "That's quite an achievement. Congratulations. Only he is my son, you lying bitch, and I love him just as much as you do. Just make less fuss about it. And who the hell are you?" He turned on Andy. "How dare you upset my wife?"

Andy showed his badge.

"That bad, eh?" Mark looked out of the window, his face set. "I thought it might be. Not much point staying, then."

She crossed the room like an arrow then, hitting Mark full force and sending the grey, livid coffee into his face, into the policeman, into all the anodyne posters on the walls advising about 'flu jabs, and quitting smoking, and pregnancy, and violence both domestic and in the hospital.

Then she fell on the floor howling. Andy moved to help her.

"Get off," Mark said, surprisingly gently. "I'm her husband. For better or worse, now. Come on, love. Selina's here. She's come home for Christmas."

Bitterness twisted Yuri's mouth. It was hours since he realised he'd been duped. It would be months before his anger subsided. Years. It wasn't for himself that he had agreed. For his mother; his grandmother.

'Marigolds'! Gloves for women's housework . . .

He didn't know how the trick had been done. He didn't care. If he hadn't been so scrupulous, checking it again and again, he could have blown up the building for nothing. Been able to do nothing about it afterwards.

The value started falling before it was even light. At first Yuri assumed he must be mistaken. A minor fluctuation. Still worth doing the job even for a tenth the amount.

He stayed at his post, looking it up incessantly, right up until the hour. Long after he realised there was no money in it. No answer when he rang the cheat who'd contracted him.

Did the man take Yuri for a fool? It was wrong to destroy a church.

His family would be opening presents already. Chinking glasses. He hated this godless country, where they didn't start Christmas till the next day.

That was the end of his Marigold money. On vodka. Nearly gone.

He picked up the bottle and stumbled outside.

They all said the UK didn't do snow. He stared at it. He would go home.

He slipped on the ice and fell full length along the pavement. His palm, holding the neck of the glass, stained the ground. The last of the spirit poured away.

There was a carol. Red berries: drifts of white.

A bloody rose lies crushed and broken on the virgin snow.

The goose was stuffed, the bread and cranberry sauces under clingfilm, Brian's brandy butter in a bowl, parboiled potatoes and parsnips in trays of goose-fat in the larder, sprouts prepared, chestnuts peeled, Christmas cake iced and mince pies laid out like Boy Scouts on parade. They would eat the first ones tonight, when Theo was home.

If he remembered. And came in before midnight.

Ann had finished most of the food preparation as she listened to the service on the radio. She didn't usually like the specially-commissioned carol but this year it was by Bob Chilcott, an old boy of the school and choir. And so beautifully tuneful in an old-fashioned way! The readings were better than usual, too. Considerable improvement there.

Charlie and Brian were, unusually, watching the telly together. Perhaps she would join them. She picked up the last few spices to put them away.

"Boo!"

"Theo, you idiot!" She turned and surveyed the powdered cinnamon clouding the floor. "Why didn't I hear you come in?"

She threw her arms around the son who was so much bigger than she was, now dutifully holding her till she was ready to release him. "So good to see you." She shook her head, smiling. "Several hours earlier than expected. Ooh," she spotted his only luggage apart from his laptop. "Have you brought me a fiddle for Christmas?"

Chapter Forty-Two

CHRISTMAS DAY

"Charlie," his mother said. "You do know that's really rude?"

Unusually, Ann hadn't drawn the curtains of the French windows. The flames of candlelight jittered in the glass, gold against the luminous silver garden which was wearing a soft, ghostly gown. The table was littered with Ann's half-eaten pudding, blackly delicious and perfectly formed from its spherical bombe; and Brian's over-sweet brandy butter, his one contribution to the meal other than polite appreciation and opening bottles.

Theo, who like his mother didn't have a sweet tooth, had concentrated on the mingled burnt flavours of the figs and almonds, allspice and nutmeg. "Dried mango," he said at last, with an air of Poirot solving a particularly tough case. Ann nodded, pleased.

"And ginger," said Brian. "Crystallised ginger. By the way, Theo, I've cracked your PIN number."

"Dad, she always puts ginger in. And the ginger's really easy to taste." Charlie didn't look up from his iPhone.

"Well done," Theo said. "No one else has."

"No one else has tried," Charlie said dismissively. "And Dad spends his life doing crosswords."

"Remind me what it was again?" Ann asked.

"'How many novel steps can you spy to the meaning of life?'" Theo repeated.

"Ooh, give me a moment!" she said. "Don't tell me."

"Thirty-nine forty-two," Brian said.

"Thanks Brian," Ann sighed.

"It was a bit too easy," Theo apologised. "I'm not used to unmathematical clues. Maybe I should have said the smallest zeroless pandigital number when combined with its quadruple."

"You don't really expect a normal human being to understand that?" Ann asked.

"Multiply the answer by four," Theo suggested. "Charlie, lend me your telephone a mo."

"Oi. I was using that."

"Sorry, but I need the calculator. Look." He showed Ann. "At both answers together," he added.

"Ah," she smiled, nodding. "Pan. Digital."

"Talking of solving things," Theo continued, giving his brother back his property, "I've just had rather an exciting breakthrough."

"In your thesis?" Ann asked.

"Does this mean you'll get your doctorate at last?" Brian said.

"Steady on, Dad." Charlie resumed his message.

"Well, it's not part of my thesis," Theo confessed. "It's ... um ... rather more exciting."

"You've got married," Charlie suggested, still thumbing. "Talking of miracles."

"Shut up, Charlie. Tell us," Ann urged.

"I've discovered how to prove the existence of an odd perfect number."

"Well that's not difficult," Charlie pointed out. "You're an odd, perfect, number-theorist. In Mum's eyes. The rest of us just think you're odd. Anyway." He had at last finished his message, and looked up. "It's surely a lot more rude not to contact your girlfriend on Christmas Day."

"I thought you'd only known each other a few weeks?" Ann said.

"So?"

"So you could give us your full attention, at least till the end of the meal."

"The meal's ended, look. And I wanted to know if my presents had arrived. Thorntons, pink fizz and a bouquet. Smooth."

"Hope she's worth it," Brian said dourly, stacking plates.

Theo pushed his chair quietly back from the table. "Excuse me," he said. "May I get down?"

It was one of the unfairnesses of life that if Charlie had asked the same, Ann would have insisted he help clear the table and stack the dishwasher. On the other hand, Charlie would have taken a couple of plates into the kitchen and gone to the loo for twenty minutes, returning just in time to say, "Do you want any help?" as the table was wiped clean.

When Theo was eight and Mr Richard had given him an old BBC computer, nobody had taught him how to use it: he devoured the manual as boys once consumed *The Beano* or stories of Desperate Dan. Ann, not having any way of measuring whether his time was being usefully spent, had prised him off it to do piano practice or homework. On Christmas Day, however, his time was (he presumed) his own. When he eventually came downstairs, he was confronted with the dual difficulty of wrapped up parcels he was expected to show an interest in even though he had no idea what was inside them, and distressed grandparents who thought he should have been pleased to see them. Theo never forgot a lesson. It was rude to use a computer on Christmas Day.

But there were other things, he now knew, which were rude on Christmas Day.

What he had been longing to do all day was see what had happened to Marigolds. Just before he went to bed they had been rallying. Since the all-time dive to almost nothing at around midday yesterday, they had climbed back up to nearly a pound. If they kept going, the family business in China might not be utterly ruined. Indeed, his own savings might one day be worth something, though probably never again the deposit for a small terraced house out in a village somewhere, let alone Grantchester Meadows. However, far more exciting even than Li's solvency – or his own – was how digital currency might behave in a situation which history hadn't seen before.

But he had not come upstairs to satisfy his curiosity. He was still looking for what he needed when Ann brought him a mug of tea.

"Can you get anything delivered on Christmas Day?" he asked.

"Doubt it," she said. "Do you want help?"

He shook his head.

"Don't take Charlie too seriously," she advised. "If she cares about you, she won't mind that you haven't remembered Christmas."

"Not much consolation, really."

"Then why . . ."

"Don't say it," he said.

"What?"

"That you don't like Clare. However subtly, even with a question."

"Okay." She smiled carefully. "I'd love to hear about your odd perfect number. There's tea for you."

"Thanks."

Ann left the room. Still, after nearly three decades, mystified. She could perhaps come up with some neurotypical explanation. Maybe, given his Christian principles, he felt he had made a commitment already?

It still didn't make sense. Why couldn't someone of Theo's intelligence . . . but she knew she was going down a blind alley.

After a long search, Theo found a website that could deliver wrapped gifts on Christmas Day for £150. Provided the order was put in by midday.

He gave up. He would ring instead. He reached into his pocket for his telephone. Odd. Not by his bed, nor anywhere obvious in his room. He was about to go looking for it when he remembered another world: the first fallings of snow, the churning Mill Pond, the dreadful, deafening detonation, and the silverfish flash of his iPhone tumbling into the Cam.

Ann had told him last night what it was. Explosion in the lab near Tennis Court Road. He wasn't surprised. A chemistry lab is a building-sized box of fireworks. You'd only need one match: a few cylinders of hydrogen anywhere near would take the building down. He had an idea she'd said someone had been inside. So although it was annoying to be without his telephone, he obviously couldn't mind something so trivial.

Numbers were Theo's friends. He fetched the landline handset, took it back to his bedroom and dialled from memory.

It was answered almost immediately.

"Hello," he said.

"Hello," she replied.

"Oh," he said.

Charlotte, too, had been alone in her room. Guy liked to have smoked salmon, oysters and crayfish with champagne at lunch time, and dinner in the evening for which they were expected to dress up. She still had plenty of time and was sitting on the floor in her towelling dressing gown, listening to music.

"Happy Christmas, Theo."

"Ah," She said. "That's little Lottie Louise!"

"Yes." she hugged her amazement to herself.

"I didn't mean you . . ."

"Oh," she said.

"Mistake," he explained.

"All right."

"Still, I can wish you a happy Christmas too. Happy Christmas."

"Thank you. Is it?"

"What?"

"A happy Christmas?"

"I don't know. I'm not there."

"I mean, your end."

"Oh, I see. Yes, that makes sense."

There was a comfortable lull in the conversation.

"You still haven't told me," she reminded him.

"Told you what?"

"Whether you're having a happy Christmas."

"Oh. Um . . . The snow is pretty."

"Yes."

"I think I was. Until I realised I hadn't done something. That's how I rang you by mistake. I thought you were someone else."

"Well, it's nice to hear from you anyway."

"That's bollocks, isn't it?"

"Is it?"

"I didn't think you were Clare at all."

"No?"

"I thought your number was Clare's."

"I think I realised that's what you meant. How is your odd perfect number proof?"

"That's interesting."

"What is?"

"Ann wanted to know, too. I can't work on it today. It's Christmas Day here."

"It is here, too," she said.

"Or buy Marigolds either," he sighed, a little sadly. "I don't think there will be such a good opportunity again."

"Did you like the Christmas present I gave you?"

"What was that?"

"A CD. Donald McClean."

"Ah. Thank you. I didn't give you one. Does that matter?"

"Not in the slightest."

"I didn't think it did. I lost it, I think."

Charlotte laughed. It was so . . . Theo. With a flash of self-awareness she understood: his losing her present was why she loved him.

There. No going back now.

There was something – this was ridiculous: he was old enough to be her teacher – there was something so *vulnerable* about Theo. He was almost naked. How could anyone be cruel to him? It would be like bullying a child.

As if his soul had no skin.

Theo was still staring at his screen. At the florist who would get orchids to your beloved, even on Christmas Day provided you placed your order by midday. 'Tell her you love her,' it said, with a picture of a smiling girl answering the door to Father Christmas holding a bouquet. Ann had told him that you have to keep telling your wife you love her even on your Golden Wedding anniversary. It doesn't count to say it once, when you propose, and assume she knows it still stands unless you've informed her otherwise. He hadn't said it to Clare, yet.

"What?" Charlotte said.

His mind came back. "What did I just say?"

She couldn't possibly repeat it. Was that for Clare too? Even for Theo, that was quite special.

"Sorry," he said. "I was thinking something else. Did I just say the wrong thing?"

She was in far too much confusion to answer.

"I do like having you as a friend," he clarified.

"Good. I like being friends with you, too."

"Perhaps we might see each other again. One day. You never know."

"Theo." She was composed now. "We live in the same college. Eat in the same dining hall. Collect our post from the same P'lodge. Worship in the same Chapel, though I admit it's quite big. Still. And you have my violin."

"Ann's been playing it. Ann's my mother," he explained.

"I'm glad. I'm sure it likes to be played."

"She said it's rather good."

"I'm glad about that, too. We'd have to try quite hard not to see each other. Our rooms are only about . . ." she wondered how far.

"A couple of chains," he suggested.

"Sorry?"

"A fifth of a furlong. Forty-four yards. Approximately."

"Really?"

"It is only a guess."

She glanced reluctantly at her bedside clock. Guy would say it was an insult to her mother to be late. She had already abandoned blowdrying her hair. But she did need to put a dress on.

Soon Guy would be tapping his fingers on the mantelpiece and looking at his watch.

"Theo . . ."

"I have to go, don't I? Or you do. I was supposed to be doing something."

"Ringing Clare."

"Thank you." She wasn't sure whether she heard a sigh.

"Happy Christmas then." In a moment of inspiration she realised the only possible comeback. "'So do I,'" she added.

"Very good," he laughed. "Silly old bear."

She waited until he had hung up.

Theo stared at his empty tea mug. He longed to finish his odd perfect number proof. And check the trajectory of Marigolds, to work out what they might do tomorrow. If he bought today he might still buy his little house. But both activities would be rude. On Christmas Day.

Nevertheless he had a sense of having done something satisfying.

He picked up his mug and went downstairs.

It was two minutes to seven. Drinks at seven: dinner at half past. Guy was all right, really: her mother was probably happier than she had been with her father.

She threw over her head a long blue velvet dress her mother had bought her when she was fifteen, for her first black tie party. She could put on some mascara while she listened to the track one more time: her mother would notice, if no one else.

Starry, starry night.

Her mascara was clogged. She threw it back into her makeup bag, and found some pink lipstick.

How you suffered for your sanity. How you tried to set them free.

Sod the makeup. She sat back on the floor, arms around her knees, enjoying the lyrics. Three minutes past seven. Her stepfather could wait. Strange how potent cheap music is . . .

They would not listen, they're not listening still. Perhaps they never will.

Ridiculous, that she was so happy and yet her eyes were pricking. It expressed exactly what she wanted to tell him. What she suspected his mother had already spent his lifetime telling him.

The song came to an end and she went downstairs for Christmas dinner, singing softly on the stairs the only lines which mattered:

This world was never meant for one as
Beautiful as you.